- To Ann

HANG FIRE

Inspired by a True Hollywood Story

Anthony Mora

To Ann for her sharp feedback and constant encouragement throughout this journey. Special thanks to Fifi Klein, whose meticulous proofreading and thoughtful editing helped shape this work into its final form. To Daxton Dubach for bringing the book's vision to life through his remarkable cover design; to Amanda for her insightful feedback that helped refine this story; and to Stella for her continuing reminder. Finally, with deep appreciation to my publisher, Andrew Zettler, whose guidance and dedication went far beyond what any author could hope for.

The Royal Penny Press

ISBN 978-0-9912370-3-6
Printed in the U.S.A

Chapter 1

I was wondering—if I told you I'm thinking of killing someone, would you have to report it?"

Dr. Kimberley Goodman stared at Jerry. An eyebrow raised.

"Not that I am," Jerry quickly added, before she could respond, "but if I was, and I told you, would you have to report it? Or," he continued hurriedly, "if I wasn't and was joking about it, or just tossing it out hypothetically, would you have to report that? Or, do you have to report the mere fact that I'm asking a hypothetical about wanting to kill someone—simply asking out of curiosity?"

"Are you thinking of killing someone?" she asked.

"That's not the point. If I say yes, will you have to report it?"

"Are you thinking of it?" she repeated.

Jerry stared down, searching for a fixed point on the floor to focus on. "No."

"Then why would you bring it up?"

"To understand how this process works." Jerry took a beat and looked up at her. "To see how safe my information is here."

Dr. Goodman leaned forward and stared at him. "That is a disturbing question. Why would you ask that?"

"Like I said, I just want to see how private this is, how safe I am here. I mean if you have to report every silly idea I have here, how can I feel free to express myself? Let's say I tell you that I'm considering offing myself. Let's say that I tell you I've mapped it all out, have a game plan set, ready to execute it—so to speak."

"Have you?"

"That's not the point," he repeated adamantly, an irritated expression on his face.

Dr. Goodman leaned towards him. "Jerry, is there really something going on here?"

"It's hypothetical." Jerry paused, folded his hands. Taking a beat, he stared appraisingly as he leaned towards her. Dr. Kimberley Goodman was medium height, blonde with sea-blue eyes. Somewhere in her mid to late thirties. Attractive. No, more than attractive, he thought as he studied her. Stunning. Could be mistaken for an actress or a model. She was wearing a form-fitting white blouse and green skirt that stopped right below the knees. Jerry had debated over what to wear to the session, hoping his wardrobe would make a statement but resigned himself to his well-worn jeans, gray T-shirt, and gray hoodie and sneakers. "It's for a script I'm writing," he continued. "I want to know how it works—what you people have to report. This conversation isn't about whether I want to do anything, but whether you keep what I tell you here between us or report it. Trust is an issue my character is dealing with."

"A script?" She sighed and leaned back. "A strange way to use our time. Why didn't you just ask me directly? Why the subterfuge?"

Jerry smiled. "You'd give me a canned answer if I just asked. If I told you it was all for a script, I wouldn't get the realistic response I needed." He paused. "So, it could be a slippery slope, right? If I told you I wanted to kill myself or someone else you'd have to report that."

Dr. Goodman sat erect. She stared at Jerry. "We're wasting time. Forget the script. Let's talk about you. Unless this is about you."

Jerry sighed. He stood up and walked to the large window that overlooked San Vicente Boulevard. Dr. Goodman's third-floor Brentwood office was small, but the sparse amount of furniture—a desk, two chairs, and a small couch—combined with the large bay window, gave it a sense of space. Clasping his hands behind his back, he leaned towards the windowpane. "Why do people jog in that island between lanes?" he asked. "They're just inhaling fumes from the passing cars. All those health-obsessed joggers sucking in exhaust like human vacuum cleaners. Seems counter-productive, doesn't it? Some kind of ultra-fit death wish."

"Quite a lot of talk about death today," Dr. Goodman replied, writing in her notebook as she studied his body language.

"It's been on my mind. The character in my script is a bit— unhinged." Jerry paused, turned towards her, and stared down at her legs. "I appreciate you wearing that short skirt."

Dr. Goodman glanced down. "It's a conventional length."

"Maybe a tad on the short side," he replied, returning to his chair. "It's attractive, but it can be distracting."

Dr. Goodman's expression hardened as she uncrossed her legs and sat upright. "I'll keep my attire in mind for future sessions."

Jerry shook his head. "I'm not complaining. I mean I appreciate it. It's, just… distracting. Doesn't matter, you're distracting even without the short dress."

Her eyes lasered on Jerry, she took a long, practiced psychotherapist pause. "What is going on with you today, Jerry?"

"Nothing." Jerry paused and gave a clipped laugh. "Is mine just one more drab vanilla session in a dreary day? While we're talking are you thinking about what you're having for lunch and how much

7

longer until it's over? Should my issues be more interesting?"

Dr. Goodman sat back, put her hands together as if in prayer. Then, placing them on her lap, she leaned towards him. "You're deflecting, asking meaningless questions so you don't have to talk. How about you stop with the smokescreen and really talk? What's really going on?"

Jerry sat back, took a deep breath, and began. The story he had initially told had very little to do with him. It was the backstory he'd written for the protagonist in his sci-fi screenplay. The character had a difficult, challenging relationship with his father. Jerry left out the fact that in the screenplay the father in question was from another planet and had been sent to earth on a reconnaissance mission. He got more involved as the story unfolded, making mental notes of plotlines to incorporate once he got back home. Jerry wasn't there for therapy.

Dr. Goodman glanced up at the clock strategically placed behind the client's chair. "We can explore this further in our next session. Our time is just about up now and we need to stop." She closed her notebook and placed it on the table.

Jerry winced. "I don't like these abrupt sudden stops. They're jarring. Just as we start to really talk and you shut your notebook and announce—'time's up.'"

Dr. Goodman nodded sympathetically. "I understand. We can review that at our next session."

Jerry began to stand, but sat back down, letting his body fall into the chair. "You were an actress, right?" he asked as he stared at her. "I mean, before you did this. You acted and modeled, right? When it comes to looks, you beat Nicole Kidman, Charlize Theron, or Amber Lake hands down."

Dr. Goodman reacted with a tight smile. "We're not here to talk about me." Standing, she walked to her office door and opening it, ushered him out. "Same time next week? Or are you going away for Thanksgiving?"

8

"Same time, same place," he replied as he headed towards the open door. "Not going home this year. Trumpism has changed the holidays. Talking politics at the Thanksgiving table while holding a knife doesn't seem like a good idea right now." Raising his eyes, he looked at Dr. Goodman. "Next session, a short, egg-blue skirt would be nice."

"I'll see you next week, Jerry." She motioned towards the waiting room, signaling his time to leave. Jerry gave a slight smile, nodded, and exited.

Closing the door, Dr. Goodman walked to her desk, sat down, and opened her laptop. Pausing, she glanced out the window and watched as a mockingbird landed on the sill and insistently pecked on the pane as though it had an urgent message to share. Sitting back, she called up Chrome on her computer, Googled her name and searched for her images. Her modeling and acting shots were still up. She hadn't posted them, her agent had. Her eyebrows furrowed as she studied them. They were probably what Jerry had searched and found. Some of the lingerie photos were perhaps a bit too much, a bit too suggestive, unprofessional for a psychotherapist to have online. They needed to come down, she thought as she stared at the images; that would probably be for the best. There must be a way to do that.

She then placed the word "nude" after her name and hit search again. Someone had photoshopped an image. Her face was superimposed over a nude shot. The photoshopped image looked real. As she stared at the image, Dr. Goodman wondered who had taken the time and the interest. A stranger? A client? An acquaintance? An ex? Jerry? He'd obviously Googled her online, seen the images, had known she'd been an actress before he'd brought it up in the session. They all had to come down. Other clients could find them, anybody could see them. Still, they were attractive she thought as she carefully studied them. Jerry was right, she could give Nicole Kidman, Charlize Theron, or Amber Lake a run for their money.

She glance up at the clock on the wall. Jason was next. He was a producer. Up-and-coming. Might have good contacts. He could possibly refer some heavy hitters her way. She could use a few celebrities. It always helped; the media liked to pick up on that sort of information. After Jason was Marie, an African American model with an eating disorder, and then Kimberley would be done for the day.

She sat in her office, reviewing notes before her next client arrived. Calling up her Google calendar, she studied November. It was generally a busy month, at least until Thanksgiving. It picked up again after the holiday. Most of her colleagues slowed down during December, but that's not what she'd experienced. Holiday angst and depression was in full swing by then. Many of her clients were single, some were actors, creatives. December brought all of the usual holiday dread, but it also signaled year's end, growing older, one more flip of the calendar where success had eluded them.

Then came the new year. That was always a good time for her. People declaring a new beginning, outlining changes and resolutions which they seldom followed through on. The first week in January was generally slow, but that was understandable. Most were just getting their bearings, returning from holiday trips. January 1, 2020, fell on a Wednesday. A ready excuse to not officially start up again until the following Monday, meaning nothing would really start until the sixth.

But Kimberley was getting ahead of herself. It was still pre-Thanksgiving and she was already thinking well past the new year. She had a tendency to do that. She again glanced up at the clock on the wall, strategically positioned behind the client's chair. There were ten more minutes before Jason arrived. Enough time to quickly check her bank balance. But that could be depressing. She'd do that after her session, she thought, as she again Googled her photos. Leaning forward, her eyes narrowed as she appraisingly moved from shot to shot.

10

Chapter 2

J erry sat at the Circle K Tavern waiting for James to arrive. A local Santa Monica tavern, known for its beer and burgers. It acted as Jerry's and James's informal office. He smiled at the waitress as she placed his drink on the table in front of him. She was new, brunette, shapely, wearing the bar's trademark shorts and a tight blouse. Expertly holding a tray with three beers whose destination was two tables over, she wore the expression of someone who was unsuccessfully trying to appear interested. Jerry glanced at the large Mickey Mouse clock on the wall as he impatiently waited for James. The two had been friends since high school and were working on developing film projects together, plotting ways to succeed in Hollywood, hit the big time. At least Jerry was. All James wanted was to write novels. He'd had one book published and another on the way, which was a bit disconcerting for Jerry. The two had been on the same footing for most of their lives. Now James was two moves ahead. His first novel sold poorly, and it didn't look like his second novel would fare better, which Jerry found at least somewhat comforting. But still, the scorecard now read James two—Jerry nothing.

And it could get worse. A hustler, a fringe quasi-producer named Lanier, whom James described as a fast-talking cross between Morticia Adams and a bowling ball, had contacted him about possibly adapting his book as a film. Initially Jerry found that distressing. That would push James even further up the ladder. But giving it further thought, he realized it could be a plus. Jerry could catch James's tailwind and fly with him. They'd succeed as a team, coproducers, form their own production company. Jerry could use the opportunity to shoot through that small crack into the inner world of the industry. He'd be a player. They'd both be players. From the little Jerry knew about Lanier, albeit strange, she could be real. She was annoying, that was a given, but she could be more than just another Hollywood, glad-talking dead-end trip to nowhere.

Lanier had connections, knew Nicole Kidman, Margo Robbie, Peter Stangerson, Amber Lake. At least she said she did. According to Lanier, not only was Peter Stangerson interested in directing a film based on James's book, there was talk of Amber Lake or Margo Robbie playing the lead and Nicole Kidman costarring. Chris Hemsworth, Matt Damon, and Bradley Cooper were apparently all being considered as the male lead. Those were names. Real names. Big names. A-list names. Jerry wasn't naive. He knew Lanier could simply be tossing out names to impress. Everyone in Hollywood did that. But, they could be real. And a Google search showed that she had a track record. She was listed on the credits of a Peter Stangerson film. Granted that was five years ago. But still, although well past his glory days, Stangerson remained one of the biggest director's names out there. He was real. And the actors Lanier listed were bankable, certifiable names that could green-light a project. When that light turned green, Jerry wanted to be ready to slam his foot on the accelerator, push it to the floor and speed in before anyone could ask for credentials. He'd make his own rules and round home base before anyone even knew he was there.

Trouble was it all revolved around James's book, and James was disinterested in the film world. All he cared about were his books. He didn't understand that novels were passé, over, done, simply flares to shoot up to get someone to notice you existed. The success, the money, the fame—those came with film deals. And now, with streaming services, it was the wild west. Producers were falling over themselves for content. James's novel could be the flare, the gleaming shot in the dark that catches fire. Jerry looked up and smiled as James sat down. Turning towards a waitress as she passed, he held out his hand, stopping her mid-stride, "You're new."

"First day," she replied with a smile.

"An auspicious day. Your lucky day. I want I introduce my partner, James Lansing," Jerry looked up at the waitress and nodded towards James. "Note the name, time, and place. This is life changing for you."

The waitress stared wearily from Jerry to James. This was L.A., where every nobody posed as somebody.

James looked at the waitress with a weary smile. "My friend here deals in fiction."

"Not true," Jerry insisted. "This is real—I'll fill you in later," he added, as though she was anxiously waiting to hear his story. "Right now, I urgently need to talk some sense into my friend here. Maybe we can meet later. Until then, two beers please."

"Right." Raising one eyebrow, she smiled and walked away.

James shook his head as he watched her exit. "That's it? You're not going to hit on her?"

Jerry sighed, carefully studying the waitress's ass as she headed towards the bar. "That's how important this meeting is. And that," he added pointedly, "that is a great ass, a walking definition of a great ass." Taking a beat, he looked back towards James. "So, fill me in. Do we have a deal?"

James shrugged and looked out the window. "I'm just wasting time. The meeting Lanier set up yesterday with Peter Stangerson and Dunhill Jr. was a total waste. A complete dud."

Jerry sat back, his eyes widening as he stared at James. "You met with Peter Stangerson and Dunhill Jr.? You're bullshitting me. You met with Peter Stangerson and Dunhill Jr.," he repeated, "and didn't tell me?"

"Nothing to tell," James replied with a shrug. "Like I said, a total waste."

"You actually fucking met with…" Jerry paused and looked up as the waitress returned and placed the beers on the table. "Perfect timing," he announced. "My friend here just met with Peter Stangerson and Dunhill Jr. We're about to close a deal, a big deal. This could be big—for you."

"Right. This is all about me." She shot James a smile and walked to the next table.

Jerry stared wistfully; his eyes locked on her ass. "They're all getting so jaded now."

James nodded. "Don't believe a good lie anymore."

"But this is no lie," he quickly added. "You actually did meet with Dunhill Jr. and Peter Stangerson—with a direct line that eventually leads to me, which could, if our waitress friend played things right, could lead to her."

James glanced at the waitress. "Right. Like she said, this is all about her."

"Don't be sarcastic," Jerry snapped. "This is serious."

"This is all bullshit. It's like a merry-go-round. It just spins and goes nowhere." James paused and grimaced. "I've been going to meetings with her for over a month now. Lanier only likes to meet at the Polo Lounge, or the Four Seasons or the Beverly Wilshire and she leaves right before the check comes. I end up paying every time with money I don't have. And nothing ever comes of the meetings. Like I said, bullshit!"

"Bullshit?" Jerry asked pointedly. "You just met with Dunhill Jr. You met with Stangerson. That's like meeting with one of the Gettys and Spielberg. You know how many people would pay for the chance to…"

"I am paying," James interrupted, his voice rising to emphasize the point. "I've been paying all along. These people are fucking richer than God, and I'm left with the bill. Like I said—bullshit! Next Lanier wants me to fly to New York to meet with Stangerson, Nicole Kidman, and Amber Lake. I'll fly there, pay for dinner, they'll ignore me, and I'll fly home." He paused and shook his head. "Not happening."

"New York? Amber Lake!" Jerry cried in a near yell. "You're meeting with Amber Lake? I worship Amber Lake. She's not a person, she's a goddess! You're crazy if you think I'm going to let you pull the plug when it's all just coming together." He paused and slowly, enunciating each word, repeated, "You are going."

James took a drink. "I already met with Stangerson and Dunhill Jr. and I was treated like a potted plant—some inanimate object which no one noticed while Peter and Dunhill Jr. just rambled on…"

"Peter!" Jerry interrupted, "listen to yourself, you're on a first name basis with Peter Stangerson. Next it will be Steven or Marty or Quentin. This is fucking amazing."

"You don't get it. They just talked to Lanier or to each other. I didn't exist."

"Of course you didn't exist," Jerry explained, feeling he was stating the obvious facts of life to a slow learning ten-year-old. "You're a fucking mortal sitting up with the deified where the air is rarified. But you're in the game, man. Lanier got you inside. Stangerson and Dunhill, Jr., right? The Dunhills fucking own most of New York. Old money. Up there with the Rockefellers."

"A lot of good that did me," James complained. "Dunhill Jr. is nuts, dresses like a maharaja, uses a megaphone to bark out orders at his minions. I don't think he even knew I was there. He, Peter, and Lanier spent their time discussing things that had nothing to do with my novel or the project and then he got bored and dismissed us. I mean, literally. He closed his eyes and waved his hand, shooing us away."

"But you were there. In his house," Jerry insisted. "No one gets in there. Plus, I Googled Lanier. She's worked with Stangerson before. She's in the game, or at least she was, and If she can make the introductions, get you this far… it's all worth it."

"Maybe she was in the game. Ancient history. Lanier is bipolar and Dunhill, Jr. is nuts. Certifiable."

"Of course he's nuts. It's his job to be nuts." Jerry paused and leaned in towards James. "Old money. The best kind. Nuts is part of the job description." Jerry leaned closer in. "So he's in? He's going to finance the film, right?"

"Finance?" James asked incredulously. "They didn't even mention the project while I was there. This has all been a lot of nothing. A lot of meetings, where nothing ever happens. I came away with a photo. That's it. Like some fucking stupid fan boy. I'm done."

Jerry slapped his hand against the table, this time loud enough to cause heads to turn. "Snap out of it! It's who you know in this city. That's all it is. You're golden." He then paused and asked, "What photo?"

James shrugged. "Dunhill Jr. had some half-naked girl there, who kept walking through the room with a dog the size of a horse. She said she'd just gotten a new iPhone and wanted to see how the camera worked. Said she wanted to take some photos to try out the camera. Dunhill Jr. waived her off. But Stangerson smiled and agreed, mainly I think just to piss Dunhill Jr. off. Stangerson went over and put his arm around Dunhill Jr., grinned, turned to the girl and directed, 'Lights, camera action!' She asked me for my phone because she wanted to compare the quality of the shots on her phone to mine. Then Stangerson, to annoy Dunhill Jr. even more, motioned me over and grabbing me by the arm, pulled me towards Dunhill Jr. He wrapped one arm around him and pushing me down on the couch, his other around me, turned towards the girl and shouted, 'Hurry. Shoot! Shoot!' The girl laughed and got a couple of shots with her phone and a couple with mine before Dunhill Jr. pushed us away, stopping it all and barking her out of the room. The girl laughed again, winked at Stangerson, walked over to me, handed me my phone and left, followed by her horse of a dog."

16

Jerry sat up, his eyes widening. "You've got photos then, on your phone? Photos of you and Stangerson and Dunhill Jr.? It's documented? You've got them?"

"A lot of good they're going to do me." James replied. "I write novels. I'm not a fucking screenplay writer. I wouldn't want to be a part of that world even if I could get in. They're nuts."

Jerry leaned towards James. "But you've got the photos, right?" Taking a beat, he held out his hand. "Give me your phone."

James shook his head. "They're embarrassing. I didn't know what was going on and I look like an idiot—deer-in-the-headlights stuff."

"Show me," Jerry insisted.

James groaned. Taking out his phone, he pulled up the photos and, leaning towards Jerry, held it out as he scrolled through the shots.

Grabbing the phone, Jerry stared wide-eyed as he scrolled and enlarged the images. "Fucking A! Fucking A!" he repeated, continuing to stare at the photos. "Stangerson has his arm around you. And in this one he has one arm around you and the other around Dunhill Jr. Everyone is smiling. This is amazing! Fucking amazing. You're one of the club," he added, texting himself the photos before handing James back his phone. "My best friend and partner is best friends with Peter Stangerson and Dunhill, Jr. You're golden, man."

"Friends?" James repeated, grabbing the phone out of Jerry's hand and slipping it back in his pocket. "Stangerson just pulled me in to piss off Dunhill Jr. It was a joke. A lark. Dunhill Jr. literally shoved me away."

"That's not the stories these photos tell. Perception creates reality and we are creating our own reality."

"You do it. Have fun. I'm going back to my novel. That's what I do, remember? I write."

"What is it with you?" Jerry asked. Sitting back, he folded his arms and stared at James. "Novels are analogue. Twentieth century. Hemmingway, Fitzgerald, Salinger—that's all fading. Put the nail in the coffin. Write your fucking novels, but then sell them as films so you can eat and pay the rent and your friend here can become famous—and get laid," he added, glancing back towards the waitress. "Ride this one out. Don't fuck it up."

"There's nothing to fuck up because—there is no there there. Besides, I'm supposed to start the job at the ad agency in three days. If I'm not there, I lose it. I'm broke," he added with a grimace. "I need that job."

Jerry took a drink and grinned. "The problems of the rich and famous."

"Like really broke," James repeated, picking up his glass and taking a drink, "I've been paying the tab on credit cards at all these fucking meetings with Lanier. Paying with money I don't have. I can't do it, not anymore."

"You fucking met with Peter Stangerson and Dunhill Jr." Jerry paused and leaned towards him. "Nobody meets with one of them, much less both. Lanier is setting you up in New York to meet with Stangerson and Amber Lake. Wake up! You don't have a choice. You gotta go to New York," he insisted. "Tell the ad company people that you came down with the flu. Push your start date back a week. Or tell them there's a funeral you have to go to. Tell them anything, but you gotta go to that meeting." Jerry sat back and stared at James. "Do not fuck this up. Go to New York, meet with Amber Lake, Nicole Kidman, and with your friend Peter Stangerson. Your book will then become a film—which in turn will sell your book and give you the freedom to write your next book. You won't ever have to think about a copywriting job again. We're almost there," he concluded. "You're racing to the finish line."

Looking away, James shook his head. "I'm not racing anywhere."

"Listen, you're doing great," Jerry said, sounding like a trainer encouraging his weary boxer in the late rounds. "All's good. Just see it through." Taking a beat, he glanced down at his phone. "Shit. I'm late. I gotta go." Standing up, Jerry pulled out his wallet and glancing inside grimaced. "I'll pay next time. I'm tapped out."

"What else is new?" James asked, picking up his drink and taking a sip. "What are you late for?"

Jerry glanced down and grinned. "Therapy."

"Shoulder acting up again?"

"Not that kind of therapy. Therapy therapy."

James laughed. "You're seeing a shrink? You?"

Jerry picked up his glass and emptied it. "Don't laugh. It's serious. You should see her. She's fucking gorgeous."

"Oh, that type of therapy session." James shook his head as he pulled out his wallet and took out his credit card. "Find a hooker. Probably cheaper and you know it's a done deal."

Jerry held his hand to his chest as though he'd been shot. "You wound me. I take therapy seriously. Working out my life problems. Plus, where is the accomplishment in nailing a hooker?"

"She's a therapist," James said pointedly. "She'll see right through you."

Jerry's grin widened. "She wore a short skirt to our second session. Kept crossing and uncrossing her legs."

"Oh, right, that's a sure sign," James replied, a sarcastic lilt to his voice. "I don't know how to break this to you, but lots of women wear skirts."

Jerry replied with an adamant shake of his head. "It's not only her skirt, it's her body language. Her tone, her look." Jerry pulled out his phone and searched for the lingerie photos of Kimberley. "Look!" He passed the phone to James, as though presenting evidence at a trial. "Is she hot, or what?"

James took the phone and studied the photos. "*This* is your shrink?"

Jerry nodded proudly. "I told you. Gorgeous. A goddess. I checked Psychology Today's listings for female therapists in Los Angeles," he explained, proudly staring at the photo of Kimberley and smiling. "They have a short description and a photo. I then searched through, I dunno, maybe a hundred different listings looking for the most

19

attractive twenty. I narrowed that to ten, then five, and, eventually, Kimberley won. Hands down she is the most gorgeous therapist in Los Angeles."

James stared at Jerry. "You searched Psychology Today listings looking to get laid?"

"It's more than that," Jerry explained.

"Yeah, right." James shook his head. "You seriously use Psychology Today as a dating app?" He paused, his eyebrows furrowing as he stared at her photos. "She has images like this online?"

"She used to be an actress and a model. These shots are from back then. This isn't just any gorgeous shrink. She probably still wants that, to be an actress—a star. They always do."

James looked at Jerry and gave a clipped laugh. "So during your shrink session, you'll subtly let it be known that you're just the guy who could restart her stalled career."

Jerry smiled. Reaching over, he took the phone back from James and stared at Kimberley's photos. "That's probably all she's ever wanted. Therapy was her fallback, plan B. What if she sees that I can offer her a way back to plan A? She'd be grateful, right? What if I drop enough breadcrumbs in our sessions where she starts to see I could be her ticket? Let's say that mid-session I just happen to mention that my partner is off to New York for a meeting with Peter Stangerson, Amber Lake, Nicole Kidman, Matt Damon?"

"Keep me out of it," James snapped. "And how did Matt Damon get into the picture? Besides, with her looks, she's getting that kind of come-on every day of the week. She'll see right through you. Blow you out of the water."

Jerry shook his head. "But my story's real. Except for Damon. That I just threw in to give it a bit more heft. But it's real and she'll see that. Besides, she'll want it to be real…"

"Keep me and my meetings out of it."

"Just reporting what's happening," Jerry replied. He again stared down at her photo. "Maybe you can help land her a small role, an under-five in a Peter Stangerson film. I mean, she has the looks, right?"

James stared at Jerry with a look of disbelief. "Land her a role? You're beginning to believe your own bullshit. Get a grip. There is no fucking film."

"But there will be," Jerry replied with a grin. "It's going to happen. And that's some incentive, for her, right? A role in a Peter Stangerson film." He again stared down at Kimberley's photos. "That could work. That's genius," he added, looking up at James. "I'll owe you big time." He glanced up at the clock on the wall. "Look, I gotta run. I'll pick up the check next time." Jerry turned towards the waitress as she passed their table. "James will fill you in," he called out. "And we need to talk about a film role. Give James your number." Turning towards James, he smiled. "It's all good. We're golden." He then grabbed his backpack, slung it over his shoulder and hurried out the door.

The waitress looked down at James and smiled as she placed the bill on the table. "Your friend is… different."

James laughed as he placed down his credit card. "I could think of more appropriate adjectives."

"He always in such a rush?" she asked, glancing towards the door.

"Late for therapy."

She paused and looked at James with a perplexed expression on her face. "Therapy? Him?"

Chapter 3

J erry silently practiced his rehearsed script as he entered the waiting room for Dr. Kimberley Goodman. After his meeting with James, he had new ammunition. He could now run the table. Start by gradually shifting her attention from his issues and deftly begin to zero in on hers. But James was right, she was a trained psychotherapist, so he had to be careful, subtle, tactful. Taking a deep breath, he walked over to the buzzer next to the name "Dr. Kimberley Goodman" and pushed. He then sat down and waited. Kimberley opened the door, smiled, and motioned for him to enter. Jerry frowned, glancing down at the billowy pink blouse and grey pants she was wearing. With a disappointed sigh, he walked past her to his usual chair. Sitting down and taking a drink of water, Kimberley placed her pad and pen on her desk and turned towards him. "So what do you think?" she asked positioning the fingers of both hands together in a steeple and resting her chin against them. "Should we have an actual session today? No more games?"

"Yeah. Right. Okay. Okay," he repeated, trying to remember his rehearsed speech, making sure he hit all of the salient points. "You were right. I am dealing with an issue, a personal problem that I've been avoiding. It's," he paused and dramatically looked away, "it's James."

"James?"

"Yeah. My friend. Best friend. He's also my production partner." Jerry leaned back, looked out the window. "We've been trying to develop projects for a while, but nothing has taken hold. Now he's published a novel, has a second one coming out, and some lunatic who calls herself a producer—maybe she's not as big of a lunatic as she seems, or maybe you have to be a lunatic to be a producer in this city—regardless, she's set up meetings with Dunhill Jr. and Peter Stangerson. They loved the project so much that they're flying him to New York for a follow-up meeting with Stangerson, Amber Lake, and Nicole Kidman. Amber Lake is being considered as the lead in the film adaptation of his book with Peter Stangerson set to direct." Jerry paused, reviewing his mental check list, assuring that he'd correctly set the bait, hit all the high points.

Kimberley sat back. She crossed her legs. "Those are big names. So where is the problem?"

"It's petty, I know," Jerry replied, folding his arms, and slightly shaking his head. "I mean it's silly feeling this way, particularly since I'm going to be one of the producers of the film." He paused, giving Kimberley some time to process the information. "But still, James is the one whose career is taking off. It's his novel. His project. His film. It's going to be a big. A-list director. A-list actors." He put his hands on his knees and leaned towards her. "I'm just a producer on it. James is the writer—it's his project," he repeated.

"The word 'just' doesn't quite seem to fit when talking about an Amber Lake, Peter Stangerson film," Kimberley said with a smile.

Jerry shook his head. "I know. It sounds silly. Most people would kill to be in my situation. But the film is going to be his. His baby. That's what I wanted. He got there before me. I lost."

"I didn't realize this was a competition."

"It probably shouldn't be, But… I'm jealous," he admitted, surprised at how true the words rang.

Kimberley nodded. "That's natural. But can you feel happy for your partner and grateful for the position this puts you in, right? Like you said, you're in a place most people could only dream of."

Jerry responded with a somber nod. It was working. She was making his case for him. "I keep telling myself that. This has opened an amazing door—and not only me." He paused. Maybe he was moving too quickly. Maybe a slower build was what was called for. Patience never being his strong suit, he continued. "This is also good for people I work with." Again he took a beat. He had to tread carefully here. Make the delivery subtle, matter of fact; not directed at her. "I'll be able to land some people positions on the crew. And," taking a breath he looked away, "I have some say in the casting. But still," he paused and then continued with a rehearsed sigh, "it's James that's the star. And," he added, his tone sounding angry, "he has another novel coming out." Taking another beat, he looked up and concluded, "He's the one taking off. Not me." Jerry flinched. The rehearsed scene hit too close to home when he delivered it.

Kimberley sat back and stared at him. Her gaze intensified, as she studied him. "You're focusing on what didn't happen instead of what did. It looks like you could be a producer on an A-list film. Could you have thought that possible a month ago?"

Jerry shook his head. He remained silent, waiting for her to continue.

Kimberley uncrossed her legs and leaned towards him. Although disappointed the powder blue skirt hadn't been worn, Jerry's eyes still followed her movements as if pulled by a magnet. "You're in an amazing position right now," she continued. "Consider being grateful, not resentful."

Jerry nodded. "Yeah, you're right." Pausing, he glanced down at her shoes. They were baby blue. The color of the skirt he'd asked her to wear. He took that as a sign. Smiling, he looked up at Kimberley. "And the real upside is it puts me in a position to help others. I can

24

be of service." He winced. That was perhaps a bit too much. But maybe not. He continued. "Like I said, I was able to land someone a position as a production assistant on the project and…" he paused. "And, I landed an actress I've worked with in the past, a small role. Nothing big, but on a film like this…" He stopped, letting the words hang.

"All the more reason to celebrate."

"Right," he agreed. He stared intently at Kimberley, unsure whether she was taking the bait. "This might sound nuts but…" Jerry swallowed hard. He was moving too quickly. He could feel it. This was not how he'd planned it. He was pushing too hard and too fast. But once he started, it was hard to stop. "In the film, one of the roles is that of a psychotherapist."

Kimberley picked up her water glass, took a drink. Her eyes narrowed as she stared at him.

"They're looking for an on-the-set consultant to work with the actress who plays that part. I suggested you. They're interested." Jerry cringed as soon as the words were out. It was rushed. Hurried. He'd moved too quickly. Hadn't given it enough of a buildup to seem plausible. His timing and delivery were all wrong. But, at least he'd had the sense to start with the consulting position—not an acting part in the film.

"I appreciate it, but I don't think so," she replied with a slight smile.

Jerry nodded and continued. "They need someone to work with Nicole—Kidman. She'll probably be the one playing the psychotherapist. Costarring," Jerry added. He had jumped into the deep water and now his best bet was to put his head down and swim. His words sped up as he spoke. "I don't know if they've completely locked it down yet, but it's either going to be Nicole Kidman or Charlize Theron. The role is an attractive, high-powered, Beverly Hills therapist to the stars. They need someone on set to act as a consultant, to make it realistic. James and I had a short conference call yesterday—with Peter."

Jerry paused and clarified, "Stangerson. He's looking for someone who knows how your world works. You're perfect for that, right? Well, except for the Beverly Hills part, but you're in Brentwood. I mean that's just a few miles away. And," he continued with rapid, machine gun delivery, "you could help whoever they choose for the role because you have the look. You know what it's like to be a very attractive therapist. You could advise her on what she'd encounter on that front. A male consultant could never do that, nor could a plain female who had never experienced that." Jerry paused and inhaled. He leaned further forward and added, "Plus, they… we… have one heck of a budget. It would pay well."

"I appreciate the thought, Jerry. Let's get back to your feelings about James."

"It would be a great opportunity," Jerry continued. "Peter's interested. He'll probably want you to meet with him. Who knows," he added with a shrug, "at the very least, you can maybe get them as clients. From the little I've seen of that world, they need it."

Kimberley laughed. "Thanks again, but we're here to talk about you."

Jerry gave a sullen nod. He'd blown it. He'd moved too fast. "I know. I know. But if the roles were reversed, wouldn't you advise me to, at the very least, investigate it? Wouldn't you tell me to give it a chance?" Continuing to hold her gaze, he sat back. "Just think about it and if you're interested…" He paused. "Look, I'm not supposed to do this, everything is under wraps, very hush hush, QT, NDA type stuff, but…" he paused, dramatically glanced towards the closed door, and conspiratorially leaned in closer. "I can get you a copy of one of the therapist scenes. You could read it and get some sense of the project. If you're interested, I'll introduce you. If not, that's fine, but at least give it a look. Dunhill Jr. is the executive producer," he added. "Like having Getty or Rockefeller money behind a project."

Kimberley stared at Jerry. After a beat, she leaned back and folded her arms. "Let's get back to our session."

Jerry nodded. Time to slow down. Back off. Give her space. "Right. Maybe we can revisit it later." He paused, waiting for an objection that didn't come. His body relaxed. She didn't say no. She was thinking about it now. The bait was in the water and she was circling. For the rest of the session Jerry talked about his fears of James succeeding while he was left behind. The more he talked, the more real the fears grew and the more depressed he became. The therapy process seemed counterproductive. His anxiety grew as he spoke.

As the session concluded, Jerry stood to leave. Pausing, he turned to Kimberley. "Look, it's crazy not to at least read the scenes they're using for the psychotherapist role. If you're interested, we can take it from there. If not, all you've lost was a few minutes reading it." Pushing his fictional narrative, he added, "I'm meeting with Amber Lake and Peter Stangerson at Dunhill Jr.'s home next week. Depending on who they've decided on, Nicole or Charlize will be there." He thought using first names added credibility. "Maybe nothing will come of it," he added to give it a stronger sense of realism. "But it's worth a shot—isn't it? Look, don't say anything. I'll email you that scene," he continued, like a dog refusing to release its grip. "Just give it a read. Who knows?"

Kimberley stood up, walked to the door, opened it. "I'll see you next week, Jerry."

Jerry gave a resigned nod. "Right. Same time, same place," he replied as he walked past her into the waiting room. Again, there was no direct "no" on her part. Although he wasn't quite sure, she seemed to have replied with an almost imperceptible nod. Opening the door to the lobby, he paused and stared back. "I missed the skirt," he said, turning to exit before she could reply.

Chapter 4

Setting her alarm and climbing into bed, Kimberley pulled the covers up over her shoulders as she rolled on her side. She began to drift as she thought about Jerry's offer. He was transparent. His ploy was obvious. More creative than most, but still—a ploy. Although, it was L.A., and she'd seen stranger things than that happen. And, what if it was real, if Jerry actually could arrange for her to meet with Peter Stangerson, it would be foolish for her to not at least explore it. It could all be a ruse, a client's ramblings. But it could be real. Jerry's story seemed to hold together. And, if Peter Stangerson was involved, the funding was in place, and Amber Lake and Nicole Kidman were on board... well, that was real. It probably wasn't. She knew that—but what if it was? The worst that could happen was she'd look foolish. And wasn't that what she encouraged her clients to do, take some risks in life, chances? If they ended up looking foolish at least they had tried.

Adjusting the pillow, she let go, feeling herself sink, drift. Her thoughts returned to Jerry. If it was real—she knew that "if" was a big one, but if it was—who knew what else it could lead to, what doors it could open? All she'd ever needed was a chance. Maybe the consulting could lead to something more. She could act. She had the looks—a gift that didn't last, a finite gift. Gone in a blink. Like a bank account with daily withdrawals.

Her thoughts were taking a depressing turn. She repositioned herself, grabbed her pillow more tightly, and began doing breathing exercises, slow even breaths through the nostrils, exhaling through the mouth. Again, her focus returned to Jerry. She wasn't seriously considering his offer; it was just a game to help her fall asleep.

Instead, her mind raced. If it was real, Jerry was right, she'd make a perfect consultant for the film. The role was tailor made. A practicing psychotherapist. She was attractive, some said beautiful. Jerry said gorgeous. She was in good shape, heads turned when she passed. It would be a waste not to take professional advantage of it. A consultant on a Peter Stangerson film starring Amber Lake and Nicole Kidman could just be the beginning. She'd hire a PR firm to get that word out. The media, particularly TV, liked their experts to be attractive. And she wasn't just attractive, she was also eloquent, funny, made for TV. Given a little time for research, she could talk about any topic they threw at her. She could probably work her way to a regular guest spot on a local news outlet and then from there—a regular on a national morning show, or cable news outlet. Not many have her looks, a Ph.D., and had worked as a consultant on an Amber Lake, Nicole Kidman, Peter Stangerson film. That could open doors.

Kimberley rolled on her right side, again adjusting her pillow. She felt her body begin to give way as she again began to drift. But her thoughts continued as her defenses gave way. She'd be the ideal consultant. In a perfect world, she'd play the role herself. She was an experienced actress. She'd done theatre, some commercials—they had required acting. And there was that horror film early on. Embarrassing. But still, although the film was horrible, she had done good work. It would probably resurface once her career began to take off. Those things always seem to, particularly now. No one can do a nude scene now and not have it come back to haunt them. She smiled at the thought of being haunted by a horror film. But, nude images had become so ubiquitous that no one really cared anymore. Not only actors, the internet was overflowing with nude images. Some of her clients seemed to be sexting all day long. Film nudity was nothing compared to the sexting and revenge porn that flooded the net. If it became an issue, she'd hire a reputation management firm. But there was nothing to worry about a few topless scenes. Tame in this world.

Kimberley winced slightly, embarrassed that she was allowing herself to fanaticize about actually playing the role. Still, she often told her clients that fantasizing was healthy. A tool she regularly recommended. It was good for the psyche to let it run free, open the gates, and let it gallop. The trick was to remain judicious. Realize it was fantasy while keeping a solid grasp on reality.

Reaching out, she grabbed for one of the extra pillows and positioned it between her knees Her best bet was to keep Jerry around, go with it, at least for a bit. Give herself time to discover what was what. If that involved a short skirt and crossing her legs now and then, why not? Plus, Jerry had issues and she could help. Their sessions would give her a chance to work with him, help him. He was in therapy for a reason. If he came with perks, well—why not, she thought. It was probably all a ruse, she again thought as she drifted off—unless it wasn't.

Chapter 5

Jerry sat at his desk, working on his laptop. He was already behind schedule. His plan was to have his sci-fi horror script ready. Once James's film got the green light, they needed to have another project that was good to go. The Hollywood machine needed to be constantly fed and Jerry was more than willing to oblige. Plus, he needed his sci-fi script ready for Comic-Con. That wasn't until late July and it was still late November, but time quickly slipped away. It would be 2020 before Jerry knew it. A friend of a friend said he could get Jerry an introduction to one of Marvel's top execs. His sci-fi horror script would be perfect for them. It was fresh, new; it would make a great comic book turned blockbuster series. If he could make an entrance at Comic-Con with a Peter Stangerson/Amber Lake project in the works, landing the sci-fi deal would be a slam dunk. He had four other equally good script ideas. Ideally he'd have two or three other projects on the conveyor belt once James's film had been given the go-ahead. They were a team. A film-making machine.

His eyebrows furrowed as he reviewed his revised script. He had changed the female lead so that she'd look and sound like Amber Lake. She now was Amber Lake. If they could lock Amber to a two or three picture deal, that would be perfect. That would shoot their flair high into the Hollywood sky. While James grumbled and complained, Jerry was preparing them for success. The industry demands product and Jerry had it in spades. Once all was in place, they'd be set. For now, he needed to focus and write the fictional psychologist scene he'd told Kimberley about. The nonexistent, never-to-be-used scene about a drop-dead gorgeous sex-starved Beverly Hills psychotherapist to the stars, played by a drop-dead gorgeous psychotherapist. Given the chance, it could improve James's film, add a seductive backstory, and a sexy eye-candy element to the project. The more Jerry thought of it, the more realistic it sounded. It would be foolish not to use it in the film. The scene not only gave him a leg up with Kimberley but offered the film new marketing possibilities. Kimberley had feigned disinterest, but she had taken the bait. Jerry saw that. She wanted his story to be real.

Saving his sci-fi horror film script document, Jerry opened a new page in Final Draft and, smiling, went to work on his Kimberley scene. The words flowed. The scene moved. Kimberley came to life as he typed. After an hour, he took a deep breath. He read and reread the scene. It was good. It would work. Taking a sip of coffee, he picked up his phone and called James.

"She's crazy," James blurted out, before Jerry could say hello. His tone was angry, accusatory, as though whatever he was referring to was Jerry's fault.

"Who's crazy?"

"Lanier. She is crazy. Certifiable."

"Oh, her. Of course she's crazy. They all are. Crazy works in that world. Crazy is a prerequisite." Jerry paused. "So how was she crazy this time?"

"She started screaming that if I don't go to New York for the meeting not only is she never talking my calls—which would be nice—she's suing me."

"Suing you for what?"

"Who knows. She never got to that. She was too busy yelling. I can't talk to her anymore."

"Tell her to calm down. And, of course you're going to the New York meeting. Problem solved." Jerry took a beat, waiting for James to contradict him. Hearing silence, he smiled as he continued. "You already met with Stangerson and Dunhill Jr. Now Stangerson and probably Nicole Kidman. Nobody gets meeting like that unless they're in. You're golden man. It's happening."

"Nothing's happening," James replied with a shake of his head. "She wants me to fly out on Thanksgiving weekend. That's the worst possible time to fly. Busiest weekend of the year," he added pointedly. "First Lanier said we'd be going to New York on Dunhill Jr.'s private jet. Now it turns out he's sending his jet to London to pick up some new shoes so I'd have to fly commercial. On Thanksgiving weekend! And I have to fly coach!"

"Right, as though you've ever flown first class." Jerry took a deep breath, working to keep his voce calm, measured. All James could do of late was create problems, throw out roadblocks. "Plus, she's not ordering you to fly on Thanksgiving. She's looking out for you. Setting you up with Amber Lake and Peter Stangerson. Who gets a meeting like that? She might be crazy, but she's doing you a favor. Big time."

"She's not offering to pay for it," James snapped. "I don't have money to fly to New York and rent someplace to stay. Besides, I'll just be ignored by all of them, just like before, and will end up paying the check with money I don't have. And I'll lose the copywriting job. I'm not going," he repeated.

"Slow down," Jerry replied, as though talking down an over-hyped child. "Lanier introduced you to Dunhill Jr., right? To Stangerson. She's setting up a meeting for you to meet with Stangerson and Amber Lake. You'll probably meet with Nicole Kidman and Bradley

Cooper while you're there. How many people get meetings like that? No one doesn't go to a meeting like that, no matter where or when it's held. This is real. This is our in. They're going to make your fucking book into a film. You cannot not go," he added, continuing to speak in double negatives. "You're going. End of story."

"Yeah? And how do you propose I pull that off? My new job starts next week. If I don't show, I lose it. I'm broke. Don't have money for the rent. I need the job." James paused and with an audible sigh added, "It's a moot point anyway. I don't have money to pay for a trip to New York. And a hotel. You know how much that costs? Even Airbnb over there is high. There's no way."

"There is always a way," Jerry insisted. Taking a breath, he tried to keep his responses steadied, measured. "Meeting with Amber Lake and Stangerson—that's like meeting with Scarlett Johansson and Scorsese. You're going."

"She's calling again," James said as he watched Lanier's number light up on his phone. "She's crazy. Amber Lake and Stangerson probably won't even show up. It's all just bullshit."

"She introduced you to Dunhill Jr., to Peter Stangerson, right?" Jerry asked, as though leading the prosecution's questioning. "Yes, she did!" he replied firmly, answering his own question. "Look, she's a bit crazy, but that's just how these people operate. It's their MO. They take a circuitous route to get there, but they do get there. You can't bail, Not now."

"I can and I am. I'm a novelist," James declared, as though planting a flag. "I don't want to make films."

"Yes you do," Jerry insisted, his voice rising as he spoke. "We do. You're in some kind of denial, a fear of success, self-sabotage mode. Breathe deeply and it'll pass." Standing, Jerry began to pace. James was complaining, acting like a spoiled kid. He had a meeting with two of the most powerful people in the industry and still he was whining. "Snap out of it," he ordered. "Let's come up with a New York game plan. This is it. Your ticket. Our ticket." He paused, waiting for James to respond. There was silence. Jerry felt the tide ebbing, taking his connections to Amber Lake and Peter Stangerson out to sea—and with it, his connection to Kimberley.

He continued to pace. "You're almost there. Just steps away. You can all but see the finish line. Peter Stangerson, Amber Lake, Dunhill Jr. A dream-team. You can't bail now. I won't let you. I know your focus is your book," he added, quickly switching his approach. "This will get your book made into a movie and that in turn will sell more books and land you another book deal. It's all of a piece."

He paused by his kitchen window and, staring out, exhaled. His thoughts went to the new scene he had written. It was good. It could work. One look at Kimberley and Stangerson would be on board. And James was selfishly throwing it all away. "You fucking have to go to New York!" he declared. Taking a deep breath, he closed his eyes, frowned, and unable to stop his words declared, "I'll pay. I'll pay for everything. An investment in our future."

James winced. "That's crazy. You can't pay. With what?"

Feeling his body stiffening, Jerry focused on his breathing. "I'll pull from my inheritance?" The words sounded more like a question than a statement.

"You fucking crazy? It's not that much and it's the only savings you've got." James took a beat and added. "Besides, I'll still lose the job if I go."

"Fuck the job!" Jerry all but yelled. "If I'm willing to risk losing my savings, don't moan about losing a fucking copywriting job. Don't make this all about you, okay? Who knew my crazy uncle was going to leave me anything anyway? This is what it's for. This is our future. Our careers. Forget the fucking copywriting job! Check on flights and a place to stay and call me back. Go red-eye and find some cheap Airbnb. I'll cover it. This is going to happen." Jerry's pacing intensified.

James began to respond but Jerry quickly interrupted.

"Stop being so negative," he ordered. Negativity breeds negativity.

I'm paying. There's no excuse now. You've got to go." Again James began to respond but remained silent. Seeing a ray of light in James's hesitation, Jerry continued. "You're focusing on being a low-rent copywriter and I'm focusing on launching your film career—on changing your entire life. Perspective!"

"You really want to gamble your money on this New York trip? That's crazy."

"Doing nothing is crazy and it's not a gamble. It's an investment." Stopping his pacing, Jerry sat back on his couch. Focusing on his breathing, he continued. "We're going to remember this call. In a couple of years, I'm going to drive up to your home in the Hollywood Hills overlooking the city and say, 'remember when you wanted to cancel that meeting with Amber and Stangerson? Remember when you were going to go to the copywriting job instead?' And you'll laugh and thank me as you walk me out to your five-car garage to show me your new Jag."

James laughed. "You're batshit crazy."

At the sound of James's laugh, Jerry sat back and smiled. "Check the flights and Airbnb and call me once you set things up." After a pause he asked, "So we're good, right? It's a go."

"This is crazy."

"Smart crazy. I'm paying for it and it's happening—right?" Jerry paused and then repeated, "Right?"

"I'm just going to the meeting and then flying right back. I'm not staying," James insisted.

Jerry exhaled, "Yeah. Right. Sure," he said, running his hand through his hair. "Whatever you want. Or stay a day, an extra day, and catch a play or something."

"Flying right back," James repeated. "New York is crazy, packed with people during the holidays. And it's cold!"

"It's almost Christmas. Is should be cold. Call me once you've set it up. This is it, man, this is our ticket. We're speeding down the runway.

2020 is our year."

"It's crazy," James repeated, as though chanting a mantra.

"Grab a pen and I'll give you my credit card information." Pulling out his wallet, he took out his card. His hand shook as he gripped the card tightly and read out the numbers. "Let me know when you've set it up. This is going to work," he said, hanging up before James could argue.

Disconnecting the call, Jerry put down the phone. It was a done deal. James would go. They were so close now. Once the film got the green light he'd figure out some way to get Kimberley a meeting with Stangerson—at least for a meet-and-greet. She'd see Jerry was real. That would change all the dynamics They'd each have something that the other wanted. She was primed now, had gone for the bait. She tried to pretend she hadn't, but as he left her office, he could see it in her expression. A look reflecting that maybe, just possibly, Jerry was telling the truth—a crack in the door had opened. Both Kimberley and a film career were in his sights.

He'd have to keep a tight rein on James, Jerry thought as he stood and headed towards the kitchen. He didn't understand how the industry worked. Jerry was made for the game. He'd watched from the outside long enough to see it. Know it. James was right about Lanier. She was nuts, but all of those people were nuts. Crazy was compulsory. Hollywood rewarded crazy. Got on its knees for crazy. The crazier the better. James didn't get it. He was like a kid looking at grown-ups, thinking that they must know what they're talking about, that they must be sane. The tagline was they didn't have a clue. They were all running downhill blindfolded, insisting they could see where they were going.

Jerry poured a coke in a glass of ice—he hated drinking from the can. His body felt as though it was racing, as though he were on speed. Maybe it would be best to forget Kimberley, at least for now. Focus on the film. A crazy gambit to begin with. As James asked, who uses the Psychology Today site as a dating app? But quickly the answer came that he did, and Kimberley was an integral part of his end game. She was gorgeous. Sexy. Alluring. Seductive. Jerry wasn't delusional. He realized he'd have no chance with her if the dynamics didn't drastically change.

But now had a game plan. A strategy. A good one, one he was betting part of his inheritance money on. A Peter Stangerson/Amber Lake film was a better, wiser investment than any mutual fund or ETF. He had exponentially upped his game. James's New York trip was an investment. It would take a bite out of his savings, but, the payoff would be massive. If he needed to, he could pick up some freelance gigs to pay himself back, replenish his savings. That sounded good, made him feel better, but he knew that would never happen. Once he withdrew the money, it would be gone. There would be no payback. That's just who he was. But the investment would be worth it. It was a solid plan. Smart. The payoff would be huge. For now his mission was to keep his eye on the prize.

Jerry walked into his bedroom and opened his desk drawer. Taking out a notebook and pen, he returned to the dining room, sat at the table, and began to compile a to-do list. This was a very delicate time in his relationship with Kimberley. One false move and his whole plan could unravel. And so much depended on other people. A fact Jerry hated.

Jerry wrote "James" at the top of the first blank page. He stared at the page for a bit then tore it out of the notebook, crumpled it, tossed it in the trash can. Staring down at a new blank pristine page, he began to write.

Tomorrow's to do list:

1.   Call Kimberley and make an appointment ASAP.

2.   Write out talking points to review with her before the session. Practice my delivery.

3.   Finish the psychotherapist scene and email it to Kimberley before the session—make it good!

4.   Tell her that Peter Stangerson has seen her photos and after listening to my pitch is definitely interested. Deliver the news matter-

of-factly. Make it believable.

5.   Explain that after seeing her photos and listening to my impressive pitch about how great she is, Peter completely surprised me by asking if I thought Kimberley could play the role herself. This is pushing it, but time's wasting. Emphasize that it was Stangerson's idea.

6.   Practice delivering that information so that I show how surprised I was by Stangerson's question. Again emphasize that the idea came from him, not me (call him Peter instead of Stangerson—has a better ring).

7.   Explain how I further interested Peter in the idea by mentioning that if Kimberley played the role instead of Nicole Kidman, Peter would have a great PR hook—gorgeous therapist to the stars playing herself. Gives it a truer ring. Also say that I mentioned that Kimberley could save them quite a bit of money, since, being new, she wouldn't charge nearly what Nicole would. (Maybe rethink on that one. That might be pushing it.)

8.   Maybe add that Stangerson asked if Kimberley would be willing to do a nude scene, maybe topless, something tasteful and I said I wasn't sure but would ask. That could make it sound more realistic—although, that might be pushing it even more. (SCRATCH THAT!—for now…)

9.   Tell Kimberley that Peter asked if she'd take a preliminary meeting with me and James before James goes to New York. Then Peter would like to meet her himself—that will set up a meeting with me outside of her office, which will make it feel real.

10.   Somehow get James to agree to be there (at least at the start of the meeting)—to make it seem real, legit—and then exit to give me some time alone with Kimberley.

11.   Make it sound urgent, which it is. Let Kimberley know that there isn't time to think or consider, that these doors only open for a second or two before slamming shut again.

12.   Play it by ear from there.

He then moved on to his Kimberley to-do list:

1.   Google Lanier and find out more about her. What projects has she worked on? How real is she? What do her weaknesses seem to be.

2.   Google interviews with Amber Lake. Look for dissatisfactions with her career. Roles she hasn't played that she's hoping for. Come up with script ideas that James can pitch her at his New York meeting that feature those type of roles.

3.   Call James and give him meeting talking points for the New York meeting—do some role playing with him to make sure he gets it (he never will).

4.   Make sure James has set up the New York trip. If he hasn't, immediately buy him a round trip ticked and find an Airbnb or hotel. Don't give him time to think about it or reconsider. Leave him no room to wiggle out of going.

5.   Check out getting Stones tickets for their May 8th concert in San Diego. Who know how much longer they'll be around?

6.   Decide whether to stay in L.A. and drive to Comic-Con on July 23rd or find a cheap hotel in Anaheim—if there are any rooms left.

7.   Figure out the upcoming holiday schedule. Go to sister's for Thanksgiving. Explain to family why I can't go home for Christmas—this is no time to be away.

8.   Start putting feelers out for jobs or freelance gigs—until the production money comes in, especially with the holidays—money is going to get tight—but then the floodgates will open.

9.   Get the number from James of that waitress at the Circle K Tavern.

10.   Get a haircut.

Chapter 6

Kimberley drove into the underground parking lot of her Brentwood office building, parked in her assigned slot and, grabbing her purse out of the backseat, made her way to the elevator. She stopped in front of a mirror in the small waiting area and quickly studied her reflection. She was wearing light blue slacks, a pink flared blouse, and a blue jacket. Her hairdresser had squeezed her in the previous day. She looked good. Her makeup was subtle, not too heavy. Her jacket accentuated her sea blue eyes.

As the elevator door opened, she turned and walked in. A man hurriedly followed. He smiled, nodded, and nervously looked down. She'd seen him before, figured he worked in the building. They'd never said hello. He'd always glanced at her and then self-consciously looked away or stared down at his feet. She could sense him trying to inconspicuously look at her, muster up the courage to say a word or two. He'd tried before, but never quite did. As the elevator reached her floor and the door opened, Kimberley looked at him, smiled, and offered, "Have a good day."

The man looked up, his eyes beaming. "You too," he said, the words catching in his throat.

Again she smiled as she headed down the hallway. She'd done her good deed. Made his day. Walking into her office waiting room, she rearranged the magazines, made sure there was no trash on the floor or on the chairs, and straightened a painting that seemed to always tilt to the left. She then walked through the waiting room to her office. Kimberley shared offices with Carla, another therapist. Kimberley's office was the larger of the two. Not by much, but definitely larger. The two therapists seldom saw each other, seldom spoke, only shared pleasantries, which was fine with Kimberley. She preferred it that way. Best share offices with a stranger and let the stranger stay a stranger.

Kimberley turned on the lights, checked the temperature and, walking to her desk, sat down, and powered up her computer. It was a light workday. That was good—it gave her time to do errands, pick up her shoes and clothes from the cleaner, and have a more leisurely lunch than usual—but the light schedule was also problematic. She was getting low on patients. People were making their holiday travel plans. Most of Kimberley's clients had family outside of L.A. and, instead of having family come to them, they were the ones that left. Thanksgiving week was slow, but December was looking unusually dismal. She was hoping that the Trump effect would work in her favor. The man was a buffoon, but overall, he had been good for business. The first two years, she'd been fully booked with terrified progressives who hadn't see him coming. Those first Thanksgivings had been good, lots of fireworks, political issues that came up at family gatherings, families divided, unable to utter a single word to one another, particularly during the holidays. People were coming to blows, conversations became battles, families disintegrating. Living in Los Angeles, her clients would often be viewed with suspicion as they ventured back to their beet-red southern and middle-American hometowns. They'd be greeted with suspicious glances. Had they been enlisted? Brainwashed? They were probably now part of the progressive cabal. The pedophile ring run by Hollywood moguls and the Clintons. It was fodder for interesting sessions.

She was hoping, with the 2020 election around the corner, some of her patients would be dealing with even more heightened issues. But the topography had changed; it now generally came down to clients spending the holidays with family members that were on their side of the political divide or cutting off communication completely.

Kimberley pulled out her phone and opened December 2019 on her calendar. People would probably start leaving on Friday the thirteenth. That sounded inauspicious from the get-go. That weekend would start the mass exodus, leaving slim pickings on the client side. And, with January first falling on a Wednesday, people would use that as an excuse to stay away until Monday. 2020 wouldn't really start until the sixth.

Her practice always slowed around the holidays, but this one was going to be bleaker than most. Apart from Jerry and one or two other regulars, those few weeks would be dead. Things generally picked up mid-January. February was usually a stellar month. New Year's resolutions were already being shattered by then. The shock of a new year with still-unfulfilled dreams began hitting home in February. But that was months away. Kimberley generally saved an emergency fund for these times, but this year her client load had been slower than usual and there had been unforeseen bills.

Keeping a full client load seemed to always be a problem. Some would up and leave after a session or two. Others would just disappear, ghost. She was generally good at convincing clients to stay longer than they needed to. Once the mundane issues were dealt with, they could move on to life's existential problems. There was always something. She had come up with a system where if clients bought twelve session, they got the thirteenth free. Offering the free session was worth it. It kept them on board It helped knowing she had a client locked in for a bit. But feeling that she had to continually feed the beast was exhausting. Networking. Digital marketing. Social media. Hustling. The hellish part of her job description.

Most of her clients came through referrals, which was nice.

But referrals were nothing she could count on. They were like rainstorms; they came when they came. PR could help, she thought as she studied her sparsely filled booking ledger. Getting on TV, radio, magazines, newspapers, establishing herself as a celebrity therapist. Particularly TV—the camera loved her. Social media was what she should be doing. But she loathed social media. Everyone posing, pretending to be someone they weren't. It was annoying and time consuming. And, when she had done it in the past, no matter how vanilla the photos of herself she'd posted, she had gotten trolls, or come-ons, or someone would dig up some of her old modeling shots and send them to her along with suggestive, often disgusting DMs. She should hire someone to handle that, delete those photos, one of those reputation management companies. But they weren't cheap. More expenses. Besides, she thought as she carefully studied the images, they were flattering. She'd think about it later.

Kimberley checked her messages. One from an associate; two sales calls. Sam, a long-standing client, asking if he could change his three o'clock session to following day and a call from Jerry. She hit the listen button. "Hi Kimberley, I mean Dr. Goodman. It's Jerry, I know this is last minute, but would it be possible to shoehorn in a session today? I'd very much appreciate it. There are some issues I really need to talk about. Important issues."

Kimberley walked to the window, folded her arms, and stared out. It probably wasn't just coincidence that she heard Jerry's message just as she was thinking how she needed to get into the media. Life often happened that way, at least in her experience. It wasn't simple luck. Not merely serendipity. She'd tracked that, both in herself and in her clients. If you focused strongly enough on something, things shifted. Then it was up to you whether you take advantage of it or not. Most people didn't. Either they didn't see the opportunity in the first place, or they saw it, it frightened them, and they recoiled. She'd watched clients do that. It was not a mistake she'd make. Holding that thought, she again listened to Sam's message, followed by Jerry's.

She would normally charge Sam for not giving her the 24 hours' notice she required, but he had been a client for a while. Plus, he'd be staying around during the holidays. No sense antagonizing him. She'd be magnanimous and waive the charge. This freed up her three o'clock slot. She could see Jerry and not have to rearrange her day. For all she knew, Jerry could be a harbinger. Foolish not to see it through.

Kimberley realized it was silly to think it could actually lead to anything. Then again, stranger things had happened. Best prepare, she thought as she stared out onto San Vicente Boulevard. See it through. Give herself a shot. If she didn't follow up, she'd never know. That's how opportunities were lost. Besides, he wasn't technically a client, not really. He didn't come for therapy. This was his form of Tinder or online dating. He was upfront about that. Didn't hide it. It was probably her modeling shots that did it. But it wasn't as though she was the only therapist with an IMDb page. Chances were that removing those images would hurt her more than help. Her SEO would probably take a hit. And, what if Jerry was on the up and up, they impressed Peter Stangerson. If certain clients, or even non-clients had trouble with her because of her looks, that was outside of her control. She was not about to start apologizing for being attractive. Not now. Not ever. And people did indeed want her to apologize. They always had. A colleague had once commented on how she dressed, suggesting that her clothes were too form-fitting, her dress perhaps an inch too short. Whose issue was that?

She couldn't let other people's discomfort affect her. She should lean into her strengths. That was the advice she'd give her clients. It was a part of her overall philosophical construct. She'd had clients who had received large inheritances and felt incredibly guilty because of it. It was Kimberley who helped them see it was a gift they should embrace, enjoy. No difference. Beauty was an inheritance. A gift. Nothing to feel guilty or apologize for. Trouble was, it was a fleeting gift. One to use or lose.

After lunch, before her session with Jerry, she'd have time to go to the cleaners and pick up her powder-blue skirt. Walking back to her desk, Kimberley returned Jerry's call and left a message saying that she could see him at three and to please call back to confirm. She then studied her Google calendar and reviewed her notes preparing for the first client of the day.

Chapter 7

Jerry arrived at 3 pm sharp. Entering the small waiting room, he pushed the button for Dr. Kimberley Goodman, sat down, picked up a copy of the New Yorker—the New Yorker seemed to be essential at therapists' offices—and waited. After a few minutes, Kimberley opened the door and motioned for Jerry to enter. "It worked out. I had a 3 pm cancelation right before I got your call," she explained.

Jerry nodded, noting she was wearing a short sea-blue skirt. He smiled, his eyes traveling down as he took her in. "I appreciate you making the time." Walking into her office, he sat in his regular place directly across from Kimberley's larger leather chair—the designated power position.

"So," Kimberley asked, sitting down, and crossing her legs, "what had you call before our regular appointment?"

Jerry glanced down following the movement of her legs. He was going to comment, thank her for wearing a skirt, but thought better of it. Kimberley's expression stayed constant as she watched him watch. Sitting upright, he cleared his throat and began. "Two things. First, I've been feeling particularly anxious and agitated since our last session." He figured he needed to clarify that he was there for therapeutic reasons and not just because of the project. "James is going to New York to meet with and cement the deal with Amber Lake and Peter Stangerson. They have a green light. The film is a go," he added, figuring that slight exaggeration would give his story more gravitas. "Like I said last time, watching his career take off is pushing my buttons. It's moving more quickly than I thought it would." He paused and theatrically ran his fingers through his hair. "This could really launch James's career. I know I should be happy for him. But—he's outpacing me. I feel I'm being left behind?"

Kimberley's eyebrows furrowed as she stared at him. "But you said you were a producer on the film."

"I am," he nodded sullenly, working hard to downplay the fact he'd indeed be a producer on an A-film. "But it's not the same. It's his project. Based on his novel."

"You're both moving forward. Together," Kimberley explained. "Maybe you're being a tad self-indulgent here. Feeling sorry for yourself instead of being grateful. Keep your focus on where you're going, not on James. Keep the focus on your forward motion, not on comparisons."

"Right," Jerry nodded. He did not appreciate being called self-indulgent.

Kimberley took a beat as she studied Jerry's body language. "And the second?"

"Second?" Jerry asked.

"You said there were a couple of reasons you came today. What's the second?"

"Oh, yeah, right." Jerry nodded, pretending that he had forgotten the second point, that it was an afterthought. Sitting up, he again glanced down at her legs. "I had a call with Peter—Stangerson. I talked to him about you." Jerry paused and glanced out the window, allowing time for that bit of information to sink in. He then looked back at Kimberley. "I hope that's okay. I didn't tell him I was a patient."

"I wish you hadn't—and I have clients, not patients," Kimberley corrected.

"Client, right," Jerry replied with a nod of his head. "I don't know how that would look if they knew I was a client. I mean I told James but he's family. I asked him to tell the others that you and I know each other socially." He looked at Kimberley and smiled. He liked the sound of that. "Hope that's okay."

Kimberley stared silently studying how he was holding himself. He was tight, rigid. It all could be an elaborate lie. Just one more come-on.

"So," Jerry continued, filling the silence. "I took the liberty of sending Peter…" Jerry went with Peter again, instead of Stangerson. Using his first name sounded more intimate, more real. "… the link to your IMDb." His story was somewhat factual, although he hadn't shown her IMDb page to Stangerson, but he had to James and James knew Stangerson. His story was nearly on-point. "Peter was impressed," he added veering back to the realm of fiction. "Even more impressed after I told him about you, explained you were a psychotherapist and had been an actress." Jerry paused and then added, "I also sent him a few of your online modeling photos," he exaggeratedly cringed to show doing so without her permission made him uncomfortable. "Hope that was okay," he repeated.

Kimberley sat back in her chair. "You should have asked me, Jerry."

Jerry replied with an understanding nod. "I know. But when I was talking to Peter and you came up and… it all happened so quickly. That's how these things happen. I was talking to him about bringing you on board as a consultant, and he asked… to see photos of you and then everything changed. He wants to meet you now." Jerry paused and again looked out the window. "It's the way things happen in that world."

"What do you mean everything changed?" Kimberley asked,

continuing to hold his gaze.

Jerry stood up, walked over to the window and looking out took a deep breath. He was pushing too fast, too hard, putting all his chips on one roulette spin. Turning towards her, he continued, "Don't freak out on me, okay?"

Kimberley's eyes locked on his. "I'm not following you."

"When I got off the call with Peter, I emailed him your pictures." For effect, he paused and stared back out the window. Turning back towards Kimberley, he soldiered on. "Peter called me back immediately. I mean, right away. That's not like him. He's not one to call back right away unless it's important—really important." Jerry again paused to consider his next sentence. He turned toward the window, closed his eyes, and jumped into the deep end. "Peter said he wasn't interested in you as a consultant." Opening his eyes, he turned and looked at Kimberley. "What he's interested in is reading you for a role in the—our—film."

Kimberley felt her pulse quicken. She sat still, reminding herself, he was a client, a client with issues, a client with an agenda. It was probably all a ruse, an elaborate lie, but still… "I don't act Jerry, not anymore."

"I know, I know," Jerry interrupted, "and I'm sorry if I overstepped, but I had Peter Stangerson on the phone. How many times can someone say that? As soon as he saw your images he was interested. It happened that fast. It wasn't something I planned on. He immediately called and asked, no, not asked, demanded, to know if you could act. I lied," Jerry confessed, his voice falling dramatically. "I told him I'd seen you in a play and that you were amazing. I know. I know," he quickly added, before Kimberley could respond. "It probably wasn't the right thing to do, but… I'm sure you are a great actress and he was interested. I mean really interested."

Jerry continued, barreling on, allowing no space for Kimberley to interrupt. "Peter went on about how the PR angle could work—a genuine gorgeous Beverly Hills psychotherapist playing a gorgeous Beverly Hills psychotherapist to the stars—particularly now when reality TV is so hot. I mean that's the zeitgeist now; we elected a reality star as president, right?" Jerry continued, not waiting for a reply. "Peter hit pay dirt that way with one of his other films. Remember Charlette Rains? She played that expensive escort in his film, *Exposed*. And in reality she was an escort. Peter put her in his film playing herself. Then she landed that reality TV show. It happened. It's worked before. Peter sees that with you—he can hit pay dirt again," Jerry concluded, convincing himself than this was more than a gambit. It was real.

"I don't run an escort service," Kimberley replied.

"I know," Jerry said. "That's just an example. But you know what I mean, it's worked before. Peter sees it can work again. There is no more perfect time. He wants to set up a meeting with you. But first he wants you to meet with James before he flies out to New York to meet with Peter, Amber Lake, and Nicole Kidman."

Kimberley gave an overly dramatic shake of her head. "Not happening, Jerry. Let's get back to why you're really here. Let's get back to what you were saying at the start of the session. You've been particularly anxious and agitated. That's why you're here. Let's get back to the session," Kimberley continued, tabling the current discussion to buy her time to think.

"Peter said he'd be calling James to discuss setting up the meeting with you," Jerry said forging on. "I'd be there. James and I can review everything with you then. We could meet at the lounge at the Beverly Wilshire. But it has to be soon. I mean, like Friday. James leaves for New York on Saturday. Peter is interested. Really interested. This could work," he added with an anxious expression.

"Let's get back to the session," Kimberley repeated, her tone measured, delivery stoic, expression unchanged.

Jerry frowned. She was either buying time to consider her options, or didn't believe his story. If it was the latter, he'd blown it, pushed too hard, made the story too fantastical, too unbelievable. Jerry paused. Best bring out his ace card. "You're right," he said, staring down and nodding. "I'm a bit of a mess. Everything is moving so quickly. Almost too quickly. I can't fully get a handle on it. Last week I was a struggling writer and next week I'll be a producer of an Amber Lake/Peter Stangerson film. But, like I said, the project really belongs to James. I talk to Peter, but James is the one hanging out with him. He's the one going to New York."

Deciding the time was right, Jerry pulled out his phone, called up the photos and, leaning towards Kimberley, showed her the photos of James with Peter Stangerson and Dunhill Jr. "See, Stangerson, Dunhill Jr., and James. He's completely in their inner circle now. Enlarging the photos as he scrolled, he continued. "See? He's at Dunhill Jr.'s home with Peter. He gets invited over socially. Not me. It hurts, you know," he added dramatically, "feeling left out like that." Jerry paused giving Kimberley time to study the photos, take in the reality of it all. She glanced up at Jerry. Her expression shifted. Seeing the photos had made an impact.

Kimberley stared, her eyes narrowing. After a pause, she leaned in towards him and asked, "What is this really about?"

"Don't you see my dilemma?" Jerry said, putting his phone back in his pocket as he turned the conversation from Kimberley to James. "Sure, I'll be a producer, but James is the star. It's his project. You told me to talk about my issues and I am. I'm having anxiety attacks. I'm anxious all the time." Jerry stood and walked to the window. "It's hard to eat. I can't sleep." He wondered if he was laying it on a bit too thick as he stared down at the cars on San Vicente. It wasn't a complete lie. He was anxious. That was a plus. It helped his story ring true. Actors had to believe their lines. Maybe he'd rushed it, should have waited a few more sessions, given them time to form a bond. But urgency gave it a sense of reality. That's how things worked in that world. And besides, James was about to go to New York.

Jerry turned towards Kimberley and continued. "And then there was the whole thing with you and the film and Peter. That too makes me anxious because you probably think I'm lying to you." He took a beat, shifting into a confessional tone. "I didn't know Peter would be so interested. But what I'm telling you is real and things like this happen in a flash in that world—overnight. Look what happened to James." He took another measured beat. Pensively biting his bottom lip, he continued. "James is living proof of that. You saw the photos. I know it sounds like some fantastical story I'm making up. But Peter is interested. It is real."

Kimberley placed her notebook back on the side table and took a sip of her water. She then looked at Jerry. "Maybe it would be best if I referred you to another therapist." Leaning back, she again picked up her pen and notebook, writing gibberish as she decided her next move. She didn't want to end up feeling duped, played by a manipulative client, but the industry often did work that way. Careers had been launched by chance meetings. It would be foolish to let an opportunity go simply because she didn't want to embarrass herself in front of a client.

Jerry shook his head. He walked back and sat down. "I'd like to keep coming to see you, but if it doesn't work..." he shrugged, leaving the sentence unfinished. "But then," he added hopefully, "if I am stopping, if I'm no longer your client, then I can set up a meeting with Peter. It won't matter then, right? No client-therapist relationship will be compromised. Take it as my parting thank you. You can then get rid of me."

Kimberley replied with a clipped laugh.

Jerry grinned hopefully. That was the first smile he'd seen since the session started. "I'm serious, if you want, I'll set the meeting and that will be that. I'll stop our sessions. Peter is interested," he repeated, continuing with his mantra, "really interested. Worst that could happen is that you waste a meeting and come away with some new A-list contacts that could help you down the line."

Kimberley folded her hands. She looked out the window and then turning back to Jerry asked, "This would be your last session?"

Jerry's body tensed in anticipation "That's your call. I'd prefer it not be. It's helped me, talking to you—but if it that would make it easier for you to follow through with this, then, yeah, this is our last session." He took a deep breath and added, "James leaves for

New York on Saturday to meet with Peter and Amber and probably Nicole." Jerry liked the sound of referring to them by their first names. "Peter asked that I set up a preliminary meeting with you, me, and James—and, if all looks good, he'll then fly out here to meet with you. But for any of this to happen, the next step is for you, me, and James to meet Friday night." Taking a beat, he held his breath knowing her response would decide whether there would be a next step, or whether this session was it and he'd be dismissed. He discreetly glanced down at her legs, hoping this wouldn't be one of his last opportunities to do so.

Kimberley glanced up at the clock. "Our session is over."

"Right." Jerry sat motionless. He then soldered on. "So, Seven? Eight? Whatever works best for you. It'll be short. James can then fill you in on the project."

Kimberley put her pen to her lips and stared down. After a long pause, she looked up at Jerry. "An hour at most."

"Of course. Sure. An hour is plenty. More than enough time." Jerry's fist clenched. His nails digging into his palm, his eyes widening as he struggled to contain himself. "Whatever works for you."

"Seven," she repeated, standing to signal time was up.

"Right." Seeing he was being dismissed, Jerry nodded, stood up and headed towards the door. Taking hold of the doorknob, he stopped and turned towards her. "So Friday at seven. At the lounge at the Beverly Wilshire?" The words tumbled out like a hopeful question.

"I can refer you to another therapist," Kimberley replied.

"Thanks. I'll think about it." He was about to thank her for wearing the blue skirt but kept himself in check.

Kimberley stood motionless until Jerry exited. She walked into the waiting room and locked the door. Heading back to her desk, she sat down, opened her laptop, and Googled Amber Lake and Nicole Kidman. She then called up her images. She couldn't tell anyone about the meeting, she thought as she studied them. At the best it would be seen as inappropriate, at worst completely unprofessional. But, she'd be foolish not to follow through. Find out if it was real. Chances were it was a ruse, a game Jerry was playing to see her outside of a session. Then again, there was a chance, an outside chance, that it was real.

Chapter 8

Jerry sat at the Circle K Tavern waiting for James to arrive. It annoyed him that he needed James on-board for the Kimberley game plan for it to work. But it was James's presence that made the project real, or at least appear real. He was Jerry's key to both the Stangerson film deal and to Kimberley. Without a film deal, or at least a semblance of a deal, there would be no Kimberley He glanced up as James entered. Smiling, he raised his hand in greeting as he silently reviewed his talking points. Jerry had sold Kimberley and now he needed to convince James. Motioning to the waitress he ordered another beer. Best loosen James up a bit. She nodded, smiled at James as he sat down, and headed towards the bar.

Jerry watched as she walked away. "Not nearly as good an ass as the other one," he began with an assessing stare. "Not a bad ass. But definitely not in the same league." Smiling, he looked at James. "So, everything set for New York? The conquering hero set to depart?"

"This is crazy." Glancing up, James smiled as the waitress returned and handed him his drink. "I'd have to leave to the airport at four-thirty in the morning!"

"Early morning is good. And two days after Thanksgiving. What could be more apropos? You'll miss the holiday rush and who wouldn't give thanks for a meeting with Peter Stangerson, Amber Lake, and Nicole Kidman?"

"Maybe Nicole Kidman," James corrected, as though that minimized the importance of the meeting. "I'm going to drag myself out before dawn and fly across the country, listen to them babble and ignore me and then head back. That's a waste. Crazy and expensive."

"Bur you're not paying," Jerry reminded him.

"Yeah, well, it's a waste anyway. Let Lanier take a copy of the book and pitch it. If they go for it, great. If not..." James paused and shrugged.

"You need to be there," Jerry insisted. You need to sell it." He paused. "You've made the plane reservations, right?"

Again James shrugged and looked away.

"Make the reservations," Jerry insisted. "Today. Now. This is your book we're talking about. Your novel. You have to be there. Not Lanier. Lanier's nuts. You have to go. I'm paying, right?" he asked leaning in towards James. "It's my money. If it doesn't work you'll be out some time, but I'll be the one who loses. But I won't lose because it will work," he added assuredly as he leaned closer. "This is the real deal. A meeting with Amber Lake, Nicole Kidman, and Peter Stangerson—who gets a shot like that?"

"Maybe Nicole Kidman," James corrected.

"I'll tell you who," Jerry continued, "fucking nobody—nobody gets a shot like that. You get a chance like that and you grab it. If you don't," he paused and shook his head, "if you don't—that is just... dumb," he said, searching for the right word. "That's just stupid. It's suicide is what it is."

James picked up his beer put it to his lips, paused and placed it back down. "The trip's not going to be cheap."

"It's an investment," Jerry replied sharply. "An investment in us—in you. The best investment I've ever made." He pulled out his wallet, opened it, took out a credit card and held it out. "Here, take this. Make plane and hotel reservations—today! Keep the card. Take it with you. I'll give you my pin in case you need to pull cash while you're there."

James stared at his outreached hand. He frowned as he took the card. "You're nuts."

Jerry shook his head. "Shrewd," he corrected. "This investment is a slam dunk. Our production company will pay me back once the deal is inked."

"What production company?" James asked. "There is no production company. You're just throwing away money."

"But if it works…" Jerry paused and stared at him. Again he leaned in. "When it works," he corrected. Groaning aloud, he threw up his hands. "You're such a pessimist. You think that keeps you from being disappointed in life. Think that keeps you safe. You're wrong. All it does is keep you depressed. This is going to work," he insisted. "End of story." Jerry let out a dramatic sigh. Picking up his drink, he took a sip and looked around the bar, still searching for the waitress. "Take Jet Blue. Find a reasonable Airbnb If you have to pay for the lunch, do it. Like I said, it will be a company write-off."

James began to respond, but simply shook his head.

Jerry stood, picked up his drink and finished it. "It's the ninth, bases loaded, you're at bat and you want to just walk away? No way. We do this. Buy the tickets. Make the arrangements—go!" He placed the glass down on the table as though he was pounding a gavel. "Call me once everything is set. I'm paying for the whole thing. The very least you can do is go, but…" Jerry paused and looked hesitantly away, as though searching for words.

"But?" James repeated, eyebrows raising.

"I need a favor. A small favor. A nothing favor. You need to do something for me before you leave."

James stared, a weary expression on his face. "What kind of something?"

"I need you to meet with me and Kimberley. Goodman. Dr. Kimberley Goodman," he added, his words racing as he spoke. "I need for you to meet with me and Dr. Kimberley Goodman and tell her that you're flying out to meet with Amber Lake, Peter Stangerson, and Nicole Kidman about making this movie and that you and I are partners," Jerry stopped, his eyes squinting as he held James's gaze.

"Who the hell is Dr. Kimberley Goodman?"

"I told you about her. My shrink. I need you to meet with me and my shrink and tell her about the film project."

James took a drink and sat back. "Why the fuck would I do that?"

"Like I said, as a favor." He paused and added. "Tell her we need a consultant for the film. And," Jerry continued before James could interrupt, "that we're also casting the role of a psychotherapist."

James stared hard at Jerry. "You're fucking kidding me." After a beat, he burst out laughing. "Tell me you're fucking kidding me."

Jerry cringed, took a deep breath and continued. "We're not offering her anything," he explained. "Not really. We're just telling her she'll be considered. That's all. It'll take ten minutes of your time. I'll tell her you have to go to another meeting. It will be over in no time. Ten minutes tops. Then it's over. Done. You'll enjoy it. She's fun to stare at."

"There is no psychotherapist in my book. There is no role for a shrink in this film—and there is no fucking film."

"Yet," Jerry added.

"No, not—'yet.' There never was a shrink in my book," James insisted. "There never will be. Okay? I am not about to go to the meeting in New York and say, 'oh, by the way, my friend wants to fuck his shrink so…' "

"Partner," Jerry corrected.

"Whatever. Not gonna happen."

59

"I don't expect you to actually pitch her at the meeting," Jerry forged on. "Is that why you're acting so weird.? You think I want you to actually pitch her. Of course you're not going to pitch her. I just want you to meet with her, assure her that you are flying to New York to meet with Stangerson and Amber Lake, that you and I are partners, and…" he added, his voice lowering, "that we're looking for a consultant and there is this role we think she just might be perfect for. That's it. Done. You're finished, outta there. She'll fill in the rest herself. And before you respond with, 'but there is no fucking shrink in the film…'" Jerry picked up his bag, opened it pulled out a short scene he'd written, put it on the table and slid it towards James. "It's rough, but it works. It actually would help the movie. Modify it anyway you want. Call it yours. I don't want any credit or payment. Just let Kimberley know that she's being considered. Nothing will come of it, I know that!" he added, his voice raising insistently. "We know that—but, well, that's Hollywood."

James stared at the pages. "You actually wrote a scene?" He looked up and shook his head. "Jesus, you're seriously losing it."

Jerry pulled his phone out of his pocket and called up images of Dr. Goodman. "Look," Jerry directed, standing and walking over to James's side of the table. Bending down, he placed the phone in front of him, again showing him the images. "Her modeling shots. She's a bit older, but she looks even better now," he announced proudly as he scrolled down, photo after photo.

James's eyes narrowed as he stared at the images. "Okay, she's a hot shrink, but still there is no way…"

"I know that," Jerry interrupted, his tone dismissive. "There is no way. I know it and you know it, but she doesn't know it." He moved his fingers enlarging what he considered the money shot. "Look. She's gorgeous, right? Blows Blake Lively, Scarlett Johansson, or Naomie Watts out of the water. As a favor, okay?" he pleaded as he carefully studied the image. "You don't have to do anything but sit there for ten minutes, go along with me, nod, and leave. Ten fucking minutes. Over in a flash."

Looking up from his phone, he leaned in towards James. "Look,

I told Kimberley we'd meet and the Beverly Wilshire at 7 pm on Friday. You have nothing else to do, it's Thanksgiving weekend. You'll already be packed. Ready to go. It'll be fast. Just a quick hello/goodbye drink. They must know you at the lounge by now, after all of your meetings with Lanier there. That will work in our favor. You can pay for drinks with the card I gave you."

James shook his head. "Even if I did this, she's a shrink, right? She'd never buy this."

Jerry smiled. James was softening. "That's the beauty of it. She's a shrink, but she wants this. Wanting blinds people, even shrinks. Trust me. All you have to do is show up. Stay for a few minutes and you're done. I'll write out a script for the meeting, so you don't even have to think, or come up with anything. If she throws you a curve ball, I'll handle it. It can basically be a monologue on your part and then if she starts asking any tough questions, I'll take them, or," he added with an excited nod, "I can call your cell. You can pretend you're getting a call from Amber or Stangerson and have to leave. You can then exit, head home and get ready for your meeting in New York—which I'm paying for—to launch your film and literary career."

James took a last glance at Kimberley's images. Looking at Jerry, he shook his head. "Either focus on getting the film made or getting laid," James instructed. "Pick one."

Jerry gave a final glance at his phone, closed the browser and walking back to his seat, looked at James. "Friday night 7 pm, the lounge at the Beverly Wilshire. You'll be out by 7:15. If nothing else, like I said, you'll have fun staring. She's already agreed," he added wide-eyed as though he could barely believe it. "She'll be there." He stared at his phone with an expression of disbelief. "Just this one favor. I'm paying for you to go to New York and launch your career. I need your help on this one."

"Even for you, this is nuts." James stared down at his drink, took a deep breath, shook his head and looking at Jerry asked, "You paying for parking?"

Jerry laughed, "You're the best," he replied with a Cheshire grin. "The night is on me. Come to think of it, starting that night it's all on me—our meeting with Kimberley, your New York trip, the whole thing. I'll call you later and see you Friday. She's worth it. You'll see. And not only that," Jerry announced, his smile broadening, "I think I've scored some tickets for South by Southwest. March 13. Write that down. We own 2020."

"How'd you get those? And who's going to pay for the flight to Austin and the hotel?"

"This boy is connected," Jerry replied with a clipped laugh. "We'll figure that out when it gets here. By March we won't have to worry about who's paying. We'll be golden. Friday, seven sharp," Jerry repeated. Standing, he held up his hand for a high five. James sighed and reluctantly obliged with a lukewarm clap. "We need to work on your enthusiasm," Jerry said. "Smile. Life is good." With a full grin, he turned to exit. Pausing, he looked back at James. "Make the reservations. Now!" Giving a military salute, he headed out the door.

Chapter 9

Jerry high fived himself with a resounding clap as he headed towards the car. It was on. James would show up. It would all look real. Sliding into the driver's seat he reached into his pocket and pulled out his phone to call Kimberley to confirm. He stopped mid-dial; a text confirmation would be best. He'd feel awkward calling her and if she answered and began to question him, he'd be too nervous and could screw it up. He'd be giving her another chance to back out. The phone wasn't his strong suit. He was more of an in-person person. He'd text her and then drive home and write up a quick script for James. The less left to him, the better. James was a writer not a talker. Jerry should be the one going to New York, but it was what it was. After fifteen minutes of sitting in his car, perfecting his Kimberley text, Jerry settled on: "Dear Dr. Goodman, Jerry here. I'm confirming our meeting on Friday at 7:00 at the Beverly Wilshire. We will be meeting with James Lansing, my production partner who will be leaving the following morning to New York, for meeting with Peter Stangerson, Amber Lake, and who knows? Maybe Nicole Kidman to discuss the production schedule. I look forward to meeting with you and reviewing our project."

The original text had been much longer, and had addressed her as Kimberley, consecutive versions growing considerably shorter. He finally decided on starting with Dr. Goodman. The current version covered all of the important points and was the text to use. He gave it one final read, took a deep breath, and hit send. Less than sixty seconds later, he received a one-word response, "Confirmed."

"Yes!" he cried aloud, slapping the steering wheel. He read the reply five more times before placing the phone on the passenger seat and driving home. Jerry hurriedly parked, dashed up the stairs and entered his apartment, then going directly to his computer. Sitting down, he called up a new Word document and began writing talking points for James to use at Friday's meeting. It continued to weigh on him that he wasn't the one flying to New York. James had no faith in the project or the process. James didn't see the possibilities. He never could. All of his creativity was used in his novels, none in his life. James was the anti-Oscar Wilde.

Jerry wrote and rewrote James's talking points. There could be no adlibbing. James was not one who thought on his feet. Kimberley was incisive. It was her job to be insightful, to ask questions, to dig, excavate. James would never stand up to scrutiny. He'd fall apart. Jerry could just hear him saying, "I'm lying. There is no film. It's all a ruse, Jerry just wants to fuck you." Jerry shook his head, negating that scenario. He had perfectly set the bait, but the slightest of tugs could unravel everything and off she'd swim. Jerry finished writing his bullet points, stared at them for a bit and hit print.

Chapter 10

J erry stood in front of the full-length mirror he'd bought at the Silver Lake flea market. He'd positioned it on his bedroom door, facing the bed, believing that strategic placement would help his sex life. It hadn't done much of anything, he thought as he stared at his reflection. He hadn't gotten nearly as much use out of it as he'd planned. Shrugging, he tried on a tie, stared appraisingly in the mirror, took it off and grabbing another tie, repeated the process. He was not one to wear ties. It had been over a year since he'd last worn one and he couldn't remember what the occasion was—a funeral? A wedding? A job interview? Not wearing ties was one of the perks of working as a freelancer and living in L.A. Still, it might impress Kimberley if he showed up at the meeting sporting a tie and jacket. But, he didn't want it to look forced, contrived—trying too hard. And if James saw Jerry wearing a tie, he'd either start laughing or make a derisive joke or snide remark. Jerry'd feel like a kid dressed up for church. That would start everything off on the wrong footing. He nixed the tie. The sports coat and jeans would work with an open-collar pink shirt.

He dressed and gave himself one final assessing look in the mirror. Walking into the bathroom he spot-sprayed the top of his head to keep his cowlick from acting up. He then exited his apartment and headed down the stairs towards his car.

Traffic was more congested than usual and trying to find a parking place within walking distance of the hotel was all but impossible. Valet parking was anathema to Jerry, but after several minutes of crawling around the neighboring blocks in search of a non-existing parking spot, he relented, drove up to valet parking, reluctantly handed the attendant his keys and hurried into the Beverly Wilshire.

Kimberley and James were seated towards the back of the lounge. "Shit," Jerry muttered to himself as he walked towards them. That was an inauspicious start. He should have arrived twenty to fifteen minutes early to ensure that he directed the conversation. By now James had probably broken down and confessed that it was all a ruse, Kimberley had convinced him not to go to New York, and he'd decided to abandon the film project and accept the ad copywriter position. Kimberley was most likely waiting for Jerry to arrive to call his bluff and, leaving him shame-faced, exit. Taking a deep breath, Jerry checked his posture and headed over to the table.

James stood and, smile beaming, extended his hand. "We were just talking about you."

Kimberley looked up and smiled. She was wearing a sheer tight-fitting aqua marine dress. Jerry's eyes widened.

Jerry took a seat and after an awkward beat, James continued. "I was filling Kimberley in on the project while you were being fashionably late. I was telling her a bit about the film, particularly the psychotherapist role. Jerry actually wrote this particular scene," he added, glancing up at Kimberley and smiling. "At first, I was a bit wary—it's not in the novel, but when we tried it, it worked, it moved the narrative. It was important to have the psychotherapist's perspective and then I saw how we could have the male lead—we're considering Mark Damon and Amber has worked with him before—become attracted by the psychotherapist that's probably going to be played by Nicole Kidman. So, we need a consultant, someone to work with her. Someone who knows how an attractive, Beverly Hills psychotherapist to the stars would act, feel, think."

Glancing from Jerry back to James, Kimberley replied, "I'm not a Beverly Hills psychotherapist."

James smiled. "I know. Brentwood. What's a few miles? But, you know what I mean. Nicole will need someone, an expert to help walk her through what her character thinks, feels. So, we needed a consultant. At least that was our original thinking."

"Was?" Kimberley repeated.

James nodded. "Right,. Jerry brought you up on a call we had with Peter who asked to see your photos, and everything changed."

Kimberley sat silently. An eyebrow raised.

"Peter, Jerry, and I had a conference call about whether to hire a consultant," James continued. "We were reviewing the script. Peter was saying what the project needs is something to add more tension between Damon's and Kidman's characters. And then Jerry jumped in," James paused, nodding in Jerry's direction. "In the script, Damon's character is in a relationship with Kidman's character, right?" James stared at Kimberley who replied with an unsure nod.

"Right," he continued. "So then Jerry asked, what if Damon, well, his character, has an affair with another therapist, a therapist who shares Kidman's office—that adds a whole new layer. It adds a different dimension to the story. For that storyline to work, we need a second psychotherapist. But," he paused dramatically, "for it to work, we'd need an actress that would plausibly pull Damon away from Kidman. I mean Kidman is attractive, right? The audience would have to believe that Damon's character would make that move. Peter liked the idea and was thinking Charlize Theron. Then Jerry jumped in and said we should consider a different approach, a fresh, more organic approach. 'What if we cast a real psychotherapist?' he asked. And, before Peter could respond, Jerry—who had already emailed Peter links to your photos—explained that you were not only a psychotherapist, but had previously had an acting career. Peter was silent for quite a while. I thought the line had gone dead. Thought we'd lost him." He turned to Jerry and gave a clipped laugh. "I know Jerry was nervous. Doesn't take much to piss Peter off. If he doesn't like an idea, he makes sure you know it. Then Peter simply pronounced, 'I like it.' He insisted the three of us take a preliminary meeting, before setting up a meeting with him and—well—here we are."

James sat back and raised his hand to catch the waiter's attention. "Drinks anyone?" Jerry stared at James, eyes widening. He was veering off script, charting into the unknown.

But his version held together, rang true, his delivery was flawless. Even Jerry was beginning to believe the story. And he was performing like a player, not the awkward James that Jerry knew. The waiter came over and chatted a bit with James, welcomed him back and asked where Lanier was. The effect was perfect, playing as though the scene had been rehearsed. The three ordered drinks. The waiter exited and James turned towards Jerry. "Did I cover it all? That's it in a nutshell, right?"

Jerry responded with a silent nod.

Kimberley glanced at Jerry. "I thought we were meeting about my possibly working as a consultant."

"You're right," James said, "the meeting was about the consultancy. That's still on the table but when Jerry brought you up at our last conference call and Peter saw your photos, everything changed. That's Peter." He paused and taking a drink, added, "He's sold on adding this new therapist role and when Jerry said that it could be played by a real therapist—that intrigued him. He's a marketer and sees all sorts of PR possibilities going this direction. That's the way his brain works. When Jerry showed him your photos and added that you act, well…" James paused as he held her gaze. "That sealed it. Peter exclaimed 'that's it. That's the look we need.' You'd still be the consultant, inform the script. Let Nicole know what it's like, not only how she needs to deal with her patients…"

"Clients," Kimberley corrected.

"Right," James nodded, "clients. See," he added with a smile, "you're already earning your money. Peter said that with you we'd have a two-for-one, a consultant who knows the field, and an actress who can play the second psychotherapist role."

Kimberley sat back and crossed her legs. "I'm flattered," she replied with a slight smile. "And I'm interested in finding out more about the consultant role." She paused, picking up her drink and taking a sip. "I don't act. Not anymore."

"But you did, right?" James asked. He leaned towards her, his voice lowering conspiratorially. "The consultant position is pretty much a slam dunk. You're perfect. But the other, the role… that's why I'm really here. Peter loves the idea. He did similar casting with his film *Exposed*. It worked. If you remember, it was a huge hit. To quote him after I showed him your photo—'it proves lightning can strike twice.' He's excited about this. It's not a done deal. It might not happen. This is Hollywood, right? But I think it will—happen."

James picked up his scotch, which was yet one more stunner for Jerry—James never drank scotch, and announced, "To success!"

Kimberley and Jerry both stared at his outstretched hand. Jerry glanced at Kimberley, looking to follow her lead. She took a beat and then, holding up her glass, clinked it to James's.

"Success," Jerry squeaked, clinking his glass to theirs.

"I think I could do a good job as a consultant, but as to the other…" she shook her head as her voice trailed off.

"You'd be perfect, you'd fit this like a glove," James insisted. "The final decision is obviously Peters, but, once he meets you," James shrugged indicating it was a done deal. He shot a quick glance towards Jerry. Whose eyes widened with disbelief at James's performance. "Right now, we just want you to consider it, nothing more. Meet with Peter and see where it goes."

Kimberley stared at her glass pensively and all but imperceptibly nodded.

Taking that as his cue, James pulled out his phone. "A text from Peter's assistant. They come with regularity," he added with a laugh. "You'll find that out." He looked at Kimberley and smiled. "I really need to get back to her," he added, staring down at his phone. Putting it back in his pocket, James began to stand. He then sat back down, paused, and leaned in towards Kimberley. "Look, I have to be honest, I wasn't really on board with this whole idea when Jerry brought this up. Like I said, there was no therapist in my novel—and now we have two, you and Nicole. Jerry warned me, that's what Hollywood does with novels; rips them up, reworks them." He looked up at Jerry and grinned. "I hate to admit it but this time I think it works." After a long pause, James concluded with, "You'd really be perfect to play the role."

Kimberley's left eyebrow arched. She stared at James. "You've never seen me act."

"No," James agreed, "but Jerry has. Said he saw you in a play and you knocked him out. Jerry knows talent, knows acting."

Kimberley turned towards Jerry who gave a wincing smile and looked away.

Again standing, James looked down at Kimberley. "You literally are the role. That doesn't always work in acting, but this time I think it would. Peter's already coming up with his PR campaign—a gorgeous Beverly Hills psychotherapist to the stars playing a gorgeous Beverly Hills psychotherapist to the stars. I mean, a Beverly Hills-adjacent, therapist to the stars," he corrected with a grin.

Kimberley laughed.

James looked from Kimberley to Jerry. "I've never known him to be this quiet."

Jerry smiled, still shellshocked by James's performance. "Just listening. I wanted Kimberley to hear where things stand and get her feedback." Jerry glanced at Kimberley and took a drink. James had been stellar, enthusiastic, but measured, cool. Very take-it-or-leave believable. But he was driving too close to the edge. Jumping that quickly from consulting straight to her acting in the film was pushing too much too soon. Jerry had planned a more gradual, stealth approach. If he saw even a glimmer of interest on Kimberley's part in the consultant role, he'd seize that opening and then slowly move her towards the possible acting role. Like a boy scout building a fire, he'd tend it, carefully fanning the flame until it grew. James started by pouring gasoline.

James nodded. "Got it. Well," he continued as he glanced towards the exit, "I'll let you two discuss it. We don't have much time though. I'll need to know if you're interested before I go to New York. If it's a go, I'm sure Peter will want to meet with you." He took a beat and smiled at Kimberley. "I hope it's a yes. Well," he continued, again pulling out his phone, "I really have to go make this call." Bending down, he picked up his drink and finished it. "Peter's hoping to shoot some basic footage in March to take a teaser with him to Cannes. He's looking to shoot in 2020 and release the film in 2021. That's cutting it close, but that's his game plan."

Staring up, Jerry wanted to leap up and hug James. His delivery had been flawless, an Oscar-worthy performance.

"Wonderful meeting you," James said. "Hopefully we'll work together on this project." He turned to Jerry. "I'll call you before I go," he said as he pulled out his wallet and slipped out Jerry's credit card. "On me. You two want anything else before I go?" he asked, holding up the card.

Both shook their heads.

"I'll take care of it on the way out."

"Jerry stared at his credit card in James's hand. "Appreciated," he replied.

"My pleasure," James said with a broad grin. He turned towards Kimberley. "Wonderful meeting you."

Kimberley smiled, "My pleasure."

James then gave a slight nod towards Jerry, turned and walked towards the bar.

"Thanks. For meeting," Jerry said.

"You told him you saw me act?" Kimberley asked pointedly.

Jetty cringed. "I just wanted to help seal the deal. Sorry if I overstepped. It was a white lie. A lie in a good cause. I should discuss this tendency with my therapist."

After a beat Kimberley laughed. Picking up her wine glass she sat back and again crossed her legs.

Jerry exhaled. All was right with the world. Everything was falling into place. None of it was impossible.

Kimberley took a final sip and placed down her glass. "I have to go," she said. "Thank you for setting this up."

"Right. Think about it. You'd be perfect," Jerry said, his pulse racing. He paused and then added. "If you haven't eaten, well, I mean, we can grab something here. You know, discuss the project, go over everything." As the words came out he regretted them. He'd gotten everything he wanted out of this meeting. He'd made it to the first rung. He needed to back off. Relax.

Kimberley stood and looked down at Jerry. "I appreciate you making the introduction. Let me think about it, but this business, Jerry, not social."

"Right. I know," he replied, realizing he had—pushed it too far. "I just thought, we're here and if you were hungry…"

Kimberley glanced at the exit. "I really have to go. You don't need to see me out. Stay and finish your drink."

Jerry began to stand, but sensing it was best not to walk her out, stayed put. He watched the men turn as she passed, their gazes longingly following her. Smiling, he motioned to the waiter and ordered another drink. She said she'd think about it. She was hooked. He could sense it. Her body language, her voice, the look in her eyes.

The project would never happen, at least not for Kimberley. He knew that. But, maybe he could get her a small role, maybe he could land her some celebrity clients. That could be worth it for her.

The main thing was that now there was an opening, a way to set up other meetings, drinks, next time alone—maybe dinner. Who knew where that could lead. That's how Jerry worked. His focus was on opening a door. There was no game plan after that. From there life took over. And the door had opened. He needed time to take it all in, how perfectly it had all gone, how seamlessly James had played his role. He had been so unexpectedly credible; made it all sound so believable—as though it was real.

Chapter 11

O nce home, James found himself strangely energized by the meeting with Kimberley. Jerry was right, she was stunning, but that wasn't what James found so compelling. It was the pitch itself, the game. Playing the successful Hollywood screenwriter had been seductive. Kimberley was bright, savvy, wary and yet she bought it. He sold her. James brought a legitimacy to the pitch that Jerry couldn't. He felt himself change as the meeting went on, his posture felt more erect, his voice more assured. By the end he believed he actually was making the film with Amber Lake and Peter Stangerson, was convinced that he did have to rush out to take an important production call before flying off to New York. He was a player.

Following up on his promise to Jerry, James walked into his bedroom, sat at his small desk, turned on his computer and began searching online until he found a relatively reasonable Airbnb on the lower east side. Using Jerry's credit card, he locked it down. He next went on the Jet Blue site and bought a round trip ticket to

JFK. Maybe Jerry was right, he thought, still flying high from the meeting; maybe it was real. Lanier had taken him to Dunhill Jr.'s house. James had been basically ignored by both Stangerson and Dunhill Jr., but still, he was there. He was in. That alone would impress most people. It impressed Jerry enough that he was willing to bet a chunk of his savings on it being real. And that was just step one. Next came New York.

But, the more James contemplated the situation, the more his feelings began to shift, his high deflate. Reality resurfaced. Lanier was a fraud. Jerry would lose his bet. The trip would be worthless. He'd fly to Manhattan, be ignored, pay for the lunch, and fly back. There was no chance James would return from New York the triumphant warrior clutching the gold ring.

Hearing the distinctive phone-tone he had set for Jerry calls, James picked up his phone. Jerry's voice was almost breathless. "You were great," he gushed. "I mean like perfect. You fucking aced it." he added with a laugh. "I actually believed we were going to cast her."

"But we're not," James replied, his voice somber.

"But we could," Jerry answered pointedly. "There's always a chance. She's closer to meeting Stangerson now than she was before our meeting. Only one step removed after having met you. At the very least she got a free drink with two of Hollywood's brightest up-and-coming filmmakers. If it doesn't happen, it doesn't happen, that's Hollywood. But I gave her a shot, right? She'll remember that. So," he asked, changing topics, "you packing? Everything set? Ready to go?"

"I got the plane tickets and have a place to stay." James paused and added, "My going is a waste. It's crazy."

"Crazy is what's going to make it work. As a reward for landing us this film deal, I've scored us Coachella tickets. So block April tenth. And you're welcome. It will be our first official appearance in 2020 as Hollywood producers."

"You really are nuts." After a beat, James asked, "How did you score tickets?"

"I too have connections," Jerry replied emphatically. "So when does the flight leave?"

"Early. Disgustingly early. I should make you drive me."

Jerry replied with a shake of his head. "That's why God created Uber. Call me when you get settled. No," he added emphatically, "call me when you arrive."

Chapter 12

James stuck his hands deep into his pockets and soldiered, face-down, through the New York cold towards The Seine, a trendy new restaurant on the west side that James had never heard of. But that was par for the course. James hadn't heard of most restaurants in Manhattan. Lanier had left him a phone message warning him not to be late. "They can be late, not you," her message concluded. James grimaced, eyes squinting, as the wind stinging, as he marched up Fifth Avenue towards Fifty-seventh. The holiday lights and Christmas music would normally bring a smile. Manhattan embodied Christmas, something L.A. could never do. As he trudged through the cold, all James could think of was that it was all a waste. Still, if nothing else, he'd be able to say he had lunch with Amber Lake and Peter Stangerson—not many could say that. But that meaningless boast would be the extent of it. A lunch, a dismissive goodbye, the check left for him to pay, and back to square one with Jerry the poorer and James out of a job.

He was greeted by the maître d', was escorted to a table, explained he was waiting for his party, ordered a diet coke, and sat and waited. At 1:45, he broke with protocol and dialed Lanier's number. No answer. At 2:10 he saw Amber Lake enter the room accompanied by two men. She was royalty even by Hollywood standards. Begrudgingly, even the most jaded eyes were pulled in her direction, if only for a second.

James watched as the fawning maître d' escorted Amber Lake to a table. Her entourage carefully scanned the room and went to sit in the back In person she was even more striking than in photos or on screen. He considered walking over and introducing himself, but instead sat and waited. Amber Lake would have no idea who he was. She'd feel accosted. Probably have him tossed out, or worse, arrested for assault. Five minutes later. Lanier hurried in, dashing directly to Amber's table. The star stood, unleashed one of her legendary gleaming smiles, and the obligatory air-kisses flew. Lanier glanced around the room, spotted James, shook her head, and waved him over. Standing, he took a deep breath, picked up his diet coke and headed towards the table.

"What were you doing over there?" Lanier asked with an impatient scowl. "We're sitting here." She then turned and announced, "Amber, let me introduce James Lansing, the writer of the novel I was telling you about. James, this is Amber Lake."

Amber remained seated. She looked up at James and held out her hand. The closer the proximity, the more stunning she became. For a second, her smile was on high beam. "Hello, James." She then turned back to Lanier. "Is Peter coming?"

"He is. But then again, you know—it is Peter."

"You said he would be here," Amber replied, a distressed tone in her voice. "That's why I'm here. I need to talk to him. My agent heard a rumor about *Ultra's Return*. A disturbing rumor."

"*Ultra's Return*," Lanier repeated. "Was there a previous Ultra film? I must have missed it."

"No there wasn't a previous film," Amber snapped impatiently. "It's part of the marketing strategy. People will think they missed the first one. But Peter guaranteed me that role. I need one of those stupid superhero roles. It's mine," she insisted.

Lanier looked up at James, impatiently signaling him to sit. "No worries. Peter will be here."

Amber scowled. "My publicist heard they were considering Naomi or Margot."

"No worries," Lanier repeated. "And, speaking of films," she turned towards James with a nod, "James's novel is perfect for you. It's dark but funny. It's human, personal. Strong female lead. It's perfect, has indie gritty Oscar written all over it? It's the kind of thing Jessica will snap up if she hears of it."

"Jessica?" Amber asked, a surprised tone in her voice. Turning towards James she frowned. "Jessica won't touch it. He's a male—a male writer. Besides," she continued, again looking at Lanier, "I've been there and done that with indie films. No offense," she added, smiling at James. "Good for the ego, I suppose, but nobody goes to those. I'm not in the market to become the indie darling. Superheroes are now. You're there or you don't exist. *Ultra's Return* is mine, I need this film," she declared, turning towards Lanier. "It's mine. Where is Peter? He gave me a guarantee. He is not going to fuck me over. Not again."

James sat in silence. Depressed at his project being dismissed out-of-hand yet captivated at his proximity to Amber Lake.

"Speaking of," Lanier stood and waved towards the doorway. James turned as Peter Stangerson entered. A mid-sized, heavy-set man in his late sixties, he wore his sunglasses over his head, as though a separate set of eyes were staring at the ceiling. Spotting Lanier's wave, he smiled broadly and walked in clipped, decisive military strides to the table. Lanier stood and the two air kissed. James stood and was ignored.

Amber remained seated and glared at Stangerson. "You are not going to fuck me over Peter."

Stangerson's smile grew. "Well no. Not here."

"I mean the film."

"Of course. The film." Stangerson looked from Amber to Lanier. "You know what she's talking about?"

Lanier smiled and shrugged.

Ambers' stare lasered on Stangerson. "Don't play dumb."

"I'd say I'm not playing, but my sarcasm doesn't have much currency here." Stangerson pulled out a chair, silently nodded at James, and turning towards Amber continued. "Take a deep breath and let's start at the beginning. What are you talking about?"

"The role is mine. Do not fuck with me," she repeated.

James watched silently, fascinated by the fact that he was sitting in a trendy Manhattan restaurant watching two industry luminaries battle. Even more fascinated to be sitting next to Amber Lake as she used the work "fuck."

Stangerson turned towards James as though noticing him for the first time. Leaning over, he held out his hand. "Peter Stangerson," he announced, shooting a well-practiced "I'm famous and important" smile.

James reached out, nervously shaking his hand. "I'm James. We met at. …"

"Do not change the subject, Peter," Amber snapped, interrupting James mid-sentence. "This is not happening."

Stangerson nodded. "Of course, it's not." He paused and looking at Lanier asked, "What's not happening?"

"*Ultra's Return*," Amber's delivery was sharp, definitive. "It's my film. My role."

Peter gave a dismissive waive. "Oh that." He dramatically paused and added, "It's gone. Over. Done. Dead in the water. There is no film."

Amber's eyebrows furrowed. "Of course there's a film. It's my film." She paused and added, "What do you mean there's no film?"

"Just that. Well, at least there is no film as far as I'm concerned. They tried to make it sound flattering," he continued, turning to Lanier with a grin. "Made it sound like the best thing in the world. 'Peter,' " he continued in a high-pitched sing song voice, " 'you direct such wonderful indie films—it would be a shame for you to sell out and make a blockbuster superhero project just for the money.' "

He paused and looking at James pointedly added, "In English it means that I'm out. They're going with younger, fresh-out-of-Sundance, cheaper meat. Maybe even a woman, better yet a woman of color. In best of all worlds, they'll find a trans person of color on the spectrum. Good PR." Turning towards Lanier, he smiled. "A few weeks later, God meted justice and they lost most of their funding. It's now a low budget straight-to-Prime project." Turning to Amber, he grinned. "They couldn't afford you or me even for a week now."

"But you were set to direct," Amber added, her tone accusatory. "It was in the trades. I was the lead. It was my film."

Stangerson shrugged. "To quote a very wise man whose name eludes me—'shit happens.' "

"No," Amber declared with a shake of her head. "Not to me it doesn't. I need that film."

Again Peter shrugged. "No worries, I'm putting together a project. I'm directing and you're starring. Sci-fi. Robots, AI, all sorts of weird futuristic sex. Has blockbuster written all over it."

James turned towards Lanier, a pained expression on his face. It was happening again, he was there, but didn't exist. Was invisible. His project forgotten. Lanier met his glance and looked away.

"No nudity!" Amber insisted. "It's in my contract."

"Really?" Stangerson replied sarcastically. "You looked online lately?" He glanced up as the waiter approached. "Take care of my friends here," he commanded. "Lunch?"

Amber ordered a wine spritzer, Lanier her regular, and James held up his diet coke, signaling he was fine. "Looks like we're drinking our lunch," Stangerson smiled. "A Manhattan."

81

"Certainly Mr. Stangerson." The waiter paused and added, "It is an honor to have you and Ms. Lake—and your friends. Nothing to eat?" There was probably a minimum, James thought. He'd end up paying either way. Stangerson shook his head. The waiter nodded and exited.

Lanier turned towards Stangerson. "James has that novel I told you about. Robert is interested in it."

"Robert?" Stangerson asked.

"Dunhill," Lanier replied. "Dunhill Jr."

Stangerson grimaced. "No one calls Dunhill Jr. Robert." He turned towards James, his eyebrows furrowing as he placed the pieces together. "Right, yes. You were there, weren't you? At Dunhill Jr.'s. We've met. We took pictures," he declared.

James smiled and nodded.

"Those photos made Dunhill Jr. crazy," Stangerson laughed. "He hates being photographed. No one calls him Robert," he repeated, again looking at Lanier.

"The family calls him Robert. We're related you know," she announced, a slight grin on her face as she scanned the table, searching for a reaction.

Stangerson stared at her, tempted to ask for an explanation, but, apparently thinking better of it, continued. "Dunhill Jr. is interested?" he asked with a sarcastic lilt. "He didn't seem interested. I don't even remember the topic of the book coming up. Is the offer in writing? Is it notarized? In blood? Do you have bags of cash that he's given you? Because that's the only way I'd work with that lunatic."

He turned towards Amber. "And it won't be full nudity," he explained with a smile, returning to the topic which was of most interest to him. "Maybe topless. But not gratuitous. It's important to the storyline, furthers the narrative," he added with an exaggerated grin. "Plus, it will help with foreign. Clevis is going to produce. He wanted to know if I could get Margo, but I told him you could act rings around her but…" Stangerson paused. "Margo is available."

Amber replied with an exaggerated pout. "*Ultra's Return* was set to go." She glared at Stangerson. "That's the role I want. I need that type of role. I need to be a superhero," she declared emphatically. "Look at Scarlett. Look what those roles have done for her."

"Forget *Ultra's Return*," Stangerson insisted. "If it ever gets made, it's going down in flames. It's finished. Over. With the two of us on board, this new project is a done deal." He turned towards Lanier and added, "I can cast some Blacks, Asians, and Latinos—or is it X now? for marketing. Maybe add a woman to the screenplay credits. Perhaps even dig up a trans cinematographer."

Amber stared at Stangerson, a skeptical expression on her face. "How old is my character?"

Stangerson paused. "Twenty-five?" he asked, doing the verbal equivalent of throwing darts.

"Not more than twenty-four," Amber declared. "I don't even know how old I am anymore," she added, turning towards Lanier. "My agent had me change the date on my passport when I started acting and now I don't remember…"

"Twenty-four then," Stangerson nodded. Looking up he smiled as the waiter arrived with the drinks. "This project was tailor made for you," he added holding up his drink in a toast. "Made with you in mind."

Amber sat motionless, staring at his raised glass. "I was counting on *Ultra's Return*. I have other offers on the table. Do not fuck with me, Peter."

Stangerson glanced at Lanier and winked. "I love when she talks dirty. This project is definite, wrapped with a bow and Amber Lake is the star."

Amber picked up her phone and stared at it. "Send the script to my manager. I'll consider it."

"I hate your manager," Stangerson replied, as he downed half of his Manhattan in one drink.

Amber laughed as she picked up her phone and studied her texts.

"Everyone hates my manager. That's her job."

"Being hated? In that case, she excels."

"I have to run," Amber announced as she returned a text. "I'd tell you who I'm meeting, but…" she stopped and looked suspiciously at James. Quickly finishing her drink, she turned towards Stangerson. "Get me the script to your project. If it's not a big budget superhero project and I'm not the lead, don't even send it." After a beat, she added. "If we are going to work together again, it can't be like last time."

"Can't and won't," Stangerson agreed with a dismissive wave of his hand. Finishing his drink, he looked up at her. "I'm a changed man. Haven't touched any type of substance in… a long time."

Amber motioned towards his Manhattan. "What do you call that?"

Stangerson glanced down with a surprised expression, as though seeing it for the first time. "This? Water. Distilled. You can't get rid of all your vices." He took a drink and, placing his glass down, looked back up at Amber. "Do that, and one of these days you'll simply blow up," he slammed the table with his free hand for emphasis, "Explode."

Amber stood and turned towards Lanier who quickly rose, preparing for another round of air kisses. "Call me," Amber said, her tone bored, disingenuous. "We'll do lunch."

"Perfect." Lanier smiled. "And, as always, you look gorgeous."

"Gorgeous?" Peter asked. "Stunning, striking, ravishing. We need new adjectives created simply to describe you."

Amber shrugged. "It's my job." Turning to James, she smiled. He froze and stared wide eyed. "Don't stand." Amber continued, turning towards Stangerson. "After a certain age you have to conserve your energy," she added pointedly.

Stangerson looked up with a razor-filled smile. "I'm covered. You know us Hollywood elites. Q nailed it. Drinking young blood at those satanic rituals keeps one fit as a fiddle."

Amber grimaced. "That's not funny."

"No, but it's effective."

"Before you go," Lanier jumped in, "we should talk about James's novel. It will make a dynamite script."

Amber turned towards James as though assessing a foreign life form. "Another time. Maybe."

James stood and nervously pulled out one of the cards that he had made specifically for the meeting. "It's been a real pleasure meeting you." His hand shook as he held the card out. "It is really an honor to…"

"I'm sure," she interrupted, staring down at the card suspiciously. After a beat, she took the card and dropped it in her bag. Turning towards Stangerson, she offered a farewell nod. "Peter."

Standing, Stangerson grinned. "I'll get the script messengered. It will be amazing. Like old times."

"Old times? Then it's a no go." Moving away, she added pointedly, "No time for a hug." Amber Lake then turned and made a slow measured exit, turning every head, pulling all eyes with the force of her gravity field.

Stangerson watched as Amber paraded out of the room. "She must practice her exits for hours." He then looked at his watch, which he made a point of letting everyone see and admire. "Seems that I have to run as well." He stood and extended his hand and smiled at James. "Been a pleasure."

Stangerson was leaving. The meeting was over. James had called it. It had gone as expected. James's time and Jerry's money had both been wasted. Taking a deep breath, he hurriedly spoke, making one last-ditch effort. "As to my novel," he chirped, "I can modify the script so that it works. I can change…"

"Yes," Stangerson interrupted dryly, "I'm sure you can. Have Lanier send me the novel. My reader will give it a look."

James glared at Lanier. She had assured him that not only had

Stangerson read it but that he was interested in optioning it. "You've read the book, right?" James asked.

Stangerson shot a weary glance at Lanier.

She forced a smile and turned towards Stangerson. "I told you about it. I'm sure I sent you a copy."

Stangerson shrugged. "Yes, well… I'm sure it will make a wonderful film. I really have to go."

"I've added some new scenes for the screenplay," James added in desperation. "Action. Visual."

"Wonderful." Peter turned towards Lanier, arching an eyebrow.

"A new character. A psychotherapist," James continued, his words picking up steam careening wildly as he spoke. "She's blonde, gorgeous, sexy…"

"Well that will never fly," Stangerson looked at Lanier and gave a clipped laugh. "Not if you want Amber involved. There is only so much gorgeousness to go around in an Amber Lake project."

Lanier glared at James and subtly waved her hand, motioning for him to stop.

Ignoring her, James continued. "She wouldn't be a threat to Amber. She's—older. And she's not just an actress," he added, deciding to jump all in. " She's a Beverly Hills psychotherapist to the stars. You remember the Sharon Stone scene in Basic Instinct. The new scene I wrote is like that, only edgier, more graphic. A scene Amber wouldn't want to play anyway, with the nudity clause and all. Plus," he continued like a car without breaks, "the fact that she's a real blonde Beverly Hills psychotherapist, who is gorgeous and used to be a stripper, well the PR value alone would be…" James stopped mid-sentence as though the tank was suddenly on empty.

Lanier glared at James. "Sorry, Peter. James is tired, just flew in. Didn't get much sleep."

Stangerson paused, sat back down, and picking up his glass and took another drink. "A gorgeous, blonde, Beverly Hills psychotherapist to the stars who used to be a stripper?" he repeated, staring hard at James.

James nodded. "And can act. I've seen her act," he continued as if channeling Jerry. "She's amazing. Incredible. And, because she's a sex therapist, she's more, well—open then most. She'd have no trouble doing an edgy nude scene."

Stangerson's eyes narrowed.

"It's not really part of the book, Peter," Lanier said, glowering at James, thrown by his veering into unknown territory. "He's more tired than I thought. Babbling a bit. Just throwing random ideas out there—bad ones. I know you have to go. I'll get you the novel and we can…"

Stangerson waved his arm at Lanier to silence her. "She can act?" he asked, his eyes locked on James.

"Amazing actress. Just never got the right breaks, so she went into psychotherapy. You know, plan B."

Stangerson paused pensively. He again began to stand. James was losing him. "We're shooting a video—of her scene," James quickly added. "I can have video to you. Looks-wise she's up there with Amber, Scarlett, Margot. She's mistaken for Charlize Theron all the time. That caliber. Look." James hurriedly pulled his phone out, willing his thumbs to move as quickly as possible to find her online photos. The good ones. The ones Jerry referred to as the money shots.

Stangerson turned towards Lanier with a questioning expression. She forced a strained apologetic smile, unsure whether to allow the conversation to keep going, or stop it now. She hadn't a clue where James was heading, but saw that Stangerson was listening. His interest had been piqued.

"Look," James proudly announced, holding his phone screen out towards Stangerson.

Stangerson took the phone, again sat down and slowly studied the photos. "She's a Beverly Hill's sex therapist? And you have video?"

"Being shot tomorrow," James replied with a tentative nod.

Deciding to put a stop to whatever was going on, Lanier motioned for James to put away his phone. "I'm sorry about this," Lanier apologized. "James doesn't mean to waste your time. I know you have to go."

James shot a hard look at Lanier. Her stare was cold, searing. Continuing to hold the phone, Stangerson looked up at James. "How old is she?"

James shrugged. "Thirty-five? Thirty-seven?" He cringed as he spoke, knowing that was ancient in Hollywood. That fact alone could have just ruined the entire pitch. That could be a deal killer.

"And she used to be a stripper?" Stangerson asked, scrolling through the photos.

James replied with a slight nod. "And she's now a Beverly Hills psychotherapist to the stars."

Lanier leaned over and grabbed James's arm, squeezing tightly. "Don't waste Peter's time talking about an old L.A. shrink."

Stangerson, ignoring Lanier, again looked down at the images on the phone. "Give me two of those cards—the one you gave Amber."

James pulled his arm out of Lanier's grasp. His hands shaking more than before, he hurriedly pulled out his wallet, took out two cards and handed them to Stangerson.

"And a pen," Stangerson directed, taking the cards and handing James back his phone.

James leaned down, grabbed his bag and hurriedly rummaging through it, pulled a pen out and handed it to Stangerson.

Stangerson put one of the cards in his shirt pocket. He turned the other card face-down, placed it on the table, and wrote his email and phone number. He stopped mid-motion and looked at James with a steely stare. "I don't give this information out freely and I trust you will safeguard it."

"Yes. Of course. With my life," James gushed, his eyes widening as

Stangerson continued writing.

Stangerson handed James the card. "Email me the link as soon as you get the video." He then turned towards Lanier and smiled. "Time to go. Don't bother standing," he added. Taking his sunglasses out of his pocket, he again slipped them over his forehead.

"You're interested in an aging shrink?" Lanier asked her eyes narrowing as she looked up at Stangerson.

Stangerson replied with a caustic smile. "I'm late." Raising his sleeve, he glanced at his watch, making sure it was on full display. Looking at James he continued, "If we do something, I'll need you to write a scene that takes place at the Japanese Olympics. I have an in with NBC. I can shoot at the games. Late July. The stripper shrink could have an affair with one of the athletes who's actually a spy."

James stopped mid-breath, hearing nothing more than the words "if we do something." "Sure. Yes. Of course."

"Maybe a sex scene in a training room," Stangerson continued. "Or in the stadium, during the games. Don't think that's ever been done." He paused, looked at Lanier and winked. "Chow." Only a few heads turned as Stangerson exited.

Lanier glared at James. "What the hell was all that about? We had never discussed you bringing up anything about some fucking stripper shrink. You can't just start making things up on the fly. What the hell's wrong with you? You ruined the whole meeting."

"What meeting?" James asked, his frustration mounting. "I wasn't in any meeting. I was just sitting here once again listening to people talk and being ignored. No one even knew that I or my book existed. You told me they'd read my book, that they were interested. That's why I flew out here."

"They talk in code, shorthand," Lanier explained with a slight shrug. "You'll learn it."

"Their code is to avoid the topic?"

"Pretty much." Lanier glowered at James. "Never do that again."

Folding his arms, James looked away and sat sulking in silence.

"Robert is sending his plane back to London to pick up some shoes he left there," Lanier continued, her anger fading. "We can use the plane. I can introduce you to Bowie and some other people. Important people. We leave in the morning."

James winced. "London? I can't just up and go to London. I can't do this anymore."

Lanier picked up her drink, sat back, took a sip, and smiled. "I'm beginning to sense a lack of gratitude. I don't want to be harsh James but you're nobody. The waiter here has more currency than you do. No one knows you, which means no one will miss you. I liked your novel, thought it had a chance, thought I'd help. Came on board as producer. I arranged financing, I put a director in, placed a name star…"

"Really?" James interrupted. "Well they sure don't seem to know about it. I'm no further along than before we met. I'm just poorer."

"I'd stop now." Lanier demanded her voice sharp, almost shrill. "Had Peter Stangerson ever handed you his email and phone number before you met me? You ever been to Robert Dunhill Jr.'s home before me? Had you ever had a drink with Amber Lake? Had you ever even had a fucking glass of water at the Polo Lounge? Those are rhetorical questions, James. I've allowed you into my private world and your response is to throw tantrums and make demands." She leaned in towards him. "I am not the one who needs you." With that, she finished her drink and stood up. "Think about it." She paused and looked down at him. "This gorgeous shrink of yours—is she real or just a ridiculous make-believe effort to interest Peter?"

"She's real," James replied with a shrug. She's a psychotherapist."

"And you're actually shooting a scene?

Picking up his glass, he paused and took a drink. "Jerry just wrote a scene," he offered, a slight grimace on his face. "There is no video."

"Jerry?" Lanier's eyes narrowed as she stared at him.

"My partner. I've told you about him a hundred times, but you've never listened."

"Because he's never mattered."

James shook his head. Lanier decided what mattered. "The therapist's character is not even in the novel," James explained. "Not a part of the project."

Lanier stared towards the doorway. "From Peter's reaction I'd say she is the project."

James glared at Lanier accusingly. "You told me he loved my book. Neither of them even heard of my fucking book."

Lanier's smile was almost imperceptible. "Let me fill you in, James. No one cares about your book." Lanier paused and watched as James winced and looked away. "But…" after a long pause, she continued. "Thanks to the meetings I've arranged, that could change. Thanks to me, everything could change in a flash. Get me the video," Lanier instructed. Standing, she looked down at James. "Don't fuck it up. Email me the video. Me, not Peter. Everything goes through me. Every email, every idea, every photo, every video goes to me first," she commanded, glaring down at James. "Do not deal directly with Peter under any circumstance."

"There is no video," James repeated.

"Make one. That video is the only thing Peter cares about." Lanier glanced down at her drink, seeing it was empty, she took a beat, shrugged, and exited. As if on cue, the waiter walked over, placed the check next to James, smiled and walked away.

Chapter 13

James was in a daze as he walked back to his Airbnb. He wasn't quite sure what had happened. He felt he'd turned the meeting around. He had Peter Stangerson's phone number and email in his pocket. Stangerson had not only listened—he stayed; he was interested. And it wasn't because of Lanier. She'd been no help. It was James. He felt stunned having successfully completed that high-wire act solo. Maybe the Kimberley meeting had prepared him. But what had he actually accomplished? Amber had left showing no interest in his book and he'd managed to grab Stangerson's interested with some made-up story of a nonexistent video of an ex-stripper, psychotherapist. There was still no talk of his novel. His book had once again been sidelined. Opening the door, he walked in, sat on the couch, and turned on the TV for background noise, so as not to feel alone. He had promised Stangerson a video—a nonexistent video. Muting the sound on the TV, he pulled his phone out of his pocket and called Jerry.

"Fill me in," Jerry said, picking up the call on the first ring. "You did it, right? Sold them. We're in."

"Peter Stangerson wants to see video of Kimberley," James announced.

"Don't fuck with me. Seriously, how did the meeting go? Did you really meet with Stangerson? Did he show up? Did you meet Amber Lake? Did you …?"

"Stangerson wants to see video of Kimberley," James repeated.

Jerry's eyes widened. "You brought up Kimberley?" Jerry sat up; his eyes narrowed. "You actually pitched Kimberley at the meeting?"

"Stangerson wants to meet her. But first he wants to see the video," James continued, his voice monotone.

"That's great! Amazing!" Jerry replied in a near yell. "You did it! After a pause, he added, "What video?"

"The one you're making. He wants to see it ASAP."

Jerry stood and began to pace. Not only was the train on track. It was speeding. "Jesus. This is amazing. You're a genius."

James paused. He frowned, remembering there had been no talk of his book. Stangerson hadn't read his book. Once again, Lanier had delt in fantasy. Stangerson had never seen James's book. There was only interest when James had pivoted to the gorgeous blonde sex therapist to the stars—who used to be a stripper. Stangerson hadn't been sold on the novel, but on Kimberley. She was all that had piqued his interest. "I don't think Stangerson or Amber ever read the book," he said, his tone lowered, his voice muted.

"Amber?" Jerry repeated, slowing his pace as he talked. "Listen to you. You call her Amber? You're on a first name basis with Amber Lake. How fucking cool is that? Next it will be Scarlet or Margot. You met Amber Lake and Peter Stangerson. We're golden, man. We are in!"

"Stangerson didn't read the novel," James repeated, feeling the full weight of the words. "It was just like the other meeting. They talked about everything but my book," he continued, becoming more deflated as he spoke. "They completely ignored me during the meeting. Amber left and Stangerson was about to go. I was grasping at straws. Finally, I blurted out the Kimberley story, showed him her photos. And suddenly Stangerson's all over it, he asks for my card, gives me his phone number and email, asks that I get him video of Kimberley ASAP."

"Fucking A!" Jerry yelled with a whoop, his pacing accelerating. "You did it. I always knew you could…"

"It had nothing to do with my book," James interrupted, "It was a waste."

Jerry stopped, mid stride. "Are you crazy? This is the best. You met with Stangerson and he wants video on Kimberley. Then they'll be dying to read your book and green-light the project. It's one of those two-birds-with-one-stone deal. Kimberley's going to flip," he added with a full-on grin. "This is so fucking amazing. You aced it!" Again his pace quickened as he all but trotted around his apartment.

James sat up, put the call on speaker, placing his elbow on his knee as he rested his face on his hand. "There is no sex therapist to the stars in my novel. That character is something you dreamed up to get laid. The scene has nothing to do with anything. And there are no spies in my book, none, no chapter where a sex therapist has sex at the Tokyo Olympics."

Jerry stopped. "What?"

"Stangerson wants to shoot a scene—a sex scene at the Olympics in Japan. There is no Olympics sex scene in my…"

"The Olympics. Genuis! Amazing!" Jerry interrupted, pumping his fist into the air. "He's a genius." He took a beat. "Earth to James. Will you lighten up? Peter Stangerson asked you for a scene. Peter Stangerson. The Peter Stangerson!" he repeated, saying the words slowly for emphasis. "A sex scene at the Olympics. I love it. I can write that. Consider it done. And the 2020 Tokyo Olympics are in July man. He's fast-tracking this. He'll probably want us to go— and Kimberley. For sure Kimberley. This is fucking real! This is the best."

James silently shook his head.

"Film versions of are never books verbatim," Jerry continued reassuringly. "This is going to be a film based on your novel. And we have the psychotherapist scene. I wrote it. We shoehorn it into the film. He needs a spy; we give him a spy. Happens all the time. I'll write a Tokyo sex scene, Stangerson's interested," Jerry insisted. "Focus on that. We'll figure out the rest. Tie the scene into the story. It's our backdoor in. Who cares how we sell it as long as it sells?"

"I fucking care!" James exclaimed. Pointing the remote at the TV, he pushed the off button with all his might, as though shooting it. "There is no sex therapist in my novel."

"We're not talking novel, we're talking film." Jerry loudly sighed. Intentionally loudly. Even with all that was happening, James was playing the precious, petulant artist. "We zigzag from Kimberley's scene to your novel. She's a tangential story that leads us back to your book. It's part of the process. Happens all the time. It's all good. We're in."

"It's not tangential," James barked. "She's becoming the whole fucking project."

Jerry modified his pace, walking more slowly, deliberately. He had seen James go dark and gloom-and-doom before. It was probably physical, he thought. Maybe a tad bipolar. But this was no time for that type of drama-queen antics. Trying to affect a calming tone, he continued. "This is the process. This is how it works, When you sell a project to Hollywood you've got to give and take. Particularly with a first project. Next time we'll have more pull. Get a Stangerson/ Lake film under your belt—then you can call the shots. For now, we go with it."

"You fucking go with it," James barked.

Walking back to his couch, Jerry sat down and closed his eyes. He'd have to do his breathing exercises to calm himself down after the call. "I will, we will," he quickly added. "Look, one of the biggest directors in Hollywood is interested. You had lunch with…"

"Drinks—drinks that I paid for."

"Drinks that I paid for," Jerry corrected. "You had drinks with Amber Lake and Peter Stangerson. Stangerson is interested enough to give you his phone number and email. Shit, it doesn't get much better than that—and you're depressed because he wants to see a video? You just won the lottery and you're fucking moping? Wake up! We'll get him the video, get him to green-light the film and your book is on the way to the screen. The doors have swung open." He paused and added, "Do not fuck this up."

James remained silent. Picking up the phone, he stood and walked towards the kitchen, looking aimlessly around as though not quite sure why he was there. Sitting down at the kitchen table, he ran a hand through his hair. "I don't even know why I'm here," he said, glancing around the Airbnb. "I can't do this."

Jerry sprang up and again began to pace. "Of course you can do this." Walking into his bedroom, he passed by the mirror hanging on the bathroom door, stared at it and silently mouthed the words, "Fuck you, asshole." He then continued pacing. "You're tired, man. A lot has been thrown at you. Look, even if you hate this, even if you want to walk away —just see this part through. The scene Stangerson wants is done, it's already written. Ready to go. I'll contact Kimberley and shoot the video. No problem. Let's just take the next step. You don't need to worry about him ruining your work. Hell, even if he options it, chances are it will never get made," he added cheerily, taking his argument in a new direction. "You'll have nothing to worry about. But, they pay to option projects. You'll make money off the deal. You can use that to buy time to write your next book. It's your project," he went on, continuing to play the cheerleader. "This is real." Jerry took a beat and then continued. "I put all my savings on the spin of the wheel and our number came up a winner. It did! If you want out, at least wait until the project is locked down. I can't lose that money."

James winced. "Don't lay that on me."

96

"It's true," Jerry insisted, now opting for the guilt card. "I need to get that investment back. I'm busted after this. Tapped out. You can't just leave me hanging. The ball is in your court. I trusted you. You hold all the cards."

"The ball is in my court and I hold all the cards? Who mixes metaphors like that?"

Jerry exhaled. He could hear a slight hint of a laugh in James's question. He was coming out of his sulk, edging off the ledge. "I don't just mix, I shake and stir," Jerry replied. "Look, we both need this. It's right there—in our hands. Let's just get him the video. Don't worry. Let's just see where it goes. I'm going to shoot the video. I'll get it to you. You then send it to Stangerson, and we can figure out…"

"Hold on," James said, hearing the beeps and looking down at his phone, "someone's calling. I don't know the number—212 area code."

"That's New York. Take it," Jerry instructed. "It might be about the project. Call me back."

James accepted the call, and answered with a suspicious, "Hello?"

"James?" asked a measured, silky female voice.

"Yeah," he replied wearily. Standing, he headed towards the refrigerator.

"James, it's Amber, Amber Lake. We met with Lanier and Peter," she added as if needing an introduction. "You gave me your card."

James stopped mid-way to the fridge, walked to the kitchen chair and sat down. "Amber?" he repeated, his voice rising uncontrollably.

"It was great meeting you, James. I'm sorry I didn't have more time to talk to you about your project, but I had to run to a meeting. You know how those things are?"

James nodded. "Yeah. Sure, no problem."

"Listen James," she continued, her voice lowering, "Lanier told me that Peter asked for you to send him a video of a scene you shot."

He silently nodded.

"Are you there, James?"

"Yes, right. Sorry," he replied, continuing to nod.

"I want you to send it to me first."

"The scene? It's really nothing. It's not even in my novel. Probably just a throwaway scene that won't even…"

"Peter wanted to see it, right?" she asked, cutting him off.

"Well… yeah."

"I want you to send it to me first." Her voice tightened, her words sounding more like a command than a request.

James's voice fell to a near whisper. "Right."

"Look James, to be honest, I don't even know if we're going to use Peter for this project." She took a beat. "He's in the running, but, well, you know how these things go."

James's eyes widened. He was tempted to ask, "What project?" but remained silent.

"He can be… well… difficult," Amber continued. "I was thinking fresh blood would be good for this. A new director." She paused and then added, "A new writer/director making his debut on an Amber Lake film, we could get a lot of mileage out of that PR-wise."

"Right…" The words stopped as his voice trailed off.

"This project could launch your career, James."

"I'm not a… a director," he stuttered. 'I… I write novels. I really don't know a thing about…"

"Everyone wants to be a director," Amber replied dismissively. "I want to be a director," she added with a slight lilting laugh. "It's easy. You really wouldn't be directing anyway; you just have to sit and bark orders and look important and let the PA's assistant, ADs and cinematographer do all the work. No worries." After a beat, James heard a soft sigh. "Send me the video, okay?"

James, mouth open, obediently nodded.

"James?" Amber asked, the irritation gowning in her voice, "have I lost you?

"No. No. I'm here."

"You don't talk much, James."

"I'm just… this is all so…"

"Get me that video," she directed. "Then we can go from there."

"Yes. Sure. Of course," James again nodded.

"I'm going to give you my email and cell phone number—which you will never, ever share with anyone."

"No, of course, I wouldn't dream of…"

"And don't hit call-back or use the number that comes up when I call you. That's just a ruse. I think it sends you to some sex call center." She paused. "Ready?"

"Wait. Just a sec. Hold on," James said, leaping up, he ran to the bedroom, grabbed his bag and pulled out a pen and a letter he was supposed to mail. It was the only piece of paper he could find. "Okay, got it."

Amber, speaking slowly and clearly, gave James her information. "When can I expect the video?" she asked, her tone indicating she was ready to hang up.

James eyes widened as he stared at his scribbling. " I, uh, I have to check with my… team, I think it's still being edited. Soon?"

"When?" she snapped.

"Tomorrow? Night? I'll get it to you by tomorrow," James replied definitively, not wanting to disappoint.

"And it comes straight to me and nowhere else. You're sending this to me, not to Peter."

"Right," James agreed. He paused and then added. "But, like I said, it's really not even a part of the…"

"And don't mention this call to Lanier," Amber interrupted. After a pause, she added. "Lanier thinks she's going to be a part of this project. But… well… you know how these things go."

James nodded.

"We have a new rule, James," Amber commanded. "When I say something to you, you respond vocally. Understand?"

James nodded and hurriedly added. "Yeah, sure, of course. Sorry."

"Good. So—the video is coming to me, not to Peter, and you're not going to tell Lanier about our calls, right?"

"Right," James agreed a bit too loudly, his blood racing at the suggestion that there would be other calls.

"Send me the video and we'll go from there."

James took a deep breath and closing his eyes asked, "Did you get a chance to read my novel?"

"Novel?"

"My novel," James repeated. "That's why Lanier set up the meeting with you and Peter."

There was a pause. "Your novel. Right. Congratulations. I'm sure it's great. So," she continued, "you'll get me the video tomorrow."

James sighed. She'd never seen his novel. "Yeah. Sure. I just need to check on the editing and…"

"We have an agreement now, right? This is our project. No moves on your end without consulting with me first."

James ran his hand through his hair and nodded.

"James!" Amber snapped.

"Sorry."

"It's annoying."

"Right. It won't happen again."

"So this is strictly between us."

100

"Right." After a pensive pause, James continued. "Peter is expecting me to send it to him tomorrow. He was very clear about the fact that he needs to see it ASAP. What do I tell him?"

James heard an impatient sigh. "There could be an equipment malfunction. A problem in editing. That happens. Happens all the time. You're the writer, James. Not me. Come up with a believable story. I have to go. Send the video to me, not Peter."

With that, the call ended. James stared at the phone and placed it on the table. After staring at the wall for an extended period of time, he picked up the phone and called Jerry.

"Finally! Who was it?" Jerry asked, noticeably impatient that it had taken James so long to get back to him.

"Amber Lake," James replied, a sound of disbelief in his voice.

"I'm serious. Who was it?"

"Amber wants to see the video before Peter does." James walked to the refrigerator, pulled out a beer and taking a sip, continued. "She says Peter might not be a part of the project. She gave me her cell phone and email address to send the video to. She asked if I was interested in directing the film."

"You're bullshitting." Jerry paused as he tried to take in all James was saying. "You don't direct," he pointedly added, "I direct."

"I told her I didn't direct. It didn't seem to matter."

"You're serious?" James silently nodded. Hearing a familiar silence, Jerry continued. "Fucking Amber Lake gave you her cell phone number and..." he paused again. "Then there is a project, right? It's real. Amber Lake is on board. We have a green light. We're fucking in!" he cried, high fiving the wall with a loud thud. "I direct," he repeated. "Did you tell her you don't direct, but your partner does?"

James picked up the beer, stared at it and placed it back down. "She hasn't read the novel. I don't think even Lanier has read the novel. It's all about this fucking nonexistent video. Lanier told Amber that Stangerson was interested, so suddenly Amber wants it. She knows Stangerson is interested, so she wants to get it before he can. It's just a game."

"A game that is going to launch our careers," Jerry said as he tried to soak in the fact that both Peter Stangerson and Amber Lake wanted to see his video. "It's all a game. They want to see it, that's all that matters. This is amazing. I can tell Kimberley that both Peter Stangerson and Amber Lake separately requested to see the video— and I won't be lying," he added, a tone of surprise in his voice. Staring up at the ceiling, he exclaimed, "Thank you, God!"

"I'm flying home. No one even knows my novel exists," James said. "I'm done."

"Done? We're just starting," Jerry insisted. "Things are just starting to gain traction. Wait until I send you the video." Pausing, he ran his hand through his hair. He had to relax. Talk slowly. Patiently. Use kid gloves. This was no time to push James over the edge. Standing, he again began to pace. "It's all good. Having Amber Lake and Peter Stangerson both interested, gives you street cred. Your stock is going to soar. You'll end up with a multi-novel multi-film deal. Play this smart. You're going to be a fucking star. I'll call Kimberley and set up the shoot ASAP—she is going to fucking freak," he added with a grin. "I'll get the video to you—you send it to them and that's our ticket in. We're on track—we're golden!"

Jerry paused, considered sitting down but continued pacing. "How is Kimberley ever going to buy that both Amber Lake and Peter Stangerson want to see her video?" he continued, talking more to himself than to James. Sounds too far-fetched. Sounds like something I'd make up—which even I wouldn't have the balls to do. It doesn't sound real, does it? I mean I barely believe it. I don't want to freak her out. Scare her off. Then we all lose." Jerry paused, brows furrowing.

"I got it!" he exclaimed. "Get Amber or Peter to email you asking to see the video. Then I can forward it. That way Kimberley will see that it's real, that I'm not just bullshitting."

"I don't care what Kimberley thinks."

"Well, start to fucking care," Jerry snapped. "This video is our in."

He took a beat. "But if I forward her an email, with their contacts, she'll be able to contact them directly. That could backfire. Not that I don't trust her, but… Let's do this," he continued as his pacing increased. "Shoot me an email explaining that Stangerson and Amber Lake want to see the video of her. Make it urgent. Add some direct quotes from them. I'll then forward her your email. She'll have the information, but no way to directly contact them. That will work. Send me that email now ASAP. We need to get the ball moving."

"I didn't come here to pitch a Kimberley video. I came here to meet about my book. Dumb idea. Nothing happened, again. I'm going back to L.A., I've had it." With that, James disconnected the call.

Jerry groaned aloud. He started to call back but stopped. James was in one of his moods and nothing Jerry could say would change that. But the moods pass. They always did. The important thing was the train was in motion. It was happening. James would calm down. Eventually come to his senses. Jerry hurriedly pulled out his phone and taking a deep breath, called Kimberley. Hearing her voicemail message, he exhaled, left a controlled, modulated message asking her to call him back, adding it was urgent. Siting on his couch, he closed his eyes and breathed deeply. So much was happening so quickly. And it all could unravel in an instant. James was ready to bail. And how could he ever get Kimberley to believe it was real? Jerry barely believed it was real.

He had to be smart. Come up with a game plan. Standing, he walked to his computer, called up a blank Word document and began writing a to-do list. As he wrote, an email came in from James. It was the email Jerry had requested explaining James's meeting with Amber Lake and Peter Stangerson and that both had asked for a copy of Kimberley's video. He emphasized that both had expressed urgency. Again Jerry took a deep breath and smiling, exhaled. James was back—at least for now.

Chapter 14

Jerry stared at his phone, his brows furrowed as he willed it to ring. After about fifteen minutes, the call came. "Kimberley?" he said, working to keep his voice steady, modulated.

Kimberley considered correcting him, replying, "Dr. Goodman." Instead she simply said, "I'm returning your call."

Jerry inhaled deeply and began. "I'm sorry to bother you, but James had his meeting with Peter Stangerson and Amber Lake and..." he paused wondering what the best approach would be, questioning the direction he had decided on before the call.

"Yes?"

"Well I'm not sure about the consultant idea but..."

Kimberley felt her body slump. She had bought into Jerry's story more than she thought. "But?" she repeated.

"You know, the therapist role that we talked about at our meeting?"

Kimberley remained silent.

"Well… Stangerson loves the idea," Jerry tried to keep his tone cool, his delivery composed. "A gorgeous Beverly Hills psychotherapist playing a gorgeous Beverly Hills psychotherapist. That's what he told James. He loves it. He's all in."

Kimberley was about to interrupt, correct that she was not a Beverly Hills psychotherapist, but remained silent.

"Peter," Jerry continued, making a mental note that referring to Stangerson by his first name made it sound more believable, "he's sold on the concept. I mean, like really sold. To be honest, James was a bit pissed off because apparently from that point on there was no more talk about his novel. All Peter was interested in was seeing the video of you."

"What video?"

"That's why I'm calling. Peter asked if we had video that we could send him. If he likes it, he wants to fly out and meet with you." Jerry paused. "Amber called James after the meeting. She's now interested in seeing the video because she knows Peter's interested. That's how those people work. Now they're both interested. I know it sounds crazy but it's real."

Kimberley walked over to the mirror and stared appraisingly at her reflection. "But there is no video," she replied.

"I know. That's why I'm calling. When James was talking to Peter, he reviewed what the three of us had discussed. He emphasized that you're not only an actress, but also an actual therapist. He showed Stangerson your pictures, the ones online, and now Stangerson wants to see video of you acting, ASAP. He asked James if we had video and not knowing how else to respond, he said yes. He was afraid if he said there was no video Peter's interest would wane. I know it sounds crazy. But it's real. We need to shoot a video and get it to James, so he can get it to Peter and Amber. Right away. I have the scene. I have the equipment. It can be short, seven to ten minutes."

Kimberley remained silent as she stared in the mirror. Stranger things had happened. She remembered the media coverage around *Exposed*, the film Stangerson made with the escort. That was real. Not only real, it was a hit. It launched careers. She walked back to her desk and sitting down at her computer Googled her photos. Chances were it was all a ruse, but what if it wasn't? Besides Jerry wasn't a client. Not any longer. She wouldn't be crossing any ethical lines. Not really. Well technically she would. Technically she was supposed to wait a year or two. She couldn't remember the guidelines. But, from her perspective, all that really mattered was he was no longer a client. James did know Peter Stangerson. She'd seen proof. The worst that would happen was that nothing would come of the video and she'd feel embarrassed, foolish. But no one would know. No one but her. And if anyone did find out, she had simply shot a short video. What was the harm in that?

"We have the scene I wrote," Jerry said, breaking the silence. "You've read it. We just need to shoot it. It'll be a fast shoot. Over in half an hour—less. Peter asked if we could get it to him tomorrow. It will be short, like I said, between five and seven minutes." Jerry held his breath as he waited for a response, praying to whoever was out there who would listen.

Kimberley remained silent as she Googled photos of Nicole Kidman, Charlize Theron, and Amber Lake. Her eyes narrowed as she compared their photos to hers.

Unsettled by Kimberley's silence, Jerry soldiered on. "I'm forwarding you an email that James sent me filling me in on what happened at the meeting. I'm sending it now." Sitting down at his computer, Jerry called up James's email. He had rewritten it a bit to add a greater sense of urgency and also added some fictitious quotes from Stangerson. He then hit send and continued. "I don't mean to push, but James is pushing me because Peter is pushing him. This is all moving so quickly." He took a beat and asked, "Did the email come through?"

Kimberley took her time reading the email. "What would the next steps be?" she asked.

Jerry tightly closed his fist, pumping it in the air in thanks. He exhaled. "We set up a time to videotape it. I then edit it, upload it to Vimeo, send it to James and James sends it to Peter. Once Peter sees it, he'll want to fly out for an in-person meeting. Guaranteed." And he would, Jerry thought. This wasn't another fabrication, another one of his stories. This was real.

"Email me the scene again. I'll give it a read and call you back."

"Right," Jerry agreed with a sharp nod of his head. "I'll email it to you as soon as we hang up. I'll stay by the phone for your call. Not pushing, but like I said, Peter is pushing James and…"

"Email me the scene," Kimberley repeated.

"Sure. Yes. Doing it right now." Disconnecting the call, Jerry put down his cellphone, went to his computer, called up the scene and quickly reread it. The scene worked. It was a good audition scene for her character. Dr. Sawyer, the gorgeous psychotherapist, confronts Henry, the film's male lead. The two have been having an affair. They are in the psychotherapist's office. She is wearing a short skirt and bra. Dr. Sawyer picks up Henry's phone and reads a compromising text. She tosses the phone down and angrily confronts him. Henry's character spends most of the scene reacting and defending himself. The scene belongs to Dr. Sawyer. A good actress could ace it. Kimberley could ace it.

The writing wasn't up to James's quality. Jerry knew James won out on that front, which annoyed him. But it worked. It was good. He wrote Kimberley a quick email explaining that he was attaching the scene and asking her to call him as soon as she read it. He then hit send and practiced a couple of visualization exercises, imagining Kimberley's swift positive response. Less than ten minutes passed before she called.

"What would be next steps?" Her voice was sharp. Direct.

Jerry leaped out of his chair and threw a congratulatory fist in the air. He would have preferred it if she'd congratulated him on the scene and his writing, but her interest was congratulations enough. "You can knock it out of the park." he replied, trying to sound as collected as possible. "Trouble is, we have to get it to Peter by tomorrow night. We don't have much time." He loved using the word "we" when speaking to Kimberley. "James said if I could get it to him by tomorrow evening, that would work. I have the equipment, camera, lighting and all," he quickly added. "We could run lines a few times, then shoot it. I can then send it off ASAP. We'd need to get it shot tomorrow, the earlier the better, so I can see if it needs any editing. The scene takes place in a psychotherapists office. So we could shoot it at your office. That would be perfect."

Kimberley called up her Google calendar. "One-thirty."

Jerry was going to ask for an earlier time, but figured that could be pushing it and he was already ahead of the game. "Perfect," Jerry repeated. "See you then. I could get there early and run lines with you."

"Not necessary."

"Got it," Jerry replied, disappointed by her quick response. "Okay then, tomorrow at one-thirty." Hanging up the call, he sprang up out of the couch, leaped up and in a loud voice cried, "Yes!"

Chapter 15

Jerry drove to the drugstore to pick up hair mousse. He wanted his hair somewhat spiky, but not over the top, not that hair-shooting-to-the-sky thing that Millennials do. Once back at his apartment, he studied his meager outfit choices. Starting with dress slacks, one of his best shirts, and sports jacket, he next went to jeans, his second-best shirt, and a jacket, to simply jeans and a shirt. Wanting to look casually professional, he ultimately decided on his good jeans and a dress shirt. The identical outfit he'd worn to the meeting with Kimberley and James.

He packed his video equipment in his car and, turning Spotify on high, drove towards Kimberley's office. The dynamics were going to be different this time. He was no longer a client going for a session. He wasn't paying to see her. He was now Kimberley's white knight helping her achieve her dream. Parking in a visitor space at her office building, Jerry lugged his lighting and video equipment into the elevator and up to Kimberley's waiting room. Pushing the buzzer announcing his arrival, he sat down and nervously waited.

Looking down at his phone he saw a text coming in from James which read, "I'm coming home." Jerry frowned and quickly responded. "Stay put! It's all good. Hang tight. Shooting the scene now. Get it to you in a few hours. This is our ticket! We're golden! Don't go anywhere." That wasn't fair, he thought as he angrily slipped the phone into his pocket. He shouldn't have read a text like that right before the shoot. It put him on edge, ruined the mood. He looked up as Kimberley opened the door wearing a form-fitting turquoise blouse and short white skirt. All was right with the world. "Have camera will travel," he smiled and standing, gathered his equipment and followed Kimberley into her office. "I just heard from James. Peter just called, to confirm that we will be sending the video today. He's anxious to see it."

Kimberley stood by her desk wondering if she'd just fallen for a fantastical scheme. There was no one she could tell about the video shoot. Her colleagues would be appalled if they knew she had a client in her office preparing to shoot an audition video. Not only would they see it as foolish on her part, but also as unethical, breaking every client/therapist rule. There wasn't even a friend she felt comfortable telling. It would all sound like such an obvious scam on Jerry's part.

Yet there were stranger Hollywood success stories. She had seen the photos of James with Peter Stangerson and Dunhill Jr. Those weren't simply fan selfies. James was in. And he had been published. She'd bought his novel. It was real. Still, she realized it could all be a ruse, all lead to nowhere, she thought as she picked up the scene and glanced at it. Plus, she knew herself, knew she'd feel even more the fool if she didn't follow up only to learn down the line it had all been real.

"Apparently James's entire meeting with Peter was about you," Jerry said as he set up the camera. "To be honest, he's a bit bummed, since throughout the conversation his book had been sidelined. But he's a pro and knew enough to stick with the pitch that works. They reviewed your photos, James told Peter about your practice, your expertise as a psychotherapist, your acting background, how you would be a perfect fit. It worked. Peter wanted to see video ASAP."

Jerry paused and picking up his camera, looked at Kimberley through the viewfinder. "You mind standing over there?" he asked as he positioned the lights.

After a beat, she somewhat begrudgingly followed his direction.

He nodded and, placing down the camera, began positioning the lighting, setting up the tripods, and plugging in the power chords. "It'll just take a second," he said. Feeling her impatience, he hurriedly worked to set everything up. Again picking up the camera, he waved Kimberley to the left as he looked through the viewfinder.

"A bit over there," he directed, feeling a sense of power as Kimberley followed his lead. "There, that's perfect," He paused, his eyebrows furrowing as he contemplated the shoot. "Sit there. Good. A bit straighter." He looked up and nodded. "This will be great. As soon as we finish, I'm going to see if it needs editing. I'll then upload it and get it to James who will immediately shoot it over to Peter."

Kimberley simply nodded. She had been right to leave her photos online.

"Do you need to read the sides? "Jerry asked. "Since you weren't given much notice, I think that will be okay if you're still on book on video."

Kimberley shook her head, as she placed the scene down on the table. "I have the scene memorized."

"Great," Jerry replied. "A pro."

Kimberley sat erect. She crossed her legs, picked up the scene and glanced down at it for one final read. "I'm ready," she said, again placing it on the table.

"I'll feed you the male character's lines off camera," Jerry said, taking a quick glance at her legs. "Let's review the blocking. We don't want you sitting there through the whole scene."

"I'll just wing it the first time," Kimberley replied. "If it doesn't work we can shoot it again."

111

"Right," Jerry agreed somewhat begrudgingly. He paused and took a breath. This was his scene to direct. He was the one calling the shots, not Kimberley. But, he needed to be patient. The best directors weren't dictators, they found ways to tease the best performances out of their actors.

"The scene starts with you standing," he explained. "You pick up Henry's phone and read a text that just came in. From the text, you find out he's been seeing the character that Nicole Kidman probably will be playing. You realize he's been cheating on you. That text changes everything. And that's where the scene starts."

Kimberley stood and placed her phone on the table. She then turned and nodded at Jerry, signaling that she was ready.

He glanced up. "When the scene starts, well, they were just about to... I mean... they are in the therapist's office getting ready to... well..." He paused, took a deep breath and continued, "Your character wouldn't have her blouse on." He winced. He was pushing too hard. Taking it too far. "Forget it," he hurriedly backtracked, "we can just play it as is. This is just a read-through, an audition. But that's where the scene starts."

Kimberley again glanced down at the script. She looked up at Jerry. "Let's do the scene," she said impatiently.

Felling the blood rush to his face, Jerry winced and looked away uncomfortably. "Of course we'll just do it as is. Like I said, it's an audition. No problem."

Kimberley walked to the mirror studying her hair and make-up. Returning to her mark, she looked up at Jerry. "Let's shoot. We're wasting time."

"Right. Of course. Ready," Jerry answered, doing his best to stay focused. "Let's review some basic blocking. Like I said, you want this to look natural. You don't want to stand in one place through the whole scene."

"I blocked the scene when I was rehearsing," she replied. "Let's just shoot it." Her tone made it clear it wasn't a request.

Jerry paused. He'd be magnanimous, let her do it her way first. That would build a sense of trust, a connection between actress and director. Then they could shoot and reshoot until he got what he wanted. The more they shot the longer they'd be together and the more they'd bond. "Right," he agreed. "Camera is on. I'll serve you the first line. Ready?"

Kimberley stood erect. Glancing one final time at the sides, she tossed them on the floor so they wouldn't be in the shot, looked up and nodded.

"And action." Jerry stared in his viewfinder, still disbelieving where he was or the image he was looking at. Thinking he could happily die on the spot. Framing Kimberley in the viewfinder, he stood erect and delivered his line.

Chapter 16

J erry felt he couldn't drive fast enough as he headed back to his apartment from the shoot. Once parked, he hurriedly unpacked his camera equipment, ran up the stairs, dashed to his computer and uploaded the video. After viewing it five times, he paused, sat back, and viewed it again. That time he watched as a professional, with a critical eye, studying how she moved, spoke, reacted, played the part. She was good. Believable. Better than good. She could act. Jerry got up and began pacing, talking aloud to himself as he walked back and forth in his small apartment. "This can work," he declared, hitting his fist into his open hand. "It's happening. It's really happening. But you gotta be smart. You can't fuck it up."

Jerry was still on the periphery, on the outside. He needed to move quickly but carefully. And he needed to take the reins. He was the one who should be taking the meetings with Amber, Stangerson, and Dunhill Jr., not James. James was losing it. All he cared about was his book. He could ruin things. It was time for him to either step up or step down. But for now, he held all the cards. It was his book they were ostensibly meeting about and his connections. But no one had even read his book. Jerry doubted whether Lanier had even read it. What grabbed Stangerson was Kimberley, not the book and it was the video that would cement the deal. And that was because of Jerry. It was Jerry, not James, who now held the cards. If not for Jerry, there would be no Kimberley, no video, no interest—no project.

Kimberley brought her own issues. Jerry had to be careful on that front. What if Stangerson bit, offered her a role, and cut out Jerry? That could happen. That happened all the time in Hollywood. What if Jerry put it together, did all the work and ended up nowhere, watching Peter, Amber, and Kimberley sail off to success. Jerry adamantly shook his head. Stopping his pacing, he sat on his couch and stared hard at his camera lying on the floor. "I gotta be smart," he said aloud. "Gotta make sure that…" A call from James interrupted his solo conversation.

"Hey," Jerry answered. "I was about to call you,. We did it. I shot her scene. She's fucking amazing man. She can act. Really act." His voice raised, revealing his surprise. "She looks incredible. I've uploaded it and am about to send it. But I was thinking," he took a beat, "we're on thin ice. There's no agreement. We have nothing in writing. Stangerson could just take the video and Kimberley and run with it. Then we're fucked. I should call Kimberley. Tell her I need her to sign something, before we submit it, right? Maybe you should set up another meeting with Stangerson while you're there to iron things out." He stood and began to pace.

"A little late for that."

Jerry came to a dead stop. "What do you mean?"

"I'm back in L.A. I called to tell you last night—to tell you I was taking the red eye, but you didn't pick up."

"I was editing," Jerry said. "I was editing our film."

"Your film. I just got back and already have two texts from Stangerson asking about the video. Your video."

Jerry grinned. "He's anxious. Bingo! Perfect. Tell him we're just about ready to send it. I'll get to you. She's a pro. Doesn't even need editing." Jerry paused and then continued. "You should have stayed. But, whatever. You're back. Okay. But, like I was saying, we need to protect ourselves. We need something in writing, or all our work could be for nothing." Jerry waited for James's response. When there was none, he added, "I'll take care of it. Don't worry. I'll wrap Kimberley up." Again he paused waiting for James to jump in. "Hey, you there?"

"Since when did this project become about Kimberley?" James asked, the tension in his voice palpable.

"It's not. I just meant this is step one and that since they want to see the video of her, we should protect ourselves. I'm going to write up a basic agreement that outlines..."

"I'm just a currier now, that it? A delivery boy getting Stangerson Kimberley's video. He probably just wants to get laid. This is all bullshit." James's voice was dry, brittle.

"No," Jerry replied slowly, distinctly, as if talking to a child. "This is real. This is about your novel, not Kimberley. She's just the eye candy. You've met with Dunhill Jr. You just got back from New York where you met with Stangerson and Amber Lake. How many people can say that? You're now on a first-name basis having phone calls with Amber Lake and Peter Stangerson. You're in, man. This is real." Jerry sat down, running his hand through his hair as he spoke. He was exhausting himself, sounding like a broken record. Saying the same things again and again. Instead of being excited by where they were, all James could do was wallow in his "poor me—no one's read my novel" drama. "Don't blow this. This is fear of success. Your brain is fucking with you."

"I'm out." James paused and then added. "I called the ad agency. Told them I came down with food poisoning, which is why I didn't make it, but I'd be okay in a couple of days. They were cool. They bought it. Said if I could start next week I'd still have the job. I need the money. I can work nine-to-five like a normal person and finish my new novel at night and during my off time. This other stuff, these stupid meetings, it's all a fantasy. None of it's real. It's all bullshit."

Jerry cringed and began to pace more quickly. He could feel everything unraveling in front of him. "Back up. Back up. You're exhausted. All of this traveling back and forth has burned you out. Forget nine-to-five and living like a boring normal person. There's nothing normal about you. A couple more days and we're across the finish line. I'll get you the video of Kimberley and..."

"You don't get it," James's voice rose as he spoke. "I don't even know what the fuck the scene is about—and I don't care."

Jerry stopped leaned back against the wall and with small movements, banged his head against it. "But I do," he replied. "A lot."

"Then you do it," James replied. "You take over. I'll give you Peter's and Amber's emails and phone numbers. I'll tell them I'm out and you're taking over."

"No! You can't just..." Jerry stopped mid-sentence. He paused, eyes widening. That was the answer. The best thing that could happen. If James were to bow out and introduce Jerry, he could take the reins, interact directly with Peter and Amber. James could be involved as much or as little as he chose, but he'd no longer be the front man. Life was offering Jerry a gift. James could stay in the background, write his novels. That's what he wanted. Jerry should step up. Take the workload off of James's shoulders. It was only fair. This could be his chance. Jerry's time to shine. And... and—he could launch Kimberley's career. James was right. Jerry should step up. Best for all.

"Look," Jerry continued, easing into his new role, "I'll take over all of the bullshit stuff. I'll deal with the headaches, with Stangerson and Amber—and Lanier. I'll deliver the video. I'll handle all of that. But we're still partners. This is still about your novel."

James shrugged. "None of them even know I have a novel. You take it from here."

"Right." Jerry smiled, sensing the best of all worlds had just opened for him. "It's only fair that I take this off your shoulders," he continued, convincing himself he was doing James a favor. "You've been doing the heavy lifting. My turn, right? No problem. So, what do you think is the best way to handle this—phone introductions? Email introductions? We have to comfortably make this transfer; let them know that I'm taking over the project—but that nothing has basically changed. Don't want to make them skittish. And," he added decisively, "they have to take me seriously, or it will all just fizzle out. Introduce me as your partner. Tell them I wrote and shot the Kimberley scene—and I was the one who discovered her. Let them know you're not out, you're still involved but now I'm the point man."

"Not that anyone's interested, but I'm not just handing over the rights to my novel."

"No. No. Of course you're not," Jerry replied with a shake of his head. "Just tell them I'm handling the rights for the film, for this particular negotiation." He paused and added, "And let them know I'm Kimberley's manager."

"You let them know." James took a beat. "Remind me how this all got to be about Kimberley?"

"It's not," Jerry insisted, "not really. Like I said, she's just a flashpoint, eye candy, a marketing hook. Kinda like the shark in Jaws. It's not about Kimberley, but she's the door opener. A lot of Hollywood projects come about back-door or tangentially. Who cares, as long as it happens."

"I care. This whole meeting was supposed to be about… Forget it." James's voice trailed off. "I'll email separate introductions to Amber and Peter. You take it from there."

"Thank you, God!" Jerry silently mouthed looking up at the ceiling.

"And then I'm done."

"You're not done," Jerry replied with a shake of his head. "You're just writing your next novel while I do the negotiating, the bullshit work. We're still a team. Okay, let's do this. I'll wait for your emails."

James silently nodded and disconnected the call.

118

"You there?" Jerry asked. "Hello?" James was gone. The call was over. Jerry sat on the couch, put down his phone and rested his chin against his hands which were folded together as if in prayer. He had to be smart, he thought, as he closed his eyes. Life had just dealt him a royal flush which included Amber Lake and Peter Stangerson. A-list players. Industry superstars who got projects green-lit. He opened his eyes and glanced down at his video recorder. He needed to protect himself now. Picking up his phone, he called Kimberley, who unexpectedly answered on the second ring.

Taking a deep breath, Jerry began. "The video looks great. Amazing. I'll email it to you when we get off. A lot is happening—James has asked me to take over the project, to be the point person, so I'm now dealing directly with Amber and Peter. Great news, right?" Jerry stood and began to pace as he spoke. "James just wants to be involved as a writer. The rest, the production, the negotiation, everything like that—that's all me now." Jerry paused, waiting for Kimberley's congratulatory response. She remained silent. Frowning, he continued. "This is great news. But—I need for you to…" he grimaced and stopped mid-sentence. This part was tricky, dangerous. If she refused, he had no follow-up move.

"Need for me to what?" she asked, an impatient tinge to her voice.

"I need you to sign a…" he winced, nervously running his hand through his hair, "just a basic one-paragraph agreement saying that I'm representing you, acting as your manager, at least for this role. Just a short, basic paragraph," he repeated. "I'll whip it up. And email it to you. It will protect us both."

Kimberley hesitated. "I don't need protection and if you're producing the film, why do you need me to sign anything?"

"I am," Jerry replied, almost too forcefully, "producing. But, I've never dealt with this group before. You know what Hollywood is like. We need to protect ourselves. I mean I'm sure everything is fine in this case, but you know… I'm a businessman. Like to dot the I's and cross the T's." His pace slowed as he spoke. "We just need a basic agreement before I send Peter the link to your video. I can email it as soon as we hang up. Like I said, I want to protect us both."

"I don't need protection," Kimberley repeated, "and we don't need to sign anything," Googling her images and studying them while they talked, she added, "You're not managing me."

"I know. I know," Jerry replied. "This agreement will just be for this project. It's just how it's done. It will be very specific. It won't be locking you up for anything else. Just this. Very specific," he repeated, his voice beginning to race. There was an uncomfortable silence, during which Jerry closed his eyes so tightly they hurt. "I just need to get it signed before I send Peter the video."

Glancing up from the computer screen, she stared at the clock, her next client would be arriving soon. "Jerry," she said, his name coming out loudly, like a full stop.

"Yeah."

"I'm not comfortable signing anything. This is your project. Yours and James's. You're covered. Send Peter Stangerson the video and we'll go from there."

Jerry stopped his pacing and exhaled. "But I really need you to…" Stopping mid-sentence, he tried to convince himself everything was okay. Besides, no one-paragraph agreement would stand up against Stangerson's attorneys. In the end, he'd have to trust her. That's what it would all come down to. "Okay," he concluded.

"Good. Anything else?"

Looking down at his laptop, Jerry checked his email. As promised, James had sent two separate emails, one introducing him to Amber Lake and one to Peter Stangerson. Both emails arrived separately and neither party was cc'd on the email to the other. "Yes!" Jerry silently mouthed. He had entered Valhalla. "No. No. That's it. Okay then. You're right. We're good. I'm going to contact Peter now."

Preparing for her next session, Kimberley picked up her phone and walked to her side table, carefully arranging her pad, pen, and water glass. "I need to see the video, before you send it to anyone."

Jerry grimaced. "Right," he replied reluctantly. He knew he'd send it regardless, but might as well email it to her first. "I need to get it to Peter now, ASAP so stand by your computer. I'll email it to you as soon as we hang up. You look great in it. Amazing."

"My next session is about to start. Send me the video. I'll get right back to you." Disconnecting the call, she walked to her computer and waited for Jerry's email.

"It's not her call to make. This is my video. My film." Jerry muttered aloud, as he headed to his laptop. Sitting down, he pasted the Vimeo link with the password into an email and, sending it to Kimberley, took a deep breath as he impatiently waited for her response.

Her email came more quickly than expected. Jerry braced himself as he opened it. Her reply was short. Two words. "Send it." Jerry exhaled. All was good to go. But there was no thank you from Kimberley. No comment on the quality of the direction, on what an expert job he'd done, on the opportunity he was giving her.

Jerry shook his head. He was wasting time, thinking negatively, acting like James. His world had just opened, opened wide. There were green lights as far as he could see.

He carefully studied James's emails. His initial email brought Jerry up to date, explained that Amber and Stangerson had two separate parallel agendas, neither knowing what the other was doing and that Lanier was out in the cold, but trying to control things. It ended with, "I'm going to introduce you in my next emails and then I'm done. You take it from there."

James's second email introduced Jerry to Stangerson, explaining that Jerry was now going to act as the point person on the project. James then sent an identical email to Jerry and Amber. James had done his part. He'd come through.

Jerry responded to James's initial email with "Thanks. Got it. We're golden." He then composed a short introductory response to both Amber and Peter. He paused, staring at the screen. He was emailing Peter Stangerson and Amber Lake. He was playing with the A Team. His time had arrived. Inhaling deeply, Jerry held his breath as he hit send on both emails.

Within minutes, a response had came from Peter Stangerson. Jerry had steeled himself, preparing for an angry response. By taking over for James, Jerry was changing the game plan and sudden changes generally upset people, especially those like Stangerson, who craved control. But the email was cordial, thanking James for the introduction and telling Jerry he looked forward to speaking with him. It ended with a directive. Jerry was to email the video link ASAP.

Stangerson sent a very different email to James, followed by an irate voicemail, his anger in full force. James did not read the first and chose not to listen to the second.

Again Jerry watched the video. It worked. Kimberley was almost more mesmerizing on video than in person. She had timing, nuance. She became the character. Although, as the writer and director, Jerry had to take a certain amount of credit there. He had written a strong scene. His direction was subtle, but flawless, and it was clean, well shot. Very basic stuff, but the camerawork was steady, the lighting worked. He made sure you could see her figure, her legs, how her eyes popped on screen. It all came together like clockwork. Without his guidance, Jerry's, it would just be another video of a gorgeous blonde. Now it was a star-turn. Now it was set to launch both Kimberley and Jerry. Parallel tracks. Stars aligning.

Jerry read and reread the email Peter Stangerson had emailed him. He stood and walked around the apartment, saying "yes" aloud. He then stopped in front of his mirror and high-fiving his reflection, yelled "Yeeessss!" Returning to his desk, he sat down, pasted the password-protected Vimeo link to Stangerson's email, wrote a short introduction, and hit send.

Chapter 17

Kimberley sat at her kitchen table, reading texts as she waited for her coffee maker to finish its cycle. She smiled when she thought of Jerry pressuring her to sign a document. She'd won. She was loath to sign anything but, if Jerry had not given in, if he had forced the issue, she might have signed. She'd already gone that far. Best see it through. Kimberley refused. Jerry relented. And she won. But, then again, so did he. A lot of her male patients had tried to find a way to get close to her. It never worked. Well—it seldom worked. Jerry found a way in. If it all stopped there, Jerry would have achieved his goal, or at least come close. And he'd have a video memento.

Jerry wasn't all bad. There were times Kimberley almost found him attractive. "Almost" being the operative word. He was tenacious but not in a stalkerish way. Not in her league, but maybe in another time, another place? Kimberley grimaced shaking her head as she stood and walked towards the coffeemaker. No, not even then. He was too much of a wanna-be, a hungry Hollywood hopeful waiting for the big spin to come his way. She'd seen that too many times, watched too many of her clients stuck there, like addicts waiting for a fix. She'd too been there. But not for long, she'd grown out of it.

Still, she remembered the dreaming, the yearning, the belief that the fantasy would actualize, the life-changing role would materialize, and life would magically change. Sometimes she missed that feeling, the excitement of almost, of maybe. But there had been too many maybes, letdowns, too many scams, too many guys with business cards that said manager or producer who were just out to score. A life lived in almost.

Yet, she thought as she poured her coffee, she'd watched, as almost turned into realities for others, she'd sat on the sidelines as others landed roles in soap operas, independent films, studio films. It did happen. She'd been in the proximity of a lightning strike, but never close enough. Never quite there. And it had beat her down. She knew she could act. She was good. She had the looks. Heads turned. Many called her beautiful. Jerry said gorgeous. Even now people compared her to Amber Lake, Scarlett Johansson, said she was a dead ringer for Charlize Theron. But those comparisons were as close as the lightening had come—until now. And now? Now Kimberley was back at almost. Back to yearning. Why not? Nothing ventured… But still, she had changed. She was a realist. She wasn't jumping all in, not really, she still had her feet firmly planted in the real world. She just took a meeting and shot a video. That was all.

Taking a sip, Kimberley walked to her home office desk. Sitting down, she opened her laptop, called up the Vimeo link Jerry had emailed her and typed in the password to access the video. She put down her cup, leaned in towards the screen, hit the video link and watched. Initially, it had been confronting. Watching it seemed awkward, almost silly. But she looked good, looked better than she would have imagined. And the more she watched, the better it played. It worked. She could still act. She sat back, hit replay, and watched it again.

She then walked to her bedroom and stopped in front of her full-length bureau mirror. Turning towards it, she smiled and let her body move, striking poses as if for the camera. Standing erect, she stared intently. People were right. She could go toe-to-toe with any actress. She was in that class, in that league. She should have made it. Years ago. Maybe it was just part of life's plan that her journey took a circuitous route, took a bit longer. She had done good work as a therapist. Helped others. And it was that experience that now piqued Stangerson's interest. That now separated her from the rest.

It would be good fodder for the media, create a buzz. She was unique. And that was what Peter Stangerson saw. Kimberley's time was now.

Chapter 18

After sending emails introducing Jerry to Amber Lake and Peter Stangerson, James composed one final email to Lanier explaining that he was stepping away from the project. He read it, reread it, stared at it again and then hit delete. Why intentionally upset a hornet's nest. She'd lose it, raise hell at his introducing Jerry to her contacts, at being left out of the loop. James didn't have the emotional bandwidth to deal with her rants. Besides, all she'd done was make introductions. Nothing more. He would ignore her calls, texts, and emails. She'd eventually fade away. James was done with all of it. Not one of them had read his book, not Lanier, not Peter, not Amber. And his novel was what mattered.

James paused as he stared at his computer screen. What if Jerry was right? What if this was how it worked? What if another chance like this never came? He'd read stories about people who hadn't recognized their shot when it was offered to them. They hesitated, balked, and disappeared. What if that's what he was doing by walking away? Disappearing. James shrugged, canceled that thought, and checked his email.

Stangerson texted again, demanding he immediately call. James had considered calling him, thought it was the proper, professional thing to do. But Stangerson's anger was legend and James would rather sidestep a frontal assault. Silence was probably his best approach. Out of sight, out of mind, eventually disappearing. And, to a large degree James was right. Once he sent Stangerson the email, James quickly began to wane. His place in Stangerson's world was fading.

Feeling his phone vibrate, James took it out of his pocket. Best just turn it off, he thought as he checked the caller. It was probably going to be an assault from Stangerson or Lanier. His eyebrows knitted as he stared at the name on his screen. James took a deep breath and answered.

"James?"

James's eyes widened at the sound of her voice. The voice. A dream. One that would probably never be revisited. He hurriedly searched for and pressed the record function on his phone. "Hi, Amber."

"I don't understand your email."

James sat back and closed his eyes. "My partner, Jerry, he's the one who shot the video, so he's going to be the one handling things from now on."

"I don't like this, James. You gave my email to a stranger. I specifically told you that you were not to…"

"Not a stranger," James protested. "He's my partner. He's handling the business side of things."

After a pause, Amber asked, "Are you still involved?"

James felt a shiver run through his body. Amber Lake wanted him involved. "Sure," he lied. "Of course."

"Have Jerry email me the video ASAP," she continued, her voice turning more clipped, officious. "Tell him not to share it with anyone else, not Peter, not Lanier, no one. Understood?"

"Right. Sure. Got it."

There was a beat as though she was contemplating saying something else, but ended with, "Goodbye, James."

"It was great meeting you, Amber," James said, figuring this was his farewell call and hoping to prolong the sound of her voice, if even for a few more seconds. He was hoping for, "it was great meeting you too," but the call disconnected. She was gone.

Chapter 19

J erry sat at his desk and watched Kimberley's video three more times, fascinated by the thought that he could now call it up whenever he wanted. The creation was his. He had written, shot, and directed the video. It was like a short film, a micro-film. Those were made now in days. They were shown on streaming services. There were film festivals devoted to them. Then again, there were film festivals for just about anything.

Switching to his email, Jerry read Amber Lake's response. It was short, terse. "Jerry, please send me video link ASAP. Do not share with anyone else. Thank you, Amber Lake." Jerry read and reread the email. He Googled photos of Amber Lake and glanced back and forth between the images and the email. Amber Lake had emailed him. Jerry was in her world. It was disappointing that she hadn't introduced herself, or said it was a pleasure meeting him, but still, she had responded.

He needed to prepare to write emails to both Peter and Amber.

Walking to the bathroom, he washed his face and combed his hair He then changed his shirt, putting on something a bit more upscale. These were auspicious emails and deserved special attention. Walking into the kitchen, he put some ice in a glass, opened a bottle of Perrier, poured it, and walked back to his desk. This was a momentous occasion. Not to be taken lightly. It deserved a formal ceremony. Taking a drink, he put down his glass, placed his fingers on the computer keyboard and began. His first email was to Stangerson. He introduced himself, said how much he had enjoyed Stangerson's films and that he was a real fan. Pausing, he reread it, deleted the fan part, and continued. He explained that there were some technical issues with the video and that he'd get it to him as soon as they were resolved. That seemed like the best approach. Jerry needed to buy some time to figure out how to best play things. Should he send the video to both Stangerson and Amber Lake, or pick one over the other? If he was going that route, he needed to decide whether Stangerson or Amber would be his best bet. He had to be smart. Judicious. If he played it wrong, he could end up alienating them both.

He should wait a bit, he thought, as he reread the email. Step away from it. Give himself time to think. He closed the screen on his laptop. He'd give his mind a break to sort things out. He could work on his sci-fi horror script. But he'd never be able to concentrate. Not now. His brain was lit up like a pinball machine filled with zooming balls and lights flashing. Maybe a walk, or an early movie. The gym. That's where he'd go. The gym followed by a sauna. Then a movie. Keep moving. Keep busy. But he'd have to decide quickly. Needed to make a decision as to where to initially send the video soon. Maybe call a psychic. It couldn't hurt.

Jerry again opened his laptop and went on the Bank of America site to check his accounts. They were dwindling. His eyes widened seeing the amount of money James had burned through in the last few days. Maybe it had been crazy for Jerry to have agreed to the New York trip. He'd not only agreed, he'd encouraged it; pushed James, like a parent, sending a reluctant child off to camp. But it was the right call. An investment. Jerry was usually frugal.

In the last few months, his only real luxury spend had been on his therapy sessions. His insurance didn't cover them, so he was paying full fee—and Kimberley was not cheap. But that too was an investment. And all his investments were coming to fruition. Still, things needed to move quickly; his freelance gigs wouldn't be enough to keep him going for long. In the worst of all worlds, he'd have to follow James's route. Get a job.

Standing, Jerry shook his head, dismissing the thought and began to slowly pace. His brain was squirming, dashing around like a caged squirrel. The money was well-spent, he insisted to himself. An investment. An amazing investment. If he hadn't paid to see Kimberley, there would have been no video. If he hadn't sent James to New York there would have been no interest in the video. If he hadn't made precisely the choices he had, he would not be in email conversations both with Amber Lake and Peter Stangerson. That was not money foolishly spent. They were genius strokes on his end.

His decisions placed him on the doorstep, an inch away from success. His money had not been wasted, but shrewdly invested. He sat back down and called up his email in-box. He looked at the emails from Peter Stangerson and Amber Lake, both directing him to email them the video immediately.

He stood up, walked into the kitchen, grabbed a diet coke, and began to argue the pros and cons of emailing Kimberley's video to Stangerson, or Amber, or both. He made convincing arguments on both sides. Sitting down, he made an executive decision. James had promised Amber the video and Jerry would much rather strike up a relationship with Amber—for a number of reasons. But, Amber was only asking for the video reactively because Stangerson was interested. Jerry wasn't sure if Amber knew or cared what the video was about, and, from what James reported, she had shown no interest in the novel. Hers was purely a defensive move. Her sole objective was to one-up Stangerson. Lock up a project so he couldn't have it. Stangerson, on the other hand, was interested, really interested. Having seen Kimberley's photos, there was the obvious sexual predator aspect, which seemed to be his MO, but beyond that—he was interested in it as a project. A similar approach had worked for him before with *Exposed*. Plus, Stangerson was hungry. He needed a hit. Executive decision made. Stangerson would be Jerry's starting point. His first move. Jerry could keep stalling Amber for a bit with the video's technical problems story. If he alienated Amber that would be rough, he'd want to stay in her good graces, but that was business and you could never make everyone happy when it came to this type of deal.

This was no time to go to the gym, he thought, as he again sat at his computer. This called for decisive action. Jerry closed his eyes, took three deep breaths, rewrote the email to Stangerson, added the link to Kimberley's video and, taking one more deep breath, exhaled as he hit send. He'd then go for a run. Clear his brain. Waiting for a response was unrealistic. People like Peter Stangerson didn't react quickly. They took their time, made you wait, even if only to make a statement about who they were. Jerry probably wouldn't hear back until the next day at the earliest. He walked into his bedroom and changed into shorts, tee shirt and running shoes. Passing his laptop on the way out, he glanced down. Stangerson had replied.

Jerry sat in front of his laptop, eyes wide. He winced as he prepared to click on the email and read it. His finger stopped as he lightly touched the mouse. It was probably a no-go, a "get lost never contact me again" response. What would Jerry tell Kimberley about the rejection? If worst came to worst, he could always lie, tell Kimberley that Amber was interested, convince her to stay on board for a bit longer. Let her know that's how these things work in the film world. That would at least buy him a bit more time to consider his options.

But once Kimberley heard Peter and Amber both passed it would all be over. Jerry would have no other options. She'd move on, would probably never speak to him again and he'd be out in the cold. He was no longer a client. He'd be out. Completely. The money he spent would be wasted, the project would be dead, Kimberley would be gone, Peter and Amber would demand that he never email them again. He wouldn't even have a therapist to discuss this with. Why even look at Stangerson's email?

He stood up and did some jogging in place, shook his body, took a deep breath and, covering his eyes with his left hand, clicked the mouse with his right index finger. Then, squinting, he opened his fingers enough to see the screen. Stangerson's email read, "We need to talk. ASAP!"

Jerry's eyes widened as he removed his hand and stared at the email. He read it four times, the last time aloud and slowly. He couldn't tell what Stangerson thought from that response. Stangerson was the kind who seemed to like to yell at people. Maybe that's what he wanted. To scream at Jerry for wasting his time. But if he wanted to talk, there would be more to it than that. Stangerson wasn't the type who wasted time talking to people like Jerry. At the very least, there was some kind of interest.

Jerry sat at his computer and slowly composed his follow-up email. He figured it would probably be pretentious to ask Stangerson to give out his phone number, so he thanked him for getting back to him, added his phone number, and invited Stangerson to call at his convenience. He then hit send. Jerry stood up, cleared his throat, and practiced using the right tone of voice. "Hello, Peter, wonderful to meet you via phone. James has told me so much about you." No. That was stupid. Everyone knew about Peter Stangerson—he was a celebrity, a world-famous director. He was a star. Jerry wouldn't have learned about Stangerson from James. He began again. "Peter, hello, I'm a real fan of your work." No, too kiss-ass. He was probably tired of everyone telling him that. Too obvious. Too mundane. Again he began, "Hello, Peter…" A call then came. The call. Jerry flinched as though hit with an electric charge.

"Hello." Jerry's voice crackled cricket-like.

"Jerry, Peter. Peter Stangerson." His voice was firm, loud. Not booming, but close to it.

"Peter. It's great to mee…"

"I want you to set up a meeting with Kimberley," Stangerson commanded.

Jerry stood and began to pace. "She's in Los Angeles. I mean I know you're in New…"

133

"Set up the meeting."

As excited as he was by being on the call with Peter, Jerry could feel it all begin to slip away. He'd introduce Kimberley to Stangerson and that would be that. He'd simply be a go-between. His role would be over. He had no written agreement with Kimberley. If Stangerson came to her with a whole new idea or concept—if it wasn't James's book, Jerry was out, as integral to the project as a bat boy in the World Series. He couldn't allow that. "I wrote the scene," he offered, his voice almost too soft to be heard, "the one in the video."

"How soon can you set up the meeting?" Stangerson's tone was demanding, impatient. Jerry glanced down at an incoming email from Amber with her number asking that Jerry call immediately He stared at the email, eyes widening, mouth open. 'Don't worry," Stangerson added gruffly, sensing Jerry's hesitation, "If anything comes of this, you'll be taken care of."

Jerry flinched. The man was psychic. He stared at Amber Lake's phone number. Taking a deep breath, he ran his hand over his face. "Thank you."

"She a sex therapist?" Stangerson asked.

"Well," Jerry replied, forgetting exactly what James had told Stangerson, "she does do sex therapy."

"I need her to be a sex therapist," Stangerson insisted. "And she was a stripper—before becoming a therapist. She'll do nudity, right?"

Jerry winced. Both concerned and aroused by the question. "Of course," he fumbled, not sure how else to respond. "I'm sure. Yes. Of course."

"Set up the meeting." Stangerson ordered. "I'll be in L.A. the day after tomorrow."

"Right." Jerry frowned, uncomfortable at the thought of leaving Kimberley alone with Stangerson.

"Are you and Kimberley… involved?"

Jerry paused at first, unsure what was being asked, and then flattered by the question. "Well, I mean… I don't really talk about… it's not something I generally…"

"Don't stammer."

"Well, I mean it's complicated."

"So you're not involved."

"Well, I mean…"

"Look, if you're gay, I don't care," Stangerson said, cutting him off mid-sentence. "It's L.A. LGBTQ and all.. Did I get all those letters right?" he asked with a bit of a snicker.

Jerry flinched. "No, I mean yes, as to the letters, but no I'm not…"

"I genuinely like fags," Stangerson added with a clipped laugh. "Wrong term right? But I'm old school. The industry needs them. We should be more like Broadway."

"But I'm not…" Jerry stopped, mid-sentence, maybe keeping that possibility on the table could work in his favor, help down the line. "You're right," he agreed, "there should be more inclusion, more representation of the community. Did I mention that I wrote, directed and shot the scene that I sent you?"

"Twice," Stangerson replied curtly. "Set up the meeting. And, this is strictly between us—Lanier, Amber, Dunhill Jr., none of them are to know about this." He paused and then added. "Understood?" Not waiting for a reply, Stangerson ended with, "Set it up and get back to me right away." The call then disconnected.

Jerry put down the phone and stared at his computer. Closing his eyes, he took a deep breath and slowly exhaled. He was in their orbit now, in their gravity field, talking to them, emailing them—not yet one of them, but in their solar system. Jerry rubbed his hand over his face.

He should call Kimberley. Set up the meeting. But call Amber first. Who in his right mind would keep Amber Lake waiting? He had promised Stangerson that he wouldn't tell anyone about the meeting. But the promise was about the meeting, not the video. He never promised not to share the video, just not to tell anyone about the meeting—at least that's how he decided to interpret the call. But Stangerson wouldn't understand it that way. If Jerry shared the video with Amber and it got back to Stangerson, which it would, that could ruin everything. If Jerry were picking sides, business-wise, the best bet would be to side with Stangerson. Stangerson's interest was genuine. He was in need of a hit.

Still, best call Amber. Pique her interest. Keep two balls in the air. Set up two possible deals. Jerry was a businessman and that was the smartest business approach. Standing up, he stretched, shook his body, and made guttural sounds to open up his vocal cords. Sitting down, he took a deep breath, picked up his phone and dialed.

"Yes," answered an officious male voice.

"Amber Lake please," Jerry squeaked.

"This is?"

"Jerry. Jerry Greenfield."

The was silence followed by, "Jerry?" Amber's voice was smooth, silky, hypnotic.

"Hi," he replied, almost too softly to hear. "Wonderful to meet you—via phone. I'm a real fan. I thought you were incredible in…"

"Have you sent me the video link yet?" she asked, her voice turning stern. "I haven't seen it."

'There, uh … there was a problem."

"Problem?"

"The video…" Jerry hesitated, frowned, took a breath and continued. "There were… technical problems. We have to reshoot."

"Reshoot?" Amber repeated sharply.

Standing, he began to pace as he talked. "Something happened. We'll have it reshot in no time. I didn't shoot this one," he quickly added, making up the story as he spoke. "I was busy wrapping another production and sent one of crews. If you want something

136

done right…" he paused and then continued. "I'm going to reshoot. I'm going to do it myself this time."

"I thought it was shot," Amber replied suspiciously. "Lanier said you had video and that Peter was interested. I need you to send it to me—not Peter."

"Right. It was… shot, but like I said, technical issues. I'll have it reshot in no time." He could hear Amber sigh impatiently.

"When?"

Jerry frowned, wondering if Amber even knew what the video was. The fact that Stangerson was interested was probably all that interested her. "Soon. Very, very soon. It's, uh, James's project," Jerry replied fumbling over his words. "It's based on his book. That's what the scene I'm shooting with Kimberley is for."

"Kimberley?"

"Right," Jerry replied, Amber's question confirming she had no idea what the video was about. "She's a therapist. I mean she's an actress—a therapist who is an actress. She's very good and…"

"A therapist?" Amber repeated with a laugh. "This is a video of a therapist? You can forget this call Jerry. I think we're wasting each other's time."

Jerry flinched. He was losing her. "She's also an actress," he repeated. "Stangerson is thinking of her for the lead, She's a therapist, but also an actress, used to be a… stripper. It'll be like *Exposed*. She's gorgeous," he added. Amber was silent. His pacing quickened. Inhaling, he waited for her reply.

"What else has she been in?"

Jerry exhaled. "She did some acting, a few years ago. She's new but not—new, if you get what I mean."

"How new? How old is she?"

"You know how that is." Jerry explained. "Actresses hate to give out their ages. And rightfully so," he added. "Plus, I kind of manage, I mean I do manage her, and I have to be careful about…"

"How old is she, Jerry?" Amber repeated. Her voice more forceful.

"To be honest, I never asked her." Jerry grimaced at his weak response.

"Guess."

Frowning, he continued his pacing as he ran his hand through his hair. "I'm not really good at guessing people's ages."

"Try."

"Right," Jerry replied, coming to a full stop. "Well, I'd say thirties. Mid-thirties. But like I said, I could be wrong."

"Thirty-five?"

"Uh, yeah. Maybe. I guess."

"Maybe thirty-six?"

"Well, maybe," Jerry replied, uncomfortably following her lead. "Like I said, I'm not very good at…"

"Possibly thirty-seven?"

"Well… I'd just be guessing, I don't really…" Jerry paused. He felt like he was at an auction where forty would be the definite winning bid. "But," he added, talking more slowly, "it's possible." He could all but feel Amber's smile broaden as Kimberley's age increased.

"Don't show this video to anyone else," Amber interrupted. "Not Lanier, not Peter, especially not Peter."

"Right," Jerry replied, exhaling at her being back on board. "I'm being very careful who I show it to. And now that I'm handling all of the negotiations for James's book…"

"James's book?" Amber paused. She'd forgotten about James and his book. "Has Stangerson secured the rights?"

Jerry came to a dead stop. "Not yet," he replied sensing an opening. "But, I think he's ready to make an offer. We're… negotiating."

"Set up a meeting with James," Amber demanded. "He's still in New York, right?"

138

"Well, he was," Jerry replied. "He's actually…"

"He's either in New York or he's not," Amber snapped. "Set up the meeting. Today. Tomorrow at the latest." Amber paused. Thinking it was best to change approaches, her voice softened as she continued. "This could just be our first project together. Who knows where it will lead? I need that video and I need to meet with James. You'll set that up for me, right?"

Jerry closed his eyes, his smile broadening as he listened to the lilt of Amber Lakes voice mention the possibility of their first project together. "Right. But, I have the rights," he replied, hoping she'd see that James was now superfluous. "I'm negotiating for him now. I can handle any negotia…"

"I need to meet with James," Amber interrupted, her tone more insistent.

"He's, uh, he had to fly back to L.A." Jerry flinched, worried that information would upset her. "I had to bring him back. I set up a meeting for him. Important business."

Again Amber took a beat. If she optioned the rights to James's book, everything else would be immaterial. The video in question was a scene from James's book, which she'd own. She could lock up the book rights for pennies. She'd beat Stangerson and could then decide whether to produce it or shelve the project. Stangerson would lose. The project would be hers. "Have James come back to New York. Now. Today."

Jerry winced. "But he can't just—I mean, he's…"

"I don't work with people who use the word can't, Jerry. Have James fly back. Now. I'll cover the cost. And you're just talking to me about this, not Lanier and especially not Stangerson."

Jerry came to a dead stop. His eyes widened. She will cover the costs. He was being offered an exclusive with Amber Lake.

"I'm going to hang up now," Amber said, making it clear he was being dismissed. "My assistant will call you to set up James's flight back here. I want to meet with him tomorrow, the next day at the latest." Her voice again softened. "You'll take care of that for me, right Jerry?"

"Yes. Sure. Of course." At this point, Amber could have asked him to drink arsenic and he would have cheerily agreed. "Don't worry. Not a problem. You can count on me."

"I appreciate that, Jerry." Early on in her career, a life coach had taught Amber that repeatedly using a person's first name could work to her advantage. Having a star repeat one's name was intoxicating.

"Of course, sure. Not a problem. I appreciate the opportunity to…"

"Send me the video and set up the meeting," Amber repeated. "And this is just between us, Jerry," Amber added conspiratorially. "You understand that, right?"

"Don't worry. I get it. This is just between us, you and me." Jerry sat down, almost swooning at having delivered that sentence.

"My assistant will call you." She put her finger over the phone to disconnect. Pausing, she added, "Who knows where this could lead us, Jerry. Bye bye."

The call then disconnected. Still holding the phone to his ear, Jerry sat back and stared at the blank wall in his living room. He blinked hard, as though assuring himself that he was awake. "Who knows where this could lead us," he repeated softly. "Me and Amber Lake," he added as though addressing someone else in the apartment. "That was fucking Amber Lake—talking to me! Asking me for help." Placing down his phone he stood, walked over to his laptop, and staring down at the screen he clicked on an email from Lanier ordering him to call immediately, spelling out U R G E N T in spaced capital letters. Jerry deleted the email. He didn't have time for that lunatic.

His phone rang. Unknown number. He was going to let it go to voicemail, but this was an auspicious day. Who knew who it could be. He answered and an officious sounding male voice introduced himself as Sam. He explained that he was calling on behalf of Amber Lake and would be making the flight and hotel arrangements for James. He needed James's information and schedule so he could make the arrangements. He emphasized that Amber had stressed that it was urgent that she meet with James as soon as possible. He then asked Jerry for James's direct contact, so he could review dates and times with him. Jerry took a beat; that would never work. James didn't have a clue what was going on. Without being prepared, a call from Sam would backfire. Jerry said he would immediately contact James. He'd then call Sam back. Writing down his number, he hurriedly hung up the phone.

Jerry walked to the kitchen, opened the refrigerator, and took out a Perrier. He took a sip from the bottle and leaning against the sink, placed it on the counter and walked back into the living room. Picking his phone off the couch, he headed to his desk, sat down, opened his laptop, and began to again watch Kimberley's audition scene.

He needed to think this through. James would be in no mood to fly back to New York. James would simply refuse. And he'd do it gleefully. He was like that. Jerry consoled himself thinking that regardless of what James did or didn't do on the Amber front, Stangerson was still interested. That was a bird in the hand. But, played right, they could have Stangerson and Amber interested. Jerry could deal with Stangerson and Kimberley in L.A. and James could fly to New York and lock down a deal with Amber. That didn't seem quite fair, Jerry dealing with Stangerson and James going to New York to meet with Amber. But that's what it was. They could then play Amber and Stangerson against each other. Or, better yet, come away with two different projects. But for that to work, he needed James on board. James needed to be part of the team.

It was Jerry's job to save James from himself by positioning this trip in urgent terms that he'd understand. Best keep Kimberley and the video out of the conversation. It had to be presented as all being about James's book. That was the key. Two Hollywood A-listers were vying for James's novel. He would have to come back on board. He'd have no choice.

Jerry glanced at his phone—another text from Lanier. She was the wildcard, a loose cannon. James painted her as being unhinged. Still, she had been the catalyst for all of it. She had made the introductions and had brought James into that world. Without Lanier there would be nothing. At the very least she was owed a call. It would prep Jerry for the call he had to make to James. Besides, Lanier had been defanged. Now that Jerry was dealing directly with Amber and Stangerson, he held all the cards. Sitting up straight he shook his body and, like a swimmer about to dive into an ice-cold pool, he took a deep breath and called.

"Lanier, this is Jerry," he announced when she answered the call. "I'm James's partner and…"

"I don't care who you are. What the fuck is going on?" Lanier demanded in a near yell. "What the fuck is James doing?"

Jerry took another breath. He decided he would use a martial arts approach, falling back with the verbal blows instead of resisting, "James told me a lot of great things about you. Nothing's changed. It's just that I'm the one who's handling the business end now and…"

"You have nothing to do with this," Lanier interrupted. "You the one who brought in the Beverly Hills shrink stripper?"

"Kimberley?" Jerry asked grimacing at that description, while at the same time finding it arousing. "I wouldn't describe her exactly that way, but yes. She's really quite…"

"I sold Peter on the Scarlett Johanssonesque shrink-gone-stripper idea. Me!" Lanier's voice was sharp. Cold.

"Actually, she was a stripper before she was a therapist," Jerry corrected. If that was the story people were going with, they should at least have the right timeline.

"Peter was walking away from the project, and I saved it." Lanier continued. "Then I told Amber that Peter's interested and now she wants it. I get two Hollywood heavyweights on the line, primed, ready to go—and then James fucking disappears. And now you crawl out of the woodwork. This is bullshit. This is my fucking project. Give me Kimberley's phone number. I'll take it from here."

"Nothing's changed," Jerry repeated, trying to sound as calm and assured as possible. "I'm just taking over for James while he writes. It's all good."

"All good because you're not involved," Lanier snapped. "You're out. I didn't bring this project this far just to have an amateur nobody ruin it. James stupidly emailed your information to Amber and Peter. They'll probably contact you now. Email them back explaining that I'm handling everything—and cc me. Introduce me to Kimberley. I need her to fly out to New York no later than tomorrow."

"She has a practice. I can't ask her to…"

"Give me her phone number," Lanier steamrolled. "Send me that video—and then disappear."

"I have to reshoot it—the video. Something went wrong. A glitch."

"A glitch?" Lanier repeated. "Real pro." Jerry heard a snort followed by, "James should never have given them your information. Those are my contacts. That's illegal. Actionable."

"Like I said," Jerry insisted with a grimace, "nothing's changed. I'm handling the business for James. He's a writer, not a business guy. You know James."

"Apparently I don't." After a pensive pause, Lanier forced a smile and tried to shift to a more pleasant tone. "When this goes down I'll makes sure you're taken care of. That's all you care about, right?" Taking a beat, her smile faded. "I'll take care of you, okay. A finder's fee. Just get out of the fucking way. I need to talk to that shrink. Now."

Jerry winced, insulted by the term finder's fee. "Yeah. Sure. Right, of course." Jerry nodded, agreeing to anything in order to get her off the phone. "Let me get the video shot and I'll get back to you."

"You do not want to fuck with me Jerry. Trust me."

"Right. Nice talking to you." Jerry disconnected the call before Lanier could respond. He all but dropped the phone on the desk as though it were radioactive. Walking back into the kitchen, he picked up the Perrier bottle and took a long swallow. He was unsure whether his overriding feeling was excitement or fear. He decided on excitement. He'd ignore Lanier and she'd go away. All was good. He was where he'd always wanted to be. At least on the threshold. Now it was up to him to make it all real. His film career, Kimberley, working with Amber Lake and Peter Stangerson—it was all in his grasp. Lanier had no place in the picture. She had simply made introductions. Nothing more. Maybe James owed her something, but not Jerry. Lanier was unnecessary, superfluous—and annoying. But she could also be trouble, a loose cannon.

Jerry took another drink, walked back to his computer, and again watched Kimberley's video. He watched it objectively. With a director's eye. She was good, mesmerizing. The camera could not get enough of her. He leaned back in his chair and smiled. Everything was set, in place. He just needed James on board; needed him to fly to New York and meet with Amber. He picked up his phone and dialed. "I need you to meet me at the Circle K," Jerry demanded when James picked up. "Now. Right now. It's important. Really important."

"I'm writing."

"It's important," Jerry insisted. "Right now. This can't wait. This is huge. You're going to love this. I'm on my way. Leave now." Jerry disconnected the call, put his phone in his pocket and headed out the door towards the Circle K Lounge.

144

Chapter 20

J erry sat at their regular table impatiently waiting as he practiced his speech. Best not let James talk or interrupt, at least not at first. Best soldier through until James fully comprehended the importance of what Jerry was saying and agreed to next steps. This would be a good test of Jerry's persuasive abilities. Looking up, he smiled as James entered and walked towards the table.

"What's so important that you couldn't tell me over the phone? I was writing," James scowled as he sat down.

"You will understand when I lay this out for you." Jerry explained "This is amazing. The best. Your dream come true."

"Yeah. Right."

"First we order. On me," he added.

"I was writing," James repeated.

Jerry scowled at James's unappreciative response. He then smiled at the waitress as she walked up to their table. She was new, attractive, on the cusp between cute and beautiful. Medium height with long auburn hair and blue-green eyes. "I don't think we've been formerly introduced. I'm Jerry, and this," he added turning towards James, "is James. James is Hollywood's next Wunderkind."

The waitress smiled. "Hi, Jerry and Wunderkind. I'm Violet, what can I get you?"

"Violet," Jerry repeated, extending his hand, "an awesome name. A name made for a film marquee."

James grimaced as he looked down and shook his head.

Violet laughed. The two ordered their regular, a hamburger well done, a cheeseburger, a coke, a diet coke, and one order of fries. Violet nodded as she wrote. "Got it. Be back in a sec."

Jerry held up his hand. "Wait. If I were to tell you that my friend here wrote a novel that Amber Lake is interested in producing and starring in with Nicole Kidman costarring, to be directed by Peter Stangerson, what would you say?"

She looked at James searchingly. "If it's real, I'd say that is awesome."

"Oh it's real." Taking out his phone, Jerry called up his photos. "Exhibit A," he pronounced, holding the phone up towards her. "Look. My best friend—and partner—is also best friends with Peter Stangerson and Dunhill Jr., which extrapolates to my being Peter Stangerson's best friend, which lead us to your big career break."

Violet carefully studied each photo. "This is Peter Stangerson." She looked from the phone to James. "And he has his arm around you."

James gave a weary shake of his head. "It's not what it seems."

"It is much more than it seems," Jerry corrected. "James is good friends with Stangerson and Dunhill Jr. What you don't see is Amber Lake who wants to make a film based on his novel. Who wouldn't jump at that opportunity, right?"

Violet continued to stare at James. "It's real? Nothing in this town is real," she added, looking back at the photos.

"And neither is this." James shook his head and looked away.

"It is certifiably real. Believe me," Jerry announced. "In the past few hours, James's world has shifted. Transformed. And you know it now, even before he does."

James looked at Jerry with a puzzled expression. "Yeah?" he asked, as if issuing a challenge. "What's changed?"

"What would you say if I told you I just got off two calls, the first Peter Stangerson and then Amber Lake?" Jerry asked, ignoring James and addressing himself to Violet. "And what if I told you, Amber Lake not only loves James's book, she wants to fly him to New York to meet with her ASAP. All expenses paid—the flight, hotel, everything—because she's that interested and wants to cement a deal. What would you say to that?"

"You really just spoke with Amber Lake?" Violet asked.

"Half an hour ago." Jerry grinned, impressing himself by the declaration. "Sounds like a story someone would make up, right? But—it's true. I did. And she wants to fly you out," he added turning towards James. "It's all about your novel," he added. "She wants to make your novel into a fucking Amber Lake movie."

"That is so cool," Violet's eyes widened as she stared at James. "Congratulations." Taking a beat, she glanced back towards the kitchen. "I better get back."

"No, don't go," Jerry held up his hand as though he was directing traffic. "I might need reinforcements. Help talk sense into my friend. Help me talk him into going to New York."

James gave a definitive shake of his head. "I don't have a clue what you're talking about. I'm not going to New York." His voice was stern. "I just got back from New York. It was a waste. I'm not going."

"Yes you are," Jerry insisted "Aren't you listening? Amber Lake wants to pay for you to go to New York to make a deal on your novel. It's happening, man. It's fucking real."

Violet nervously looked back towards the kitchen, "I better get back to work."

Jerry quickly grabbed her by the wrist. "Just a couple of secs." He then turned towards James. "Amber Lake is going to pay to fly you to New York and to put you up in some A-list hotel while you're there." He paused and then continued, saying the words slowly. "And you're going to sign a film deal based on your novel. This is what you wanted." Still holding her wrist, he looked up at Violet. "Tell him he has to go."

Violet gave a tug. "First let go of my wrist."

Jerry quickly released his grasp. "Sorry."

"Thank you." She turned towards James. "If it's real, you're friend's right. You have to go. You can't pass that up."

"Bingo!" Jerry exclaimed slamming his hand on the tabletop. "The right decision from a beautiful impartial observer. You cannot pass that up. Look, Amber's assistant is impatiently waiting for me to get back to him with your information so that he can book the flight and set up where you're staying." Jerry quickly glanced up at Violet. "Just stay through the call. You're my good luck charm—our good luck charm. We'll double our order, so you don't get in trouble. Plus, this is going to launch your career." He pulled his phone out of his pocket and dialed.

James grimaced. "This doesn't make any sense. All Stangerson was interested in was Kimberley. Why is Amber Lake suddenly interested in my…"

"She is, okay? It's all about the novel." Jerry snapped, waiting for his call to be answered. "Tell him not to fuck this up," he added, looking up at Violet. "Hey, hi," Jerry continued, talking into the phone. "It's Jerry. I have James here. He can give you his information for the flight and the hotel. Right. I'm passing the phone over to him now."

James took the phone and glanced up at Violet, a scowl on his face.

She smiled broadly and nodded. "Do it," she mouthed.

Putting the phone to his ear, James glowered at Jerry as he robotically gave out the necessary information. He nodded; eyes furrowed as he agreed to fly out the following day. He explained he didn't have a favorite New York hotel and would leave that up to them. He then said goodbye, disconnected the call, and handed the phone back to Jerry.

"Yes! Bingo!" Jerry exclaimed, standing up and hugging Violet. "You are my lucky charm."

Violet winced, squirming away from Jerry's grasp. "I really gotta go or I'm going to be in trouble. Congratulations," she added, looking back at James. "An Amber Lake film. You can't do much better than that."

"And you were there," Jerry declared, smiling at Violet. "You are now a part of Hollywood lore. And, like I said , this is going to be big for you too."

Violet laughed. "Right. I'll be back." She then turned and hurriedly walked back towards the kitchen.

"I'm not going," James gave an adamant shake of his head. "I just agreed to get whoever that was off the phone and to shut you up."

"Of course you're going. She's hot," Jerry added, watching Violet as she walked away. "You have to go," he continued, turning towards James. "I just landed you a film deal with Amber Lake. She's flying you to New York, putting you up—all expenses paid. Amber Lake is making your novel into a film. And, you're welcome."

James looked up towards the window. "I have the copywriting job at the agency. I miss that date again and it's gone. I need that job. I'm broke. I need the money."

Jerry shook his head and laughed. "Your priorities are so fucked up. Snap out of it. Forget the copywriting job. You're coming back with a film deal. You're golden."

Violet returned and placing their drinks on the table, looked at James. "The whole place is impressed. The owner says if you can bring Amber Lake in for a drink, he'll comp you for life."

"Of course he will," Jerry agreed with a grin. "You can't buy that type of PR."

149

"Congrats," Violet smiled at James and walked away.

"Your first groupie," Jerry stared longingly. "I want my manager's percentage."

"You're not a manager."

Jerry grinned. Picking up his beer he took a drink. "You just need to get cards made and—poof, you're a manager. I'm managing Kimberley," he added. "Sorta."

"Right. Has anyone informed her of that?"

"I am," Jerry insisted. "Can you believe we're having this conversation?" he asked as he leaned in towards James. "We're talking about you flying to New York to meet with Amber Lake and me meeting with Peter Stangerson about Kimberley. It's unreal"

"Because it's not—real."

Jerry folded his arms, sat back and frowned "Don't be negative." He paused and took a drink. "The only thing I'm worried about is at my meeting with Stangerson and Kimberley, he wants me to leave early so he can speak to Kimberley alone. Doesn't seem right, does it? Him asking me to leave? I set it up. I'm the reason the meeting is happening. I'm her manager. I should be there through the whole meeting. He could just run with it. Cut me out completely. Then I'm fucked."

"Don't be so negative," James replied sarcastically.

Jerry shrugged. "I've bottled lightning. You saw the video. She's gorgeous. She can act. She's good." Picking up his diet coke, he took a drink. "After the Stangerson call, Amber called. Amber Lake called. Me! Is that a fucking amazing sentence? And then Lanier called." He winced as he said Lanier's name. "She's a freak. I hung up on her. But Amber—I spoke with Amber fucking Lake, who's not only cool and one of the biggest stars in Hollywood, but drop dead gorgeous. I mean we're talking as high up the food chain as Scarlet Johansson or Margot Robbie. And she wants your novel. This is real."

"I am not flying to New York. I'll get there and it will all be about

150

Kimberley's video…"

"No, no, no," Jerry jumped in before James could finish his sentence. "This meeting is about your book, not the video. That's what Amber's interested in—the book, your novel." He smiled and pulling his phone out stared down at it. "I'm saving Amber's voicemails." His grin widened as he held up his phone. "How cool is that, having voicemails from Amber Lake? They're probably worth money." He took a beat and frowned. "Lanier sounds kinda spooky. Her texts and calls get more and more threatening. What the fuck is wrong with her? Her deal was with you, not me. Even Peter said she wasn't involved."

James shrugged. "None of this would have happened if it hadn't been for her. Stangerson, Amber, Dunhill Jr.—they're all her contacts. Without her—nothing."

Jerry took a drink. He then looked around the bar pensively. "Forget Lanier. Concentrate on Amber. She's huge. A star. We don't even need Stangerson now. But," he paused and leaned in, "if we play it right we could come away with two projects; one with Amber, one with Stangerson. We'll be on the map. We'll be players."

"You love this shit, don't you? Hollywood cloak-and-dagger," James gave a weary shake of his head. "God, it's such bullshit."

"This is real," Jerry replied with conviction. "Amber Lake will star; Nicole Kidman will costar and Kimberley will be introduced to the public in a featured role. Or," he leaned conspiratorially closer, "we end up with two separate projects. Stangerson does the Kimberley project with Emma Stone and Bradley Cooper and Amber Lake produces and stars in the adaptation of your novel with Nicole Kidman and Chris Hemsworth and…"

"You're losing it," James interrupted. "Emma Stone, Bradley Cooper, Chris Hemsworth? They have nothing to do with any of this."

"Come on. You know who Amber was dating," Jerry shot back, delighting in using first names, "They were an item. You know that."

"Why would I know that? Why would I pay any attention to who Amber Lake is dating?"

"Well you better start," Jerry instructed. "Once we begin producing, we have to know who has been hooking up with whom before we start casting. If you don't know that, you're asking for trouble. Just saying."

James took a drink and glancing across the room towards Violet, caught her eye and smiled. He then turned towards Jerry. "Why is Amber suddenly interested? What's really going on?"

Jerry grinned. "It's the business. It's how Hollywood works. Amber knows Stangerson is hot for the video but, since the video is based on a scene from the book, she realizes the book is the thing. If she lands the rights to the book, she not only lands her next film project—which she both produces and stars in—she beats Stangerson to the punch. She wins. But," he added quickly switching gears, "it's more than one-upmanship now. She's read the book and loves it. Now it's all about the book."

"Amber read the book?"

"And loves it." Jerry smiled. A lie, but only a temporary one. Eventually she would read the book—and love it.

James looked at Jerry suspiciously. "If she read the fucking novel, she'd know that the Kimberley scene has nothing to do with it. There is no blonde psychotherapist in my book."

"Look, it's a game, man. That's how it's played." Jerry picked up his coke. "Adapted books are always changed, new scenes added. That's how it works. So we play it—and we win. We're inches from the finish line." He grinned and held up his drink. "To your book becoming a huge Amber Lake film."

James shook his head dismissively. "So," he asked, changing the topic, "did you get a signed agreement with Kimberley?"

"Kinda. Sorta. Verbal mostly."

"Verbal?" James replied with a shake of his head. "If Stangerson's hot for her and he thinks you're with Kimberley, he'll want you out of the picture. Without an agreement if he wants you out, you're out."

Jerry smiled, flattered that Stangerson could think he was sleeping with Kimberley. He then looked away and shook his head. "No problem there. He thinks I'm gay."

James laughed, almost spilling his drink as he took a sip. "Why does he think you're gay?"

Jerry shrugged. James's laugh signaled a thawing, an opening. "Not sure to be honest," Jerry replied. "Somehow he ended up thinking that. Probably for the best. But we're missing the big picture here." He again leaned in towards James. "I've got Stangerson interested in Kimberley, and you're meeting with Amber Lake. This is it. Our time. We have to focus, strategize. If you told me we'd be having this conversation a week ago, I'd say you were crazy."

He picked up his drink and finished it. "So, we're good, right? We're set. You're getting another all-expenses paid trip to New York, this time courtesy of Amber Lake." He stood, paused, and stared down at James. "You leave tomorrow night. The 2020 train is leaving the station and we're in the driver's seat. This is our year, man. This is it!"

James shook his head. "I can't go. I need that copywriting job. I'm fucking broke. If Amber Lake wants to talk have her set up a phone call or a Zoom meeting."

"Zoom?" Jerry asked. "Nobody does Zoom. Hollywood's all about meetings. Real meetings. This has to be in person. We're talking about Amber Lake. Amber fucking Lake!" Jerry repeated, accentuating each syllable. "You're flying out to sign a film deal with Amber Lake. And I set it up. We're golden, man." Jerry stared down at James. "Smile. You're launching your career—not going to a funeral."

He paused, pulling his phone out of his pocket. "I'm texting you Amber's assistant's phone number. He'll take care of everything." Quickly sending the text, he looked back at James. "This is a dream—a dream come true." Jerry looked towards the bar and raising his hand waved Violet over.

"The check?" she asked, as she walked up to their table.

"I couldn't have done this without you," Jerry smiled. "I personally will see to it that you get, at the very least, an under five in the film."

Violet laughed. She turned towards James. "You really going to New York?"

James shrugged.

Violet's eyes widened. "That is so cool. You're going to New York to meet with Amber Lake. That's amazing." She turned towards Jerry. "So you're buying right? A bon voyage gift to your friend."

"You're dangerous. He'll pay but with my credit card. Long story," Jerry explained. "Give her a large tip," he added, turning to James.

Violet laughed. "Be right back with the check."

"An even better ass than the other one," Jerry pronounced studying Violet as she walked away. "Again, you owe me. Not only have I landed you an Amber Lake film, you now have your first groupie. Call me before you go," Jerry added turning back towards James. "We have to strategize. Get things in place." He took a pensive beat and reluctantly added, "Keep my card for expenses. So, we're good, right?"

"I'm going to lose this fucking job."

"And walk away with a seven-figure film career. You're going to thank me forever after this. Build a shrine in my honor. I gotta go. Call me. Keep me in the loop. Twenty-four seven, I'm there for you man." With that, Jerry smiled, turned, and headed out.

Violet returned and placed the bill on the table. "Your friend's— different."

"That's one way to describe him," Jerry said with a smile. "He's hoping to entice you with a role in our new big budget film—which doesn't exist."

Violet grinned. "Flattering. The only downside is I don't act. But it does exist, right? Everything he was saying is real. You really do know Peter Stangerson, and Dunhill Jr. You're really flying to New York to meet with Amber Lake. It's all real, isn't it?"

James shrugged. "I've met them. I've met them, but I don't know them," he corrected. "There's a difference. I guess I'm flying back. But I don't know why. It won't amount to anything."

Violet's eyebrows raised. "Come on! Amber Lake. That's Impressive."

James shook his head. "Not really. Jerry thinks proximity equals success. So you didn't come to L.A. to make it big as an actress."

"What makes you think I'm not from here."

"Nobody's from L.A. and nobody walks in L.A."

"You're funny." Violet glanced back towards the kitchen. "I better go. Good luck in New York," she added. "Bring back an autographed Amber Lake photo for me."

"That's probably all I'll come back with."

Chapter 21

Jerry inhaled deeply, picked up his phone and dialed Kimberley's number.

"I'm going into a session, Jerry," Kimberley answered.

"I just spoke with Peter," he said, a tingle of excitement running through him at using Stangerson's first name. "He wants to see the video and he wants to set up a meeting. Like right away. Amber called," he added. "Amber Lake. She wants to see the video." Kimberley remained silent. Jerry could sense she was growing weary, unsure. The story was fantastical, but it was real. Taking a breath, he soldiered on. "What I mean is they're both interested, but they're not working on this together." He spoke quickly, trying to get the whole explanation out before he lost her.

Walking to her laptop, Kimberley sat down, called up the video and hit play. She pensively bit her bottom lip as she watched. It worked. She had the look. The only difference between her and Amber Lake was access. Jerry's story was almost too messy to be fabricated. If it was a lie, he would have made it more alluring, less complicated. Being a practiced liar, he would know that if it sounded too convoluted it wouldn't work. Besides, stranger things had happened. And, she'd seen the photos of James with Peter Stangerson and Dunhill Jr., smiling, arm in arm.

"You there?" Jerry asked.

She'd gone this far, she thought, as she continued to watch. They'd already shot the video. It would be silly to back out now. "I could give a better performance," she said. "Maybe we should reshoot before you send it."

Jerry smiled. She was on board. All was right in the world. "What we have is fine. It's great." His words surprised him. At any other time, he'd leap at the chance to reshoot the video, to again be alone with Kimberley. But Stangerson and Amber were waiting. "I sent it to Peter first, He's our best bet. He's definitely interested. "One thing," Jerry added, "Lanier, the one who introduced James to Peter and Amber, found out about you and the video. She's a bit... off, unbalanced, unhinged. She thinks this is her project, her deal. I don't want her involved, but she could try to contact you directly. If she does..."

"My job is to deal with the Laniers of the world," Kimberley replied. "She won't cause us problems."

Jerry smiled. They were now an "us."

"Call me when you hear from Stangerson." With that the call ended.

Jerry took a deep breath, pasted the video link to an email, addressed it to Peter Stangerson and hit send. Within ten minutes, Stangerson replied "I'll be in L.A. tonight. Make the reservations for 1 pm tomorrow. The Four Seasons." Jerry stared at the screen, reading, and rereading the text. It was real. "Done," Jerry replied and hit send.

He quickly called Kimberley. "I sent it to Peter," Jerry said, his voice racing. "He wants to meet. Tomorrow at one at the Four Seasons. That's the only time he can meet," he added, to emphasize it was nonnegotiable. "We should meet there a bit early to prepare."

157

After a long pause, Kimberley said, "I'll meet you there at 12:30." She then disconnected the call.

"Yes!" Jerry cried. He then called the Four Seasons Beverly Hills and made reservations for three at 1 pm. He and Kimberley would get there early. They'd need to get the lay of the land, to plot, brainstorm. Walking to his computer, he watched and re-watched Kimberley's video. "This is going to work," he said. "It's happening."

Kimberley again played the video. She'd be meeting Peter Stangerson tomorrow, she thought as she watched. It might lead nowhere, but she was going to meet with a legend, one of Hollywood's most renowned directors. She wanted to call someone; excitedly tell them that she was meeting with Peter Stangerson. But who could she tell? Who could she confide in? Carla, her best friend, was also a therapist. If Kimberley honestly explained the situation, Carla would remind Kimberely that Jerry was a client and therefore out of bounds. She'd remind her of advice they'd both given to delusional clients who they both knew were going off the rails. Carla would not share her excitement, but offer a lecture.

She couldn't tell her therapist, particularly not about Jerry. Years ago she had confessed to having an affair with one of her clients and she remembered how that played out. She'd escaped being reported, being reprimanded, possibly losing her license—but barely. Besides, if nothing came of it, if it was a trail to nowhere, she'd feel the fool. No, until Kimberley found out if it was all real, she was on her own.

Chapter 22

Jerry arrived at the Four Seasons at noon. He wanted to give himself time to get a sense of the place and to go over the game plan with Kimberley before Stangerson arrived. To be on the safe side, he begrudgingly valet parked. Entering the hotel, he took a quick look inside the restaurant. Walking back to the lobby, he found a seat that faced the front door, and sitting down took to checking his phone approximately every thirty seconds. He hadn't heard from Stangerson since their call. All was probably fine, but Jerry was worried. Stangerson could have already lost interest. What if he didn't show? That wouldn't be unusual. Not in that world. Stangerson could have forgotten about it. Something more important could have surfaced. After all, he was Peter Stangerson. What would Kimberley think of Jerry if Stangerson was a no-show? His heart sank as he waited. At 12:30 sharp, wearing a short, tight, one-piece, red dress Kimberley entered. She saw Jerry and headed his way. Heads turned, following her as she walked. Jerry stood, trying not to gawk. "You look… amazing," he stuttered, unsure whether it was more appropriate to

159

shake her hand or hug her.

"Thanks," she replied, resolving his dilemma by doing neither and sitting down. "Do we have a particular agenda here? Anything I need to know that I don't know now? He knows I haven't acted in years, right? Knows that's not what I do."

"Yeah, definitely. He knows you work as a therapist."

Kimberley nodded, sat back and crossed her legs, "And if James comes up in the conversation—I don't know a thing about him or his book."

"That's okay," Jerry replied, trying not to stare at her legs. "Stangerson knows I just brought you into the project. Plus, I'm not sure the book is still the project. It's all moving so fast. And, well, there is one thing, it's nothing really, probably won't even come up but, just in case…" Jerry paused and uncomfortably looked away.

"What?" Kimberley asked.

"Well, in case it come up." Jerry fidgeted in his chair as he sat, "Stangerson might think I'm gay."

Kimberley stared at Jerry. "Why would he think that?"

"I'm not sure," Jerry continued, trying to recall the conversation he'd had with Stangerson. "I really don't know, but he might."

Kimberley gave a clipped laugh. "And are you looking to set him straight? So to speak."

"Not sure. I was thinking, it could work in my favor. I think he believes my pitch more, feels it's more on the up-and-up if I'm pushing you so hard and I'm not straight. It feels more like…" Jerry let the sentence fall.

"Like there's no ulterior motive."

Jerry responded with an embarrassed smile. "And…" Jerry paused and frowned, "one more possible small, insignificant mix-up— Stangerson might think that you might have… in the past, that you could possibly have been a…" Jerry winced. Pausing her stared down at the floor, unable to finish the sentence.

160

"Been a what?" Kimberley asked impatiently.

"He might think that once, a long time ago, you might have, maybe you had possibly... worked as a stripper." Jerry tossed the word like a live grenade. His head slightly dipped as though dodging the oncoming eruption.

Kimberley frowned and stared at him. After a prolonged pause she burst out laughing. "A stripper?"

"Not my idea," Jerry quickly continued, relieved by her laugh. "James was just trying to make the story sound more compelling. He figured it might pique Stangerson's interest a bit more if he thought that, well... that you had..."

"How did he find out?" Kimberley asked, leaning towards Jerry conspiratorially.

Jerry stared back, eyes wide, mouth ajar.

Kimberley sat back and smiled. "That was a joke."

Jerry nervously laughed. "Stangerson might have already forgotten that James mentioned it. Probably in one ear and out..."

"I seriously doubt that. I'll have to let him know James was mistaken." She paused and staring at Jerry added, "Or, like you being gay, is this another piece of misinformation you think could help?"

Jerry gave a nervous shrug. "Well... what if he thinks that could help sell the film? Maybe we should wait... just a bit, you know until..." He glanced up towards the front door, saw Peter Stangerson entering. Jerry had seen his image countless times, in magazines, newspapers, film clips. Decades ago, he had been the wunderkind who took the indie film world by storm.

For a while there he could do no wrong, there was no project he couldn't steer to success. He launched careers. No A-list stars refused him. He came up as part of the club, the short list—Stangerson, Coppola, Scorsese, Spielberg, DePalma. And he came out of the gate the fastest. But after the home runs came myriad lackluster outings, and one total bomb. That descent was followed by online buzzes of sexual impropriety. *Exposed* then hit which resurrected his career, but that had been a while ago. He was still a player, still in the game, there was no one in the industry who didn't know him, his films, or his history, but the projects came less frequently, the funding less easily.

In his late sixties, he looked shorter, heavier, and balder in person. His large sunglasses, which sat on top of his head, gave the look of a caricaturish sixties Italian director. A bit of an anachronism. He stopped as he entered and scanned the room. His eyes locking on Kimberley, he moved towards her with a measured, confident stride.

"Here we go," Jerry whispered, standing as Stangerson closed in.

Stopping in front of Kimberley, Stangerson beamed a fully lit smile and held out his hand. "Kimberley."

Kimberley reached up, took his hand and, smiling, stood to greet him.

Continuing to hold her hand, Stangerson's eyes shifted to Jerry. "You did her a huge disservice."

Jerry stared, a confused expression on his face.

"Gorgeous is much too timid, too pedestrian a word."

Jerry replied with a relieved smile.

"Thank you," Kimberley said as she all but imperceptibly pulled back her hand.

Stangerson turned slightly, offering his hand to Jerry. "Peter Stangerson," he announced. Turning to Kimberley, with a slight bow, he waved her towards the restaurant entrance. Kimberley and Stangerson walked together. Jerry uncomfortably trailed a couple of feet behind. As the trio entered, the maître d' looked up and seeing Stangerson, stood at attention and smile broadly. "Mr. Stangerson," he announced. "I had no idea you'd be joining us. It's such a pleasure to see you again."

"Christian," Stangerson boomed, once again extending his hand. "It's been too long. What's it been? Two weeks?"

Christian laughed warmly.

162

Jerry cleared his throat and announced, "The reservation is under the name Jerry…"

"This way," Christian gave a slight bow, cutting Jerry off and leading them towards a table. "This is Mr. Stangerson's table," he explained, pulling back the chair for Kimberley.

"She's a vision, isn't she?" Stangerson asked, glancing at Christian with a smile. Kimberley sat and the others followed. "You're seeing Hollywood history in the making," he continued. "You will have been present at Peter Stangerson's first meeting with Kimberley…" he paused and looked expectantly at her.

"Goodman."

"Right. My first meeting with Kimberley Goodman," he continued, looking up at Christian with a grin. "We might have to change the name," he whispered, looking back at Kimberley. "Something with more of a ring."

"I am honored," Christian smiled, as he passed out the menus. Looking up, he motioned to a waitress. "She is indeed lovely," he continued, turning his gaze back to Kimberley. "I look forward to seeing your projects. And this," he said, nodding towards the smiling woman now standing at his side, "is Serena. You have the honor of serving Mr. Peter Stangerson and his guests, including Kimberley Goodman. Serena will take care of you," he continued, looking back at Stangerson. "Please let me know if there's anything you need. Again, it is always a pleasure and an honor." Stangerson smiled and nodded. Christian gave a slight bow and walked back to his station.

Without consulting anyone, Stangerson ordered for the table. The wine arrived, was poured, and Stangerson raised his glass and stared at Kimberley. "To an auspicious meeting," he pronounced. "A life-changing meeting."

"To change," Kimberley replied, clinking her raised glass with Stangerson's and then Jerry's.

"Not just change," Peter corrected. "Change is inevitable. To life-altering change." Again, the three clinked glasses and drank. There

163

were a few minutes of small talk, Stangerson asking Kimberley about her life, her practice. Sharing a bit about a film he'd recently wrapped. He then paused and turned towards Jerry. "Your name never came up at the meeting with Amber, Lanier, and… what's his name?"

"James," Jerry replied. Although happy to finally be included in the conversation, he felt suddenly put on the spot. "He wrote the novel. We're production partners."

"Right. James. Yes, I think Lanier mentioned a novel," Stangerson agreed. "What have you worked on?"

"A few projects," Jerry fumbled, "most in preproduction. This one. The adaptation of James's novel will be the most high-profile project."

Stangerson took a drink and nodded. "So, do you have funding? Is it cast?"

Jerry responded with a confused frown. "We… um… James was handling the business side. I just took it over. I, uh, was under the impression that the book adaptation of his novel was what you had met James about."

"Really?" Stangerson asked, sitting back as the waitress brought their orders. His question sounded more like an accusation. "What grabbed my interest was Kimberley—I don't know a thing about the novel." After a beat he said, "And don't really care. Amber could be—interested. But I doubt it. Lanier probably told your friend we were meeting about his book. That's Lanier. She can be useful. Just don't believe a word she says," he added with a clipped laugh.

Jerry forced a smile and nodded. James and his book had again been sidelined. The game had changed and Jerry's connection to whatever reason they were there for was growing ever more tenuous.

"But let's not talk shop now. Let's eat," Stangerson continued, turning to Kimberley, "I want to learn about you." He asked Kimberley a few preliminary questions about her practice and her work as an actress, responding with knowing nods as she replied. He then paused, picked up his fork, and pointing it towards Kimberley, grinned. He leaned in towards her as he began with his well-worn Hollywood stories. Stangerson had told, retold, and embellished them so often he no longer knew what was true. Kimberley smiled, nodding at the appropriate times. Jerry ate in silence. Finishing his meal, Stangerson sat back, folded his arms, and continued with his long-ago Hollywood stories as the table was cleared and coffee delivered. Picking up his cup, he took a sip and turned towards Kimberley. "A Beverly Hills sex therapist to the stars must have some… interesting stories to tell."

Kimberley held Stangerson's gaze. "I would think so. But, I'm Brentwood-based, not Beverly Hills, not a sex therapist, and don't really work with stars—still," she added with a smile, "I know what you mean."

Jerry winced. Kimberley contradicting Stangerson was not part of the game plan.

"I like her." Stangerson turned towards Jerry. "She's funny. A comedian. You know what I mean," he continued turning towards Kimberley. It's not only an actress that I'm looking for here. I want you, your stories. True-life, in the trenches, stories from a beautiful, sexy, Beverly Hills sex therapist to the stars." Stangerson paused, as though waiting for Kimberley to correct him. She remained silent and he continued. "You will play," he paused and raising his cup, motioned towards her, "you. I don't see this just as a feature film," he added with a shake of his head. "I'm envisioning spinoffs, a series, who knows—it could be its own cottage industry. Maybe Barbie-like dolls for the girls." As he took a beat, his grin widened, "And life-sized ones for the boys."

Kimberley's eyebrows furrowed as she stared at him.

"A joke," he laughed.

"I can't share real client stories."

"I know," Stangerson dismissively waved his hand, "but the public doesn't know what's real and what's not. You make it up. You pull from some experiences you've had, embellish them, turn them on their head and no one knows. That way your patients can't call foul and the public thinks they're being let into your inner sanctum."

"Clients," Kimberley corrected.

"Whatever," Stangerson replied with a wave of his hand. "Just picture it," his eyes widened as he held up his right hand as though writing on air —"True Life Confessions of a Beverly Hills Sex Therapist to the Stars! A bit long for a marquee, but I'll work on that."

Kimberley glanced at Jerry. "This isn't about James's book?"

Stangerson shrugged. "This is about you, not a book." Placing his coffee cup down, he picked up his wine glass, raised it and turned back towards Kimberley. "You have…" he paused and leaned towards her, "something. I saw it in the video. I see it here, now. What I am interested in is you, not a book. You can't carry a film yet, you're still a nobody. I'll bring in some star names to do the initial heavy lifting. Nicole, Margo," he took a beat and reluctantly added, "Maybe Amber. With all of the different streaming companies falling over themselves for content, this won't be a tough sell. But," he added emphatically, "I want to launch it as a feature film, on the big screen, not on phones. Who in their right mind watches a film on a phone?" he asked glancing towards Jerry, who uncomfortably nodded in agreement. "We'll say 'based on a true story' as our tag," Stangerson continued, his voice rising. "Confessions of a Beverly Hills Sex Therapist to the Stars," he announced, holding his hands apart as though showcasing a film marquee. "That will be the subtitle, not the title, and then an over-the-top seductive shot of you and—'based on a true story.' "

"I'm not a sex therapist and…"

"You worry too much," Stangerson said, cutting Kimberley off. Turning towards Jerry, he asked, "Based on a true story—do you know what that means?"

Jerry hesitated, not quite sure what the correct response would be.

"Of course you don't," Stangerson replied, his voice booming. "No one does. What's the formula? Four percent has to be true in order to use that phrase? That could mean anything," he added with a laugh. "That's why everyone uses it. Jackson could have come out with Lord of the Rings,—based on a true story. Why not?" Stangerson laughed, took a sip of coffee and sat back. "So," he continued again looking at Kimberley, "that's why I asked for this meeting—you! That's what this is about." He paused, put down his coffee cup, picked up his wine glass and, taking a sip, leaned in towards her. "Interested?"

Kimberley sat back and took a drink. Her eyes locked on Stangerson. "I'm flattered."

Stangerson grinned. "You damn well should be."

"I'm not a sex therapist," she repeated.

"Any of your patients ever talk to you about sex?"

"They are clients, and yes, but…"

"Case closed. Secrets of a Beverly Hills Sex Therapist—based on a true story."

"I don't really work with stars."

"She always this difficult?" Stangerson asked, his eyes sliding towards Jerry. "What do you mean you don't work with stars? You're working with me, right?" Stangerson sat back and laughed loudly. "Let me worry about the particulars," he continued. "You just help with the stories, with the ideas, and seduce them on the screen. I'll take it from there. We'll write it together."

"Jerry is a writer." Kimberley smiled and turned towards him as though offering a lifeline.

"Who isn't? This city is lousy with writers," Stangerson said, picking up his fork and pointing at Jerry. "Don't worry, my friend, you'll be taken care of," he added dismissively. Looking down at his watch, which he took time to put on display, he announced, "I need some alone time with Kimberley." He stared up at Jerry and smiled. "To get to know her a bit better."

Jerry winced. "Yes. Sure. Right. After a beat, he continued. "As I explained on the phone, apart from the production company I have with James, I manage." He spoke quickly, unsurely. "That's how Kimberley became involved in the project. I manage her." Not meeting Kimberley's eyes, Jerry looked away, silently praying Kimberley wouldn't contradict him.

As though not having heard Jerry, Stangerson turned towards Kimberley and smiled. "If you drove her," he said, turning back towards Jerry, "I can have my driver take her home."

"I drove," Kimberley explained.

Stangerson smiled. "Perfect."

Jerry felt his body tensing, sensing the ship leaving port without him. "Well," Jerry stood, wanting to make his exit on his own, before Stangerson again dismissed him, "I suppose I should go." He paused and added. "Uh, so you'll fill me in on whatever…"

"Good meeting you," Stangerson interrupted. His tone was clipped, hardened.

Jerry nodded. Taking a deep breath, he added, "Amber and Lanier are waiting for me to get back to them. About Kimberley, the tape."

Stangerson's eyes narrowed. "I'd suggest you don't."

"Amber was insistent," Jerry continued trying to make it clear that he had other options, other moves, other places to go with Kimberley.

Stangerson smiled. It was a hard, almost cruel smile. "Leave Amber to me. Lanier is not involved. Good meeting you, Jerry."

Jerry nodded. He looked down, a defeated expression on his face.

"Then again," Stangerson added before Jerry walked away, "if all goes well, you'll soon be free to send that video to Amber—to anyone. In fact, I'll urge you to. Once Kimberley and I lock up a deal…" he turned towards her and winked, "I'll want everyone to know about it."

Again Jerry nodded. He glanced down at Kimberley.

"I'll call you," Kimberley said, smiling. She stood and leaning in gave him a tight, reassuring hug.

Jerry closed his eyes, concentrating as he memorized the feel of her body.

Stangerson remained seated and reached out his hand. He glanced at Kimberley and grinned. "She's in good hands."

Jerry shook Stangerson's hand, staring at him with a pained smile. "I look forward to working with you."

Stangerson silently held Jerry's gaze. With an awkward nod, Jerry turned, and walked towards the door.

Stangerson watched as Jerry exited. "Doesn't have a clue. That's not a putdown," he explained turning towards Kimberley. "Most of them don't. It's not like there's a manual you can use. You know, follow these steps and you end up with a movie."

Kimberley nodded. "You seem to have done okay."

"Just okay?" Stangerson grinned. "You wound me."

"I think your ego can take it."

Stangerson laughed. "Is that a diagnosis? That's you're specialty right, the ego, the psyche. See," he leaned towards her, his voice lowering, "that's what I want to explore. The mind's inner workings, the shadow side, from the perspective of a Beverly Hills shrink," he paused and added, "a beautiful, sexy, desirable shrink. I'm not saying that as a come-on—it's business, a cold objective fact— and that's what we'll be selling. Your character in the film," he continued, picking up his fork and pointing it at her, "she will know what makes people tick, know all about these cravings, desires, lusts, but," taking a beat he raised his eyebrows, "when it comes to her life, she is completely controlled by her cravings. That's what will make this work. You bring reality, authenticity."

Kimberley smiled. "Who launches an acting career at thirty-seven years of age?"

Stangerson's eyes widened. "You tell your age? Amazing. Incredible. Normally I'd tell you never to mention that number in public, but not in this case—in this case your age is part of our PR campaign. Part of our pitch. That's what will make this story work. The campaign will be three-pronged. One," he said, picking up the salt shaker and placing it in front of her, "I'm introducing a stunningly gorgeous new actress to the world. Two," he said, repeating the action with the pepper shaker, "I'm bringing true-to-life stories from the inner sanctum of a real Beverly Hills sex therapist, psychiatrist to the stars. And three…" he continued, picking up the sweetener tray.

"Psychotherapist," Kimberley corrected.

"Whatever," Stangerson replied dismissively, his eyebrows furrowing. "And three," he concluded, putting the tray next to the pepper, "I'm launching a new star, one who is not sixteen, or eighteen, or twenty. No! I'm launching a thirty-seven-year-old mature woman at the peak of her sexuality. I'm changing the rules, breaking glass ceilings, redefining Hollywood—helping women's empowerment! Me Too, Time's Up, you name it. I'm leading the charge. Follow?" he asked with a wide grin.

"This is a new time," he continued before Kimberley could respond. "A new Hollywood. Hollywood puts actresses to pasture at thirty, while the Liam Neesons and Tom Cruises of the world go on as action stars no matter how long-in-the-tooth they are. Well, Peter Stangerson is turning that narrative on its head, he's single-handedly remaking Hollywood. Peter Stangerson discovered and launched Kimberley Goodman, thirty-seven-year-old Kimberley Goodman. We might want to change your last name," he added. Sitting back, he folded his arms and nodded, as if in agreement with himself. "So," he said, leaning forward and placing a hand on her forearm, "Interested?"

Kimberley instinctively winced and pulled back.

"I'm a toucher," Peter explained, letting go of her arm and sitting back. "Women, men, children, dogs, cats—I touch. Not a good time to be a toucher, eh?" he added with a laugh.

"I'd probably cut down on it."

"More professional advice?" he asked with a grin. "I'll work on it. So, like I was saying, before Jerry sent me your video, I was looking to launch a film, an adult sexy thriller. You don't launch that type of film like you do a big budget super-hero movie. This is the type of film you launch in the fall, a prestige project, Oscar contender— doesn't make a billion, but makes money. Figured I'd throw in an ingenue—a sexy new actress at the start of her career. But, after James brought you up at the meeting, I got to thinking." He paused and leaned in towards her. "What if I turned the whole formula on its head? What if the ingenue role isn't a new twenty-something star? What if the star-launching role is a psychologist played by an actual shrink who is on the other side of thirty-five?"

Stangerson leaned closer and again reaching out and taking hold of Kimberley's hand, smiled. "No one ever thinks of launching a female actress in her late thirties. That's when their stars are fading. So?" he asked, leaning back, picking up his knife and holding it high, "what does Peter Stangerson do? He defies expectations. He launches a new female star who is thirty-seven. He launches the career of Kimberley Goodman. Revolutionary!" Stangerson sat back, folded his arms, and stared at Kimberley, a self-satisfied grin on his face.

Kimberley smiled. She studied the tone of his voice, his body language, trying to read what was true, as opposed to what was simply a show to impress.

"You need some work, but…" he shrugged and smiled, as his gaze traveled up and down her body. "And then, the coup de grace, the piece de resistance? " he added, his grin going on full tilt. "You're a gorgeous shrink who was a stripper. A stripper!" he repeated in a near whisper. "A gorgeous, Beverly Hills, psychiatrist to the stars, who was a stripper. Based on a true story!" he exclaimed. "That's our magic bullet, our secret weapon. That is a game changer. That's paydirt! It's titillating for the men, and empowering for the women. You went against the grain. Made your own decisions. Your own choices. Instead of being subjugated by the male gaze, you used it. You chose to become a stripper—'chose' being the operative word. That's what got you through college, right? Landed you your degree. Paved your way to this successful practice. You did it your way and got what you wanted. You gamed the system and look where you are now. You won." He picked up his glass and holding it towards Kimberley announced, "As will we. If we're going to do this, we have to move quickly. It's a funding issue, If we don't shoot in 2020, we don't shoot."

Kimberley held her smile. She began to speak, to set the record straight. She had never been a stripper, wasn't a psychiatrist, wouldn't spill client secrets and wasn't in Beverly Hills. Instead, she picked up her glass and looked at Stangerson, a subtle smile on her face. "Why not?"

Chapter 23

Jerry sat on his couch, staring at the incoming call from Stangerson on his phone. He didn't have the emotional bandwidth for the call right then. He considered letting it go to voicemail. Then, later in the day he could fortify himself with a few drinks before listening to the message. It wouldn't be good news. Not after Stangerson had spent time alone with Kimberley. Jerry was superfluous now. Stangerson was calling to let him know he was out of the picture, dismissed. But, he'd eventually have to speak with him, learn his fate. He took a deep breath and, bracing himself, took the call.

"Jerry," Peter's voice snapped. It was loud, authoritative.

Jerry stood and taking a deep breath began to pace. "Hi, Peter. How did your meeting with…"

"Kimberley told me that you two had some kind of agreement."

Jerry's eyes widened. "Yeah," he fumbled, unsure of what story she had told Stangerson.. Right… I'm, uh," grimacing, he forged on.

"I'm managing her and…"

"You're not," Stangerson interrupted decisively. "You will be taken care of," he added, "You'll get a finder's fee. But you are not involved in her career. Understood?" It was more a statement than a question.

"But…"

"Understood?" Stangerson repeated, his voice rising.

"But… I guess."

"Don't guess," Stangerson instructed. "I need to hear a clear definitive 'yes' and then I can move on to the second reason I called you."

Jerry took a long pause. Pushing Stangerson would get him nowhere. "Yes."

"Good," Stangerson replied, as though closing a book. "That is settled. So, moving on. The scene Kimberley shot for the video— you wrote it?"

Jerry began to pace, bracing himself for an attack on his writing. "Yeah," he replied, his response sounding unsure.

"It's," Stangerson paused and followed with an unconvincing, "okay. I might give you a shot on the writing team," he continued. "There is nothing guaranteed. But, your dialogue was… okay. Kimberley thinks you might be able to write for her."

Jerry's pace quickened, his strides getting longer, his speed increasing. Kimberley had gone to bat for him. "That's—great, that's really…"

"No guarantees," Stangerson repeated. "I'll get back to you." Stangerson paused and then added, "You don't need to call Kimberley about any of this. It's all been taken care of. So, we have an understanding? Everything's clear?"

"Right. But…"

"There are no buts Jerry."

Jerry sat back down on the couch, eyes furrowed as he stared at the floor. "I'm supposed to call Amber. About the video."

Stangerson laughed. "Ignore her. It's my project."

"But… I can't just ignore Amber Lake. And Lanier keeps calling."

"Lanier doesn't exist," Stangerson's voice was sharp, pointed. "She's not involved. I have another call coming in. I'm glad we were able to clear things up. Ignore Amber." With that the phone disconnected.

Jerry placed the phone on the table next to him. His excitement at Stangerson's writing offer quickly faded. When it came to Kimberley, Stangerson was only offering Jerry a finder's fee. He was simply swatting away a fly, cutting him out. Jerry'd be nothing more than an afterthought. He'd remain a nobody and would be powerless to do anything about it.

Closing his eyes, he sat erect and, putting his right hand over his left nostril, took a deep breath. Holding it for thirty seconds he exhaled though his mouth and then repeated the process closing his right nostril. He visualized himself driving a cherry red Jaguar on his way to his home in the Hollywood Hills. He felt his body sinking into the car's leather seat, his foot pressing down on the accelerator, as he rolled down the window feeling the wind on his face. He continued visualizing until the image was as real as possible. That was the trick. Making it real.

Opening his eyes, he stood up and raising his hands up over his head, slowly brought his arms down his sides in an arc, moving the energy. He then shook his body, like a soaked dog who had just been caught in a rainstorm. "It's all good," he said aloud. "It's all working. Peter Stangerson is offering me a writing gig. The Peter Stangerson is offering me a writing gig. The Kimberley project will be green lit, and I'll be a part of it—somehow."

His eyes narrowed, the air seeping out of the balloon at the word, "somehow." But he was now in the game. Even if the writing gig didn't work, it would be his calling card to other projects. He was now a writer for Peter Stangerson, *the* Peter Stangerson. He should be ecstatic. He hadn't yet won—but he was winning. Besides, Stangerson wasn't the only game. Amber was flying James to New

York. She'd sign a deal for the book. Stangerson had no interest in the book so there was no conflict. Jerry had masterfully, albeit unwittingly, set two deals in motion. He'd be involved in both the Kimberley project and Amber Lake's production of James's book. He would skyrocket.

Jerry picked up his phone and stared at it. Stangerson had no right to tell him not to call Kimberley. She was not only Jerry's contact she was his therapist, or had been. Of course he could talk to her. Besides, he hadn't agreed not to contact Kimberley. Jerry said "yes," but his yes meant that he understood that Stangerson had made that request, not that he agreed to the request. Stangerson would never buy that line of reasoning, but still, there was a subtle but important difference. Jerry hit her preset number and called.

After two rings, she answered. "Hello, Jerry."

Jerry smiled. She recognized his call. Probably had his number saved. "I wasn't expecting him to ask me to leave," he said.

"No, neither was I."

"What happened?"

Kimberley walked over to her office window and stared out. "It may be nothing." She gave a slight shrug as she looked down towards the street.

"Nothing? Peter Stangerson is offering you a lead in his new film."

"It could be something," she said, as though making a concession. "We'll see. My next client is here," she lied. "I'll call you back, Jerry." With that the phone disconnected.

Chapter 24

Jerry picked up his phone and dialed James's number. "You're set to leave tomorrow, right?" He could hear James exhale.

"Early. Ridiculously early."

"Early is good," Jerry smiled. "Amber's probably sending a limo. No Super Shuttle or Uber this time. First-class all the way."

"After the meeting, I need to head back ASAP, but she has me booked there for three days."

"She probably has other meetings lined up. She's worked with Christopher Nolan, J.J. Abrams, Steven Soderbergh—maybe she's looking at one of them to direct now that Stangerson's out of the picture. Maybe Naomie Watts to costar. Stay as long as she wants you to. She's covering the costs and you have my card if you need it. You're set. This is it. What we've been waiting for." James responded with silence. "This isn't a fucking wake," Jerry insisted. "Get excited. We're golden."

"Golden," James repeated woodenly. "Right. I gotta pack," he added as he disconnected the call.

Chapter 25

Lanier sat on her couch and glowered at her silent phone. No one had returned her texts, emails, or calls, not Stangerson, not Amber, not James, not even Jerry—and Jerry was nobody. She was being locked out and she didn't like it. Stangerson was doing an end run. He was trying to cut Lanier, James, and even Amber out of the picture. His standard MO. She'd seen it before. Whatever he did or didn't want to do with James and Jerry was fine with her. They weren't anybody. They certainly weren't Lanier. She was the one to put the project together. She was the reason it was in motion. All roads led back to her and if Stangerson had the temerity to cut her out of her own project, he was playing with fire. She'd take it somewhere else, make a better deal. Sighing, she picked up her phone as she continued to stare at it. Her silent pep talk wasn't working. She was playing a weak hand and she knew it. Lanier sat erect, inhaled deeply, and called Amber. After a clipped hello, Sam, Amber's executive assistant, matter-of-factly informed Lanier that Amber was unavailable and that, yes, he had given her all of

Lanier's messages.

"Tell her it's important. Crucial," Lanier replied insistently. "News about Peter... Stangerson. News that can't wait. He's making a deal. Signing a new actress. It's happening now."

"Will do. Thank you." Sam seemed to yawn his reply. The line then went dead.

If Amber didn't respond to that. She wouldn't respond to anything. And, if that was the case, Lanier was out. Minutes later, a call came through. "Sam gave me your message." Amber's tone was bored, dismissive.

"Thanks for calling." Lanier worked to keep her voice upbeat, cheery. "Peter is setting up a meeting with an ex-stripper, Beverly Hills psychiatrist who is a part of James's script?" The sentence was awkward, clunky. She hadn't practiced, hadn't thought it out. She winced as the words tumbled out.

"Old news. Peter thinks he's locking up James's novel. That's so Peter. Too little, too late. If that's it—I'm busy."

"It's not about the novel," Lanier added hurriedly. "James is out."

Amber frowned. "What do you mean it's not about the novel?"

"Just that," Lanier continued, her radar picking up on Amber's hesitation. "The novel's dead. Peter's only interested in the stripper shrink."

"And she's a part of the novel," Amber insisted.

Lanier smiled. She had Amber's attention. "Her character never appears in the novel," Lanier explained. "She was just something James invented to try and keep Peter interested. It worked, but not the way he was hoping. Now she's all that Peter's interested in. James talked himself right out of a film deal," Lanier added with a high laugh. "Now it's all about Kimberley."

"You're the one who told me that Peter was going to option the novel. I moved forward on the information you gave me. Do not fuck with me." Amber's voice sounded like a whip snap.

180

Lanier flinched. "I'm trying to help. I want to help you get to Kimberley before Peter…"

The line disconnected cutting Lanier's sentence short. She immediately called back and was instructed by Sam to stop calling. Again the line disconnected.

Amber threw her phone on the couch with a thud. She turned to Sam. "I just flew James to New York—for nothing! Fucking Lanier." Plopping down on her couch, she groaned aloud. "Call James at the hotel," she instructed. "Tell him I have to cancel our meeting."

Sam nodded. "Got it. When should I tell him you're rescheduling?"

"I'm canceling, not rescheduling. And find out who that stripper shrink is."

Chapter 26

James sat on the bed at the Peninsula Hotel. He carefully studied the room. It wasn't what he was expecting, not nearly as luxurious, but still, it was as upscale New York as he'd ever get. He might as well take it in, enjoy it. Laying down spread eagle on the bed, he felt his phone vibrating in his pocket. Sitting up, he pulled it out and answered.

"James? It's Sam. Listen, Amber had something come up and won't be able to meet. If anything changes, we'll contact you once you're back in Los Angeles. Feel free to stay at the hotel until your return flight." After a slight pause, Sam added, "Amber said to tell you that meals at the hotel are on her."

James was silent.

"James?"

"Yeah," he replied with a grimace. "I got it." Hanging up, he let the phone drop on the bed. There was a perverse pleasure in being right, in proving to Jerry it had all been a waste. James was simply running in place, wasting time. He'd probably lose the copywriting job. Sitting on the edge of the bed he stared blankly at the wall. He then stood up, quickly packed his one bag, and headed out the door.

Chapter 27

Lanier felt almost giddy as she walked out of Phillips & Company's public relations offices. She still had contacts in the industry, still knew people she could turn to for information—and information was currency. Heading towards the subway, she practiced her delivery. Once home, she sat on her couch and slipped her phone out of her pocket. Her smile grew as she dialed Amber's number. "Sam," she began, "I know Amber's pissed, but I have some news for her. Important news. Tell her I just need a minute."

"Amber is not taking your calls," Sam's tone was cold, dry.

"I know, I know," Lanier forged on with machine gun speed, "but… look, tell her it has to do with James, and Stangerson." She took a beat, inhaled and, her voice rising added, "and Jessica."

"Jessica?"

"Chandler," Lanier slowly and carefully enunciated the name. "She's involved now—it's not just Stangerson."

Sam hesitated. "Hold on."

Lanier took a deep breath, nervously waiting as Sam relayed her news to Amber.

"What about Jessica?" Amber demanded. Her voice was sharp, demanding.

Lanier exhaled. "Stangerson is barking up the wrong tree—is that how that saying goes? Whatever. It's not about the hooker shrink. It's all about the book."

"What about Jessica?" Amber repeated impatiently.

"The book, James's novel," Lanier continued. "It's all about the book. Everything's changed," Lanier added hurriedly. "After it's featured on the cover of The New York Times book review, everyone who matters will be after it. And Jessica knows it. She has a window in the next few months. Her plan is to lock this down and start shooting in April 2020. If not, she's committed until 2024. That's why she's rushing to nail this down. Now. We have to move on this fast. Together. Having Jessica Chandler going after this is worse than having Reese Witherspoon going against you. Jessica's book club is bigger." She paused to let the information sink in.

"Why would it be featured in…" Amber sat down. Her eyebrows furrowed. "When?"

"Four weeks," Lanier replied. "No one knows about it yet, not Peter, not Jerry, not even James. I doubt his publisher even knows."

"How do you know?" Amber asked.

"I have—friends," Lanier proclaimed, demonstrating her worth. "It's happening. And," she took a dramatic beat, "Jessica knows it." Again she paused, but not long enough for Amber to reply. "And now, because of me, you know it. Jessica is trying to secure the rights. Now! While Peter is focusing his attention on the stripper shrink video, he's missing the big picture. Jessica has a direct line to James's publisher. She's probably already contacted them."

"But you just told me it wasn't about the book," Amber replied in a near yell. After a few seconds of silence, Amber continued. "I have a direct line to James." Turning, she hurriedly motioned to Sam. Placing the call on mute, she directed him to immediately call James and reschedule their appointment.

"I know James," Lanier replied definitively. "If you remember, I'm the one who brought you his book. I'm the one who can deliver this to you. But," closing her eyes, she took a breath, bracing herself, "I need some reassurance. I need to be sure I'm part of the deal. One call to James and I can get him to New York and lock up the rights. Get this done."

"I don't need you to call him. He's here."

Lanier winced. She took a breath and tried to compose herself. "Where?"

"Here," Amber replied with a self-satisfied smile. "Manhattan. We're meeting."

Lanier paused. If Amber was telling the truth, it was new information. Disturbing information. "Manhattan," Lanier repeated. Again she paused, as she tried to stay centered. "I know," she lied, forcing an upbeat delivery. "That makes it easier, right? He was hurt by the way you and Peter treated him at our lunch, but I talked him down. He trusts me. I'll call James and secure the rights to his novel for you, leaving Peter on the outside with his ridiculous stripper shrink and keeping Jessica out of the picture."

Again muting the phone, Amber turned towards Sam. "Tell James we need to meet now. Send a car to pick him up." Unmuting the phone, she put it back to her ear, "I need to go, Lanier. And do not call James. That is not a request."

Lanier faintly heard Sam's voice through the phone line as he told Amber, "I just tried the hotel. He's gone."

Turning towards Sam, Amber again muted the phone. "What do you mean gone?" she demanded. "Gone where?"

"Just gone," Sam repeated with a shrug. "He's not picking up his cell. I called the hotel's front desk. He's gone. Checked out. They don't know where."

"Well find him!" Unmuting the phone, she again put it to her ear. "What did you tell him?" Amber snapped. "You scared him off."

"I scared him off? I haven't even…"

"You do that," Amber continued, interrupting Lanier mid-sentence. "Scare people off. You're rude. You're too pushy, annoying, you scare them away. If I lose this whole deal because of you…" Amber's voice trailed off. "Do not call him. He's avoiding everyone now because of you."

"Me?"

"You, Lanier." Amber's voice was emphatic. "You do that to people. It's annoying. Really annoying. Stop it!"

Lanier was about to respond but held back. It would do her no good to get into a pissing match with Amber Lake. Lanier would never win. It was Amber's game. Her rules. They got that way—celebrities. Began to think they were above the fray, that they could say whatever they wanted, whenever. And they thought that because it was usually true. With fame came carte blanche. Anything was permitted, accepted. Mean, cruel vicious, it didn't matter. Battling them head-on was useless; one never won that way. "I'll get in touch with James and deliver the project to you," Lanier kept her voice calm, modulated.

"Are you deaf?" Amber barked, her voice rising. "Didn't I just tell you not call him? Do not call him. Do not speak to him. You've just about ruined this as it is. He won't talk to me now because of you. Do not call James. I'm serious, Lanier. I need you to disappear." Amber paused as she considered her next move. Lanier was exasperating but had some value. Best not to completely blow her off. "At least for a while." Amber continued, lowering her voice, modulating her tone, "Once I put this deal together, I'll see you're taken care of. But do not call him. I appreciate the information," she added as though tossing a bone, "about The New York Times and Jessica." With that, Amber disconnected the call.

Lanier sank down in her couch, took a deep breath and dialed James. The call, as expected, went straight to voicemail. It was time for a different tact. "James, you need to call me," Lanier began, keeping her tone uncharacteristically light, upbeat as she left a voicemail. "It's good news," she announced, forcing herself to smile as she spoke. "Great news. Unbelievable news. What you always wanted. Call me and I'll fill you in and we can celebrate." She then placed the phone down. She couldn't call Jerry or Stangerson. James would call her back, she assured herself. She'd just need to wait a bit. But he would call.

Amber tossed the phone onto the table and turned to Sam. "Everything's changed. You need to find James. Now!"

Sam gave an even nod. Sam was always even. He was used to the dramatic ups and downs. Unexpected eruptions. Random hysterics. He was well paid to live on a roller coaster. "I will. His flight doesn't leave for two days. But," he added with a slight frown, "he might leave sooner. It'll cost him to change flights, but if he's not staying at the hotel, it will cost him to stay here anyway. And, I'm sure he's pissed after the meeting was canceled."

"I'm the one who's pissed. Find him," Amber demanded. " Now! I need to lock this up before Jessica does and before Stangerson finds out about the Times piece."

Same gave an assured nod. "Done. No worries. I'll find him."

"And call Gavin," Amber added. "Tell him I need to see him. Tell him I'm on my way over. I'll leave my phone on; if you get a hold of James call me ASAP."

"Let me call and see if Gavin's available."

"I pay him to be available," Amber replied pointedly. Picking up her bag, she slid in her phone, headed to her bedroom-sized walk-in closet, put on her large, full-length coat, gloves, purple sock cap, and oversized sunglasses. She then headed to the bathroom, which was larger than most master bedrooms, and studied herself in the full-length mirror. She hated mirrors, but stared appraisingly at her suit of armor. Even she couldn't tell it was Amber Lake. "I need to talk with James right away," she barked as she walked back into her living room. "Make that happen." Picking up her bag, she added,

"Tell the driver to meet me downstairs. And cancel anything I have scheduled today. I'll be at Gavin's. Call me as soon as you find James." Amber then turned and headed out the door.

Chapter 28

Amber Lake sat in the back of the town car texting Sam to move her spa appointment to the following day. Pulling up in front of a brownstone on the upper east side, the driver turned, announcing they had arrived. Amber nodded, secured her sock cap, buttoned her coat, and slipped on her oversized sunglasses. Today there would be no entourage, no bodyguards. She needed to be alone. Not that she expected to truly be on her own. Even when she insisted, she knew someone was most likely trailing her. Out of sight, but there. They made sure of that. Amber Lake was an investment. She texted Dr. Gavin, to ensure the door would be open and the office empty. Then, exiting the car, she briskly walked up the brownstone's stairway, through the front door and down the hall and, passing the waiting room, went through a back door which led to his office.

Dr. Gavin looked up from his large, plush, oversized chair as she entered. "I can't work this way, Amber. You can't just appear unannounced. What if I was with a patient? You were just lucky this time. You need to give me at least twenty-four hours before we have a session."

Amber marched to her appointed chair, removed her cap, coat, and glasses and, glancing around the room to assure herself they were alone, looked at Dr. Gavin. "It's cold in here. Put up the heat. And I can't very well give you twenty-four hours when an emergency comes up, can I?" she replied dismissively. Again, she glanced around the room.

"You need to give notice, Amber." Dr. Gavin repeated. "I can't have you traipsing in mid-session."

Amber shrugged. She then sat silently staring down at the rug on the floor, studying the patterns.

"What's so urgent?" Dr. Gavin asked.

Amber looked up. "Howard Stern does analysis. He goes every day, right? Maybe I should be doing that?"

"I don't do traditional analysis," he replied. "Plus, you made it clear that you couldn't go to therapy every day."

"Yeah, well that's because I can't. Or at least I won't," she added. "That would drive me nuts. Sitting and talking about myself every day..." As her voice trailed off, she made a face as though she had eaten something disagreeable. "I'm fucking sick of talking, or reading, or seeing, or hearing about Amber Lake. Makes me crazy." Pausing, she leaned back in her chair. "I'm fucking sick of talking about her."

"It's not her, it's you," Dr. Gavin corrected. "We've talked about disassociating, about not referring to yourself in the third person."

Again Amber shrugged.

"What's going on? Why did you need to come before our scheduled session?"

Sitting back, she took a deep breath, and began. "Initially it looked like I was going to be doing a film with Peter and..."

"Peter?"

191

"Stangerson."

Dr. Gavin nodded. Picking up his pen and notebook from the side table he began to write.

Amber frowned, staring at the notebook. "Lanier set up a meeting with me and Peter to talk to James about his book and…"

"Lanier? James?" Dr. Gavin interrupted. "You're getting ahead of yourself. I'm not following. I don't know who Lanier or…"

"We didn't pay any attention to him at the meeting," Amber interrupted, ignoring Dr. Gavin's questions, "I mean, he really isn't anybody, right?" she continued, her voice racing. "But then things changed, so I flew James out here and then things changed again so, I cancelled the meeting and then I found out that The New York Times is doing a piece on his novel, and now he's left the hotel and I don't know where he is and…"

Dr. Gavin held out his hand. "Slow down. I'm not following any of this. You're all over the map right now. Stop and close your eyes and just breath for a few minutes. Center yourself. Be present. Start at the beginning. Stop and take a deep breath."

"You take a deep breath," Amber snapped.

Dr. Gavin sat back, silently staring at her.

Amber groaned aloud, took a deep breath, and closed her eyes for approximately ten seconds. "That doesn't work," she protested opening them again and continuing, her voice racing. "I need to track James down and secure the rights before Jessica does and before Peter finds out about The New York Times cover story and…"

Again Dr. Gavin held up his hand, like a cop halting traffic. "Amber! Slow down. Who is Jessica? What New York Times cover story? Start at the beginning and explain this sequentially."

"Jessica!" Amber repeated insistently, her voice rising. "It's actually a good book," she added, as though making a concession. "After I decided to fly him out I had Sam get me a copy. I read it in a night. It's good," she repeated, her tone noting her surprise. "It could make good film. Peter would just fuck it up. Anyway, Lanier said what Peter is really interested in is that stripper shrink, not the book, and since James is an unknown author, I figured it wouldn't really be worth the meeting if Peter's not interested, so I canceled the meeting with James but then Lanier tells me about The New York Times and Jessica so I had Sam call and now James is no longer at the Peninsula and..."

"Amber," Dr. Gavin said, his tone veering from commanding to pleading. "Slow down," he repeated. "Breath. Remember some of the exercises we've practiced. We might need to revisit your meds."

"You revisit them."

Dr. Gavin sat up and leaned towards her. "Let's go through each point. Okay?" After a beat, he looked down at his notes and asked. "What book? What New York Times story? Who is James? Who is Lanier? Who is Jessica? How is Peter Stangerson involved? And what is a stripper shrink? But first, center yourself. Sit up straight. Take some slow deep breaths."

"I don't have time for this." Amber shook her head dismissively. "Not now. So," she went on as she leaned towards him, "I'm sure my canceling that meeting completely pissed James off. I mean after the meeting with Lanier, me, and Peter he was already pissed to start, right? And then I cancel again once he's out here from L.A. But what does he have to be pissed about? He was flown out here all expenses paid, by Amber Lake. He should be thanking me, not sulking off somewhere."

"Third person again," Dr. Gavin warned. Looking down, he again studied his notes. "Let's start with you telling me who James is."

"I probably pissed him off from the start by ignoring him at the meeting Lanier set up," Amber continued, annoyed by his questions. "I ignored James and let Stangerson ramble on about his project, thinking there was maybe something there. But there never is with Stangerson. Not anymore. Plus, I found out *Ultra's Return* is dead. I needed that picture. And that was Stangerson's fault. I was pissed.

I fucking needed that picture." She repeated angrily. "Besides, James is a nobody. An unknown author. His book could never make the money *Ultra's Return* could have. I'd finally play a superhero—not that that makes any difference now that they've lost their funding—but, with The New York Times piece coming out, if done right, his novel has a shot at Oscar buzz. Like one of those old Miramax films."

"But without Weinstein," Dr. Gavin added with a hint of a smile.

Amber grimaced. "And without Peter.. I'm not saying he's as bad as Harvey was, but…" she paused and holding on to a strand of her long brown hair, wrapped it around her left trigger finger. "Doesn't matter. Everything's changed. Peter's trying to screw me over. But it won't work," she added, looking back at Dr. Gavin and grinning. "He doesn't know about the Times. I do."

Dr. Gavin's eyebrows narrowed. "Screw you over how?"

"By bringing in one of you people?"

"One of my people?" Dr. Gavin asked, a confused expression on his face.

"No," Amber replied impatiently, "not one of your people, one of you people—a shrink."

"They're having a psychiatrist on the set? A consultant? Didn't you tell them that I work as…"

"Not a consultant," Amber replied with an irritated grimace. "And I don't know what she is. Some kind of shrink. Not a consultant. She's going to be in the film. She's going to fucking act in the film. A lead!"

Dr. Gavin sat back; he looked down at his notes as though they would help him comprehend what Amber was saying. "A psychiatrist is going to act … in a Peter Stangerson film?"

"I didn't say psychiatrist, a shrink, some kind of ex-stripper, Beverly Hills shrink."

"Ex-stripper?" Dr. Gavin's eyes furrowed as he leaned in towards her. "An ex-stripper psychotherapist. And she's going to act in the film?"

Amber allowed her hair to unwind as she pulled her legs up onto the chair cat-like. "I know what he's doing," she said with a nod of her head. "He's trying to throw me off balance. Trying to fuck with my head. From what I hear, she's going to do a goddamn nude scene. A shrink in a nude scene! The film will probably start with it. I said no to nude scenes and it pissed him off. So now the first thing you're going to see is her—naked. That's all people are going to remember." She paused and looking down ran her hand over her right foot. "That's why I need to find James. Now!"

"Back up," Dr. Gavin instructed. "A Beverly Hills psychotherapist, who might be a psychiatrist and used to be a stripper is going to do a nude scene in a Peter Stangerson film." He put his pen and notebook on the side table. "Who is she?"

Amber gave a dismissive shrug. "Kimberley something."

"Kimberley what?" Dr. Gavin asked, again picking up his pen and pad and preparing to write.

"How the hell do I know?" Amber snapped. "Who cares? Stay focused. But she's hot. Sam showed me some of her online pictures. What kind of shrink has pictures like that online? I still don't have the video but I've seen pictures online."

"What pictures?"

After a beat she added. "She's hot—but old."

"Old?"

"Yeah," Amber replied with a slight smile. "Mid-thirties—like almost-forty."

"Almost forty is old?" Dr. Gavin asked defensively.

"It is if you're launching a film career. Nobody launches their film career at forty. This is her first film—first real film. She did some stupid horror thing decades ago. I'm having her investigated," she added with a nod. "But, anyway, this is her first real film and she's starting at like almost forty!"

"You know," Dr. Gavin said, sitting upright, "if they do need a psychiatrist consultant on the project…"

"Don't turn this into a fucking job interview," Amber snapped.

"I'm not," Dr. Gavin protested defensively. "I'm just curious. If this therapist isn't an M.D., a psychiatrist, I could…"

"Forget that. Peter's just doing this to get back at me," Amber interrupted. "I wouldn't sleep with him on the first film." Amber paused and picked at a piece of lint on her jeans. "From what I could see online, she has a really, really good body. I'm pretty sure her boobs are bigger than mine," she added, looking down at her chest. "Peter says everyone's boobs are bigger than mine. He's not the only one. Early on, one producer wanted to put into the contract that I could only have the part if I got a boob job." She glanced up at Dr. Gavin. "Do you believe that?" She paused, again glancing down. "I like mine. They're not huge. I mean, they're not like Scarlett's, but they're not… little."

Again she took a beat. "Say something," she insisted. "You're supposed to help me here. Give me advice, encouragement."

"Your body is fine." Dr. Gavin said with a reassuring nod.

"Yeah? How do you know my body's fine?" Amber asked. "You've never seen my body. Plus, if she's hot, who is going to care if she can act? And Peter's not going to have her show her boobs and all unless she's hot." Amber paused. "I'm sure he found that out."

Dr. Gavin leaned towards her. "Look, chances are they secured financing for the film because you're attached, right?" He enjoyed talking about films as though he was an insider, understood the workings of the industry. "You know there was probably no financing without you being in the film."

Amber shrugged. "I don't even know if there is a film. I don't know what anybody's talking about anymore. It's Peter, remember? I thought I had *Ultra's Return*. I beat out Margot and Naomie and… but that project isn't even happening now. It's his fault. It's Peter," she said as though that was enough of an explanation. "None of that

196

matters. Not anymore. *Ultra's Return* is dead. That's the project that interested me. Let Peter keep his ex-stripper shrink." She paused and looking down frowned, as though searching for something. "He doesn't know about Jessica, and The New York Times piece. So, I need to get to James before anyone else does and lock up the rights of the book." She looked up at Dr. Gavin and declared. "I'll fuck Peter before he fucks me."

"Interesting way to phrase it," Dr. Gavin said as he stared down at his notes. "Walk me through this again. Slowly. And, what you want to remember is that you can't control what Stangerson does, but you can control what you do and how you react to what he does."

"Why not?" Amber demanded. "Why can't I control what he does? Male directors and producers control things all the time. And if I option the book, I can—control things. Peter's the one who's controlling this shrink, right? Believe me, it wasn't her idea to do a nude scene in her first film. Control is the name of the game. It changes everything. Look at Jessica. She's got control now. She acts, produces, and her book club is bigger than Reese's."

"Reese?" Gavin asked.

"Witherspoon," Amber replied impatiently. "Stay with me. Both Reese and Jessica act and produce. That's the secret. That's what I need. Control. I need to produce." She paused and stared at Dr. Gavin accusingly.

"You should have told me that a long time ago. Giving advice is your job." She pensively stared out the window. "That's going to be my New Year's resolution," she pronounced. I'm going to produce. I'll start with James's book. But I have to move and fast. I need to be in production by March, or it won't work. Have to make sure I beat Peter or Jessica. After the Times piece everyone will be after James."

Dr. Gavin paused and, staring down, again tried to make sense of his notes. "What New York Times piece. I'm still not sure who Jessica or Jerry are and how they fit in to…"

"Jessica!" Amber repeated in a near yell. "Chandler!" Shaking her head, she impatiently looked out the window.

Dr. Gavin nodded, working to stay composed, not overreact. "And how does Jessica fit into the story?"

Amber turned back towards Dr. Gavin and glowered. "Look, I need you to follow me here. That's what I'm paying you for." She paused pensively. "I'm going to beat him—Peter," she announced, sitting back with a self-satisfied smile. "Let him stay with his ex-hooker, while I…"

"Hooker?" Dr. Gavin asked. "I thought you said she was an ex-stripper."

"Stripper, hooker, whatever," Amber replied with a shrug. "Ex something to do with sex, okay?" Her lips formed a pout as she looked away. "James has disappeared. And now with The New York Times piece coming out, Jessica is after James's novel…"

"What New York Times piece?"

Amber grimaced. "Jesus! That's what I've been explaining to you. I could lose the whole thing," she snapped, slapping her hand against the chair's arm. She glared at Dr. Gavin accusingly. "I need advice. Solutions. A game plan. A way to beat Peter."

"Don't focus on Stangerson," Dr. Gavin replied. "He's going to do whatever he's going to do. You can't control that. Stangerson is well… Stangerson. I've learned enough about him from…" Catching himself, he paused mid-sentence. "Let's just focus on you, not Stangerson."

"Really?" Amber interrupted, her eyes widening as she leaned in towards him. "Who?" she asked with a slight smile. "Which clients? What did they say exactly?"

"Patients," Dr. Gavin corrected. "And you know I can't tell you which patients, Amber," he replied, his tone direct, officious.

"Patients," she repeated. "Whatever. Okay, don't tell me who, just tell me what. What did you find out? He's a scum, right? A letch. A perv?"

"Let's just leave it at I think your assessment of the situation is correct. I don't know all of the reasons why he brought this psychotherapist on board, but one of them could be to trigger you, to elicit a response he's looking for. But you're not going to give him that response. You're going to react very differently."

"Right," Amber said dismissively. Tucking her legs under the chair she eagerly leaned in towards him. "Just tell me a couple of things they've told you about Peter. I know who you see," she added, her grin widening. "We talk, you know. It's no big major secret who your other clients are."

"Patients," Dr. Gavin corrected.

"Just tell me a couple of things. One—just one."

"Let's talk about how you're going to deal with this situation."

"Who actually slept with the guy? That's what I'm curious about," Amber continued, twisting her body into a tighter pretzel. "That's the information that nobody shares. If anyone did do it she'd be too embarrassed to tell, because what if the rest of us didn't? She'd feel like a fucking idiot, right? Look at the whole Weinstein thing. Everybody knew, but no one knew exactly who did what. Who would want to admit that?" Amber made a distasteful expression and shook her head. "I'm not saying Peter is like Harvey," she added. "He's bad, but not that bad," she paused and looked out the window. Turning back towards Dr. Gavin she smiled and leaned closer towards him, "So who gave in?" She raised her hand, Boy Scout style. "It won't leave this room. I promise."

"Amber," Dr. Gavin sat upright and shifted in his chair. "You know I'm not going to share anything like that with you. Let's focus on the issue at hand."

Amber glanced back at the clock on the wall that was strategically placed out of her view "You know one thing I do like about this arrangement. I don't have to worry about what time it is, or if our hour is almost over. One of the perks of being Amber Lake, right? I can put you on retainer and stay for as long as I want."

"Not a luxury everyone can afford," Dr. Gavin replied. "So let's take advantage of it and deal with your—issues."

"Come on," Amber grinned, leaning almost out of the chair, "just tell me one, one thing that you found out about Peter. Who did he do?"

"We are not talking about this." Dr. Gavin replied definitively. "My suggestion is when dealing with Stangerson don't get sucked into any drama. Remember you don't have to immediately act on your feelings. Be aware of them, but…"

"Easy for you to say," Amber replied, opening her bag and rummaging through it. "He pisses me off."

"Anger is a secondary feeling," Dr Gavin pronounced.

Amber glanced up and frowned. "What the hell is that supposed to mean?"

"Anger is always a secondary feeling," he repeated. "It's a reaction to the primary feeling which is usually fear or shame or guilt. So start tracking what the primary feeling is, what it is that's triggering the anger."

"What triggered the anger is that I'm pissed," Amber pronounced as she continued to dig in her bag. "Don't use psychobabble to try and confuse things. I'm angry because I'm pissed," she repeated, her voice rising, as she pulled out her cellphone. "And you're getting me off point here. I need to find James."

Dr. Gavin glared at her phone. "You know that cell phones are off-limits during the session. Please put it away."

"I considered it," Amber continued, ignoring his request. "Saying yes to the whole nude scene thing." She stared at her phone as she scrolled down her texts.

Dr. Gavin shook his head. "If you feel strongly about it, you were right to nix the nude scene idea."

"I don't feel strongly about it. I don't really care. I just like saying no to Peter. Besides, I'll have to do one sometime," Amber replied as she

200

answered a text. "Every A-actress does."

"The phone. Please."

Amber shrugged, quickly sending a second text she slipped the phone back in her bag. "It's easier on the Aussies. Nudity is different for them."

"There is no written or unwritten rule that says you ever have to do a nude scene."

"Oh, I'll have to do one," Amber nodded. "Somehow it proves you're a serious actress. It used to be you had to—do a nude scene, be in a Woody Allen film, and do one film where you look really, really ugly to be taken seriously. The Woody Allen part is out of the picture, so to speak," she added laughing at her quip. "So now it's just really the nude scene and a film where you look really ugly." She again pulled out her phone and stared at it.

Dr. Gavin glared at the phone. "Amber!" His voice was stern, like a schoolteacher admonishing a student.

"Okay. Okay," she said again putting it away. "Just habit." Amber shrugged and looked out the window. "I really wanted to do *Ultra's Return*. That would have been a blockbuster. My superhero film. I need one of those. Scarlett has done them, Brie has. I need one! And this was going to be the one. Plus, they're cash cows." She looked back at Dr. Gavin. "You know how fucking rich Robert Downey Jr. is?" she asked pointedly. "Everyone in China knows who he is. Superheroes travel. Academy Award films don't go anywhere. They're quicksand." Amber took a beat. "Why are we talking about this?" she asked pointing her phone at Dr. Gavin. "You need to keep the conversation on track here. That's your job." She paused, her eyes squinting as she stared at Dr. Gavin. "I need to move fast. Peter will find out about The New York Times, Jessica already knows. And Lanier can't keep her mouth shut."

"How about you start by telling me who Lanier is?" Dr. Gavin asked, glancing down at his notes.

"Let Peter waste his time with the stripper shrink," Amber continued, ignoring his question as her right foot began to shake. She again reached into her bag and pulled out her phone. Catching herself, she stopped mid-motion. Looking up at Dr. Gavin, she grinned and dropped the phone back in her purse. "The New York Times changes everything. I gotta move on this," she said, nodding to herself. "I gotta find James. Now!" After a pensive beat, she declared, "I gotta go. We're done."

"Let's finish talking this through," Dr. Gavin said. "Naming your fears helps to diminish them."

"Yeah?" Amber replied. "So if a guy is pointing a gun at me and I say, 'there's a gun pointed at me,' then I'm not going to be afraid anymore?"

"We both know that's not what I mean. What are you afraid of right now?"

"What I'm afraid of is that James isn't at the hotel anymore," she said, her foot swinging like a metronome gone wild. "He's gone. Disappeared. I canceled the meeting and that pissed him off. But that's the way business works, right? Meetings get canceled, rescheduled. Besides, how many people get to meet one-on-one with Amber Lake? He should be happy he got this far, act like an adult. But he just left. Now I need to track him down, before he finds out about The New York Times piece. That changes everything. Jessica knows," she added. "And she's going to move on it. And if Peter finds out…" Amber looked down pensively. "If I try going through Jerry, he'll tell Peter and that will fuck everything up."

"Who is Jerry?" Dr. Gavin asked impatiently.

"He's nobody," Amber said with a dismissive waive of her hand. She glanced up at him like a furtive animal. Looking away, she bit her bottom lip. "We're wasting time. I've got to move on this—fast. I need to track James down. I gotta go," Amber grabbed her bag and standing up, looked down at Dr. Gavin. "I could get Jerry on my side. That would be easy enough."

"Who is Jerry?" Dr. Gavin insisted, saying each word slowly.

Ignoring the question, Amber stood, walked towards the window and stared out. "Jerry doesn't have a clue. Peter will cut out Jerry as soon as he gets what he wants. He works that way," she added with a nod. "But, maybe I can convince Jerry that Peter is going to fuck him over and…" She stopped mid-sentence and holding up her right hand, stared at her nails as though looking for answers in the sea-blue polish.

"Sit down. Let's go through this sequentially."

"Jerry's a bad idea," she said, looking up from her nails and glaring at Dr. Gavin as though he had suggested it. "Say something. I need some help here…"

Dr. Gavin motioned towards the chair. "Sit down. And let's talk this through," he said, leaning towards her. "Do you really want to alienate Stangerson? Why not work it out? A Peter Stangerson film starring Amber Lake is like a Tarantino film starring Margot Robbie. It sells."

Amber grimaced. "Peter is done. Over. I just need to get James on board. Need to find him, calm him down, get him on board and we'll be good. We talked on the phone for a few minutes. He should be grateful, right? A phone call with Amber Lake? He tried not to show it, but he was pissed off because all everyone was interested in was that Kimberley video, not his novel."

Dr. Gavin sat back. "What video?"

"I told you about the video," she replied impatiently.

"No you didn't. You never once mentioned a video."

"A video of that stripper shrink. That's what started this whole thing. I told you!" she repeated impatiently.

Dr. Gavin stared at Amber with a startled expression. "There is a video of that psychotherapist stripping?"

"No, she's not stripping! Get your mind out of the gutter."

I'm not following you, Amber." Dr. Gavin pointed to the chair. "Sit down and let's talk this out."

"I'm done talking." Walking back to the chair, Amber picked up her bag, pulled out her phone and called Sam. "Tell me you found him," she demanded, as she sat on the chair's armrest. "Yeah, well, of course he's not answering, he's pissed. I'm calling Marcia. I'll put her on it. She'll find him." Amber groaned, disconnected the call and putting her phone back in her purse, stared at Dr. Gavin. "Doubt James will even talk to me now. Weird, right, someone refusing to talk to Amber Lake?"

Dr. Gavin shook his head. "You're doing third person again. Don't disassociate."

"Too late. That happened a long time ago," she replied with a clipped laugh. Taking a pause, she glanced at the window. "I gotta go," she said looking back at Dr. Gavin.

"Sit down. Let's finish the session."

"The session is officially over." Amber again stood and looked down at Dr. Gavin. "I need to walk."

"Let's finish. Besides, you shouldn't walk alone."

"I do that sometimes," she declared, as though taking a walk by herself was a most daring act. "With my sunglasses, coat and hat no one notices me. Besides, it's not L.A.—everyone walks in New York. Walking clears my head." She again glanced towards the window. "I need to find him—and then…" Not finishing her sentence, she gathered her cap, coat and sunglasses. marched towards the door and exited.

Chapter 29

Amber paused in Dr. Gavin's waiting room, quickly put on her armor and headed down to her waiting car. Walking to the passenger's side, she bent down and knocked on the window. The tinted glass slid down revealing the driver's stoic face. Her regular driver was on a two-week vacation. She didn't know this one and from the get-go didn't much like him. A change in staff always made her uncomfortable.

Amber instructed him to wait, explaining that she wanted to walk for a bit and would call him when needed. He nodded. As the car window slid up she stared at her reflection. Not even she would recognize Amber Lake in that garb. Smiling, she stood erect and headed towards Fifth Avenue. Pulling her phone out of her purse, she called Marcia, her manager, impatiently waiting while her call was put through. "I need you to find somebody," she demanded.

"Hello to you too," Marcia said with a clipped laugh. "What do you mean—find somebody?"

"If you don't know how to find somebody, call somebody who does,"

Amber directed. "Somebody who's good. Fast. I need someday tracked down today. Right now."

"Your calls are always different, Amber. Okay, give me a sec, let me grab a pen." After a slight pause, her voice returned. "Give me the info."

As she walked, Amber pulled out the card James had given her and read the information, giving Marcia his name, phone, and email. "He's here, in New York, at least I think he's still here. I flew him out here. He was at the Peninsula—all expenses paid I might add—but he's gone. Disappeared. I need to find him before he heads back to L.A."

"What's this all about? Who is James Lansing?" she asked, as she scribbled down the name. "If he's not at the Peninsula, where is he staying now?"

"If I knew that I wouldn't be calling you, would I? I don't have time for this, Marcia."

"Have you checked Facebook? Instagram? Twitter? People always stupidly post where they're going. Kinda like, 'Hey Mr. Burglar, my home is empty now.'"

"No, I haven't checked Facebook!" Amber snapped. "I never check Facebook. I hate Facebook. You check Facebook. I need him found today. Like right now."

"Okay. Got it," Marcia replied, a mildly irritated tone in her voice. "I'm on it."

"And don't just find him, track him. Find out where he is, where he goes, and who he talks to."

"Sounds like a B-grade spy movie. Okay, I'll get on it and get back to you."

"Find him and call me." Amber disconnected the call, slipped her phone back into her bag and braced herself as she walked in the December cold towards Fifth Avenue. Her thoughts were clearer when she walked, and she seldom walked by herself anymore. She missed walking in New York, missed the days before she was *the*

Amber Lake. The struggling actor days when she and her boyfriend would spend a day trapsing around the city.

She'd read memory is imperfect. What we remember is often fiction. Either way, she did, miss that time. Particularly around the holidays when she and David would wander around Fifth Avenue gazing into the decorated windows, visiting the tree at Rockefeller Center, buying a bag of chestnuts from a street corner vendor. Scouring their tiny apartment, they'd search for loose change between paydays.

The city lit up like a Christmas jewel, sometimes snow, the cold almost too bitter to walk in, but they walked all the same, laughing, singing Christmas carols. Those were the days she viewed as her normal life—hoping she'd land her next audition, worrying about paying the rent, trying to save up enough to buy David a Christmas present.

Amber smiled remembering those electric feelings of something about to happen, just out of reach. Not yet twenty-five, she was already feeling old, nostalgic. No one would get it or believe her. They'd think she was striking a pose, a rich, privileged star longing for her struggling actor days. Not a lot of sympathy to be found there. She was a realist. She knew if given the chance she wouldn't go back. She wouldn't have the guts. Amber was where most people dreamed, yearned, and schemed to be. Still, she thought, grimacing as a cold wind whipped, she was happier then. She truly was.

David was long gone. Amber wondered about him as she marched on. He'd probably be uncomfortable around her now. That would be strange. There would be no point of contact. Not anymore. Strange for her, but probably even stranger for him. She tried to imagine what that would feel like. What if his career had taken off? If she was still waitressing and he now was mentioned in the same breath as Brad Pitt or Chris Hemsworth? How would that make her feel? How would she make sense of a world where something like that could happen to David, while she was still waiting tables and trying to find an agent? Her story would now be that she used to date him. "Really," she'd insist. "I did. He was my boyfriend." How strange would that be?

His narrative was now changed forever by her success. She most likely gave him a certain amount of currency. If a conversation lulled, or if he wanted to impress, he'd have a trump card, a good story to hold until the right time. "Yeah, Amber Lake was my girlfriend. Really. I'm serious. No, I'm not bullshitting you. Of course I slept with her—she was my girlfriend." How strange would it be to be the preverbal fly on the wall and listen to his story? The questions that would follow—what was she like? What happened to them? Were they still in touch? Was he happy for her? Did he always know she'd make it? And the other questions—was she a bitch? Did she sleep her way to the top? Was it just dumb luck? Looks but no real talent? She'd never know his version of her story, or if there was a difference between the story he told others and the version he secretly held on to.

She could look him up some day, just to say "Hi"? But why? There was no place where their worlds intersected. Not now. Looking him up would be a waste of time at best and cruel at worst. He was locked out of her world and she could never go back to his. Two parallel dimensions that never converged. No going back. Ever. There was a loneliness to that thought. A deep sadness that bordered on fear. Enough of that, she thought, shaking her head to dislodge the memories. Accelerating her pace, she held on to her bag like a halfback clutching a football. Second nature in New York. She never did that in L.A. Walking in L.A. was slower, looser, freer, but not nearly as much fun and besides, you never got anywhere.

The memories didn't shake. They held on tenaciously. Embrace them, she thought. That's what Dr. Gavin would probably say. So she would. She'd retrace the steps she and David used to take, go see the windows they used to visit. Revisit their yearly pilgrimage. Their tradition—if a three-year relationship could establish a tradition. Bergdorf Goodman, Louis Vuitton, Saks, Bloomingdale's, Cartier's, a walk-through Tiffany's. Back then they'd bundle up and slowly walk past or through the stores pointing to all of the things they wanted, all of the things they tried to convince themselves they eventually would buy, could buy—one day. They'd laugh, neither secretly believing that they ever would be able to own that ring, or neckless. And there was such a freeing joy in that knowledge, knowing that the yearning was all. Was enough.

They'd fantasize aloud as they walked on, jostled in the crowds, the colors, the lights, the throngs of others huddled, laughing, hands in pockets, eyes squinted, heads down as they collectively marched through the cold. Christmas music flowing out of open doors. David said she was a sucker for it. She couldn't get enough. Except for "Silent Night." She'd never cared much for "Silent Night." David had repeatedly pointed out that "Silent Night" was the Holy Grail of Christmas songs. The sentence made little sense to her since the Holy Grail had been lost for centuries and she could call up "Silent Night" whenever she wanted, but she got his point.

Still, he was Jewish, and she told him she would not be lectured about Christmas songs by someone who wasn't even Christian, much less Catholic. He'd laugh and tell her that he was more Catholic than she'd ever be. Those times had been electric. Magical. They'd end their trek with a subway ride up to St. John the Divine's. One year they went to midnight mass at St. Patrick's. That was the first time she'd been to mass in a while. She'd stopped going to church at sixteen, angering her parents, causing familial drama. Still, she loved the theatre of the mass, the trappings, the feelings she got when she entered a church, heard the singing, smelled the incense, watched the priest in his flowing vestments.

Amber smiled as she turned the corner towards Sacks. There were lines of people two-deep in front of the windows. People jostling, smiling, laughing, children, eyes-wide, pointing, squealing, nudging their mothers to acknowledge what they had seen. Amber joined in, staring, watching, melding with the others. It felt good to be invisible, comfortable, safe. But all it would take was one. She knew that. All it would take was one person recognizing Amber Lake, pointing, calling her out. Then others would follow and all would be lost. They'd collapse on her en masse, hands out, pens ready, phones pointed like cocked revolvers to shoot photos. Her driver would have to be quick. She'd have to run for the safety of the empty back seat.

But that hadn't happened. Not yet. She was still lost in the crowd. No one had picked her out. No one was gawking. Everyone was busily jostling for position, staring in the windows. And Amber joined, comfortably enveloped in anonymity. Pretending David was at her side, imagining them laughing, she opened the large Sacks door, grinning as the Christmas music rushed past her out into the street. She was moving by sense memory.

The first stop would be the cosmetic counter. It was always the cosmetic counter. David would find a chair, or wander not too far, as she took her time searching, studying, asking the salesgirl questions, trying testers. It was like being set lose in a toy store, bright gleaming, colored containers filled with transformational secrets. After a while, David would amble back and buy her a lipstick, or an eyebrow pencil. Something that was fun but inexpensive and off they'd go exploring the rest of the store.

She'd buy herself a treat this time. Something small. Walking to the counter, she picked up an eyeliner tester, began to remove her sunglasses and stopped. She looked down at the item in her hand and frowned. She couldn't remove her glasses, couldn't take off her cap, couldn't talk to the salesgirl. That would be the end of it. Continuing to hold on to the eyeliner, she bit her bottom lip. Maybe just for a couple of seconds. Just try on one, quickly. Glancing around the counter, it seemed safe. Everyone around her was busy, lost in their searching, talking with friends or family, no one looking at her. Amber quickly removed her sunglasses and bending towards the mirror on the counter stared. The reflection startled. The familiar face now no longer stared back only in mirrors, but on posters, films, ads, billboards. Her image had been co-opted, highjacked. But here, at the counter as Christmas music played and other's attention were elsewhere, it was hers, solitarily, happily hers.

Emboldened, Amber removed her cap. She liked to drift from counter to counter, explore, search, investigate, but for now this would suffice. There was no luxury of time or space. She'd stay there, at the one counter. She'd be quick. It would be her safe haven. She smiled as placing down the eyeliner, she picked a lipstick. Looking up she saw a young woman staring at her. The woman quickly turned away, an embarrassed expression on her face. But that was enough, it signaled the end. She had been recognized, spotted, seen. Amber sighed as she hurriedly placed the lipstick down, put on her cap and slid on her sunglasses.

But it was too late to turn invisible again. Having been spotted, it was time to leave. She considered summoning her driver as she headed towards the front door. Have him meet her at the corner and drive her uptown to St. John the Divine's, where she and David ended their treks. Or maybe brave it and hail a cab. Her times with David were still the days of subways—hailing cabs had been a luxury. She couldn't chance the subway, although that would have been her first choice, racing down the stairs, the smells, the jockeying, the speeding pinprick of light that grew out of the black tunnel, the metal squealing as it came to a stop, doors sliding open, people jostling for position, talking, laughing, reading; eyes cast up or down in order to avoid other eyes.

First she'd go across the street to Saint Patrick's, Walk through the church to Our Lady's chapel in the back. It was peaceful in the chapel. No one would bother her there. But she had promised herself a gift at Saks and, glancing up, searched for the woman who'd spotted her. She was gone but the threat wasn't over. She could return with reinforcements, more gawkers. Amber should leave, she thought, as she picked up a lipstick she would never use. Walking to the woman behind the counter, she kept her eyes down, as she made her purchase. Then, glancing around the store one final time, she quickly marched towards the Fifth Avenue exit.

"Pardon me," Amber heard as she walked towards the door. Slowing, she took a deep breath, her body tightening, steeling itself. She had come so close. Probably best pretend she hadn't heard and march out the door. Instead she slowed and turned towards the voice, facing the enemy. Taking her phone out of her bag, she texted her driver to meet her in front of Saks ASAP. The woman who had spied her, now stood a couple of feet away, a pleading expression on her face. She was attractive. Looked to be in her mid-twenties, shoulder length auburn hair, blue eyes. Probably just wanted an autograph. But some were more brazen. Some had the temerity to ask for money, a role, an introduction to her agent. Amber shot an unwelcoming glare at the woman, as she dropped her phone back into her bag. She then turned and continued to walk.

"I don't mean to bother you," the woman called out, her voice tentative, as she followed Amber, "particularly around Christmas," she added. Best get it over with, Amber thought. Stopping, she turned and was about to ask what the woman wanted her to sign.

"I'm not asking for an autograph or a selfie or anything like that," the woman said, as though replying to Amber's silent thought. "I don't want to intrude or bother you. I can see that's not what you want. Can I just…?" The woman's voice trailed as Amber continued to silently stare. "God, I feel like an idiot," the woman continued. "I don't do things like this. I hate bothering you. I know what that must feel like." Taking a quick pause, she added, "Well, I really don't. I mean no one stops me in the street, but I can only imagine."

Amber continued to stare, saying nothing. She had learned from Dr. Gavin that silence is often the best approach. Just stay centered, silent, and let the other person spin-off. Stay silent, listen, and watch. Her car would be there any minute. She'd then be whisked away and free.

"I'm so sorry," the woman repeated. "It's just…"

After a few seconds of silence, Amber relented. "I'm in a hurry."

"I'm sure you are and I don't want to bother you, it's just never in a million years would I think I'd see you, have an opportunity to actually talk to Amber Lake. If you were to walk away right now, this would still be an amazingly incredible experience, me standing here talking alone one-on-one in Sacks with Amber Lake. I mean that doesn't happen."

Amber looked around uncomfortably. Standing still was a bad move. It drew attention. "But it did," she continued. "Here." Reaching into her purse, she pulled out the eye pencil she had just purchased and handing it to the woman. Anything she handed her would be special, treasured, a piece of gum, a tissue paper; the item didn't matter. It had been touched by Amber Lake. "A gift. Have a good life. As

I said, I'm in a hurry." With that she turned and quickly marched towards the door.

"Yes. Of course. Of course you are. I'm so sorry. Can I just talk to you for ten minutes? Five," she quickly corrected herself, as she followed Amber out the door. "Five minutes. I know it's a horrible imposition. You have no idea who I am. You're famous. I'm sure, you have all sorts of important places to go and I'm basically a nobody, but…"

Amber stopped on the sidewalk, ignoring the woman and watching as the car turned to corner and headed her way. "Goodbye," Amber called as she headed towards the car. The driver put the car in park, jumped out, quickly jogged towards the passenger's door and, opening it, shot a warning glare at the woman. Ushering Amber in, he shut the door, marched back to the drivers seat and the car pulled away. The woman was left, mouth ajar. She stared from the car to the eyebrow pencil in her hand.

"Thanks for the rescue," Amber said.

The driver laughed. "Kinda dangerous walking around Saks like that on your own."

"Danger is my business," Amber replied.

Again he laughed.

Amber leaned against the door and sliding down her sunglasses, stared out the window. She'd managed it. At least for a few moments she wandered alone, unseen, melded into the crowd. Hearing her phone, she pulled it out of her bag. "Marcia, tell me you found him," she snapped.

"Mission accomplished—sir!" Marcia announced in a mock military voice. "James is staying in some cheap hotel in Soho. There's a PI guy I use, ex-FBI. He retraced James's steps since leaving the Peninsula. While in New York, he's been to the same place for breakfast every morning and the same Starbuck's every afternoon. Creature of habit. Even if my guy somehow lost trace of him, he'd always find him. Have your driver take you and Sam to the Starbuck's on Broadway in Soho at 4:30—and you got him."

"Good," Amber replied, relieved James was back in her orbit. "But I can't be the one to talk to him. Not yet. He's pissed, remember? That would either get him more pissed, or scare him away."

"Then Sam."

Amber shook her head. "He's talked to Sam. Doesn't trust him, not after…"

"What then?" Marcia asked. After a beat, she added, "I got it. Let's use one of my actresses. A pretty one. That always works with guys, right? We'll give her hazard pay. She can meet James at Starbucks or someplace, come on to him. Guys like that. They always buy it. She can prime him. Soften him up. You can then swoop in and get the rights to his book."

"Let me call you back," Amber said. "Sam's calling. Marcia found him," Amber announced, transferring the call to Sam. "He'll be at Starbuck's today at 4:30. Marcia can have one of her wanna-be actresses there. A hot one. She'll come on to James." Amber took a beat. "Like Marcia said, guys always fall for that." Again a quick beat. "James is straight, right? Of course he is," she replied answering her own question. "She'll soften him up, well take it from there and lock down the rights before Peter or Jessica can."

"Too late," Sam replied. "James headed back to L.A. today. He'll be landing soon. Besides, it's not a pretty actress or sex that will bring him around."

"What do you mean back to L.A.? Marcia said he's here. She knows where he goes, when."

"Well he's gone. Forget the actress. James is broke. Money is what will work. Looks like he lost a job by coming out here. He's broke," Sam said. "Dead broke. As in can't pay the rent broke. Money," Sam repeated. "Cash. Right away. Now. That will get you your rights."

Chapter 30

J ames walked into the Red Circle Tavern and headed over to their usual table where a waiting Jerry sat, an impatient expression on his face. "What's going on?" he demanded before James had a chance to sit down. "You're supposed to be in New York. Amber Lake called me. Me!" he repeated emphatically. "Amber Lake! But all she was interested in was trying to track you down, She's pissed. Said you weren't returning her calls. You do not not return a call from Amber Lake. That's just fucking crazy."

James grunted as he sat down. "What's fucking crazy is that Amber Lake flew me to New York for no reason whatsoever. She then had one of her 'people' call to cancel the meeting. And that was it. Nothing. Nada. Zero. That's what I came away with. I was left dangling. It was a waste. A total fucking waste. And I lost the job. I should sue her."

"But then she tried to contact you. To reschedule. And you flaked."

"I left when her assistant called and cancelled. I'd had enough. It's a game to her. A fucking game. I'm not going to ask 'how high' every time Amber Lake says jump. You talk to her. I'm done."

"Look," Jerry continued, working to modulate his voice as he leaned in towards James, "she lives in a different universe. That's how those people are. It's not personal. Come on—it's Amber Lake. Amber fucking Lake!"

James looked up and scanned the room. Not seeing Violet, he motioned to a passing waitress and ordered a coke. "I don't care who she is, not anymore," James replied, turning towards Jerry. "I was told the meeting was canceled and that I should go back to L.A. And that's what I did. Maybe she then got bored and changed her mind—again. Not my problem—I'm out. Fuck Amber Lake."

Jerry's eyebrows raised. "I wish."

"Going to New York really screwed up my chances at landing that copywriting job." James stared at Jerry accusingly. "I told you I shouldn't go. If I beg and grovel maybe they'll still let me have the position."

"Forget copywriting job. That's your old life. Amber Lake is waiting for your call."

James looked out the window, his eyebrows furrowed. "I actually bought it for a while. Bought in to your fantasy. I believed the novel would be produced as a film. The option money would spell me for a bit. Give me time to write. Work on my new novel. A stupid fairyland fantasy," he concluded, all but spitting out the words.

"This is Hollywood. It lives on fairyland fantasies," Jerry insisted. Glancing up, his eyes locked on their waitress as she walked by. "I think she just smiled at me," he added, his gaze following her as she headed towards the bar. "She's new. Haven't seen her before. Amazing ass. Probably another one of those actresses that's really a waitress. If I tell her about this project, I bet that she'd be interested and…"

"Would you give it a rest?" James snapped. "I'm talking about my life here and all you care about is playing producer and nailing

216

waitresses. I'm broke. Dead broke. I need a fucking job. Now."

"But you have to admit, that is a seriously amazing ass," Jerry replied, as he stared longingly. "Study it the next time she passes by. That is a perfect ass. Look, she's heading back." Jerry craned his neck to look back towards the bar, "I'll call her over and tell her I'm producing a film based on your novel and that we're casting…"

"I can't take that now," James barked, pensively staring at his coke. After a beat, he added, "I'm out of the game, okay? I'm done."

Jerry took a breath. Talking to James when he was like this was like dealing with a weary animal. Jerry had to be patient, silently wait until James relaxed. He'd eventually get him back on board. "I'm still waiting to hear back from Stangerson," Jerry said, thinking it best to drop Amber Lake for the present. "That's what people mainly do when making films—wait. It's an art."

Jerry turned, picking up his phone as the waitress passed by. "Think I'd be pushing it if I tell her that she has a perfect look and I want to take a photo of her to show to my producer?" Jerry glanced at the phone in his hand. "Holy shit! I missed this text." His eyes narrowed as he read. "Stangerson wants to meet. With us. With you! Wants to have dinner tonight. He says you need to be there. Yes!" he announced, banging his hand against the table with a snap. "We are in!"

James shook his head. "You're in. I just told you. I'm done."

"You fucking crazy?" Jerry asked in a near yell. "Meetings with someone like Stangerson come around once in a lifetime."

"Really?" James grabbed Jerry's phone and read the message, "I met Stangerson at Dunhill Jr.'s and had lunch with him and Amber Lake a few days ago, so I guess I've lived a couple of lifetimes. And you know what Stangerson did? Ignored me, pretended I didn't exist. Ditto Amber Lake. It all amounted to nothing," he said, repeating it like a mantra as he handed Jerry back his phone.

"That's just how it's played," Jerry explained rereading the message. "It's a game. Nothing personal. Disinterest is a strategy they use.

They act bored, disdainful. That's just a trick. They try to make people think they don't care that they're ready to walk away, then they can swoop in and pick up projects for pennies on the dollar."

"Yeah, well then they're really good actors because I'm completely convinced that they don't give a shit about me or my book. Look," James continued, again taking the phone from Jerry and reading the message, "if your theory is right, then turn the tables. Play Stangerson. Make him wait."

"No man. No. No. No," Jerry insisted, grabbing back his phone and slipping it in his pocket. "Stangerson can play it that way, not us. We don't have that luxury. Not yet. For us to try that is a sucker's game. We gotta show up. We gotta be ready to go."

"So go."

"You read the text. Stangerson specifically said he wants you there." Jerry paused, angry that James was being so dense. Leaning in, he spoke slowly. "These offers don't stay on the table. If he throws out a good offer, we take it. Then you're good. Golden. We have a deal. We're in. Play it right and 2020 is ours. You'll have your option money. You can work on your new novel."

James shook his head, picking up his coke and taking a drink. "He's obsessed with this whole Kimberley thing now. I'd be sitting there staring at the wall while you two go on about some ex-stripper shrink. No thanks."

"Well, she really wasn't a stripper," Jerry corrected. "Wish she had been," he added with a grin. "That would have been something. But it is about the book. It says right here in his text that he wants to meet about the book. You gotta come. I have Stangerson set up to meet us," Jerry said, his voice rising. "Peter Stangerson! The Peter Stangerson and you just want to blow it off. You're not just fucking yourself over, what about me?" Pausing, he took a deep breath. "Just forget it. You're some piece of work." Standing up he glared down at James, shook his head, and marched out the door.

James sat and watched as Jerry exited. Finishing his drink, he sat and stared blankly out the window. After a few minutes, his phone rang. It was Jerry. Bracing himself, he answered.

"You owe me, big time," Jerry said, his voice noticeably shaking. "I've never been yelled at like that. I thought he was going to have a stroke, or I was going to. But I rescheduled the meeting. I moved it. It's not today. We're set for tomorrow night. You owe me big time," he repeated. "Stangerson said people don't cancel on him and wanted to know who the hell you think you are. But I did it. We're still on."

"I told you I'm not going. Not today. Not tomorrow, ever. Never again."

"Something's changed, man," Jerry forged on. "He's hot for your book. Really hot. Besides, Stangerson said if you didn't show, he'd sue me for breach of contract."

James laughed. "Breach of what contract? There is no contract. There's nothing. All he's interested in is nailing Kimberley. This one is your baby not mine. You go."

"But he said the meeting was about your novel," Jerry protested. "I told him you'd be there."

"Then you lied."

"But you've got to…"

James stood, took out his wallet, pulled out some bills and left them on the table. "Give Peter my love," he said, hanging up the call. He then turned, walked out, headed to his car and drove home.

Chapter 31

Amber took the private elevator to her penthouse, opened the door with her phone, walked in and, throwing her cap and sunglasses on the couch, dropped herself on the cushion next to them. "He's really gone?" she called out.

"He's gone." Sam confirmed. Putting the video he was watching on pause, he walked into the living room. "He moved to some low rent hotel in SoHo after you canceled the meeting, then he called American Airlines and changed his flight, grabbed the next one leaving—and left."

"Is he an idiot? I was going to offer him a deal. Make his film into a book."

"He didn't know that," Sam said, assuming the voice of reason. "All he knows is that you and Peter ignored him at the first meeting, then you flew him out here and ghosted him. I tried calling, it just goes to voicemail."

Amber stared at Sam. She did not like to hear that anyone would avoid her. How could anyone not talk to Amber Lake? People jumped when she called. She considered lashing out, throwing one of her patented outbursts. But that would be useless. Sam would be her sole audience. And he was inured by then. Amber needed to make sense of the situation. Moreover, she needed James's book. "He's not done," she replied. "He just needs a push, some convincing. I'm offering him a film deal."

"He's different. He just wants to write his novels. But, like I told you, we still have an in. He's broke, dead broke, as in he's not sure how he's going to pay his rent broke."

"How do you know?" Amber asked.

"I had his phone tapped," Sam replied with a proud grin. "Well I didn't but I made some calls. You have a lot of people on retainer. Comes in handy."

"I'd give you a bonus if you weren't already so overpaid."

Sam laughed.

"So did you listen to the calls?"

He nodded.

"And?"

'Doesn't say very nice things about Amber Lake. Feels like he's been played, duped, and dumped. He was up for some copywriting job and he lost it because he flew out here to meet you."

Amber frowned. "Copywriting? I thought he was a novelist?"

"You think novelists make money?"

Amber shrugged.

"So he's back in L.A., dead broke, lost his job and doesn't know how he's going to pay the rent that's due in a couple of weeks. Money is what will do the trick here. Cash. Peter is trying to set up a meeting with him," Sam added. "He's after the book. He heard you're after it. You know Peter, he wants to land it just in case."

"Peter?" Amber said in a near yell. "Peter can't get the rights. We need to get them now. Fast. Today."

After a slight pause, Sam added, "It's worse than that." He enjoyed agitating Amber.

Lowering her glasses, she stared at him. "What do you mean worse?"

"Lanier called James—she's pissed at you too. She's trying to get him to sell the rights to Jessica."

"Jessica?" Amber replied in a near yell. "How did Jessica get into this? Does Peer know—about Jessica?"

Sam shrugged. "Not sure. I think Lanier is waiting to tell Peter. She wants to lock James up first. Get him to sign the rights to her. Giving him some song and dance that she can negotiate a better deal for him. Then she'll go to Peter. Then she'll give you a call. Let you know she owns the rights and that Peter and Jessica are both chomping at the bit. She'll be looking for top dollar."

"Shit! Shit! Shit!" Amber cried. "I had him here, ready to go. Why didn't you have me sign him? What's wrong with you?"

Sam chose not to argue the point; when something went wrong it was inevitably his fault. That was part of his job description. "James needs money," Sam replied, offering a solution. "He needs it now, like immediately. Offer him that and Lanier, Peter, and Jessica are knocked out of the game. He can't pay his rent. Can't pay his bills. He needs cash. A suitcase filled with cash. Cash he can see, deposit and spend right away. That will solve his problems and that will get you the rights to his book."

"Cash." Amber repeated. "Like in dollar bills? People still use cash?"

"Give him cash," Sam repeated. "Like in hundred-dollar bills—a lot of hundred-dollar bills."

Amber slid off her sunglasses. "As in how many hundred-dollar bills?"

"Fifty thousand dollars. Maybe seventy-five," Sam replied. "I guarantee you, he's never seen that much money. We draw up the paperwork, have it ready to sign, land the rights to the book. Give him fifty thousand upfront and some kind of negligible back-end deal. Have him sign the deal, an NDA, a receipt for the cash. And it's done. The rights are yours. Peter and Jessica will be furious and all will be right with the world."

"Twenty-five," Amber countered.

"We need to blow him out of the water," Sam said with a shake of his head. "Need someone to sit him down and open a case filled with at least fifty thousand in cash. His brain will go on tilt. A visceral reaction. He'll see his money problems solved in a flash. He'll have his life back—and a film deal. He'll sign anything at that point." Sam took a beat. "Like seventy-five thousand is going to mean anything to you."

Amber grinned. "Okay fifty."

"Seventy-five."

"Fifty," she repeated. "Call Johnathan to draw up the paperwork. Then get the cash. Take my plane. I want this done ASAP. You'll go today. Now."

"Me?"

Chapter 32

Sitting at his desk, Stangerson looked up from his computer as Genie, notepad in hand, walked into his office and sat down opposite him. "We didn't expect you back so soon," his longtime secretary smiled, using the royal "we."

"I didn't expect me back so soon," Stangerson replied. He stared up at his wall of fame, covered with framed photos of Stangerson with Jack Nicholson, Martin Short, Harrison Ford, Heather Locklear, Jennifer Aniston, Tom Cruise, and others. His eyebrows melded as he stared. The wall was dating. Time was passing. It had been a while since there had been any new additions. It now served more as a museum, than as a current snapshot of his life, a static trip down memory lane.

His career was devolving. slipping into past tense. Stangerson knew there was no reason for him to be on the lot. Not any longer. It would probably be more efficient and cost effective to have a small office somewhere else. But he liked it, liked the feeling of driving onto the lot—the knowing nod and hello from the entrance guard. Plus, there was currency in telling people his offices were on the lot at Warner Bros. It was a safe home. A home with cache. And, with one deal his life could transform from sepia back to technicolor. With one project, the Peter Stangerson would return.

Genie looked down at her notes. "The only meeting I have scheduled for you is with a Dr. Kimberley Goodman."

Stangerson nodded, still staring at the photos. "I was supposed to meet with," he paused pensively as he tried to remember the name. "James, James... something," he added, forgetting the last name. "The one who wrote that novel. Lanier brought him to the New York meeting with Amber."

Genie nodded, continuing to study her notes. "Lansing. James Lansing. You're interested in his book?"

"Not really," Stangerson said with a shake of his head. "At least I wasn't."

"What changed?"

"What changed is now Amber wants it," Stangerson explained with a scowl. He wouldn't usually engage in this type of conversation with an employee. But Genie was beyond employee status. In her early fifties with two grown kids and two ex-husbands, she was more like an accomplice than his executive secretary. Tall, plump, with an officious motherly air, she had seen him through his career highs and lows, his four marriages, his addictions, his infamous battles with the press, and his industry feuds. She had guarded his secrets and kept him on track. And through it all, even when her checks bounced, when he was abusively out of control, she stayed.

"Amber's interested. That's it?" Genie knew how badly Stangerson needed a hit, knew about his debts, the alimony payments, how hard he was working to maintain the image of Peter Stangerson.

"Isn't that enough?" Stangerson asked with a shrug. "Lanier let me know that Amber was moving to lock up the project. If she's moving on it, she knows something."

"You believe what Lanier told you?"

Stangerson glanced up from his computer. "Information is her currency. That's all she's got. If she fucks up on that front, it's over for her. No one will listen to her, take her calls. So yeah, I believe her. And if Amber's hot for the book, she must have a reason. I'll lock it down for pennies and find out why later. James has given this Jerry idiot the rights to negotiate. He doesn't have a clue. I'll grab it for almost nothing. If it's anything, I own the rights, if it's nothing, I can write off the couple of grand I spent to secure it. Plus, it will piss Amber off. That alone makes it worth it."

Genie smiled. "Is the James meeting scheduled?" she asked, looking down at her notes. "I don't have it on the calendar."

"It was scheduled. Until Jerry called to say that James was in the ER with food poisoning." Stangerson paused. "Something doesn't smell right. Something's off. Guys like that don't just cancel a meeting with Peter Stangerson." He shook his head. "They'd have the fucking ambulance drive them from the ER to the meeting. Something's off," he repeated.

"Amber?" Genie asked.

Stangerson shrugged.

"You know how Amber works," Genie continued. "She could be feeding information to Lanier to send you on a wild goose chance. She loves drama."

"Or not," he added. "I think I scared Jerry enough to reschedule right away. Call him in about an hour and tell him I need a meeting set up. ASAP." Picking his favorite pen off his desk, he wrote his name on a blank sheet of paper, as if practicing singing his autograph. "When's the meeting with Kimberley?"

Genie again looked down at her pad. "Next Wednesday. Wednesday at two. Here. At the office. You previously met with her and Jerry," she added continuing to study her notes. "Will he be at this meeting?"

Stangerson grimaced and shook his head. "Jerry's nobody. Make the Kimberley meeting sooner. This week. Tomorrow." He paused and again scanned the photos on the wall. "She has something. I could probably pull of another *Exposed* with her. Maybe spin off a celebrity-sex-shrink reality show or some kind of real-life streaming series after the film. It could have legs."

"An ex-hooker turned therapist with legs?" Genie asked, a slight smile on her face.

"You should see her legs," Stangerson replied with a laugh. "And she's not an ex-hooker, she's an ex-stripper." Stangerson paused. He looked up at Genie and grinned. "But I like that. Ex-hooker," he repeated, clapping his hands together. "Perfect! An ex-hooker's even better. Or both," he added, his grin widening. "Ex-stripper and ex-hooker. We'll use both. I'll owe you a bonus," he added with a laugh. "A very hot ex-stripper, ex-hooker Beverly Hills psychotherapist who is going to spill the beans on the sex lives of the rich and famous—and do a nude scene. That will have legs," he added definitively. Stangerson pulled up Chrome on his computer. He searched until he found Dr. Kimberley Goodman's lingerie shots. "Come here," he said, motioning for Genie to walk around his desk and stand behind him. "Look at these. She's a few years older now but just as hot. Hotter. Think of this image only better, hotter, blown up on the screen, billboards, a shrink-sex-doll that can spill all of Hollywood's secrets."

Standing behind Stangerson, Genie bent down and taking the mouse in her hands moved from photo to photo, slowly studied each shot. Standing upright, she folded her arms. "Can she act?"

"Does it matter? But, yeah, she can," he added as he called up Kimberley's video link. "Watch."

Genie bent over him as the two silently watched. Walking back to her chair, she picked up her notepad and sat down. "Be careful Peter." She only called him Peter when she truly wanted his attention.

Stangerson winced. His hands involuntarily tightened into fists. He took a deep breath and looked again at the photos on the wall. No one else could talk to him this way, not even his ex-wives. "I've learned," he replied, relaxing his hands and giving a dismissive wave. He looked back at Kimberley's image on the screen.

"Does Amber know about her?" Genie asked.

Stangerson looked up from the screen and smiled. "She will. I'll make a point of it. It'll make her crazy." He paused and looked up at Genie. "Something's changed and Amber's looking to lock down James's book rights. Could be nothing, but she could be on to something. I figure I should play it safe, sign the book and Kimberley. They'll both come cheap."

"I still don't get why Amber's chasing the book."

"Lanier probably told her I wanted it," Stangerson replied with a laugh. "She probably has the two of us chasing each other's tails." He shrugged. "I'll lock it up, hedge my bets."

"And anger Amber."

Stangerson looked up and grinned. "I like the alliteration," he replied. "Call Jerry and scare him into setting up a meeting ASAP." He paused and then added with a nod. "Then call Kimberley. Get her here tomorrow. I'll lock up both. It will then be us two, Amber zero."

Genie smiled and nodded. She liked the "us,"—that she was included.

"But I have to move quickly," Stangerson continued. "If I'm going to get the funding it has to be in the next few months. I have to be in production by May at the latest. Otherwise there's no deal."

"Funding from where?" Genie asked.

Stangerson was about to snap, "None of your business." Instead, he took a beat, and with a slight grimace on his face and in a low voice, replied, "Lenny Downs."

Genie winced at the sound of the name. Her silence said it all.

"Think of it as my *Wolf of Wallstreet*, Stangerson said with a forced laugh.

Closing her notebook, Genie stood and headed towards the door. Pausing, she turned back towards Stangerson. "Be careful, Peter."

Stangerson again felt his anger rising. Not long ago, he would have exploded. But Genie was trying to help, and years of therapy had some effect. Made a dent. He was more patient now, more magnanimous. "No worries." He a forced a smile, "I'm a changed man."

Chapter 33

Kimberley exited the 134 freeway at Pass Avenue and drove south towards the Warner Bros. lot. She had driven by it hundreds of times, had seen the back of the lot when she'd gone to the Toluca Lake Tennis Club for dinner, but had never been inside. Even during her acting days she'd never been called in for a reading on the lot. She'd gone to Twentieth Century Fox, CBS, Raleigh Studios, casting director's offices, but never Warner Bros. This marked a first. And she wasn't there for an audition, a reading, or a call-back, she was there for a private meeting with the Peter Stangerson.

Kimberley turned onto the lot, stopped at the gate, and gave the guard her name. He called Stangerson's office, nodded, smiled, opened the gate, and gave her directions to where she could park. Stepping on the accelerator, she was in. Everything had changed so quickly, she thought as she drove towards the parking area, too quickly for her to make sense of it. But it was happening. It was real. She smiled as she parked, exited her car, and walked towards the building.

The office was smaller than she had imagined, but offices in studio lots were usually somewhat cramped. Most producers and directors had their main offices off the lots and were only there during productions. Kimberley gave the receptionist her name, sat down, picked up a copy of Variety and thumbed through it as she waited. She hadn't looked at Variety in years. There had been no need, no call to. And, in those years when she did read it, she had always felt like the poor match girl pressing her face against the glass, always outside looking in. Not this time.

After a few minutes, Genie opened the door to the reception area and smiled. "Mr. Stangerson is ready to see you," she announced, motioning for her to enter. Kimberley placed the magazine down, stood up and followed her towards Stangerson's office. "Just walk in," Genie instructed as they stopped in front of the closed door, "No need to knock. He's expecting you."

Kimberley nodded, stood erect, took a deep breath, and entered. Stangerson sat behind a desk that was too large for both him and the room. Kimberley glanced at his wall of fame, photos of him with various actors and Hollywood luminaries. There was a full size cutout of Marilyn Monroe with her arm around a very young, much thinner Peter Stangerson. "That goes back to Biblical times," Stangerson explained, following Kimberley's gaze. "Years ago, a friend dug it up, made a cutout and gave it to me as a birthday gift. I'd just started in the industry. I was on the set of…" he paused and shook his head. "Well on the set of something. I saw someone with a camera, and I was ballsy enough to corral Marilyn into take a photo with me before I was—me."

Kimberley turned towards him and smiled. "And now you are you."

Stangerson laughed. "So, what would be the clinical psychological term for that behavior of my youth?"

"If I tell you, I'll have to charge you," Kimberley quipped, walking to one of the two chairs placed in front of Stangerson's desk and sitting down.

Again he laughed. "Let's wait then, until I have time for a full

231

session. Once we start production, I'll probably need a few."

Kimberley smiled, focusing on the word "we."

Stangerson stared at Kimberley. Locking his hands behind his head, he leaned back. His eyes freely traveled over her body. "For the male lead, I'm considering John Hamm, Chris Pine, Ryan Gosling… But we're getting ahead of ourselves. This is a high-concept project. And you're the concept," he added pointedly. He held up his arms, moving his hand's apart as if reading the caption on a billboard. "The inner workings of an ex-stripper, blonde, hot, over-sexed Beverly Hills therapist to the stars."

Kimberley winced at the description, After a beat, she laughed. "Maybe one of those descriptions are accurate."

"Close enough." Stangerson gave a satisfied nod. "Close enough to be able say 'based on a true story.' The rest we take some poetic license with. And," he added, "not only based on a true story, the gorgeous shrink stripper is playing herself."

"I can't stand the word shrink, and I never was a stripper," Kimberley corrected.

"But you could have been," he replied with a dismissive waive. "I bet you would have been a hell of a stripper."

"But I wasn't," Kimberley repeated, with a raised eyebrow. "How about if the stripper scenario is a part of my character's backstory instead of mine?"

Stangerson waved off her suggestion, as though chasing a fly. "Has to be yours. That's what's going to grab the audience. Don't worry about it." He paused and stared at Kimberley. "You will be my creation," he announced, as though she had no choice in the matter.

Kimberley forced a smile. Sitting back, she crossed her legs. "I'm flattered, but…"

"You should be," Stangerson interrupted.

"Is there a script I can read so I can get a sense of it? Something I could start working on?" She paused and added. "Is it based on

James's book?"

Stangerson leaned towards her. "Once this starts, I'm going to need you fully committed," he said, ignoring her questions. His tone was stern. His eyes narrowed as he stared at her. "I'm going to need all of you. I'm telling you this because I don't want you thinking you can shoot a few hours on a Peter Stangerson film and then go back to your previous life. That's not how this works. We'll be starting in a few months. 2020 is Peter Stangerson's year," he added with a smile. "We'll shoot here, in L.A., but there will also be location shots. And when we are here, you're not going to have time for anything else. This project is going to be all consuming. It's going to be your life. Understood?"

Kimberley's eyebrows furrowed. "I can't just stop my practice. I'm not even sure what the project is. This is just a preliminary meeting."

"Preliminary for you," he replied, reflexively staring down at her legs. "We went from meeting to pre-production the moment you walked in that door." He paused and added, "Understand?"

Kimberley flinched at being spoken to as though she was in grade school.

"Good," Stangerson nodded, taking her silence as agreement. "Forget about whatever small projects you worked on in the past. Playground stuff. This is your first real film."

Kimberley took a beat. She wanted to ask about specifics, contracts, compensation. There was no way she could simply stop her practice, particularly without knowing what time and money was involved. But she'd wait. Address that later. "Is Jerry going to be involved in the project?" she asked.

Stangerson leaned back in his chair and stared at Kimberley. He took a long pause. His eyebrows knitted. "Maybe I was wrong about Jerry," he replied. "Maybe he doesn't play for the other team. If there is something going on between you and Jerry, that stops. Now. Jerry is a messenger boy," Stangerson explained, his voice was sharp, deliberate. "You're the message. From this point on his involvement or noninvolvement with this film has nothing to do with you." He paused, a hint of a smile coming to his lips. "Are you two fucking?"

Kimberley winced and stared silently in response.

Stangerson grinned. "I'm direct. That's how I work. If so, lucky guy. I wouldn't think he was in your league. That's now over, understand?" he directed, more as a statement rather than a question. "And no one like Jerry is going to be involved. He's out. This is not just a film," Stangerson continued, "it's going to be a transformation. I have a dermatologist for you to see to review Botox or fillers, or… he'll know. Next week you'll also start with an acting coach and a trainer who will start you on a workout and nutritional regime. You look good, but you could look better. There is a nude scene. It will be tasteful," he added, responding to her anticipated objection. "Waist up frontal and a full body shot from the back, but, still—you don't want to disappoint the audience," he concluded with a smile.

Kimberley's body tightened. She remained silent.

"No objections. Perfect!" he said, bringing his hands together in one loud clap.

"We haven't agreed to anything."

"Sure we have." Stangerson gave a knowing laugh.

After a beat, Kimberley scanned the photos on his wall.

Stangerson's eyes narrowed as he followed Kimberley's gaze to a photo of him with his arm draped over Amber Lake. "Early in her career. Her second film. She was quicksilver then."

"Past tense?"

Stangerson shrugged as he stared at the photo. "Actresses are always past tense. They just don't know it. Like cars, as soon as you drive them off the lot, they start to depreciate." He sat back again locking his hands behind his head, his elbows pointing out like wings about to fly away. "They get to where the air is rarified, they become deified and then…" he paused and grinning added, "everything that goes up comes down. Gravity. A law of nature." He stared back at the photo and shrugged. "She was something," he nodded, his gaze remaining on the photo. "She was like a kid, funny, open, she was a

234

sweetheart."

"Again past tense. You act like she's over the hill. She's young, in her twenties. Her career is just starting."

"A fading star who needs a hit," he declared. Stangerson's stare moved down the line of photos. "They start to fade from the get-go," he added. "And they know it. That changes people."

"People can change for the better."

"Maybe in your world."

"You seem to have come out okay."

"I was ahead of the game. I started out as an asshole," he replied with a grin. Turning back towards Kimberley, his eyes moved down to her chest as though to illustrate the point. Sitting upright, his eyes moved up to hers. "So, we start. Now."

Kimberley continued to stare at the wall of photos. "Like you said, I'm here."

"So that's a yes." He took a slight pause. "There's something I want from you."

Kimberley's body noticeably stiffened as though preparing for a blow.

Stangerson gave a hard laugh. "Not that."

Kimberley replied with a smile.

Stangerson leaned closer. "If it had been, would that be so awful?"

"We'll never know," she replied, leaning back.

Stangerson replied with a shrug, as if to signify she could be wrong. "This needs to be a closed camp," he said. "The less Amber knows, the better. Which means Jerry, James, or Lanier are to know nothing."

"I don't know Lanier," Kimberley replied.

"Lucky you," Stangerson quipped. "Keep it that way. I'm talking about James and Jerry. Nothing we discuss leaves this office. Amber will know what I want her to know. That's where Lanier is useful," he added with a slight smile. "Anything I tell her confidentially makes a bee line to Amber. Once Amber sees this is happening, she'll see you as a threat and try and bury you. Or she'll pretend she wants the project herself, and offer you a deal so she can kill it."

Kimberley stared at him pensively. "Amber won't be involved?" She paused. Again her body tensed. Kimberley was unknown. She couldn't carry a film. If Amber Lake wasn't involved, chances were there was no film. The meeting was just an elaborate ruse. One more Hollywood come-on.

"Not Amber, but for this to work, we're going to need star power." Stangerson replied as if reading her mind. "I'm going to fill the project with guest starring roles." He turned back to the photos on his wall. "Nicole, Scarlett, Naomie, Ryan, Chris..." Stangerson shrugged. "I have feelers out. Their star power initially carries the film. But the PR will be centered around this unknown gorgeous, sexy, blonde, ex-stripper Beverly Hills psychiatrist-to-the-stars making her acting debut and spilling celebrity secrets."

"I'm not a stripper, not a Beverly Hills psychiatrist to the stars and I can't legally spill secrets."

Stangerson shrugged. "The public doesn't know that." Standing, he walked over to the photo of him and Amber Lake, straightened it. "This one's always a bit lopsided, always a bit cockeyed. Makes you think, eh. It's a fantasy world," he added, using his shirtsleeve to wipe the photo of him and Tom Cruise. "We get paid to give people the fantasies that they want." He turned towards Kimberley. "That in turn gives me what I want and that will let me give you what you want. That's my superpower," Stangerson continued, walking back to his leather chair, and sitting down. "Knowing what people want. And I do—know what they want," he added turning the photos on his wall. "I know what Nicole wants. I know what Tom wants. I know what Amber wants and I know what you want."

Kimberley started to respond but sat in silence.

Stangerson continued to scrutinize the wall. After a few silent seconds, he stood, and walking over to the photo of him and Amber, again straightened it. "I'll make sure Amber's hears about you, about Jerry's video," grinning, he turned to Kimberley. "I see it as a—motivator."

"There are positive and negative motivators," Kimberley replied.

"I can tell you from experience that jealousy and envy generally do the trick, at least in this world." He walked from photo to photo, straightening them as he spoke. "Fear trumps hope," he laughed. "That's what Trump's slogan should be, right? That's as on-point as you can get."

Walking back to his desk, he sat down, folded his hands, and leaned towards Kimberley. "I'm going to start the shoot with your nude scene. I'll basically make it a closed set but will make sure the press finds out about it. Get some provocative, but tasteful images that can be leaked to TMZ and People. Tasteful," he repeated with a smile. "That will create a buzz. The tabloids, social media, everyone will jump on it." He took a beat and stared at Amber's photo. "If we do it right, not only Amber will hate you, every actress in Hollywood will." He paused, leaned towards her and speaking slowly said, "I am going to make you a star."

Kimberley sat back, and again crossed her legs. "How often do you think that line has been used in this city?"

Stangerson laughed. "It's a mantra. The difference is that 99% can't follow through—I can. I don't have time for come-ons or games. I don't need them. I need a hit," he admitted. Taking a beat, he looked from the Amber Lake photo to Kimberley. "And together we're going to create one. We're not just making a film," He repeated. "We're launching a brand." He glanced down grinned and added, "One with legs."

Kimberley replied with a taut silent smile.

"We'll start with the nude scene," Stangerson repeated. "Like I said, tasteful, discreet." After a beat, he added. "You know, this is the hardest I've ever worked to get a woman's clothes off."

"Maybe a nude shot of me from the back," Kimberley replied. "The rest can be—suggested."

Stangerson waved the suggestion away. "You don't want to start by cheating your audience. Let me take care of that. I'll make you even more gorgeous than you are. I'm a magician."

A topic to be revisited, Kimberley thought. "Will Jerry be working on the script?" she asked.

Stangerson stared at Kimberley. He replied with a grunt, scowling at the suggestion.

"I'm not involved with him," she quickly added. "Not my type. But you and I wouldn't be meeting if not for him."

"So I give him a finder's fee and send him home." Smiling, he continued. "If it means that much to you, I'll give your ex-boyfriend a trial run, on the writing team for the project—emphasis on ex. He'll never cut it, but, my gift to you." After a beat he added, "You'll owe me."

"Interesting game you play," Kimberley replied. "Does it usually work?"

"Usually. But... not what I'm after this time."

Kimberley laughed. "I'd be insulted if I wasn't relieved. So I won't owe you?"

"Oh, you'll owe me." Stangerson declared. He glanced at the clock on the wall. "I have to wrap this up. Genie will contact you with a schedule."

Kimberley paused. That was the Hollywood MO—glad talk at meetings followed by a complete lack of clarity, or silence which led to nothing. "We haven't discussed specifics, the contract or terms. Shouldn't I have an agent review..." Seeing the grimace on Stangerson's face, Kimberley stopped mid-sentence She had to play it smart. Stangerson had swung the gates wide open. Angering him could slam them shut before she put her foot in.

"It will all be taken care of," Stangerson replied impatiently. His delivery was definitive, leaving no room for discussion. "I'm more

238

than fair. You'll be happy. And the clock is starting now. Like I said, we're in preproduction. It's a done deal. By March I'll need you full-time. Clear your books. Block out 2020. It belongs to me now." Again he glanced at the clock, signaling her exit.

Kimberley began to respond, explaining that she couldn't possibly close down her practice in March. Instead, she took a beat, nodded, stood, and extended her hand. "Thank you."

Stangerson stared at her outstretched hand and smiled. Standing, he walked towards her. "Welcome on board," he whispered, as he pulled her towards him and wrapped his arms around her. "I'm a hugger," he explained, as he pressed her closer. Releasing Kimberley, he held her at arms-length. "It's a shame," he concluded as he gazed at her appraisingly.

Kimberley gave a clipped laugh as she tactfully pulled away. "Better this way. And it's a dangerous time to be a hugger," she added. "Wrong decade." Smiling, she turned and exited his office.

Genie walked in after Kimberley left. Folding her arms, she frowned. "She didn't close the door."

"No manners," Stangerson replied with a grin.

"I have an update," Genie continued, "Jerry says James is recovering, but probably won't be able to meet for a couple of days."

Stangerson waived his hand dismissively. "Forget Jerry. Fuck James."

"Outside of my job description," Genie replied straight faced.

Stangerson laughed. "You're lucky. Kimberley is the project now, not James's book," he explained, as he walked to the window and watched as she walked to her car. "Forget the book. Amber's using it to send me on a wild goose chase. Draw up a contract for Kimberley," Stangerson directed.

"What is the contract for? If it's not based on the novel, what's the project?"

Stangerson shrugged. "Who cares? I'll make up a title, or you make up a title. Then we'll come up with a storyline and hire a writer to write a first draft about a hot Beverly Hills ex-hooker, stripper therapist to the stars. We'll have a shooting script in a couple of weeks. Done."

Genie nodded. She turned to walk to her office. Pausing she turned and asked. "She's letting you use that tagline—ex-hooker?"

"Not sure I brought it up—the ex-hooker tag," he replied. "We had too much to cover. But, what if a writer at In Touch has a lead on a story that Kimberley was an ex-hooker as well as a stripper? Nothing I can do about that, right? I can't control the press. But, none of that will come out yet. When it does, well, like I said, we couldn't control it, could we?"

Gennie stared at Stangerson. "She won't be happy."

"Happiness is overrated," he declared. "Call Jason and tell him we need a script. He's good, a bit of a hack but he's fast and cheap. I need someone to start working on the first draft. I'll make the working title Hollywood Secrets or Celebrity Confessions, the true-life story of an ex-hooker/stripper, psychotherapist to the stars. A bit long, but I'll work on it. I'll email him a synopsis later today and he can get started on it."

"Got it." Genie glanced down at her pad. "I almost forgot; Lanier called again."

"Keep forgetting." He took a beat and added, "Set up a call with Jerry."

"I thought we were canceling the meeting with James and Jerry."

"No James, just Jerry," Continuing to stare out the window, Stangerson squinted, hoping to catch a flash of thigh as Kimberley climbed into her car. "I told Kimberley I'd... On second thought, scratch Jerry," he added as he turned and walked back to his desk.

Kimberley entered her car, slipped on her sunglasses, and turned on the engine. Hands on the wheel, she sat motionless. If Stangerson was to be believed, her life had just changed, been completely transformed. She now lived a new reality, a new life. Taking her phone out of her purse, she called both clients who had appointments later that day. Luckily both went to voicemail, allowing her to leave short uninterrupted messages, explaining that due to unavoidable circumstances she would need to reschedule. She needed time to herself. Time to think. Slipping her phone back in her purse, she again put her hands on the wheel and sat motionless.

If Stangerson was right, she wouldn't have time for a full practice. She could maybe cherry pick a few clients, refer the rest to other therapists. Still, she couldn't make such drastic life changes based on one meeting. She'd wait, see things through for a bit. See where they went. But, she'd have to quickly clear her books if they were indeed going to be in production by March. She should at least start preparing. It seemed real enough. Stangerson's track record was real. 2020 would be the year her life changed, her Cinderella year. Putting her car in reverse, she backed out of the parking place. She'd demand a closed set for the nude scene, she thought as she drove out of the lot.

Chapter 34

L anier had repeatedly called Amber. Message after message had gone unanswered. That on its own wasn't unusual. When Amber or Stangerson called her, they expected Lanier to jump with a smile. The rest of the time she was completely ignored, tolerated, at best. But, she had her uses; she'd helped make connections, passed on vital information—information that could give them the upper hand, doled out timely gossip that either helped with their career moves or helped stifle others. Dunhill Jr. once called her "Truman Capote in drag." She'd be valuable for a time and her calls were returned. She'd then be dismissed. Shut out. Lanier was growing tired of the game, of being the hapless go-between, the messenger, the nobody. Rewarded with a pat on the head, or a few thousand would be doled out as a reluctant thank you. Scraps. Never a seat at the table. Not a producer or executive producer credit, never allowed in the game. Films had been made; production funds had been secured because of her information. Stangerson had once thrown a production assistant title her way. It ran at the end of the crawl, but she had never been allowed on set. A bone tossed to keep her happy, a bogus title while Stangerson became even more successful.

But times had changed. Stangerson was no longer at the top of his game. He was scrambling. He needed a hit. Although the Beverly Hills ex-stripper therapist concept seemed ludicrous to Lanier, worse ideas than that had worked. Stangerson seemed sold on it, saw it as his next *Exposed*. If so, it was due to her. She had introduced him to James, who introduced him to Kimberley. Without the meeting— which she had been the one to set up—there would be no stripper shrink. Connect the dots and Lanier was the prime mover. The same was true with James and his novel. There would be no James without Lanier. And now, again, Lanier was forgotten. Even Jerry, whoever he was, was suddenly further up the food chain. But Stangerson had played it all wrong this time. If he had treated her better, Lanier would have given him, not Amber, the information about The New York Times cover story on James's book, given him the chance to lock up the rights before Amber Lake or Jessica or any of them, but not now, not after, she'd—once again—been ignored, dismissed, discarded.

Now Amber was playing the same game. Ghosting Lanier. "Screw Lanier" could be a board game. Amber took The New York Times information, ran with it and tracked down James. She was now racing to beat Jessica, trying to secure the rights before the Times article ran. Lanier was being cut out without a phone call, not even a thank-you/fuck-you goodbye. Amber was worse than Stangerson, if such a thing was possible. If he found out about the Times piece, he'd swoop in and snatch it right out of Amber's mouth. Amber would never beat him. There was a chance that helping Stangerson would help Lanier, a slim chance, but still—a chance. If nothing else, it would throw a wrench in Amber's plans. That was worth something. Picking up her phone, Lanier took a deep breath and called.

"The Stangerson Group," a chipper female voice answered.

"Can I speak with Genie?" Lanier forced herself to smile. She had read that smiling made for a more pleasant delivery. "Tell her it's

243

Lanier."

"One minute, please." After a few seconds, the cheery voice returned. "I'm sorry, she's busy right now. Can I take a message?"

"Tell her I just need a minute." Lanier tried to project the urgency in her delivery.

"I'll have her call you." The cheeriness faded.

"Tell her it's important. Tell her it's regarding an Amber Lake and Jessica Chandler project."

A moment's hesitation was followed by, "Please hold."

As she waited, Lanier placed the phone on speaker, putting it on the small side table, and stood erect. Preparing for the call, she held her arms out, moved them in a large circle, expanded her chest and breathed deeply.

"What about Amber and Jessica?" Genie asked, bypassing "hello."

Hearing Genie's voice, Lanier quickly picked up the phone and put it to her ear. "Hi Genie. Great to talk to you," she said, forcing her smile to stay put. "Amber and Jessica are both chasing the same project. Falling over each other. Thought Peter might want to know. Beat them to it."

"What project?"

"If I told you that, I wouldn't have much negotiating room."

"This is a negotiation?"

"A friendly one." Lanier paused. "People seem to take what I give them and run off."

"People can be like that."

"I know," Lanier agreed. "I used to run a production company," she threw in to help establish her bona fides.

"Right—I saw your film," Genie emphasized the single digit associated with the word film. "It was... fun."

Lanier flinched at the word "fun." "It was a tough time in the industry," Lanier explained. "We had projects in preproduction. The funding dried up and…"

"Get back to Amber and Jessica."

"Right," Lanier nodded. "If I help Peter land it, I want to be attached." She paused and then asked, "Is he doing a deal with the stripper shrink? I was the one who set up that meeting." Lanier cringed and stopped. She was overstepping, pushing too hard.

"I'll tell Mr. Stangerson you called," Genie announced, signaling an end to the conversation. Her voice was ice, her delivery sharp.

"That came out wrong," Lanier quickly backpaddled. "I was just hoping it went well. Look, if he moves quickly on this, it could be a big project for him. In two weeks, it will be the buzz, it'll be everywhere. Production companies will be falling over themselves and…"

"Either tell me what you're talking about or I have to go, Lanier," Genie interrupted.

Lanier gave up on her smile. She'd already lost Amber. If Genie hung up on her it was checkmate. Stangerson would miss any chance of landing the project, but so would Lanier. "James's novel," she blurted out.

"James's novel?" Genie repeated dismissively. "Old news."

"In two weeks, the book is going to be the cover story in The New York Times Sunday book section," Lanier added quickly, before Genie could hang up the call.

Genie was silent.

"Jessica knows about it," Lanier continued. "She thinks it has a strong female lead. Thinks it would sell."

Genie's eyebrows knitted. "Jessica?" she asked. "That's like having Reese produce it. The book was written by James, a male."

"Go figure," Lanier replied. "But she wants to secure the rights and lock it down before the Times piece comes out. It has a strong female protagonist. Jessica likes that. Amber knows and is racing to beat her to it."

"Who else knows?"

"Only Jessica, Amber—and me" Lanier assured. "Not even James knows—yet."

"Jessica, Amber, you, me, and everyone at The New York Times," Genie corrected. "How did Amber find out?" she asked pointedly.

"It's urgent. I thought Peter should know," Lanier replied, sidestepping Genie's question. "I thought he'd be interested."

"I'll put you through," Genie said after a long pensive pause. "But don't make me regret this."

Lanier smiled. A host of possible responses came to her. She settled on, "Thanks."

Chapter 35

The knock on the door startled James. He never had unannounced visitors. Solicitors seldom visited his apartment; the building didn't seem to hold enough promise. He wouldn't be late on his rent for a couple of weeks, but maybe the word was out. Maybe his landlord was at the door. Or the sheriff's department was there to forcibly evict him. Maybe he'd open the door to officers with guns drawn, James worried, as he slowly headed from his desk towards the front door.

"Good to finally meet you in person, James," said an attractive, dark-haired man, looking to be in his mid-thirties. He was a few inches taller than James, putting him at about 6'1". "Sam," he announced as he shot out his hand in greeting.

James stared at Sam, wondering why he was standing in his doorway. Shaking his outstretched hand, he muttered a soft hello.

"Mind if I come in?" Sam asked. Not waiting for a response, he marched past James into his apartment. "Okay if I sit here?" he asked as he sat at the empty chair next to James's computer.

James continued to stare as Sam sat opened his briefcase and, pulling out two sets of documents, laid them on the table. He looked and acted like an actor, James thought as he studied him, a bit too attractive, his delivery a bit too upbeat, too cheery to be real. "Who are you?" he asked.

"I told you, Sam. Your contracts!" he announced, picking up one of the documents and holding it high.

"What contracts?" James replied. "I don't understand why you're here."

"I'm hurt you don't remember me, James. We talked a few days ago. Crystal Productions. I called to reschedule your meeting with Amber Lake. Then you disappeared."

James emitted a slight sigh of relief. He wasn't getting evicted. Closing the door, he walked back to the table and sat down. "You didn't call to reschedule. You called to cancel the meeting. After I'd flown cross country. There was no mention of rescheduling. And I did not disappear. I left. Came home."

Sam shrugged. "Disappeared, left, same difference. In either case you were gone."

"I think it best if you leave," James said, again standing. "I'm done with Crystal Productions, or Amber Lake, or anything to do with that world. I write novels. That's it. I'm writing now, so if you'll excuse me…"

"Sit down, James. We need to talk. I've got a deal for you. A deal directly from Amber Lake. She's going to make your book into a film. A writer's dream come true, right?"

Still standing, James stared down at Sam. "I'm not falling for this again. I'm not a pinball. Like I said, I'm writing," he added. Walking to the door, he opened it to usher Sam out.

"Amber was busy," Sam explained. "She has a lot of demands on her. She apologizes. Now grow up and let's get down to business." Sam held up both sets of documents. "One is for you and one I take back to Amber. She's already signed them. Amber seldom signs these contracts herself. This project is that important to her."

James remained standing as if rooted. "Contracts?"

"For the rights to your film. You hit the jackpot, Jimmy." James cringed. No one called him Jimmy. "Crystal productions is going to turn your novel into a film produced by and starring Amber Lake," Sam continued. "Like I said, a writer's dream. Come on. Sit down and sign and we're in business."

Walking back over to the table, he sat in his writing chair, picked up one of the contracts and started to read.

"Real as it gets," Sam said, his too-white teeth gleaming. "Just sign and we're in business."

"I can't just sign. I don't even know what the offer is. I have to have an attorney review it."

"An army of attorneys have reviewed it," Sam replied reassuringly. "It's all kosher. Good to go. Just sign on the dotted line and it's a done deal."

"I mean I need *my* lawyer to look at it," James protested.

"You have a lawyer?" Sam asked with a slight chuckle. "I already told you; the lawyers have done their work. Besides, lawyers just cause trouble. That's their job, why they're paid. A word to the wise, Jimmy, steer clear of lawyers whenever you can. Here," he said. Reaching into his bag, he pulled out a pen and handed it to James. "Sign both, you keep one and I'll take the other. Like I said, Amber's already signed it," he added with a wink. "Then we're good to go."

Continuing to stare at the document, James began to tentatively thumb through it. "I really need to have my lawyer give this a look," he said, continuing to pretend he had a lawyer.

"What did I just tell you about lawyers?" Sam asked. Pointing to the contract in James's hand, he added. "It's all kosher. All good. Your first film is an A-list, Crystal Productions project, starring Amber Lake. Things like that don't just happen. You must have been a saint in a previous life. Good karma. You've caught lightning in a bottle," he concluded with a grin.

James's eyebrows furrowed, as he quickly scanned the contract. It was voluminous, filled with legal jargon, but seemed boilerplate. His name and Crystal Productions had been inserted in all of the appropriate spaces. "Where does it outline the compensation?" James asked.

"There are some specifics that need to be added. That happens all the time. Par for the course. But it's basically all there, all good," Sam replied. "I just need you to sign, I'll leave you a copy, take one to Amber and we can get this show on the road. We start shooting ASAP and she wants this out and in theaters by 2021. You are going to be one busy boy in 2020." He checked his phone. "Would love to sit and chat, but Amber needs me back at the office. Amber calls—you go," he added with a clipped laugh. "You'll learn soon enough."

James's first inclination was to ask Sam to leave. Move on and close the door on this annoying chapter of his life. It wasn't going to lead anywhere. He'd dealt with Amber long enough to know that. But Jerry would throw a fit if he found out contracts were offered and James didn't at least explore the possibilities. "I need to study the contract," James said. "I'll have my lawyer give this a quick once-over and get back to you."

Sam's smile faded. "That's not going to work. It has to be now," he insisted. "Amber's waiting on this. She needs it signed. Now! Wait and the whole deal will fall apart. Amber will not be happy and, believe me, you don't want to know what that looks like."

"But I just can't…"

"I thought you might feel that way," Sam interrupted, "particularly after having been jerked around a bit. So," he continued, picking up the other bag, "Amber approved an advance. A cash advance. She's never paid an advance in cash," Sam added, opening the bag and tilting it towards James, showing some of the hundred-dollar bills bound in neat stacks. "Kinda looks like a drug deal," he added with a laugh.

Jamese's eyes widened as he stared at the open bag.

250

"Twenty-five thousand," Sam announced. "Sign and it's yours. Now. Today. Right now. I leave with a signed contract, but the bag and the money stays with you. That's not your full payment obviously, just a good-faith advance. Amber letting you know she's serious."

James continued to silently stare at the bills in the bag.

"All right, thirty-five," Sam replied begrudgingly. "Thirty-five thousand in one-hundred-dollar bills is yours once you sign this."

James's eyes stayed locked on the bills. He could pay his rent. Pay his credit card. Have money in the bank. Breathe.

"All right. Fifty then," Sam cried out as though he was an auctioneer. "But that's it, my final offer. Amber's going to kill me, but you're a tough negotiator."

"Fifty?" James repeated. "Fifty thousand in cash? You're carrying that much cash with you?"

"I came to make a deal. This is not a letter of intent, not just an option. It's a deal." Glancing down at James's computer he added. "Sign your autograph here. I'll leave you your cash and I'll let you get back to your writing. That's what you do, right? Write." He held his pen out towards James. "Take this, sign, and life is good."

Taking the pen, James stared down at the document. "I'll just have an attorney give it a quick review. I'll get it done today. I'll call right away," he added, figuring he could Google lawyers once Sam left. "It's just this is my first..." his voice faded. "A lot of the specifics are left blank."

"It's standard practice, Jimmy," Sam replied, his impatience evident in his tone. "That's how it's done. It will all be filled in later. You'll be more than taken care of." He paused and stared at James. "Is it that you don't trust Amber Lake?" he asked, his face darkening.

"No," James quickly replied.

"Because if you don't," Sam continued, "I need to call Amber right now and let her know you're out and I'm going to have to take back the fifty thousand. Now. Once she finds out you're backing out, who knows what else will happen. You've never seen Amber angry. I wouldn't want to be in your shoes."

"I didn't say I'm out," James insisted. He again stared down at the document. He figured the worst thing that could happen would be that he'd be paid scale—plus the fifty thousand. It wasn't as though he had other offers.

"I'm not here to negotiate, James," Sam snapped. His voice louder, sharper. "Amber sent me to get the agreement signed. If that's not going to happen, let me know now."

"Right. Right," James said, continuing to stare at the bag filled with money. The answer to all of his problems lay in that bag. The fifty was an advance. That would just be the start. That was more money than he'd ever seen. It was going to be an Amber Lake film. Most writers would do that for free. Jerry would be whooping and doing back flips. And his money worries would be over. By simply signing that agreement, his debts would dissolve, his angst disappear.

"Seventy-five," Sam's voice was stern, definitive. "But that's it. My top offer. I have a receipt here," he continued, pulling out another sheet of paper from his bag. "I'll write in seventy-five thousand dollars and sign it. You sign it, then sign the agreement and the seventy-five stays here with you. I'll throw in the bag for free. But like I said, that's it. My final offer. I'm going to start counting and if by the time I get to ten you haven't signed—me, the bag, and your money are out of here. There will be no other offers. Amber will see to it. You'll get no other offers from anyone, not Peter, not anyone." After a brief paus, Sam began, One, two, three…"

James's pulse quickened. His body seemed frozen, cemented in place as he continued to longingly stare at the bag.

"Four, five, six…"

James's eyes widened as he continued to stare.

"Seven, eight, nine…"

All but lunging toward Sam, James snatched the receipt out of his hand, picked up the pen and hurriedly signed. He then signed the mostly unread contract.

Sam shot James a bright, high-beam smile. "That was painless, right?" Picking up a copy of the receipt and signed contract, he put them and his pen back in his bag. "Welcome to Crystal Productions. Amber will be happy. And a happy Amber is always a good thing." Taking out stacks of hundreds from the bag, he counted out seventy-five thousand and stacked them neatly on the table. "I believe these are yours now. They look better there than stuck in the bag. Pulling the rest of the cash out of the bag, he opened his briefcase and stuck the bills in. "Don't worry," he said with a slight grin, "I just had a bit more left to negotiate with. You did good. Amber was hoping I'd get it for twenty-five. I told her you were too shrewd for that." Standing, he stared down at the piles of hundreds on the table. "Looks good, right? It can solve a lot of problems. Think of it as a reset. Like I said, you can keep the bag." Sam extended his hand. "Welcome on board, James."

"Thanks," James replied, a confused expression still locked on his face. Standing unsurely as though getting off an extreme amusement park ride, he shook hands with Sam, whose grip was intentionally too strong.

"The production team will be in touch to review next steps. Amber will probably call you to welcome you on board—that's rare, so show appreciation," Sam instructed. "I'll let myself out," he said as he headed towards the door. Pausing, he scanned James's living room. Turning towards James, he grinned. "Maybe time for a new apartment, eh?" Then, shooting James an actor's wink, he exited.

Chapter 36

James called up his pirated copy of Final Draft and stared at the screen. It was difficult to concentrate. Too much had happened too quickly. Everything had changed. There was no more money angst. No more wondering how he was going to pay his rent, no dreading having to start a nine-to-five sentence as an ad copywriter. His book was going to be an Amber Lake film. Sam had followed up with an email informing him that in April they'd start scouting locations. Shooting was scheduled for mid-June. It would shoot in 2020 and be released in 2021. Amber agreed to give him a first crack at the screenplay but was clear that she needed it ASAP. If his version didn't work, it would be passed on to other writers. At the very least, he'd get paid for the attempt, maybe get partial screenplay credit. He had no desire to write films, but it was worth giving it a try. It would mean more money, more free time to write his next novel. A luxury he had never experienced.

But none of it felt real. He'd be foolish to relax or let his guard down,

James thought as he glanced at the clock on the wall. He knew who he was dealing with. Knew how they worked. He glanced down at the sound of his phone. Lanier was calling. She was relentless, he thought, as he let the call go to voicemail. He had stopped listening to her messages. They were rantings, accusations, and threats. Lanier's naked Id turned loose was not pretty. Again glancing at his phone, he picked it up. It would soon be time to put an end to it. He braced himself as he listened to her voicemail message.

"James, it's Lanier." Her voice was upbeat, cheery, uncharacteristically friendly. "Listen, I'm sorry for some of my earlier messages. It's been a stressful time. I know I can be—overly enthusiastic. Ignore them. I have some good news. Great news. Wonderful news. I don't want to leave it on voicemail. I want to tell you directly. Call me. And, again, sorry for the other messages. Call me." There was a slight pause and she ended with, "It's really great news, James. Congratulations. You deserve it."

James frowned as he put the phone down on his desk. It was a very uncharacteristic Lanier message. No rants or threats. He had never heard that tone in her voice, at least not when she was addressing him. It was obviously some kind of game, a ploy, a trap—a way to get him to call her back so she could let loose with a full fury screeching banshee barrage of rants.

But, what if it was good news? How much more good news could he take, he thought with a muted laugh. He was in no mood to talk to Lanier. He'd deal with her later. Turning back towards his laptop, he placed his hands on the keyboard and stared at the empty page on the screen. Nothing came. Again he stared at his phone. After a few motionless minutes, he let out a sigh. Best get it over with, he thought. Hesitantly picking up the phone, he took a breath and called.

"James," Lanier's voice sounded upbeat, veering toward jubilant. "I'm so happy you called. I'm sorry for those other messages. It was all that dealing with Peter and Amber. They can be crazy making. I'm sorry I ever introduced you to them. But that's all behind us now."

"I don't follow." James's body tensed, preparing for the real Lanier to surface.

"Forget them," she continued, talking in her rapid scattershot delivery. "They're history. Both going down in flames. Over. Done. But I have news. Great, great news."

"What news?"

"Incredible news that will change your life forever."

"What news?" James repeated his voice more insistent.

"I can't tell you over the phone," Lanier's voice dropped to a deep whisper. "It's important. Confidential. We need to meet now."

"Can't. I'm back in L.A.," James explained.

"I know," she replied. "So am I. Perfect. Makes it easier. We'll meet at the Polo Lounge in an hour and a half."

James's brows knitted, wondering how she knew he was back, or that he'd gone, or if it was another ploy. "I can't," he repeated, envisioning another wasted meeting with him again paying to watch Lanier drink herself into a stupor.

"But we have to meet," Lanier insisted, her voice raising with tinges of the familiar irritation and condescension. "We'll meet at the Polo Lounge and I'll tell you the great news and we'll come up with a plan."

"I can't meet, Lanier." It felt good not to cower, to no longer try and placate her demands, her craziness.

"James," Lanier's voice was turning terse. "I'm telling you I have very good news—amazing news to give you, but I'm not going to give it to you over the phone."

"I have to go."

"Wait," Lanier cried, changing course, her voice again softening. This was not the James she was used to. "I understand. I'm interrupting your writing, right? That's why you're being so rude. You're a writer. A very good writer. All right then, I don't want to interrupt

256

your writing. Let's meet in the evening. Let's meet for dinner."

"I can't meet, Lanier," he said again. He wanted to say won't as opposed to can't, but he wasn't quite there yet.

"Listen, James," Lanier snapped. She paused. There was silence as she took deep breaths and composed herself. "I understand," she continued. "Alright then, what I am going to tell you is strictly confidential, between us, and when I land you this deal, I want to be brought on board as a producer, with a producer's fee, not just the title."

James thought of breaking the news to Lanier. Telling her that she was too late, that he'd already signed with Crystal Productions. But then he'd be left to deal with a completely out of control Lanier. Best wait. Instead, he simply replied, "I've got to go."

"You think it's Stangerson," Lanier forged on. "Of course you don't want to work with Stangerson," Lanier agreed. "Who does? You don't want to work with Peter or Amber." After a pause, she emphatically announced, "It's Jessica. I'm talking Jessica."

James stared down at his phone, a look of confusion on his face. "Jessica?"

"Yes, Jessica," Lanier repeated, her voice impatient, admonishing, as though she was speaking to a very dense four-year-old. "Chandler. Jessica Chandler! She wants your book. Her company wants to buy the rights, wants to make it into a film. She loves the female protagonist. She wants to go into production this summer. It's a lock."

"Jessica Chandler?" James asked, thrown by the turn the conversation had taken. He paused. "But I'm a male. I'm a male writer."

"Go figure." Lanier shrugged. "She wants it anyway. Everything has changed, and we need to come up with a game plan—quickly. That's why we have to meet. Today. This is a done deal. A slam dunk. And that's just one piece of good news."

James remained silent, still trying to comprehend the first piece.

Lanier again took a deep breath and slowly exhaled as she considered her next moves. She'd told him about Jessica. That was already out. No sense holding back. She'd show all her cards. Boast a winning hand and reel him in. "And then there's the Times. The New York Times," she continued, slowly enunciating each syllable.

"What?" James stood as though being propelled up.

"The New York Times, James."

"The New York Times is reviewing my novel?"

"Not a review," Lanier replied emphatically. "A feature. A cover-page feature story in their Sunday book section."

"What?" James repeated incredulously. Again sitting down, he place his hand on the table as if to steady himself.

Lanier grinned. She'd hooked him. Pausing, she ran various scenarios in her mind, searching for the most advantageous. "I gave them the book," she lied. "The New York Times—I got the book to them. I thought the book deserved a shot. You deserved a shot. I hope that's okay with you," she added with a grin. Since she was already in the deep end, she figured she might as well dive. "I know one of the writers there," she continued with her fictionalized account, "and I gave her my can't-miss pitch. Your publisher probably doesn't know yet. Unless it's one of the big five, the Times doesn't care about publishers. They figure small publishers are more of a nuisance than a help. It's running in a couple of weeks." Lanier paused. "This discussion should really take place in person."

James ran his hands through his hair. Holding out his phone he stared at it, as though at a foreign object. He then placed the phone on the coffee table, put it on speaker and, leaning back, closed his eyes. "But... I don't get it. I don't get how all of this is happening."

"The nature of the beast," Lanier replied, a shrug in her voice. "When it moves, it moves at warp speed and you have to be ready. I talked to Jessica," she said, continuing to fabricate her story as she spoke. "She wants to secure the rights so she can announce pre-production the same week that the article runs. She not only wants to produce—she wants to star." Lanier again paused, letting the last sentence linger.

"As soon as Peter and Amber find out they'll be after you. Try and lock the rights down for peanuts. They'll smell blood. I know them. That's how they work. Hopefully you've been avoiding their calls as successfully as you have mine," she added with a slight jab. "Do not talk to them, James. They are out to fuck you, pardon my French. They know what's happening and then want to lock your book down for a song and beat Jessica to it."

James paused, scowling as he stared at the phone. "They both know —about the Times piece? But I didn't even know." He took a pensive pause. "How did they find out?" he asked, already knowing the answer.

"Writers are low man on the totem pole in the film world," Lanier explained, sidestepping the question. "But we're going to change that, you and me—and Jessica. They know because Peter and Amber are players. They have their spies. Information is power. But I knew first because I set it up. If you had taken my calls you would have known, and Jessica would be ready to announce your deal. That can still happen, but we have to move quickly—now! I can wrap this deal up with Jessica for you in a day or two. We can then release a joint press release. Go out of the gate guns blazing. But," she added, "I've worked hard on this and need to protect myself. I'm going to write up a letter of agreement; nothing elaborate, a short, basic, concise agreement that explains our working relationship. That's why we have to meet—today."

"Jessica Chandler wants to produce a film based on my novel?"

"Isn't that what I just told you? Are you deaf?" Lanier snapped, her impatience and frustration rising to the surface. "Stay with me, James. Not only produce it—star in it. And Jessica has lined up some other names to cast. Big names. A-list names. She says you've created some wonderful strong female characters. I've put this together for you. All we need to do now is tie it up with a bow. It's a done deal," Lanier declared. "But we need to meet. Now!" she added insistently. "We need to cement this and good riddance to Peter and Amber. Maybe we'll invite them to the premier," she added with a clipped laugh. "Dinner, tonight—7:30. The Polo Lounge or wherever you want. On me," she concluded.

James sat back against his chair and stared at the wall. "Amber knows?" he asked with a wince.

"Forget who knows," Lanier said impatiently. "All that matters is that your novel is going to be featured in The New York Times and Jessica is going to produce and star in the film. Tonight, James. We have to meet tonight. This can't wait."

"And Jerry? He knows?"

Lanier replied with a loud groan. She was about to snap but stopped herself. Jerry was a wild card. If Jerry knew and didn't tell him, if James believed Jerry had lied, that could help. There would be no more allegiance on James's part. No matter whose camp Jerry was in now, James would see him as a traitor. One less problem. "Of course Jerry knew." Lanier again took a beat and added, "I told him."

"You told Jerry and you didn't tell me?" James asked accusingly.

"How was I supposed to tell you?" Lanier snapped. "You weren't taking my calls, remember? You were ignoring me. You didn't even tell me you'd left New York. I told Jerry and asked him to have you call me and tell you about Jessica and The New York Times." After a beat, she added, "I guess he didn't." She smiled, thinking she had set it all up rather nicely.

"And you told Peter and Amber?"

Lanier began to pace to keep herself centered. James was pushing it with his useless barrage of questions. "I'm working with Jessica on this. Why would I tell them?" she asked defensively. "Jerry probably made a beeline to both of them trying to see what deal he could make, trying to play them against each other—and not tell you. He's a piece of work. You need to get away from all of them," Lanier declared. "Jessica is good people. I've set it up. We'll meet tonight," she ordered. "I'll bring a short letter of agreement. We'll order champagne to toast. We'll make a deal and you'll start your new life. 2020 is your year James—because of me."

Continuing to stare at the wall, James blinked hard, as though trying to focus. "I can't." His voice was cold, distant.

"James, don't fuck this up," Lanier demanded. "You don't want to piss me off. Believe me. I have an offer on the table and…"

Disconnecting the call, James looked down at his phone. A furious text arrived from Lanier. "You do not want to fuck with me James. Call me back. Now." There was too much information to process. Too many emotions to take in. He had signed with Crystal Productions. Had a bag filled with cash in his bedroom to prove it. If Lanier was telling the truth, a cover story on his book was coming out in The New York Times and Jessica Chandler was ready to offer him a film deal. Scenarios he wouldn't have had the audacity to fantasize about were now his reality. They all knew about Jessica and The New York Times—Amber, Stangerson, Jerry. They all knew and intentionally kept him in the dark. Instead of feeling exuberant, all he felt was alone, duped, betrayed.

Chapter 37

Genie walked down the hall to Stangerson's office. She entered without knocking. "News from the front."

Stangerson looked up, one eyebrow raised. "Good news or bad news?"

"I just spoke to Lanier."

Stangerson's nose flared as though he smelled rotten fish. He brushed his hand in front of his face waving it away.

"She says it's urgent. She has to talk to you."

"That's your news?"

Genie laughed. Walking over, she sat in the chair facing Stangerson's desk. "I have some real news."

Stangerson stared impatiently.

"James signed a deal with Amber Lake. They're in preproduction. They're rushing it. They start shooting in May or June."

"Oh, that," Stangerson replied dismissively. "Probably just a letter of intent. Amber papers the city with them. That won't hold. She just wants to keep James in her hip pocket in case the project turns out to be anything. Jerry is setting up a meeting with James and…"

"No letter of intent," Genie explained with a shake of her head. "James signed contracts. It's a done deal."

Stangerson's stare hardened, as though wondering whether to believe her. "Fuck," he spat. "Lanier told you that?"

Genie shook her head. "Not Lanier. She's in the dark. She thinks she's still in the game. Thinks she's pitting you against Amber and Jessica and that somehow she'll win. Completely in the dark," Genie repeated. "It was Amber who made sure I got the news. Now that she's signed James, she wanted me to know. If I get the news— you'll get the news. The only upside is that Amber beat Jessica too."

"Jessica?" Stangerson's eyes widened. "How did Jessica get in the picture?"

"She found out about The New York Times piece, smelled blood."

"What New York Times piece?" Stangerson said in a near yell. "Why didn't I know about The New York Times piece?" he added staring accusingly at Genie.

"I didn't know," Genie replied, somewhat sheepishly. "Sounds like Lanier was somehow involved, or she made it up and told a convincing enough story to interest Jessica."

"Fuck!" he repeated, his voice louder, angrier.

"You didn't want the book five minutes ago," Genie reminded him. "Let it go."

Stangerson shook his head. "Neither did Amber or Jessica. I want it now. Fuck!" he repeated. "Get Jerry on the phone."

"Why?" Genie asked. "What for? It's a done deal. Move on. Forget James's novel. It was Kimberley you were interested in anyway. The whole, blonde, ex-stripper, Beverly Hills, psychotherapist to the stars, dishes secrets."

263

Stangerson replied with a resigned sigh. Taking a deep breath, he opened Chrome on his computer and pulled up Kimberley's photos. "Ex-hooker, stripper nymphomaniac Beverly Hills psychotherapist," he corrected. "That has a better ring." He glanced up at Genie, eyebrows furrowed. "So Amber wins?"

Genie leaned in towards Stangerson. "You win," she insisted. "Kimberley will get you more traction than a book featured in The New York Times book section. Nobody reads The New York Times book section. Nobody reads books. Not anymore. Kimberley is reality TV fodder. From the big screen to streaming. Amber did you a favor."

Stangerson stared at the Amber Lake photo on his wall. Placing his hands together as though in prayer, he grinned. "We can begin shooting some real-life, behind-the-scenes shots with Kimberley. Hot stuff. Racy stuff. We can rush into production by May. Start with a full-frontal nude scene. Maybe pretend it was real—found footage that was secretly taped like what happened to that ESPN gal. We can pretend we're furious. That we don't want it distributed or seen. That we're suing whoever released the footage. Not a bad way to start a buzz."

Genie smiled. Stangerson was back. "Kimberley's probably wondering why we haven't gotten back to her. She's probably anxious. Wondering if plans have changed—if it's really going to happen."

"I like my actors anxious."

Genie laughed. Standing, she headed towards the door. She paused and turning back asked, "You still want me to call Jerry?"

Stangerson shook his head. "Leave him out there spinning. Or," Stangerson paused. Putting his hands together, he rested his chin on his fingers. "Or," he repeated, "call him and tell him he's on board. Tell him I've lost interest in the book and I'm hiring him to work on the Kimberley project. Tell him it's green-lighted. It's a go."

Genie stared at him questioningly.

"Tell Jerry that and first thing he'll do is call James," Stangerson continued. "Amber will know in a second. It will make her wonder. Maybe she picked the wrong horse." Stangerson stared at Amber's photo, his smile growing.

Chapter 38

Walking into Circle K Tavern, James sat down at his regular table. He wasn't hungry but felt he should eat. He never drank alcohol during the day but wanted a beer.

"Hey, long time no see." He looked up and saw Violet smiling down at him. "Where's your partner?"

James shrugged. "Not sure we're partners anymore."

"What happened? Were you right? Did the film deal fall through? Another Hollywood horror story?"

James shook his head. His inclination was to agree, to tell her it had turned out to be just one more dead end street. It would then make sense for him to be so down, depressed. "No, I signed the deal." He looked up at her with a lost questioning expression. "Amber Lake is going to produce and star in the film. Nicole Kidman might costar."

Violet's eyes widened. "You're kidding."

James shrugged and shook his head.

"That's awesome. Amazing. Congratulations." She paused. "Then why so down?"

Again James shrugged. "Long story."

Violet frowned and stared down at him. "Did they screw you over —on the deal?"

James shook his head. "It's a good deal. At least I think it's a good deal. Who knows? I'm out of my depth. Amber's rushing the project. We're in preproduction. They're starting to scout locations now. Principal photography starts mid-May."

"May? Wow. 2020 is your year," Violet said with a high-beam smile. "Come on. Get excited! Whatever you're ordering is on me. A congratulatory meal."

"Thanks. Appreciated. But you don't have to do that. For the first time in my life, money is no object."

"There's a sentence I've never used," Violet replied with a laugh. "It's on me anyway," she insisted. "But I still don't get it, you should be up, excited. I'd be telling everyone. I'd be stopping strangers in the street, standing on the table screaming out the news."

"Like I said, long story."

"I like long stories."

"You'd probably be bored by this one." James looked up and smiled. "Besides, I'm not a very good storyteller."

"You better be a good storyteller," she replied. "You're a writer. Your job is telling stories."

"A writer—not a talker."

"Something to work on."

James laughed. "You're right." He paused and took a breath. "Maybe we could get coffee, or dinner, and I could practice—talking. My treat. Think of it as payment for you teaching me to talk."

After a beat, she added, "I'm off at five."

James smiled. "Great," he replied. "I think I'll pass on ordering anything right now," he said as he stood. "How about I meet you back here at five?"

"Okay, but you're missing a free congratulatory meal."

"See you at five." His smile broadened as he turned and walked towards the door.

Chapter 39

At five sharp, James returned to the Circle K. He waited at the bar until Violet finished her shift.

Waving goodbye to one of the waitresses, Violet slipped on her sweater and walked towards him. "You're punctual," she said, staring up at the clock. "I like that. Where to?"

"A secret."

Violet smiled. "I like secrets."

"So, let me guess," James said as they exited. "You're originally from the Midwest and you came to L.A. to make it as an actress. Right?"

"You're right geographically. I'm from Michigan. You lose points on the actress bit. I'm at USC studying developmental psychology. Been here for about four months. The Circle K helps pay the bills. Still finding my way here."

'You're going to be a psychologist. Perfect, Jerry can land you a lead in a movie."

Violet stared quizzically.

"A joke. Long story," James explained. "I'll fill you in at the restaurant. There's a lobster place right by the pier. How about we go there?"

"Lobster? Sounds expensive."

"Like I said, money is no object!" he declared overly-dramatically as he walked to his car and opened the passenger door for Violet. He paused and smiled. "I'm trying to practice saying that sentence until I can somewhat believe it."

"Must feel good," she said as she climbed into the passenger's seat.

"I can't imagine money being no object. Not really." Turning on the ignition, he turned towards her. "Bet you were the high school prom queen."

Violet blushed and looked down.

"You're kidding."

"Probably the high point of my life, right?" Violet looked up with a slight grimace. "All downhill from there."

"I don't think I've ever dated a prom queen."

"Is this a date?" Violet asked, a teasing lilt in her voice.

"The restaurant's not far," he explained, sidestepping the question, as he drove down Wilshire towards the beach. "Once you finish school, maybe you can take Amber as your first client. God knows she could use therapy."

"Amazing," Violet said, "You're on a fist name basis with Amber Lake."

"It's fucking strange."

"Great is what it is," she corrected. "Maybe you can get me an autographed photo."

"I might never hear from her again, for all I know. That's how these people work. You think you're close and then everything comes crashing down. It always has in the past."

"But you said you signed a deal. Got upfront money."

James nodded. "I still don't believe it. I keep thinking I should hold on to it. That any minute they're going to come to my door demanding I give it back."

Violet shook her head. "It's yours. Your money now." After a beat, she added, "It must be good—your book. For all this to happen, it must be a good novel. I need to buy a copy. Maybe I could get the author to sign it."

"If you promise not to tell the author, I'll get you a copy for free." James paused. "To be honest, I can't tell if any one of them has ever read my book. It's as though everything that's happened has nothing to do with my book. It seems to be about everything but my book. Everyone's trying to one-up everyone else. Amber's trying to screw Stangerson and he's trying to beat Jessica…"

"Jessica?"

"Chandler."

"You know Jessica Chandler?"

James shook his head. "I don't even know how she got into the picture. None of it makes any sense."

"Wow." She stared down pensively, trying to take it all in.

"To be honest, I don't have a clue what I'm doing. Things just seem to be happening. All I know is that I signed a contract, which I now think I was tricked into, and now Jessica Chandler's interested, and Peter Stangerson is very angry at me."

"Tricked how?" Violet asked. "Isn't it a good deal?"

"Well, it's the best deal I've ever had," he answered with a forced laugh. "Not to mention it's the only deal I ever had. Yeah," he nodded, as though settling an argument with himself. "I think it's a good deal. It's both. It's a good deal and I was tricked," he said. "Let's talk about something else."

271

"But this is huge," Violet declared. "Life changing. Opportunities like this don't come to people, at least not to people I know, and you're acting like…" She stopped. "Sorry. If you don't want to talk about it, that's fine."

"You're right," James nodded as he pulled into a parking place. "I should be acting like it's Christmas, New Year's, and my birthday rolled into one. It's just… yeah I have this deal, but…" his voice trailed off. He glanced at Violet and added, "Like I said, I don't even think anyone's read my book. They just want it because they think other people want it. Maybe that's just how it works. None of it makes sense." He paused, shaking his head as he turned off the engine. "The restaurant is right over there. Let's have dinner and talk about something else."

"Speaking of something else," Violet grinned as she picked up her bag and pulled out a plastic baggy which contained two expertly rolled joints.

James stared at the bag and smiled. "You come prepared."

"Maybe we can go for a walk," Violet suggested, holding up the baggy. "Before dinner."

"Sure, or… I live close by." He paused and slightly grimaced, hoping he wasn't pushing it.

Violet looked at James. An eyebrow raised. "Cool." She took a beat. "More comfortable than getting stoned while wandering the streets."

James turned and pointed east. "I live just a couple of blocks away."

"You can walk to the beach."

"Yep, I can walk to the beach, which is cool, but my apartment's pretty small. It's small—and messy."

"Now you have an Amber Lake film in preproduction. So soon you'll have a big messy apartment."

James stared down at the baggy with a laugh. "You've been smoking too much of that."

"I can sense these things. My friends say I'm psychic."

"Psychic? You were made for L.A."

"It's true. I pick up things... sometimes. So," she asked looking at him and pulling a joint out of the bag. "Whatdayasay, a before dinner joint?"

Laughing, he started up his car. "But maybe wait until we get to my place. I'm not used to it being legal. Still makes me paranoid, driving around with it." James pulled out of the parking place and drove the few blocks to Second Street and California. "It's street parking," he explained apologetically as he parked the car in front of his apartment building. Exiting the car, James led Violet to his apartment door. Stopping, he turned towards her. "Wait here for a couple of secs, okay?"

"Don't worry," Violet assured him. "It's fine. My place is a mess most of the time."

"Just a couple of seconds," he repeated. Opening the door, he entered, shutting the door behind him. He quickly moved through his apartment, hurriedly picking up clothes, papers, books and shoving them into his closet. He stashed the dirty dishes into a paper bag and, not knowing where to put them, stuffed them into the closet as well. Luckily he'd made his bed. He then returned to the front door and opening it said, "Well, I think this is as good as it gets."

Violet smiled and entered. "This is nice." She walked over to the couch and sat down. "Cozy. So this is what a writer's lair looks like, huh?"

"This is what an unsuccessful, struggling writer's lair looks like," he corrected. "I'm sure other writers' lairs look very different."

"But you're not an unsuccessful and struggling writer. Not anymore." She paused and glanced around the apartment. "You're the most successful writer I know."

James laughed. "You need to get out more. You want something to drink? Water? Sparkling water? A coke? A beer?"

273

Violet smiled. "Role reversal. You're serving me. I like that. Maybe a beer."

James nodded, walked into the kitchen, and returned with two open beer bottles. Handing one to Violet, he sat in the chair opposite her and raised his beer. "Cheers."

"Cheers," she echoed, taking a drink. She leaned towards the coffee table to put the drink down. "You have a coaster I can put this on?"

James shrugged. "It's okay. You can just put it on the table."

Violet shook her head, stood up and walked to the kitchen.

James watched, his eyes following her as she moved. He studied her body. Her shape. He looked at her as he never had before. She was in his home. All of the dynamics had changed. She was no longer someone he casually flirted with. She was now here, in his world. An anticipatory thrill shot through him.

Violet returned with two paper towels, handed one to James, and folding hers, laid it on the table and placed her beer on top of it. Sitting down, she picked up her purse, opened it, took out the plastic baggie and pulled out a joint. Grinning, she held it up like a prize. She then took out a book of matches, lit the joint and placed the used match on the paper towel. Taking a long hit, she leaned towards James and held it out.

"Thanks." James reached for the joint; he felt an electric rush as their hands grazed. "Music?"

"Sure. You pick."

Walking over to his albums, his eyebrows furrowed, he fingered through them.

"Vinyl," Violet said as she watched him. "How cool."

"Old school," James replied with a nod. "I spend way too much on these. Give me some help here. A genre, an era, something. As long as it's not disco."

"Play disco," she ordered with a laugh.

"You're no help at all." Putting the joint to his mouth, he turned away from Violet and pretended to inhale. He then turned and handed it back. He hadn't smoked pot in years. He and the drug had not left on good terms. It made him paranoid, anxious. The highs lasted longer than he liked. He'd still feel stoned the next day. Not pleasantly stoned, but woozy, anxious, light-headed. When he decided to stop, his decision made his friends uncomfortable. They would egg him on, try to get him to take a hit, as though his abstaining somehow diminished their enjoyment. Others would choose not to smoke if he didn't, making James feel he had ruined their time.

The easiest course was simply to pretend he was smoking along with them. Then no one felt awkward or judged, everyone was in it together. If he had told Violet he didn't smoke, chances were she wouldn't have lit the joint—the dynamics would have changed. He picked up an album and put it on the turntable. He then walked back towards Violet and handed her the joint. "So, tell me about you," James asked, as he picked up his beer and took a sip.

She shrugged. "I already did. I'm from Michigan. A small town where people get married young and have kids. I'm not putting that down." She gave a slight frown. "That's cool. But not what I wanted. At first I thought I wanted to try acting. I did theatre back home and everyone was telling me I should—a lot of people screw up their lives making choices like that, doing what people say they should. Then I took a psych class and that opened up another world. Gave me a direction. I think I'd be good. Think I could help."

"Of course you'd be good," James agreed. "So you're the one pretty girl who came to L.A. not to be an actress?"

After a pause, she asked, "You think I'm pretty?"

James took a beat. "Beautiful."

"Beautiful?" Violet repeated thoughtfully. Holding out the joint she stared at it. "This stuff must be more powerful that I thought."

James looked down, an embarrassed expression on his face. "You leave some broken-hearted guy back home?"

She shrugged as she again put the joint to her lips and inhaled. "He wanted to do what people do there—marriage, kids."

"What happened?"

"This an interrogation?"

James winced. "Sorry. I worked as a journalist for a while. I fall into interview mode a bit too easily. Didn't mean to pry."

She took another hit. "I'm smoking the whole thing," she said, holding the joint up towards James. "Here."

James shook his head. He held up his beer. "I'm good. Just wanted a couple of hits. I react pretty strongly to it."

"You sure?" she asked. "This stuff is strong." She paused and then smiled. "This how you Hollywood-types work? Lure unsuspecting females into your home and get them stoned?"

"We can go out—go to dinner," he hurriedly said, not sure if she was being serious or sarcastic.

"Relax," she replied with a smile. "I was kidding. "I wouldn't be here if I didn't want to be." She paused. "My decisions have been known to get me into trouble." She laughed as she took a hit. "If you don't want anymore, I'm going to put this out. I'm pretty stoned already."

James nodded. "What kind of trouble?"

"Girl trouble." Lying back, she kicked off her shoes and stretched her legs on the couch, "And don't ask what kind of girl trouble."

"What kind of girl trouble?"

Violet laughed. "The kind where a pair of track shoes comes in handy." Sitting up she curled her legs under her, cat-like, and studied James. She reached over, picked up the joint, and relit it. "One more hit. Sure you don't want any more?"

James nodded. He stood and walked towards the record player. "Okay if I put something else on?"

"Sure. But I'm a bit buzzed. Pick something a bit dreamy. Nothing too loud. No metal."

Picking up a copy of Debussy's "Afternoon of a Fawn," he placed it on the turntable.

"Perfect." Violet's eyes widening as she recognized the music. "My mom used to play Debussy when I was growing up. She was a pianist—Debussy, Chopin, Beethoven."

"What a cool way to grow up."

"It was," she agreed. "I used to play," she added, as though making an admission. "Formed a band. We played a few gigs, were gaining momentum locally. Then everything fizzled. Blew up. I had my own almost famous Hollywood story before I ever got to Hollywood," she added with a slight laugh.

"I'd like to hear it, your music." After a beat he added, "Maybe I can help."

Violet shook her head. "Past history," she replied. Her tone was sharp, firm, signaling that was not a road she wanted to go down. "One final hit," she announced, again lighting the joint and putting it to her mouth. Inhaling deeply, she reached out, handing it to James.

Putting it to his lips, he again pretended to inhale, acting as though he was holding the smoke in his lungs. He silently counted to seven and then made a show of a loud exhale and handed it back to Violet.

She looked up at James and smiled. "I'm stoned. Okay if I put it out?"

"Again?"

Violet laughed as she put out the joint. Lying back, she let her body go limp, rag doll-like. "God am I stoned. Beer and dope before eating, haven't done that in a while. I don't think we're going to make it to dinner." Turning towards James she smiled. "At least not anytime soon."

James returned her smile, unsure whether she was simply too stoned to go out or signaling something else.

Violet sat up a bit and rested on her elbows. "I was pretty sure we weren't going to make it to dinner when I decided to come here."

James continued to stare with the anticipatory look of an animal not quite sure of its next move.

"Yep," Violet added and looked towards the door to James's bedroom.

"It's kinda messy," he apologized, nervously glancing at his bedroom door, thankful he had shut it before letting her into the apartment.

"Messy can be fun."

James's eyes widened as he stared at the closed door. "Give me a sec." Standing, he quickly headed towards his bedroom.

"Take your time." Closing her eyes, she lied back. "I'm not going anywhere."

Chapter 40

James awoke with a start and checked the clock on his nightstand which read ten after eight. They had both drifted off. He turned and stared at Violet who was lying on her side, her back to him. He studied the curves of her body, the soft roundness of her shoulders, the delicacy of her neck. She was beautiful naked. He stared in near disbelief that she was there, in his room, on his bed. He edged towards her and slowly reaching his hand around her body cupped her right breast, feeling the softness in his hand. He spoke softly. "We're going to miss dinner altogether if we don't hurry,"

Violet slowly stirred and turned towards him, smiled. "It's you."

"It is."

She stretched as she slid upright in bed. "I thought we might miss dinner."

"We still have a shot if we hurry." He paused and with an embarrassed grin, admitted, "I wasn't sure."

She nodded, looking at James with the hint of a smile on her lips. "See, there are two types of guys. One would have been plotting how to get me in bed the minute we decided to go out and the second wouldn't be sure. I like the second type."

James laughed. "I'm a dope. Come on. We can still grab dinner."

"We could do takeout. I'm easy." She paused and gave a short laugh. "That didn't come out right. But, speaking of…" her voice trailed off as she moved towards James, gently pushing him until he was lying on his back. Taking his erect penis in her hand, she squeezed. She moved her body up and over his, until she was straddling him. Stopping mid-motion, she glanced down at her purse on the floor. "Shit. I put the rubbers back in my purse."

James held her arms. "Let me inside. Just for a second. I just want to feel you without… I promise I won't…"

Violet frowned and pulled away. "Don't be an idiot." Jumping off of the bed she hurried to her purse and, pulling out a small plastic package, bit the edge and ripped it open. Again climbing on the bed, she pulled the condom out of the package and slid it down James's erect penis.

James stared, somewhat startled at the precise clockwork. "Like a pro."

"Hey!" Violet cried, glancing up at him.

"Wrong! Came out wrong. That's not what I mean. I just mean you're so prepared, joints, condoms…"

"Can't rely on guys for that. Now, no more talking. At least not about that." Again straddling James, she slowly pressed her body down guiding him inside. He looked up, his eyes widening, mesmerized by her, the sensation, the way her hair fell, draping her face, gently landing on her full breasts which moved towards him. James pushed his body up, deeper inside of her. She smiled and squeezing, bent down kissing him on the lips, first gently and then more firmly. Her lips moved down to his ear, tracing the outline with her tongue. Sitting up she looked down at James as her body rocked rhythmically. James closed his eyes, trying to minimize the impact of the visual, to prolong the moment. Letting go, he gave way with a prolonged shudder. "God!" Opening his eyes, he frowned as he sank into the bed. "Sorry!" he apologized. "I usually… don't… I usually last longer."

Violet laughed. "I'll take that as a compliment. Okay. Now dinner." She took a beat and pointedly added, "I'll take my turn next time. Come on," she ordered as she climbed off him. "We still have time. Get dressed. I'm starving."

Chapter 41

Violet and James followed the hostess to their table, handing them their menus. she politely but adamantly explained that the kitchen was closing. The two nodded and quickly ordered.

Violet smiled as the hostess exited. "We're lucky they seated us. I know what kitchens can be like and there can be hell to pay if a waiter or hostess seats someone after the kitchen is set to close. They probably heard about your film deal. Want to make new Hollywood royalty happy."

"Yeah, right."

"It's true," Violet continued with an authoritative nod. "I should probably get a picture. That way, when people don't believe I went to dinner with you, I can take it out as proof."

"It's going to be more than just one dinner, isn't it?"

Violet smiled. "Is it?"

"It better be," James took a beat. "You're the first girl I really wanted to spend time with in a while."

"Girl?"

"Woman," James quickly corrected. "Is that right? What is the correct noun? What is it you people like to be called now? I can't keep up."

"Us people?"

James laughed. "I'm going to stop while I'm behind." He took another sip. "It's strange—2020 was just going to be another year of me trying to survive, slogging through as an ad copy writer, and working on my novel in the evenings. Now it's a whirlwind. I've got a film deal with Amber Lake and all of this travel coming up and..." he paused. "And now all I want to do is stay home, write, and have more dinners with you."

"You have a whole new life," Violet said. "When do you leave?"

James pulled out his phone and checked the dates. "It starts in March. There is the London book fair on March 10th. They want to start the buzz or the film there. Then Amber wants to do some preliminary preproduction work in Austin. She has some meetings set at South by Southwest and wants me and the director to be there." Glancing up, he added, "I don't know who she's choosing to direct but it's definitely not Stangerson."

"South by Southwest, how cool. I've always wanted to go to that."

James nodded, as the waitress came with their drinks. Taking a sip, he sat back and smiled. "Maybe I could bring you."

"That would probably be pushing it—you're just starting on the project."

He again stared down and nodded. "It all sounds so unreal."

"What else?"

"We're going to Coachella in April. Then on May 8th we're supposed to see the Stones in San Diego, backstage VIP, the whole bit. Not sure what any of that has to do with the film. I think Amber just likes to show the type of access she has. Likes to impress people—which it will. Then Cannes." He glanced up, an almost embarrassed expression on his face. "Like I said, unreal. It sounds pretentious even saying it."

"Cannes? Wow!" Violet's eyes widened. "It's like a fairy tale. You're the male Cinderella."

James winced. "Let's come up with another metaphor."

"I like that one," she replied with a smile. "Where else?"

"Amber says we're going to start production on June 20th," James continued. "And then in late July we're going to Comic-Con. There are talks about her being featured in some sci-fi film. For some reason, she wants to announce our project there. I don't see how my novel ties in with Comic-Con," James added with a shrug.

Violet picked up her wine glass and smiling, sat back in her chair. "Sounds like Amber Lake is keeping you close. I bet she has a crush on you."

"I think she barely tolerates me. I'm serious," James said with a frown.

Violet laughed. "I tried to get tickets to Coachella, one of the Rage Against the Machine nights. No luck."

James leaned towards her. "Come with me. I'm sure I can convince Amber…"

"Like I said," Violet interrupted, "you don't want to push it. Not this early."

"It would be so cool to be there with you." He paused, staring down at his wine glass as though a message was hidden inside. "Jerry's going to go ballistic when he finds out. He loves the Stones, and always wanted to go to South by Southwest. He thought he had Comic-Con tickets, but they fell through. He'll completely lose it when he hears about Cannes. This is his dream, not mine."

"Isn't he a part of the production? I thought you were partners."

"It's… complicated. Like I said, long story."

"Well then, he and I can sit at the Circle K and cry in our beer together while you go globe-trot." Violet stared at James with an exaggerated pout.

"Don't be silly. And stay away from Jerry." He paused. "That didn't sound right. I didn't mean that I was trying to tell you what to do. I just…"

Violet's eyebrow raised. "The jealous type?"

"No, not really," James replied with an unconvincing shake of his head. "Like I said, that came out wrong."

Violet looked up and smiled as the busboy placed bread and butter on the table. "I've been with jealous guys," she said, turning back towards James. "Didn't much care for the experience."

"I'm not," James insisted. "It's just a knee-jerk reaction with Jerry. I know what he's like.. He tries to nail everything that moves and…"

"Oh," she interrupted, as she buttered a piece of bread, "so I'm just something that moves. Something to," she took a beat and added, "nail."

"No. That's not what I meant. I mean I know he's attracted to you. He'll make a move. Plus, I'm pissed at him. He was doing stuff behind my back and…"

"What stuff?" Violet asked.

James shook his head as though he was unsure. "Trying to make a separate deal with Stangerson. Using my contacts to pitch another project with some stripper psychotherapist."

"What?" Violet asked with a laugh.

"I'd find it funny too if it wasn't pathetic. I don't know all of it. I thought he was my best friend." He paused and took a drink. "And it's not just Jerry."

"What do you mean?"

"All of 'em. Jerry, Amber, Stangerson, Lanier…" James stopped and looked away. "You can't really trust any of them. Nothing is

285

what it seems. Let's talk about something else," he muttered. Taking a beat, he turned towards Violet, smiled and raised his glass. "This is supposed to be a celebration, right?"

"To your book," Violet declared, holding her drink up. "Your book, your film, your travels—and your new life."

James clinked his glass to hers. "To us," James corrected. "I don't want to go anywhere," he added, his eyes glued on hers. "I really don't. I want to stay here with you and work on my new novel. That's what I want to toast to."

Violet took a sip and, looking up at him, smiled. "Don't be silly. You have a new film, an Amber Lake film. You're going to South by Southwest… Cannes."

James replied with a pensive nod. "I don't want to go anywhere," he repeated. "Not now."

"Once it all starts… that will change."

"I don't even think it's true. Any of it. Amber has lied every step of the way."

"You signed contracts. She paid you an advance. It's real, James."

"It's hard to believe after everything, but… if it is real," James took a long pause. "If it really is real," he continued, "I won't have to worry about money—at least for a while. The film buzz might give my novel a chance to sell and give me time to write, which would be amazing. But the rest…" He shook his head. "I don't care about the rest. Jerry's the one who wants the glitz. Cannes, Comic-Con the travel, the trappings, that's his fantasy, his dream—not mine."

Violet leaned in. "Come on. You really don't care about the film, Cannes, South by Southwest, the London Book Fair, flying first class—seeing your novel turned into a movie?"

"First class isn't so great."

"I wouldn't know. But I'd like to find out," she added with a smile. "It all sounds magical to me."

"If I could bring you with me, it would to me too."

286

"Don't move too fast," Violet said, staring down at her glass. "That can backfire."

"I'm not," he replied, thinking her warning had come too late.

The waitress came with their dinners. Once again explaining that the kitchen was closing, and it was last call for food and drinks. James ordered two more glasses of wine.

Violet leaned towards him and, grabbing his arm, shook it. "Come on. Snap out of it. Your whole life has just changed. You just landed a deal most people only dream about and you're sitting there all doom and gloom."

James forced a smile. "I know, but, it's like I'm going alone behind enemy lines. I don't trust any of these people. I don't want to go— not now." he repeated, his eyes locking on hers.

"Believe me, that will change. Take it in James. What has happened is amazing." Holding up her wine glass, she announced, "To your success."

"To us," he corrected, clinking his glass to hers. He took a beat and stared at Violet. "I've got a guitar, at my place. Maybe we could go back. You could play me some of your songs. And..." Again he paused. "And if you wanted, you could... maybe you could... stay. Easier than you having to go home." He smiled and added. "I have an extra toothbrush."

Violet looked up at James, an eyebrow raised. "An extra toothbrush? I should be suspicious," she replied with a laugh. "That sounds nice. My shift doesn't start until noon tomorrow."

James's smile brightened. "I don't have to go to work at all tomorrow." He sat back letting those words sink in. "I don't have to go anywhere. We can sleep in." Taking his glass and holding it up he added, "Or not."

Violet leaned towards him, again clinking her glass to his. "Sometimes sleep is overrated."

Chapter 42

J ames sat on his couch, staring at a blank TV as he tried to comprehend all that had happened. His life had been taken by a whirlwind, a hurricane that was hard to make sense of. Standing, he walked to his bathroom and found Violet's hairbrush. He smiled, remembering he once read that when people left things behind it was an unconscious act signaling that they wanted to return. He called to let her know that he could stop by the Circle K when she was getting off and return it—and take her to dinner. She said she'd like that.

Walking to his desk, he sat down, opened his laptop, and called up his pirated copy of Final Draft to start work on the screenplay. He stared at the page, groaned aloud. Nothing came. He blankly stared at the page some more. His fingers rested on the keyboard, unmoved. He gave an audible groan and, changing screens, called up his novel. There his writing flowed. He couldn't keep up, couldn't write quickly enough. It felt as though he was channeling, taking dictation, the words tumbling out faster than he could type.

After a few hours of writing, he checked his email, voicemail, and texts. There were five increasingly more hostile and threatening messages from Lanier and three messages from Jerry. The first angry, the second pleading, and the third inexplicably upbeat and excited. There was an email from Sam with an itinerary for the upcoming months and confirming a production meeting the next day with Amber and the staff to review the project and the upcoming timeline. An email from a writer at the Los Angeles Times requested an interview. This was someone else's life James thought as he stared at his phone. He'd eventually have to tell Jerry that Stangerson was out of the picture, that he signed contracts with Amber. Picking up the phone, he figured he'd get it over with. Bracing himself for Jerry's meltdown, he dialed.

"I'm going to fucking Cannes," Jerry blurted out, answering on the first ring. "In April. Me! Cannes!"

James paused. This was not the reaction he was expecting. "I'm not sure Amber has you on the list," James replied hesitantly.

"Forget Amber. I'm talking Stangerson—Peter," Jerry corrected. "The Kimberley project—it's a go. He's got Jennifer Lawrence and Chris Pratt interested. It's real. It's fucking real!"

James replied with a confused silence.

"I'm sorry, man," Jerry continued. "It's not the novel. Not anymore. Peter was all excited about it and then something shifted, suddenly he wouldn't even talk about it. He's probably pissed because you canceled the meeting. I warned you."

"When did Stangerson turn into Peter?"

"We're tight now, Peter and me. I know how to play him. I got a plan. Don't worry. I can get you on board—eventually. The Kimberley video did it. The hot psychotherapist to the stars ex-hooker thing. That hooked him," Jerry added with a laugh.

"Ex-hooker?"

Jerry shrugged. "Hooker, stripper, whatever. Peter has glommed on to the backstory of her being an ex-hooker, so what the hell. Why not? He's giving me a shot at the first draft of the screenplay. Me! This is the big time, man. Like I said, give me time and I'll find a way to get you on board. Not as a cowriter, but as—something. Maybe my assistant." After a slight beat, he hurriedly added, "That would just be a title, ya know. Not real. Just a way to get you in. On board. Just to start."

James ran his hand through his hair, trying to make sense of what Jerry was telling him.

"Peter wants me to shoot a sizzle reel and take it with him to Cannes," Jerry continued, not waiting for James's response. "Then in July he wants to shoot some footage at the Tokyo Olympics. Kimberley's character has morphed into nymphomaniac therapist who's hot for a Russian Olympian that's competing in Tokyo and might be a spy."

"What?"

"Crazy, right?" Jerry laughed, "but I'm serious. Peter's totally on board. He wants to shoot footage at the Olympics. It'll be a seduction scene in the locker room. Nudity—but tasteful. That's how genius directors work, right? Kimberley's still going to be an ex-hooker/stripper shrink to the stars, but he wanted to add more intrigue, add a type of James Bond twist, which is where the Olympics and Russian spy thing comes in. Who knows? Who cares? He wants me to go, Cannes and the Olympics!" Jerry cried in a near whoop. "I told you it would work! 2020 is my year." After a beat he added, "Our year."

James closed his eyes and nodded. "Right."

Jerry frowned. He was hoping for more enthusiasm, excitement. But James's disappointment was understandable. The project was no longer going to be based on his novel. "I'm sorry man, about Peter not wanting to do the book. Like I said, he was hot there for a while, insisting he meet with you ASAP. Wanting to make a deal on the spot. But you didn't show. He's not the kind of guy you put off or say no to. That must have been it. Because he then turned. Lost interest; just went stone cold. I told you to take the meeting. But, who knows, maybe another deal will show up for your book. It's Hollywood, right?"

"Right," James replied.

"It's all good. Like I said, I'm not forgetting you. I'm bringing you on board." He took a beat and added, "Somehow."

James hesitated, wondering whether to tell James the Amber deal but remained silent.

"Lanier has been calling," Jerry said. "A lot. She's threatening now; talking lawsuits—worse. Pulling out all the stops. I'm done with her. Not taking her calls. Not even listening to the messages anymore."

"Probably a good idea."

"You okay?"

"A lot to take in."

Jerry nodded. "I know, man. I get it. Listen, I'm sorry Peter's not going to do the novel. But you're working on another novel. That's what you really want, right? I mean, you're right, this Hollywood shit is crazy. It's a fucking game. And that copywriting job is probably still available," he added encouragingly. "Besides, I'm not forgetting you. I'm going to get you on this project somehow. Like I said, it might start as an assistant or something. But that's not what it will really be. Just what we'll have to call it, you know, to get you hired, get you on board. We'll still be partners."

James again was tempted to tell him everything. Instead he simply said, "I think I'll pass."

"Come on, don't be that way. Don't sulk," Jerry replied, an irritated tinge to his voice. "It's just how it's played. I told you, it's all a game. My project this time. Yours next. Get excited. We did it. It worked. The plane is speeding down the runway. 2020 here we come. We're golden."

James nodded. "Right, golden." After a beat, he added, "I'm happy for you. You always wanted to go to Cannes."

"Not just Cannes," Jerry continued excitedly. "South by Southwest. Did I mention that? Peter is taking me and Kimberley. He's going to introduce the project there. We're going to shoot some footage to

291

show. I'll be there as a VIP, not just one of the crowd. And Japan, man. Don't forget Japan. The Olympics."

"Right. Japan."

"Kimberley is a bit worried about the Japan part. The mother of one of her clients was quarantined last week on some cruise ship in Yoko-something. It's some kind of virus that seems to be spreading over there. Sounds kinda creepy. She's afraid we could catch it. Or people could carry it to the US. That could throw a wrench in the works."

"I wouldn't worry about that," James said dismissively.

"Yeah," Jerry said with a nod. "That's what I told her. Africa and Asia always get those weird kind of diseases. Then they pass and you never hear of them again. But, that could make for a good sci-fi film right? A killer virus that spreads from country to country, threatens the world—that kind of crap sells. I'm leaving myself a note to work on something like that. I could probably get Peter interested. I could bring you on board." He paused and added. "Kimberley sees me differently now. I think that there's, you know—a chance."

"That's great." James paused. "Listen, I gotta go."

"Get excited," Jerry insisted. "Get up. We're good. Golden. Besides, you called me. What's up?"

James again considered explaining why he'd called; tell Jerry contracts had been signed on Amber's film, about the cash-filled bag in his apartment. "Nothing important," he said instead. "Just touching base. Seeing if you had any news."

"Have news?" Jerry repeated with a laugh. "I am news! I'm going to make sure this pays off for both of us," he again added, not wanting James to feel left out, abandoned. "So in the interim you going to take that copywriting job? They going to give you another chance after the whole New York/Amber fiasco?"

"We'll see. I have a call coming in," James lied. "I have to take this."

"I can maybe get you into Comic-Con," Jerry added. "No promises, but I have Peter's ear now. If I play it right, I think I can probably…"

"I really gotta go."

Jerry continued talking as James disconnected the call.

James sat back and closed his eyes. Jerry was floating away. He was where he'd always wanted to be, at least on the outskirts. Their paths were heading in different directions. His eyebrows furrowed as he felt a twinge of loneliness. Picking up his phone, he dialed Violet's number. It went to voicemail. "Hey," he began, "just calling to tell you that, that I really…" he paused, "that I'll see you tonight." Hanging up, he sat back and remembered Violet stretched out on the couch, smoking her joint as she laughed, as they both laughed. She appeared in his life just as an earthquake hit. She arrived as his whole world was shifting. With Amber's film deal and the upcoming New York Times piece, everything he'd worked towards was in motion. Picking up his phone, he looked up the LA Times writer's number and dialed. Before the call connected, James hung up. His phone lit up with an incoming call from Lanier. He could palpably feel her insistence. He let it go to voicemail. He then dialed Sam to review the upcoming itinerary. Again, he hung up before the first ring. There was too much coming at him too soon. James placed the phone down on the couch and walking to the record player, put on the Debussy album he had played for Violet. He headed back to his computer and sat down to work on his novel. He'd see her that evening. Apart from that, he yearned for a pause button. To put it all on hold. For the world to come to a hard stop. He simply wanted Violet. That was enough.

Chapter 43

Amber sat in back of the town car reading her texts. The driver had initially arrived with a limo, but she directed Sam to have him come back with another car. Limos were garish, gauche, drew too much attention. They were embarrassing. The driver quickly returned with a nondescript midsized black town car. The windows were smoked, enough to make it difficult to see in, but not blackened.

Sam sat in front riding shotgun. He turned back towards Amber. "I have Sandy, the AD, and the director meeting us at the office," he explained. "I haven't called James. Do you want him at the meeting?"

Amber shook her head as she looked out the window. "We have his book locked up. That's all I need from James. I want to make sure things are on track before we leave today." She took a beat. "What time do we fly back?"

"The plane is at Burbank Airport. I figured we'd head back close to three."

"Is Gavin on the flight?"

"Yep," Sam replied with a laugh. "Reluctantly. Said he had to reschedule patients and cancel an important dinner meeting. Said he couldn't be expected to be flying from coast to coast on a moment's notice. He wasn't very happy."

"I don't pay him to be happy," Amber replied as she scanned her texts. "Besides, he should be more than happy. I've built him his own flying office." The plane's interior had been built to her specifications. It required that she buy a larger model, but what good was a plane that didn't meet her needs? At the back was a sound-proofed, scaled replica of Dr. Gavin's office. She'd often scheduled sessions there, much to Dr. Gavin's chagrin, who she kept on call 24/7. For Amber, it was a good way to utilize the in-flight time. Besides, she wasn't all that fond of flying. At times she'd terrify herself thinking of a small metal object speeding thirty thousand feet above ground. It could stall and plummet in an instant. It helped to have Gavin on board.

But today had nothing to do with flying angst. She needed to center herself. She had secured James's book but by doing so she'd alienated Stangerson, and, if Lanier was right, probably Jessica. Amber could brag that she'd won. Put up a good front. But secretly the move frightened her. This was new terrain. Foreign. Secretly unwelcomed. She'd be happy simply acting; accepting a role, playing the part, doing the media appearances, and moving on to the next project. That was what she had signed up for. It was her comfort zone, where she excelled, where she was content. But now actors also had to be producers—even directors. That was the new status symbol. It proved an actor had arrived, had gravitas, was taking control of her career.

Actors now boasted more about their production deals than their acting roles. If Amber didn't jump into the game she'd be left behind, relegated to the sidelines, a mere actor—not a player. And that she couldn't allow. Now that she'd secured the rights to James's book, she had to figure out next steps. Steps that had nothing to do with acting. She needed Gavin to help her work it through, sort it out.

During their in-flight session he'd calm her down, help her devise a workable game plan. That's why she paid him. He should be grateful for the opportunity of holding their sessions on her private jet.

"Word has it that Peter was not at all happy that you beat him to the rights of James's book," Sam said. "You got what you wanted."

Amber wanted to beat Peter, but an angry Stangerson was not a comforting thought. He could be vindictive, was big on revenge.

"He licked his wounds by signing that stripper shrink," Sam continued. "That sounds like a project doomed to go down in flames," he added with a snicker.

Amber shrugged. "It worked for him with *Exposed*. He probably thinks he can do it again,"

"Totally different project," Sam replied. "Who is going to pay to see the life of a forty-year-old shrink? Word has it that he does have Bradely, Naomi, and Jennifer interested. I don't see it, but that's what I've heard." Sam threw that out to get a reaction from Amber. Knowing Stangerson was lining up A-list actors would throw her. It wasn't that Sam was exactly being mean, but he did like to keep her off balance. A type of payback for her demanding, yelling, and barking.

"You're kidding me," Amber replied.

"That's what I've heard. But it's probably all talk, right?" he added looking back at her with a smile. "He's even got that Jerry guy on board. Giving him a crack as a writer."

"Jerry?" A slight smile came to Amber's face. "Jerry's a nobody," she replied. "Peter's grasping at straws. Jerry's about as far up the ladder as he'll get. Margot or Bradely will never sign up for a project like that," she concluded, comforted by the thought. Hearing the distinctive chime that signaled her manager, Marcia, was calling, Amber answered her phone.

"*Ultra's Return* is back on the table," Marcia announced.

Amber's eyes widened. "Peter?"

"He's out. I don't think he was seriously ever in. Tom Samuels."

"Who?"

"Samuels. Tom Samuels," Marcia repeated impatiently, signaling Amber should know the name. "He's young. New. Won Sundance last year. Being called the next Christopher Nolan. He's hot. A lot of buzz. And he's a fan. Wants you as the lead. Wants to meet tomorrow. But if it's going to happen, it has to move quickly. It has to be in production no later than April, or he'll have to push it back until after his next film, which means it will get shelved and probably never get done. It's gotta shoot in 2020. You have to move on this, Amber. Now."

Amber began to respond but remained silent.

"He wants to meet at the Carlyle," Marcia continued. "The funding's secured. It's happening. Shooting mid-summer. Studio backing. Huge budget. Samuels knows you were originally attached and wants you on board."

Amber paused, her eyebrows narrowing. "I'm supposed to start production on the film based on James's book. I'm already committed." Her tone was unsure, tentative, unconvincing.

"You're in early preproduction," Marcia explained. "It hasn't started yet. Besides, it's your project. You call the shots. You can put it on hold. This is *Ultra's Return*, Amber. Your superhero film. This is the project you wanted. It gets you in that game; will rival any Marvel film. It's here. It's yours. Samuels wants to meet you tomorrow at the Carlyle at 2 pm."

"Tomorrow?" After a long beat, Amber replied with a definitive, "Confirm it." Disconnecting the call, she stared out pensively.

Sam again turned back towards Amber as the car pulled up to the office. "That Marcia?" he asked.

Amber placed her phone back in her purse. Sliding up her sunglasses, she looked at Sam. "Maybe we could postpone the production or do it without me as the lead. Maybe cast Margot or… someone."

Sam's eyebrows furrowed. "I don't follow."

"*Ultra's Return* is back on. They want me as the lead. I want that role." After a beat she added. "I need that role."

"*Ultra's Return*," Sam gave a high whistle. "What about everything we have going here?"

"It doesn't have to stop." Amber's voice was unsure, questioning. "We could cast a new lead, right? The production can still go forward."

"It would look bad if it didn't," Sam replied. "We have stories coming out in all the trades. The New York Times is going to do a follow up story on you adapting James's novel as a film. If your first production fizzles…" he shrugged, letting his words hang. "Sharks will smell blood. Stangerson's already pissed that you snatched this one away."

"That's half the fun," Amber replied with a forced grin. "But you're right. This could backfire."

"So what do we do?"

Amber paused. That was the question she wanted Sam to answer. Again staring down at her phone, she Googled Tom Samuels. Marcia was right. His star was rising. The new golden boy. "We'll postpone this meeting," Amber pronounced. "I need to fly back. I'll review this with Gavin on the flight. Tomorrow I'm meeting at the Carlyle with Tom Samuels."

"Tom Samuels?" Sam asked.

"You don't know who Tom Samuels is?" Amber asked pointedly. "Everyone knows who he is. He's the new Christopher Nolan."

Sam shrugged. "You sure you want to cancel this late? We're already here. Everyone's on their way." Sam paused, waiting for Amber to reply. "So we just drive off?" he asked. "Shouldn't we at least go inside for five minutes, talk to everybody? Explain what's going on."

"I don't have time for explanations. Text everyone and say we're rescheduling," Amber directed. "Tell them I'll fly back in a few days. After I talk with Gavin and Marcia I'll meet with Tom Samuels.

Then I'll know my next move. Everything will sort out." Turning to the driver, she directed, "Head to the airport."

As the car pulled away, Amber heard a beep that signaled a new text. She again pulled her phone out of her bag. "Just confirmed with Samuels. He's excited," Marcia wrote. "I think he has a crush on Amber Lake" was accompanied by a heart emoji. Leaning back, Amber smiled as she slid the phone back into her bag.

The car turned right on Sunset Boulevard. As it idled at a stoplight, two teen girls peered in the window.

"It's her!" one cried.

"Amber Lake! Ohmygod! Its's her!" the other agreed with a yell.

"We love you, Amber!" they cried out in unison.

As the car glided away, Amber leaned forward, raising one hand, her graceful gesture resembling a benediction. Her smile widened as the car accelerated. Sliding off her dark glasses, she settled back into her seat. Everything was falling into place, like pieces of an intricate puzzle. *Ultra's Return* would catapult her into an entirely new stratosphere. She'd next produce and star in James's project, marking her as a true Hollywood hyphenate.

As she gazed out of the car window, Amber envisioned 2020 as her long-awaited breakthrough year, propelling her from an internationally renowned actress to veritable superhero. She was on the verge of something extraordinary.

"Drive faster," she called out to the driver, her urgency palpable. Time was of the essence.

The stars had aligned.

EPILOGUE

The most widespread coronavirus to date was discovered in Wuhan, China in November 2019.

January 9 — The World Health Organization (WHO) announces mysterious coronavirus-related pneumonia in Wuhan, China

January 20 — CDC says three US airports will begin screening for coronavirus

January 21 — CDC confirms first US coronavirus case

January 21 — Chinese scientist confirms COVID-19 human transmission

January 23 — Wuhan now under quarantine

January 25 — Stangerson secures funding for Dr. Kimberley Goodson project from hedge fund

January 31 — WHO isues global health emergency

February 2 — Global air travel is restricted

February 3 — US declares public health emergency

February 25 — CDC says COVID-19 is heading towards pandemic status

March 6 — Twenty-one passengers on a California cruise ship test positive

March 11 — WHO declares COVID-19 a pandemic

March 12 — Stangerson loses funding for Dr. Kimberley Goodson project; hedge fund investigated by DOJ

March 13 — Trump Declares COVID-19 a national emergency

March 13 — Travel ban on non-US citizens traveling from Europe goes into effect

March 14 — James introduces Jerry to ad agency; Jerry reluctantly accepts a part-time remote copywriting gig

March 14 — Tom Samuels withdraws from *Ultra's Return* project as film industry goes dark

March 19 — California issues statewide stay-at-home order

March 25 — James's film project with Amber Lake postponed indefinitely

March 27 — James and Violet move in together; with his advance for the film securely in the bank, James spends his time working on his new novel

March 29 — Coronavirus ICU patients in California double

April 1 — Dr. Kimberley Goodson is offered the lead in a reality Zoom series titled Beverly Hills Shrink Rap; She passes

About The Author

Anthony Mora is a novelist, playwright, director and producer whose writings have been compared to Fante, Cheever and Salinger. Anthony has been featured in the New York Times, The Huffington Post, CNN, the BBC and other media. His first novel was *BANG! A Love Story*. Linda Cardellini starred in the original play adaptation of *BANG!* in Los Angeles and New York. Anthony, who served as the playwright-in-residence at The Sidewalk Studio Theatre, has had several plays produced including *P.O.P.: The Principles of Perfection*, *Modern Love*, and *Silencing Silas*. His second novel, *Virtual Velocity: An L.A. Story*, was published in 2019.

In 2020 Anthony co-founded Swan Place Productions with Ann Convery. The company's first film *Exposé*, was written by Ann, was featured at over twenty film festivals and was nominated for best U.S. short film at the Seattle Film Festival. The company also produced the documentary, *An Unimportant Girl* and *The Revenge Sessions*, which is based on one of Anthony's plays.

AnthonyMoraWriter.com